Praise for No.1 New York [illegible]

CHARLAINE HARRIS

"Read more than a few pages and
you'll find yourself hooked."
—*SFX*

"Fans of Laurell K Hamilton...have a
pleasant surprise in store."
—*Science Fiction Chronicle*

"Charlaine Harris playfully mixes several genres to make
a new one that is her own bright creation."
—*Denver Post*

MAGGIE SHAYNE

"A rich, sensual and bewitching adventure of good vs
evil, with love as the prize."
—*Publishers Weekly* on *Eternity*

"Intense, mystical and lyrical."
—*Library Journal* on *Destiny*

BARBARA HAMBLY

"Masterful...ravishing...haunting."
—*New York Times* on Hambly's Benjamin January novels.

"Intricately plotted and solidly written."
—*Publishers Weekly* on *Knight of the Demon Queen*

For more information about *Night's Edge* and other new paranormal and urban fantasy fiction available from MIRA Books, visit www.mirabooks.co.uk

CHARLAINE HARRIS

MAGGIE SHAYNE

BARBARA HAMBLY

NIGHT'S EDGE

First published in Great Britain 2009.
MIRA Books, Eton House, 18-24 Paradise Road,
Richmond, Surrey, TW9 1SR

ISBN 978 0 7783 0346 6

60-1009

MIRA's policy is to use papers that are natural, renewable and recyclable products and made from wood grown in sustainable forests. The logging and manufacturing processes conform to the legal environmental regulations of the country of origin.

Printed in Great Britain
by Clays Ltd, St Ives plc

CONTENTS

HER BEST ENEMY

MAGGIE SHAYNE

CHAPTER ONE

IN THE TIME IT TOOK Kiley Brigham to submerge her head, rinse out the shampoo and sit up again, the temperature in the bathroom had plummeted from "steamy sauna" to somewhere around "clutch your arms and shiver." Sitting up straighter, with rivulets fleeing her skin for warmer climes, Kiley frowned. Her skin sprouted goose bumps. She muttered, "Well, what the hell is *this?*" and then frowned harder because she could see her breath when she spoke.

Had late Halloween week in Burnt Hills, New York, turned suddenly bitterly cold? There hadn't been any warning on the weather report. And even if there had been a sudden cold snap, the furnace would have kicked on. According to the overall-wearing, toolbox-carrying guy she'd hired to inspect the hundred-year-old house before agreeing to buy it, the heating system was in great shape. True, she hadn't run it much in the three days since she'd moved into her dream house, just once or twice during the late October nights when the mercury dipped outside. But it had been working fine.

She tilted her head, listening for the telltale rattle of hot water being forced through aging radiators, but she heard nothing. The furnace wasn't running.

Sighing, she rose from the water, stepped over the side of the tub onto the plush powder-blue bath mat and reached for the matching towel. Her new shell-pink-and-white ceramic tiles might look great, but they definitely added to the chill, she decided, peering at the completely fogged-up mirror and then scurrying quickly through the door and into her bedroom for the biggest, warmest robe she could find.

As soon as she stepped into the bedroom, the chill was gone. She stood there wondering what the hell to make of that. Leaning back through the bathroom door, she felt that iciness hanging in the air. It was like stepping into a meat cooler, she thought. Leaning back out into the bedroom, she felt the same cozy warmth she always felt there.

Kiley shrugged, pulled the bathroom door closed and battled a delayed-reaction shiver. She closed her eyes briefly, just to tamp down the notion that the shiver was caused by something beyond the temperature, then turned to face her bedroom with its hardwood wainscoting so dark it looked like ebony, its crown molding the same, its freshly applied antique ivory paint in between. Her bedroom suite came close to matching: deep black cherry wood that bore the barest hint of bloodred. The bedding and curtains in the tall, narrow windows were the color of French cream, as were the throw rugs on the dark hardwood floor. Ebony and ivory had been her notion for this room, and it worked.

"I love my new house," she said aloud, even as she sent a troubled glance back toward the bathroom. "And I'm going to stop looking for deep, dark secrets to explain the bargain-basement asking price. So my bathroom has a draft. So what?"

Nodding in resolve, she moved to the closet, opened the door, then paused, staring. One of the dresses was moving, just slightly, the hanger rocking back and forth mere millimeters, as if someone had jostled it.

Only, no one had.

She could have kicked herself for the little shiver that ran up her spine. She didn't even believe in the sorts of things that were whispering through her brain right now. And had been ever since she'd moved in.

I jerked open the door, it caused a breeze, the dress moved a little. Big deal.

In spite of her internal scolding, her eyes felt wider than she would have liked as she perused the closet's interior. Her handyman-slash-house-inspector had asked if she'd like a light installed in there. She'd said no. Now she was thinking about calling him tomorrow morning to change her answer. Meanwhile, she spotted her robe and snatched it off its hanger with the speed of a cobra snatching a fieldmouse. She back-stepped, slammed the closet door, and felt her heart start to pound in her chest.

B-r-e-a-t-h-e, she thought. And then she did, a long, deep, slow inhalation that filled her lungs to bursting, a brief delay while she counted to four, and a thorough, cleansing exhalation that emptied her lungs entirely. She repeated it several times, got a grip on herself and then felt stupid.

She did *not* believe in closet-dwelling bogeymen. Hell, she'd made her career debunking nonsense like that. More precisely, putting phony psychics, gurus and ghost busters out of business in this spooky little tourist town. And no one liked it. Not the town supervisor, the town council, the tourism bureau, and least of all, the phony psychics, gurus and ghost busters.

But thanks to the Constitution, freedom of the press couldn't be banned on the grounds that it was bad for tourism.

She pulled her bathrobe on, relishing the feel of plush fabric on her skin, and then drew a breath of courage and turned to face the bathroom again. Her hairbrush was in there, along with her skin lotions, cuticle trimmer and toothbrush. And she still had to tug the plug and let the water run out of the bathtub. She was going back in. A cold draft was nothing to be afraid of.

Crossing the room, one foot in front of the other, she moved firmly to the door, closed her hand on its oval, antique porcelain doorknob, and opened it. The air that greeted her was no longer icy. In fact it was as warm as the air in the bedroom.

She sighed in relief as she stepped into the room. But her relief died and the chill returned to her soul when she saw the mirror, no longer coated in fog, but something else. Something far, far worse.

Written across the damp glass surface, in something scarlet that trickled in streams from the bottom of each letter, were the words "House of Death."

Someone screamed. It wasn't until she was down the stairs, out the door and about fifteen yards up the heaving, cracked sidewalk, that Kiley realized the scream had been her own.

She stood there in the dead of night, barefoot, clutching her robe against the whipping October wind and staring back at her dream house with its turrets and gables and its widow's walk at the top. Such a beautiful place, old and solid. And framed right now by the scarlet and shimmering yellow of the sugar maples and poplar trees at the peak of their fall color.

Swallowing hard, she lowered her gaze, focusing on her car in the driveway beside the house. Leaping Lana was an '87 Buick Regal—a four-door sedan in rust-brown that ate gas like M&Ms and sounded like a tank.

Kiley squared her shoulders and forced herself to march over there—even though it meant moving *toward* her house when every cell in her body was itching to move *away* from it instead. She opened Lana's door and climbed in. She couldn't quite keep herself from checking the back seat first, the second the interior light came on. It was clear. The keys were in the switch, because if someone was brave enough to steal Kiley Brigham's car, she'd always thought she would enjoy the vengeance she'd be forced to wreak on their pathetic asses, and besides, who would steal an '87 Buick, anyway?

She turned the key. Lana growled in protest at being bothered at such an ungodly hour, but finally came around and cooperatively backed her boat-size backside out into the street. As Kiley shifted into Drive, she glanced up at her house again.

There was someone standing in her bedroom window looking back at her.

And then there wasn't. She squinted, rubbed her eyes. The image hadn't moved, hadn't turned away. The dark silhouette she knew she had seen simply vanished. Faded. Like mist.

"Fuck this," she muttered, and she stomped on Lana's pedal and didn't let off until they'd reached the offices of the *Burnt Hills Gazette,* and her own office there, which held three things Kiley dearly needed just then: a change of clothes, a telephone and a spare pack of smokes.

SHE WAS SO TOGETHER BY THE time the police arrived that they actually seemed skeptical. At least until they headed back to her recently acquired house and saw the message on the mirror for themselves. Kiley preferred to stay out in the bedroom—and even that gave her the creeps—while the cops clustered around her bathroom sink debating whether the substance on her mirror was blood. One opined that it looked like barbecue sauce, and another said it was cherry syrup. At that point the conversation turned to previous cases where what was thought to be blood turned out to be something else entirely, like corn syrup with red food coloring added—a tale that the officers found laugh-worthy.

She interrupted their fun by standing as close to her bathroom door as she wanted to get, and clearing her throat. The laughter stopped, the cops looked up.

"Excuse me, but shouldn't one of you be taking a sample of that? And maybe checking my house for signs of forced entry?"

"Did that, ma'am," one cop said, sending a long-suffering look toward another. "No signs of a break-in. You sure the place was locked?"

"Of course I'm sure the place was…" She stopped, pursed her lips, thought it over with brutal honesty. "Actually, I forget to lock up as often as I remember."

"Mmm-hmm. Well, at least you're aware this was the work of an intruder."

She frowned at him. "Well, of course it was an intruder. What else could it have been?"

"You know how folks get around here. Half the time we get a call like this, the homeowner insists some kind of ghost was responsible."

"Especially at this time of year," another cop said, and they all nodded or shook their heads or rolled their eyes with "isn't that ridiculous" looks at one another.

"Well, I don't believe in ghosts," she managed to say, rubbing her arms against the chill that came from within. "As to how the intruder got in, I'm not even sure it's all that important. The fact is that he did get in. And I know that because I saw him."

"You saw him? Excellent." Cop number one—his name tag read Hanlon—pulled out a notepad and pen. "Okay, where and when did you see the intruder?"

"He was standing right there, in that window, looking down at me when I backed the car out."

"So you didn't see anyone while you were inside. Only after you'd left?"

"Right."

"And can you describe him?"

She licked her lips, recalling the misty silhouette behind the veil of her curtains. "Uh, no."

"But you're sure it was a male," Hanlon said.

She narrowed her eyes and searched her memory. "No. No, I can't even be sure of that much. It was dark. It was just a shadow, a dark silhouette in the window." She sighed in frustration. "Has there been a rash of break-ins that I should know about, anything like this at all?" she asked, almost hoping the answer would be yes.

Hanlon shook his head. "We've got hardly any crime

around here, Ms. Brigham. Little enough so you'd be reading about it if there had been anything like that."

She nodded. "We're so hungry for stories we've been covering the missing prostitutes from Albany."

"You work for the press?" he asked.

"Yeah. *Burnt Hills Gazette.*" More people came in. Suits, instead of uniforms. They carried cases and headed for her bathroom. She watched them, her gaze unfocused. One swabbed a sample of the stuff from the mirror, dropped it into a vial and capped it. Another snapped photos. A third started coating her pretty shell-pink-and-white bathroom in what looked like fireplace soot in search of fingerprints.

The guy with the swabs took out an aerosol can of something—the label read Luminol—and sprayed it at the mirror, then he turned off the lights.

Kiley sucked in a breath when the grisly message glowed in the darkness.

"It's blood, all right," the guy said, flipping the light back on.

Officer Hanlon moved up beside Kiley and put a hand on her shoulder, as if he thought she might be close to losing it. "We'd probably better start thinking about who your enemies are, Ms. Brigham."

She swallowed hard. "It would be easier to tell you who they aren't, and it would make a far shorter list."

The cop frowned. Another one nodded, coming out of the bathroom. "That's probably true."

Hanlon sent him a questioning look and he went on. "Don't you recognize the name? She's the chick who writes those columns discrediting all the mumbo-jumbo types in town."

"Aah, right. Kiley Brigham. It didn't click at first." Hanlon eyed her. "Is this the first death threat you've received, Ms. Brigham?"

"You think that's what it is? A threat?"

He shrugged. "Reads that way to me."

Kiley sighed. "Yeah, it would be my first."

"Wow." His brows arched high, as if he were surprised she didn't get threatened on a daily basis.

"Look, I'm not a demon here. I don't eat babies or kick puppies. I just tell the truth." She shrugged. "Can I help it if that makes the liars of the world angry?"

"Can you think of anyone in particular who could have taken their anger this far?"

"Yeah, I can think of several. Most of them hold public office, though."

Hanlon looked alarmed by that. "I hope you're kidding."

"Maybe. Half. So what should I do?"

"Get yourself a security system," the officer said. "Something that's not going to let you get away with forgetting to lock up. In the meantime, is there someone who could stay with you tonight? A friend, relative, something like that?"

The question made her stomach ache, though she didn't know why. It wasn't as if she gave a damn that she didn't have any friends or family, that she was, in fact, utterly alone in the world. She could care less. Hell, if friends were what she wanted, she'd be out making them, instead of pissing off as many people as possible on a weekly basis. Screw friends.

"Ma'am?"

She shrugged. "I'll spend the night at my office.

There's security there. Tomorrow I'll see about that system. Thanks for coming out."

He nodded. "We'll be another hour here," he told her. "You can go, if you want. We'll lock up when we leave."

"Yeah, like *that's* gonna do any good," she muttered as she headed out of the room. And then she stopped in the hallway and wondered just what the hell she had meant by that. She shook it off, told herself it didn't matter.

She had a major day tomorrow. *Major.*

Tomorrow she was going to bust the one New Age fraud who had eluded her ever since she'd begun her weekly series of exposés. She'd planned for this, prepared for it, set up an elaborate scheme to make it happen. And nothing as mundane as a death threat written in blood on her bathroom mirror while she was standing a few feet away wearing nothing but a towel was going to stop her from seeing it through.

CHAPTER TWO

WHEN SHE WAS AROUND, the hair on the back of his neck bristled the way a cat's will in the presence of a killer dog. He always tensed up the instant before he saw her. It was *not* a case of extrasensory perception, no matter what his harebrained assistant might like to believe. More likely a case of instinctive self-preservation.

She was nearby, all right. It wasn't a scent, exactly, though now that he was alert, he could just detect a faint whiff of that aroma that always floated around her. Not a powerful fragrance—not even a perfume or cologne. Maybe it was the soap she used or something. He only knew it was unique, an aroma he equated with his biggest headache. It shouldn't seem like a sexy scent to him. But it did.

Jack lifted his head and scanned the dim room, but he couldn't see her. Candles flickered from the shelves that lined the walls. Their dancing light was refracted in the slow-turning crystal prisms suspended from the ceiling, and transformed into living rainbows that crept over the walls and floor. The purple curtains that separated this room from the rest of the shop were closed, and revealed nothing.

She was out there, though. No doubt about it. The persistent little pain in the ass.

Finally, Jack refocused on the nervous woman who sat across from him, fidgeting with her purse straps. Really on edge, this one. Even more than most people were their first time. At least now he knew why; she was just another weapon in Kiley Brigham's one-woman crusade against charlatans like him.

He barely restrained himself from cussing loud and long—not a good quality in one who purported to be in touch with the spirit world—and forced a serene smile for his new client.

"I'm sorry, Martha. I just can't seem to get a response from your dear departed husband."

"You can't?"

He shook his head sadly. "It's odd. Feels almost as if he—" Jack pinned her with his gaze "—doesn't exist," he said. "It's as if you made him up, just to—I don't know—test me or something."

She blinked twice, gaping, and Jack saw just enough guilt in her eyes to confirm his guess.

"That's impossible, of course," he went on. "You wouldn't do something like that to me, would you, Martha?"

"Of course not!"

"Maybe you'll have better luck with another medium. I could give you some names."

"No, thank you. I'll just…" She let her voice trail off as she rose.

Her small wooden chair scraped over the marble tiles, a growl of discord breaking the spell of the haunting New Age music that whispered in magical Gaelic of fairies and poisoned glens and other such nonsense.

"Don't rush off," Jack told her, rising as well. "I insist on refunding your money. I'm not a thief, you know."

She took a step backward, toward the curtain, clearly itching to get out of there. She actually leaned toward the curtain as she moved, actually reached behind her for it long before she was close enough to touch it. "You, uh, you can mail it to me," she rushed on, her feet shuffling away from him, slowly but steadily.

"All right, I'll do that. Do you want to give me your address, Martha, or shall I just save time and send the money to Kiley Brigham?"

The purple curtain flew open even as Martha kept groping for it, and he was not surprised to see Kiley herself on the other side, mad as hell, judging by the way her face was screwed up. "Damn you to hell, McCain!" Her hands were braced on her hips and she was breathing a little too fast. She did the heaving-bosom thing well. She certainly had the bosoms for it. Candlelight illuminated the hot-pink spots on her cheeks and the fire in her green eyes. Cat's eyes, she had, and hair blacker than ink. Hell, she ought to be the one running this scam. Her exotic looks would attract customers like moths to the porch light.

Well, she'd have to dress the part, of course. Those tight-fitting, faded jeans and that T-shirt that read "Keep Your Opinions Out of My Uterus" would never cut it.

But Kiley Brigham, girl columnist, wasn't interested in taking up his line of work. Instead, she was intent on ruining what he'd built into an incredibly lucrative business.

Martha, he realized, was long gone. Must have darted out of the room while he'd been perusing his nemesis, who, he realized, had been perusing him right back.

"Tell me something, Brigham," he said, relaxing back into his chair. "Were you mauled by a pack of mediums as a child?"

She sent him a smirk that should have burned holes through him, but said nothing. Her probing green eyes were busy now, scanning the room: narrow, suspicious, searching. He hated to admit it made him a little nervous to have her looking around his place so closely.

"So what do you want?" he asked to break her concentration. "You come for a reading? Want me to tell your future, Brigham? Read your palm? What?"

As planned, her gaze returned to him. "How the hell did you know I was here?"

He rolled his eyes, shook his head. "I'm *clairvoyant,* remember?"

"And I'm a Republican."

A grin tugged at the corners of his lips. He battled it and finally won. "So what do I have to do? Slap you with a restraining order?"

"You really think it would help?"

"Couldn't hurt," he said.

She bristled, but only for a moment. It seemed to him the wind left her sails far more quickly than usual. She heaved a sigh and sank into the chair the other woman had occupied.

"Did you have to scare her like that, McCain? You know how tough it is to find out-of-work actresses who come as cheap as that one?"

He did smile now. It seemed safe. Her rage was ebbing, and in record time. It made him wonder what was wrong. "You want something to drink?"

"Not if you're gonna try to foist some herbal, trance-inducing tea on me, I don't."

"Guess you're outta luck, then."

She rolled her eyes. "You don't really drink that crap. You can fool everyone else in this town, including the tourists, but you can't fool me. Why don't you drop the act?"

He pursed his lips as if thinking it over, then said, "Nah. Business is booming these days." He narrowed his eyes at her and leaned forward, flattening his palms to the table. "Largely thanks to that nasty little column of yours discrediting my competitors one by one on a weekly basis."

She leaned over the table, too, her palms on the gleaming hardwood surface like his, her face only inches away. "You make a living by feeding innocent victims a line of bull. They hand over their hard-earned money for the privilege of being duped."

"I make a living by giving people who might not listen to a therapist psychologically sound advice. I'm good at what I do. I help people. You, on the other hand, make a living putting hard-working people like me out of business. I'll take my karma over yours anytime."

"Karma, schmarma." She sat back, her palms gliding in tight circles on the small round table. "You know as well as I do that there's no such thing. No psychics, no ghosts, no magic."

"No God?" He asked the question idly, as if he could care less.

She was silent for a long moment, so preoccupied she didn't even notice him looking at her. Her eyes looked a little puffy, as if she hadn't slept. There was a tautness to her face that suggested worry.

Then, her gaze still focused inward, she said, "I don't get it, McCain."

"Don't get what?"

She shrugged. "Look at this picture. It's skewed, don't you think? You're the crook. I'm the crusader. So how come you get the adulation and I get the hate mail?"

"It's adulation you want, huh, Brigham? The love of your fellow man?"

"I don't want anyone to love me. I've scraped by without it for this long, haven't I?" She said it lightly and rushed on before he could identify the emotion that came and went in her eyes. "I'd be happy if they'd just stop with the death threats."

Jack started to laugh, but it died in his throat when he looked into her eyes. There had been no lightness in her tone this time, no laughter in her eyes. She wasn't kidding.

"You've been getting death threats?"

"Just the one, actually. You wouldn't happen to know anything about it, would you? Quaint little love note on my bathroom mirror, written in what the police department tells me is blood. Human blood, I learned this morning. Cute, huh?"

It wasn't his imagination. She shuddered when she said it, though the way she gritted her teeth made it obvious she was trying real hard not to show the slightest hint of upset. Hell, her face had gone a full shade whiter. It was as he was studying the pallor of her skin that Jack noticed his own new position. Now, just when the hell had he come out of his chair and around to her side of the table? She rose as he stared down at her, as if she didn't like having to look up at him. Or maybe it was that she didn't want him to see her teetering.

Too late for that, though.

"When did this happen?"

She shrugged, avoiding his eyes. "I was soaking in the tub last night. I got up and went into the bedroom for my robe, and when I came back it was there on the bathroom mirror. For all I know they could have been right on the other side of the shower curtain from me at some point." Her lower lip quivered, but she bit it hard and quick, then gave her head a shake. "Bastard's lucky I didn't see him."

"This isn't funny, Kiley. Jesus, have you got the police on this?"

She nodded. "Look, don't trouble yourself over it. I didn't come here for sympathy."

He wanted the animosity back. He wanted to fight with her, wanted her back to insulting his moral fiber instead of making him feel sick on her behalf. "No, you just dropped in to chat, ruin my business and accuse me of threatening your life. I love these little visits of yours." As an attempt to rekindle the banter, it was sadly lacking. But it worked all the same.

"Drop dead, McCain," she said.

Ah, that was more like it. "Same to you, Brigham."

Her head came up fast, green eyes meeting his, wider than he'd ever seen them. "You mean that?"

He felt as if she'd punched him in the gut. But she just stood there, waiting for an answer, probing his eyes with hers and looking madder than hell, capable of murder and as vulnerable as a wet kitten all at the same time. His hands came up to grasp her shoulders, never bothering to ask his permission on the way. "I didn't leave you any death threat, Brigham. Whenever I get the urge to tell you to drop dead—which is often—I say it right to your pretty little face. And if I'd been lurking on the other side of the curtain while you were soaking in the tub, the worst thing I'd have done is cop a peek. And I think you know it."

She blinked, swallowed audibly and nodded. "I didn't really figure a message in blood was your style."

"Because I'm such a swell guy?"

She smirked, a little of the old mischief backlighting the fear in her eyes. "Because you know me well enough to know I'd kick your ass if I ever found out."

"Any time you wanna try, Brigham."

No comeback. Hell, he couldn't remember the last time he'd sparred with her and she'd run out of back talk. It made him uncomfortable to know just how upset she must be to let it affect her acid tongue. And he had to change the subject, right now, before he started getting some stupid urge to help her out or something.

He cleared his throat, realized his hands were still on her shoulders, and lowered them to his sides while searching his brain for a safer topic. "So, uh, how did you manage to get in? I would have thought Chris would have noticed you lurking outside the curtain."

"You mean the scrawny kid with the quartz earring and the bright yellow dust mop on his head?"

"That's his hair."

"No shit?" She shrugged. "Anyway, he was busy humming along with whatever flaky music you have playing out there. What is that, some new Gaelic tranquilizer or what?"

"You know, if you could manage to stop being so damned *pleasant* all the time, you might attract more friendly fans." He felt his lips thin as he tried to find a way to give her some free advice without imparting the impression that he actually gave a damn. "And you might try being a little less controversial, while you're at it."

"And how would you suggest I do that, McCain? You want me to put in for a personality transplant?"

"Maybe you should try toning down your columns for a while? Find a new subject for a few weeks, give this a chance to blow over?"

Sighing, she dug a pack from the bottom of the denim backpack she carried and shook a cigarette loose, catching it between her lips. Normally, Jack would have forbidden her to light up inside the shop. It was against state law, anyway. In fact, he opened his mouth to do just that. But then he noticed the way her fingers trembled as she fumbled with her lighter, and for some reason he couldn't get the words out. Instead, he grabbed a candle from the nearest shelf and held it up to her.

She sent him a quick, surprised look. Then she bent her head to the flame and the flickering amber glow painted her eyes with mysterious light. It made her raven hair gleam. And when she straightened, her full, moist lips parted, puckered...and blew a stream of smoke in his face.

Jack stepped out of the carcinogenic cloud and replaced the candle. "On second thought, maybe the personality transplant wouldn't be a bad idea after all."

"Not possible," she said. "No more than backing off from my work is possible. That would be letting the bastard win." She hauled her backpack onto her shoulder. "I gotta go."

"I'll walk you out." He walked her through the shop to the front door.

She looked around his shop, those piercing eyes of hers searching for secrets, tricks. She wouldn't find any. Jack's tricks were all in the minds of his customers. This crap was real to them.

Brigham stopped at the front door, turning to face him. For a very brief moment he had the feeling she didn't want to leave any more than he wanted her to. Damn. He must be overworked or something. They couldn't stand each other. They *detested* each other. If someone had asked Jack to name his number one enemy, he'd have named her without batting an eye. And he had no doubt she would name him if asked the same question. She knew damned well he had about as much clairvoyance as her ancient, smoke-belching boat of a Buick. She knew it, and he *knew* she knew it. He reveled in rubbing her nose in it, and that drove her nuts!

It was strange, the relationship they'd developed over the past few years. She, always trying to trip him up. He, always struggling to stay a half step ahead of her. It was an ongoing contest with no clear winner in sight. He'd gotten kind of used to it…maybe was even beginning to *enjoy* her irritating persistence?

Nah.

He looked down at her and then he flinched at the size of the knot that formed in his stomach. For a second, he'd seen it in her face, just as plain as day: cold, dark fear. She hid it quickly, covering it up with the stubborn determination he was used to seeing there. But not fast enough. Not before he'd spotted it peering out of those sparkling emerald eyes of hers. It wasn't an emotion he'd ever seen there before. She was probably the gutsiest loudmouth he'd ever known.

She cleared her throat, reached for the door handle. "Well…"

"Yeah."

She nodded once, stepped outside into the normal world again. And he winced inwardly, because he had the feeling someone was about to drop a piano on her.

He caught the door before it could swing closed. "Brigham?"

"What?"

Jack licked his lips. "Watch your back, okay?"

"You bet your amethysts, I will. And I pity the son of a bitch who left me that message, once I find him." She sent him a wink and strode away as if she wasn't terrified of being alone.

CHAPTER THREE

JACK MCCAIN MIGHT BE the lowest form of pond slime, Kiley thought as she sat at her desk back in her office at the *Burnt Hills Gazette,* staring at her empty computer screen. But he wasn't the kind who would leave messages in human blood on a bathroom mirror.

She'd known that before she'd asked him, but hadn't been able to resist asking all the same. Just to gauge his reaction.

There was a tap on her office door before it opened, and her boss, the most gorgeous woman in town if Kiley was any judge, stepped inside. "Did you get anything on McCain?"

Sighing, Kiley shook her head. "He knew it was a setup. Smelled it like a rat smells cheese."

Barbara Benedict laughed softly, raking a hand through her pixie-cut ash-blond hair. "You ever wonder about that, Kiley?"

"About what? Whether he's part rat?"

"Whether he…maybe really *has* something. Some kind of…you know."

Kiley pursed her lips. "God, it would be one warped universe if it handed out gifts like that to guys like him."

"Yeah, he's already got the looks, the charm—you're right, it would be unfair."

Kiley hadn't been referring to his looks or his charm, but she didn't bother to correct her employer.

"So did you ask him about the, uh—the incident?"

"Uh-huh."

"And?"

"Oh, hell, you should have seen it. It was the performance of a lifetime, Barb. The hint of worry in his eyes. The concerned knit in his brow. The hand on my shoulder. It was perfect. He almost had me believing he was worried about me."

"You…you don't really think he *did* it?"

Kiley lowered her head. "No, it's not his style."

"Then why—"

"Because Jack McCain doesn't worry about anybody or anything, other than himself and his financial well-being. If he's concerned at all, it's that I'll try to pin this on him and disrupt his livelihood in the process. No, Jack is a con man. I've dealt with men like him before. I know 'em when I see 'em."

Barbara tipped her head to one side. "You talking about your ex now?"

"They're so much alike it's tough not to compare."

"What did that guy *do* to you, anyway? You haven't talked about it since you moved out here, and you have to know I'm dying of curiosity."

Kiley pushed her hair behind one ear, rising from her chair and grabbing her shoulder bag from the desk. "I gotta go find a subject for this week's column. I've got a bear for a boss and she'll skin me alive if I don't." She sent Barbara a wink, then moved past her and out of the office.

Kiley walked out through the parking lot, trying to let the slanting October sunshine lift her spirits. She inhaled the scent of dying leaves, tasted late autumn on the breeze, told herself the alarm system would be all installed by the time she went to bed tonight, and that all was right with the world. But it wasn't easy to shake off the chill that had settled into her bones last night.

At her car, she ran a hand over the warm fender. "You up for a ride, Lana?"

The car sat there, silent, ready. Her trusty steed. It was way better than the Porsche she used to drive. Lana had *character.* She unlocked the driver's door, checked the back seat and got in. Then she drove into town to have her lunch in the park, as she did every day, weather permitting. People knew where to find her. Up to now, she'd always considered that a good thing.

Now, though, maybe she should reconsider.

Still, she needed a tip, and this was her best shot at landing one. She walked to the corner hot dog stand. "Hey, Bernie. Gimme the usual."

Smiling, the compact, muscular, utterly bald vendor began putting her foot-long-with-the-works together. "Heard you had a break-in last night," he said as he heaped on the sauerkraut.

Her brows rose. "Where'd you hear that?"

"Around."

Bernie's son was on the town's police force. But she wouldn't rat him out for spreading gossip. It was a small town. Everyone knew everyone's business.

"So you okay?"

"Yeah. Got a whole new security system being installed tonight."

"Smart." He put her dog in a cardboard boat, set it aside and fished an icy diet cola from his cooler. "Three ninety-five, same as always."

She slid a five dollar bill across the top of his shiny stand. "Keep the change, same as always." She took her dog and drink and started to turn away.

"So you sure it was someone that broke in, not someone who was already there?"

She turned back to face the hot dog vendor again. "What do you mean, Bernie? There was no one there but me."

"Well, yeah, but you know the stories about that place. It's got a history."

She blinked three times. "What kind of history?"

His face changed; he looked suddenly…different. Worried, and maybe regretting his words. "I, uh—I figured you knew. Then again, it's old stuff. You've only been in town a year."

"Two years," she corrected him. "And I've only been in the house for a few days, Bernie. So if there's something I should know, then I'd appreciate you telling me."

He grinned at her suddenly and waved a hand. "I'm just picking on you, kid. You know this town, it's full of ghost stories."

"My house has ghost stories attached to it?"

"I told you, I was kidding. Go on, get outta here."

She wasn't going to get anything out of Bernie. Not that a ghost had anything to do with what had happened in her house last night. Even if her stomach did tighten up at the word, and even if it was the same theory her imagination kept posing. But if there were things she hadn't known about the place, things the real estate folks had failed to disclose, they were liable to find themselves the next topic of one of her columns.

She walked to her favorite bench, the one near the fountain, sat down and proceeded to share scraps of hot dog bun with the pigeons while she opened a notebook and dashed a note to herself to do some research on her house.

Someone sat down, right beside her. And she knew just by the way her skin prickled who it was. Without looking up, she said, "Hello, McCain. What, you didn't get enough of me this morning?"

"Don't be nasty, Brigham. I come bearing gifts."

She finally looked up at him. He had a foot-long hot dog with the works, and a diet cola. She said, "You're going to give me your lunch?"

"You telling me you could eat two of these pups?"

"I could eat three. And still have room for dessert."

He smiled. "I like a woman with an appetite."

"*You* like a woman with a pulse."

"Well, yeah. A pulse is good, too." He leaned back on the bench and took a big bite of the hot dog, giving her the perfect opportunity to do the same. God, she loved them. Probably unhealthy as all hell, but damn, so worth it.

He washed his bite down with a gulp of the cola. "I felt sorry for getting the best of you yet again this morning."

"Oh, I'm sure."

"Hated leaving you without a column this week."

"Mmm-hmm." She kept eating, pretending to be only barely listening, but in truth, she was rapt. Was her arch rival going to give her a tip? It sure seemed to be what he was getting around to.

"Anyway, I'm no more fond of frauds who cause more harm than good than you are."

"So how do you sleep at night?"

"Hell, Brigham, you wanna shut up and listen, or should I take my information and go home?"

She faced him, a serene smile on her lips, batting her eyes in mock innocence.

He rolled his in response, then brought his napkin to the corner of her mouth to dab something away. Ketchup or relish, she guessed. "There's a new player in town. He's rented out that little brick box on Main and Oak that's been vacant for so long."

"The one that used to be the barber shop?"

He nodded.

"So what's his game?"

"Oh, he starts out small. Tells people he had a dream about them, specifically, and that he has information for them. Then he gives them some cock-and-bull story about staying out of traffic on a certain day, and asks them to make an appointment for a more in-depth session. That first bit is free, but when they come back he starts really soaking them."

"How badly?"

"Fifty bucks for the first session. Then there end up being all these charms and talismans they have to buy in order to avoid disaster, and those start at a hundred and go up from there. He's calling these people at home, claiming to have urgent messages that they have to hear, convincing them to come back for another fifty-dollar session. It's all older folks. One of my regulars said her mother had laid out more than a thousand dollars in the past month. The guy's ruthless."

"The guy's a bastard." She nodded. "Okay, I'll get on it. Thanks for the tip."

He smiled. "Can't have people like him giving us legitimate psychic counselors a bad name."

"You're as legitimate as this hot dog is health food, McCain."

"Hey, if I were a fake, you'd have had me by now. You're too good not to."

"Yeah, and flattery will win me right over."

He shrugged. "Have it your way." He got to his feet, popped the last bite of his hot dog into his mouth.

"McCain?"

Still chewing, he looked at her.

"You know anything about my house?" Her brows bent together.

He swallowed, swiped his mouth with the napkin. "Like what?"

"I don't know. I heard it had…a history."

His brows rose. "What kind of history?"

"I got the feeling it was the kind that was right up your alley."

"You mean it's haunted or something?" He covered the stunned expression he wore with a grin. "Hell, I didn't think you believed in any of that stuff, Brigham."

"Oh, I haven't given up on the possibility. Just my faith in my fellow humans, and my chances of ever finding proof that there's…something more out there." She watched his face, because frankly, she had trouble swallowing that *he* really believed in the nonsense he was selling.

He swallowed hard. "Tell you the truth, Brigham, I only came to this town about six months before you did. I wouldn't know much of its history."

"I figured you probably would have mentioned it if you had."

"You're not thinking your little break-in and that death threat were the actions of some kind of ghost or demon or something, are you? Because that kind of thinking could make you careless. It could get you killed."

She licked her lips, thought about how icy cold it had become in the bathroom just before the message had appeared on her mirror. She thought about the clothes moving in the closet and the shadowy shape in her window. She almost told him about all of that. But then she pursed her lips, shook her had. "Nah. I don't think any such thing. See you later, McCain."

"Yeah. See you."

Kiley watched him walk away as she finished her hot dog and her cola. Then she headed to the library and asked for help from the librarian. The woman promptly produced a book titled *The Haunted History of Burnt Hills.* It was a local author, self-published, but amazingly, exactly what she needed.

She took the volume with her when she went to stake out the little brick building on the corner of Main and Oak Streets.

CHAPTER FOUR

JACK SAT IN HIS TEENAGE employee's rusted-out pickup truck around the corner from where Kiley Brigham's car was parked. She wasn't in it, not now, anyway. She'd sat there for a long time, with the overhead light on, reading something and smoking. Then, when Randeaux de Loup, as he called himself, had left his little brick shop, she'd gone over there.

"You think she's going to break in?" Chris asked, pushing his mop of yellow hair off his forehead.

"I imagine she's going through the garbage."

"Why do you think that?"

"Because it's what I would do. Scoot over to her car, Chris, and see if you can get a look at what she's been reading."

Chris licked his lips and sent Jack a scared look. Sighing, Jack pulled a twenty out of his pocket and handed it to him. Chris snatched it and was out of the car a heartbeat later. The kid kept to the shadows, crouching low as he ran. Moments later he was back, getting into his pickup and handing Jack a book.

"Jesus, kid, I said see what it was, not steal it!"

"Oh. Uh. Sorry. You want me to put it back?"

Jack looked up, didn't see any sign of Kiley returning to her car. "In a minute." The book had a page folded over. He flipped it open to see what Kiley had been reading.

"Why are you following her, anyway, boss?"

"To make sure no one murders her," he said.

"You like her. I knew it."

"I can't stand her. I just know damn well I'd be on top of the list of suspects if something should happen to the irritating little—hell, this is what I was afraid of."

"What?" Chris leaned over, trying to get a look at the pages Jack was reading.

Jack turned the book so the kid could see the black-and-white snapshot of the house, looking slightly newer than it did now.

"Hey, isn't that where Miss Brigham lives?"

"Yeah, and according to this, it's haunted."

"Well, yeah. Everyone knows that."

Jack just sat there staring at the kid in disbelief. "You knew she was living in a haunted house and you didn't tell me?"

"Didn't know why you'd be interested." He shrugged. "I thought you didn't believe in that stuff."

"I don't. But if you haven't learned another thing from me after all this time, Chris, you should have learned that it's not what I believe that matters." Something moved over by the brick building. Jack shoved the book back into Chris's hands. "Go put it back. Right where you found it. And don't let her see you."

"Right." Chris slid out of the vehicle again and managed to get the job done.

It was as he was heading back to the pickup that Jack heard the tap on his window and turned to see Brigham standing there, looking at him. Telling himself to think fast, he rolled the window down.

"You following me, McCain?"

"Saw your car. Thought I'd pull over for a sec. Just to watch your back."

"So you're my bodyguard now?"

"Hell, you wish, Brigham." She rolled her eyes, but he kept speaking. "Find anything?"

"Client list," she said with a smile. "Jackpot."

"Yeah? What are you going to do with it?"

"You really wanna know? Then buy the Sunday paper and find out with the rest of Burnt Hills."

"That's gratitude for you. See if I ever give you another scoop."

"Hey, did I say I wasn't grateful?"

He shrugged, glanced around. "It's getting dark earlier, isn't it?"

"It's fall, Jack. That's what happens."

"You get your locks changed yet?"

She glanced at her watch. "The workers arrived a half hour ago. They're probably still there. I really have to get home."

Something changed in her voice when she said that.

He cleared his throat, told himself to shut the hell up, but the words came tumbling out, anyway. "You want me to come along? Just to…you know, take a look around?"

She fixed her eyes on him, brows pulling together as her head tipped slowly to one side. "You really *are* playing bodyguard, aren't you."

He shrugged. "It's not a bad body. It'd be a shame if something happened to it."

"I didn't think you liked me, McCain."

"I never said I liked you, Brigham."

She smiled at him. "Actually, I *would* like you to come with me. There's something I want to talk to you about."

His throat went a little dry, because he thought he knew what it was. And he'd walked right into it, hadn't he?

"You wanna ride with me?" she asked.

"Sure." He glanced up, saw Chris frozen on the sidewalk, looking panicky. But Jack was certain Kiley hadn't seen the kid messing around near her car. He got out of the truck, waved at the kid.

"What's he doing wandering around?" Kiley asked.

"Had to take a leak," Jack said. "I'm riding with Ms. Brigham, kid. See you at the store tomorrow."

Chris said something that emerged as an indecipherable squeak and hurried to his pickup, passing them on the sidewalk as they walked to Kiley's car. Jack smiled down at Kiley. "We go for pie sometimes after work. I let him drive once in a while."

"That's nice of you."

He shrugged. As explanations went, it was full of holes, but he wasn't sure it mattered at this point. He slid into the passenger side of her car. She got behind the wheel. "Lana, this is Jack. Jack, Lana."

Frowning, Jack swung his head around, half expecting to see someone in the back seat. But no one was there. "Uh, I'm not following you, Brigham."

"What, your car doesn't have a name?"

"Oh. The car. Right. Funny."

She shrugged, started the motor and drove them through the curving lanes of Burnt Hills, beneath the canopy of autumn colors, fallen leaves stirring on the roadsides as they passed.

"So what is it you wanted to talk to me about?" Jack asked. "Finally ready to admit I'm the only legitimate psychic in town and call a truce?"

"Maybe I am."

He gaped in surprise. She only blinked at him, then glanced down at the book that lay on the seat in between them. "Have you read this book?"

He looked at it. "No."

"Well, according to it, my house has been considered one of the most haunted in the county for the past thirty years."

He closed his eyes. God, he'd had no idea it was that bad.

"I need a ghost buster, Jack. I need one that even I can't prove is a fraud. And the only one I've tried and tried to discredit, and failed to discredit…is you."

Jack swallowed the huge lump in his throat. This wasn't happening. It couldn't be happening.

"So," she went on, "I'm forced to admit the faint, extremely small possibility that you *might* actually be legitimate. And even more distasteful, I'm forced to ask for your help."

"My…help?" It was happening.

She was turning the car into the driveway now. There was a white minivan parked there with Gates Security Systems painted on the side. The old house rose up before him like a guardian at the gate of a treasure, daring him to bring it on. He could almost hear it laughing, asking him, "Just what are you gonna do now, Slick?"

He licked his lips, wished for something to drink.

"I know there's no love lost between the two of us, Jack. But do you think you could put that aside for a little while?"

He met her eyes, saw the hope in them, and the fear. "Yeah, I could do that. What do you want me to do?"

"Just come inside. Feel the place. See if you...pick up on anything."

Jack nodded, as if he'd be more than happy to help her out. But he'd already made up his mind what his diagnosis would be. He was *not* going to find any hint of any "presence" in Kiley Brigham's house. Not even if Casper himself performed an Irish jig in the living room. No way. Because if she thought there were ghosts in her house, she would ask him to get rid of them. And if she asked him to get rid of them, he would have to fake his way through it. Otherwise, she would have exactly what she had always wanted—proof that he was a fraud. Far easier not to find anything at all.

Hell, he didn't believe in this crap, anyway.

"Lead the way."

"Thanks, Jack. I appreciate it."

And he thought she really meant it. Guilt pricked his conscience. She got out of the car, then waited for him to come around to her side before moving to the sidewalk and up to the front door. It stood open, the light from inside spilling out. Men in overalls were on the other side, mostly standing around, though one of them was twisting a screwdriver, tightening a box near the door.

"How's it going?" she asked, leading Jack inside, past the men.

The worker nodded. "Just fine. We're all finished." He straightened from his task, dropping the screwdriver into a loop on his belt. Then he pulled a fat envelope from his pocket and handed it to her. "This is your manual and your invoice."

"You're not going to show me how to work this thing?"

"Oh, it's real simple. Once you set it up with your personal security code, you just hit the code, press the green button to unlock, the red one to lock. It's all in the manual. We got the whole place wired, just like you asked. Every outside door and window."

She took the thick instruction booklet from the envelope, then eyed the panel on the wall.

"You have a good night now, ma'am."

The man nodded to the others, and they gathered up their various toolboxes and filed out the front door. She watched them go, then sighing, closed the door. "It'll be morning before I get this thing figured out."

"It looks like the same system that's on my shop," Jack said. "I can probably walk you through it. If you don't mind my knowing your security code."

"Hell, if I can't trust my worst enemy, who can I trust?"

He shrugged, looking around the house, absently rubbing his arms. "So what makes you think there's anything otherworldly going on here?"

She walked on through to the kitchen, and he followed. "You want coffee?"

"Love some."

"Sit."

He took a seat at the square table. It was topped in white ceramic tiles with green ivy leaves on them. She put a clean filter into the coffeemaker's basket, then opened a canister and scooped out some coffee. And she talked.

"I was soaking in the tub last night when it happened," she said softly. "The shower curtain was closed. To keep the steam in there with me." She patted her cheeks. "Good for the skin, you know."

"Right."

She slid the basket into the maker, then carried the carafe to the sink and ran water into it. "So I'm soaking in the tub, and all of the sudden the temperature in the bathroom just plummets. Just like that. I had goose bumps. I could see my breath, Jack."

Okay, she could see her breath. He couldn't chalk it up to her imagination, then, could he? Not if she could see her breath.

"So I got out of the tub, wondering what the hell was going on. The furnace wasn't running. It should have been if it had suddenly become that cold outside. But nothing. I…I felt something. I don't know how to describe it, it's just…" She gave her head a shake. "So I went to the bedroom for my robe, but it wasn't cold in there. Just in the bathroom. And when I went back in there, those words were on the mirror."

He frowned. "So whoever left you that message did it while you were in the next room."

She nodded. "But I never heard anything. Not a footstep, not a breath. Not the door opening—and the hinges squeak, Jack. I should have heard something."

He nodded slowly. "I'm not…feeling anything now."

"No. No, neither am I." She rolled her eyes. "It's probably ridiculous. I mean, it's almost certainly some human asshole who left me that message. It's just…well, when I read the reports from other people who've lived here over the past thirty years. I figured it wouldn't hurt to make sure."

"Reports? You mean in that book you had?" She nodded. "What's in them?" he asked.

"Noises, lights going on and off by themselves, doors opening, furniture being moved. Burners turned on without warning. Music, footsteps. You name it, it's in there. The most common occurrence is the weeping."

"Weeping?" He got a chill at that word.

She nodded. "I haven't heard it. It's usually heard in the basement, and I can't quite bring myself to go down there, so that may be why. So? What do you think?"

"Like I said, I'm not sensing anything. Not at the moment, anyway."

She licked her lips. "Maybe if you stay awhile. Maybe…if you come up to my bedroom—"

He looked up so fast he nearly wrenched his neck.

"And the bathroom. Where it happened."

Slowly, he nodded. "Sure. But first, let's have that coffee, hmm?"

She seemed to relax just a little, smiling, nodding.

Then there was a sound from upstairs—something like shattering glass. Jack shot to his feet and, amazingly enough, Kiley shot into his arms.

CHAPTER FIVE

JACK COULD HAVE KICKED himself. What the hell was he doing? His hands were buried in her hair and her nose was crushed in the fabric of his shirt, not an altogether unpleasant experience. Dammit. She went to pull back, but his arms slid lower, hands cradling her shoulders, almost as if he wanted to keep her there, pressed against him, body to body.

"You can let go now," she said. Or at least, that was what he *thought* she said. It sounded more like a series of grunts with her face mashed to his chest the way it was. And frankly, the heat of her breath penetrating the fabric and bathing his chest was a little distracting.

He let her go and looked down at her, and he hoped he didn't look as confused as he felt. Because, *damn,* there had been a moment there…

He squelched the thought. Figuratively licked his thumb and forefinger and snuffed that little sucker right out. So what if it burned a little and he thought he heard the hiss? "You okay?" he asked, just so he could fill the silence and stop falling into her eyes.

"I'm fine. I'm right here in front of you, you can see I'm fine."

"I meant—"

"What the hell was that, anyway?" she asked, glancing toward the living room where the stairs were.

"I don't know."

She drew herself another step away from him. He let his hands fall from her shoulders to his sides. He hesitated only a moment before he realized she was probably waiting for him to *do* something. Then, before he could act on the realization, she said, "Well, I'm damned if I'm too afraid to go up there and find out."

She ought to be, he thought. But then he was ashamed of himself, because she was stomping off through the house toward the staircase, all alone. He followed her, caught up to her. Even put a hand on her again. He didn't plan to, it just sort of happened. His hands seemed to feel now that the ice had been broken, it was okay to touch her at will. Which, of course, it wasn't. Still, he put a hand on her shoulder, and she stopped at the bottom of the staircase and glanced over her shoulder at his face, looking mildly irritated.

"What?" she snapped.

"I'll go," he said. It came out in a deep tone that sounded rather heroic, he thought.

She rolled her eyes. "I'm going. But you can come with me if you want."

He nodded, stepped around her and started up the stairs. As if he were the big brave warrior, and she were the innocent virgin in need of his protection. What bull.

Still, he went up the stairs, down the hall. Then he stopped, uncertain which way to go.

"My bedroom is that one," she whispered, leaning closer and pointing.

"You think that's where the noise came from?" he whispered back.

She nodded, her wide eyes fixed on the bedroom door. She was scared to death and determined not to show it.

Then again, so was he. He moved toward the door, reached for the knob, put his hand on it and sucked in a breath at the iciness of the brass. Twisting all the same, he pushed the door open, stepped through—and *that* took some major willpower—and flipped on the light switch.

The first thing he saw was his breath forming little clouds in the air in front of him. He could see them. There was no mistaking it, the bedroom was that cold.

"Hell, here we go again," she whispered.

He stood very still, vaguely aware that Kiley was gripping his arm now, maybe a little less concerned about hiding her fear. He felt wind hitting him in the face and glanced toward the windows, relieved to realize there might be a very simple explanation for the cold—but the windows were shut tight.

Then where was that icy wind coming from?

"What the…?"

Suddenly, there was rattling, shaking. The lamp on the bedstand trembled, and the light fixture in the ceiling began to swing. The room exploded in sound and motion. Dresser drawers flew open one after the other, one of them so hard it wrenched itself out of the dresser and onto the floor, scattering its contents. The closet door flew open at the same time, as did the bathroom door, towels sailing through it as if hurled at them by unseen hands. The curtains were whipping like vipers.

Then—just as suddenly—the wind died and everything went still. Utterly, perfectly still. The curtains fell limply, the stands and fixtures stopped trembling, the room was silent again.

Jack breathed. Maybe for the first time since turning on the light. No steam emerged from his lips now. It was over, whatever the hell it had been.

And Kiley was still clutching his arm, with both hands this time, and her body was pressed tight to his side. Given that she'd sooner cling to a spraying skunk or a rabid badger—or both—he figured she must be pretty shaken.

"I don't like you, Jack," she said. "You know that, right?"

"Right. No more than I like you, Brigham."

"And I'm *not* afraid of this thing. I'm not afraid of *any*thing. You know that, too, right?"

He shrugged. "I've never seen you scared. I can give you that." Till now, he thought, but he didn't say that part aloud, mostly because it would piss her off and he was dying to see where the hell she was going with this.

"Good, just so we're clear on it. I wouldn't want you to take it the wrong way when I ask you to spend the night with me."

He swallowed hard, about to tell her she couldn't pay him enough to spend the night in this fucked-up house. But before he could speak, she went on.

"You're used to this, after all," she said. "You talk to the spirit world all the time, right? So you've seen this kind of shit before."

He probed those big eyes of hers, wondering for one brief moment if she could have possibly engineered this entire event, special effects and all, just to finally trip him up. And all of a sudden, he realized he had to be very, very careful.

"Right," he said. "Not that you ever really get used to it, but yeah, I've seen it before."

The relief on her face was so intense that he thought she was close to tears.

"I don't know why the hell that should make me feel any better, especially when I still don't believe you're for real."

"But it does?" he asked.

She pursed her lips. "Will you stay? Spend the night?"

He would rather stick hot needles into his own eyes, he thought. But aloud, he said, "Sure."

She sighed, lowering her head, eyes, shoulders, all at once. "Good."

"Hey, I'll expect suitable compensation for this. Don't think I'm doing it as a favor or anything."

"No, not on your life." She met his eyes again, hers hiding just a hint of a smile this time. "So do you think you can...get rid of it?"

He didn't even know what the hell *it* was. He was clueless. He'd never been within a hundred miles of a real ghost, so far as he knew. Didn't even believe in them—or hadn't, up until five minutes ago. Now he wasn't sure what to believe. "If this thing can be...banished, then I'm the guy who can do it." He was lying through his teeth.

Her shaky smile widened a little. "I'll tell you one thing, I'm not sleeping in here."

"Don't blame you there."

"Do you want to?"

"Huh?" He thought his eyeballs might have come close to popping out of his head.

She shrugged. "To get a better feel for—for whatever it is we're dealing with."

He pursed his lips. "Oh. No, there's…no need."

"Then you already know what it is?"

He nodded, deciding to say anything that came to mind, so long as it kept him from having to sleep in this room. He still had goose bumps, even though the chill had fled. "It—uh—seems like a pretty straightforward case of poltergeist activity. It's not that unusual. Not a big deal."

"Maybe not to you."

He shrugged. The genuine-looking gratitude gleaming up at him from her eyes gave him the *cojones* to move farther into the bedroom, where he bent to pick up a drawer, along with several of the items that had been flung from it. His nonchalance fled, though, when he realized he was holding a pair of thong panties in his hand. Something tightened in his nether regions, and he stuffed them back into the drawer and hoped she hadn't noticed.

"So is there a guest room or something?" he asked as he replaced the drawer in the dresser and closed all the others.

"Not furnished. We can sleep downstairs. There's a sofa bed."

He shot her a questioning look. She ignored it, swallowing something he took to be her pride when she said, "Will you wait here while I grab a nightgown?"

He nodded. "You, um…wanna shower?"

"Not in there."

He felt sorry when he saw the shudder that worked through her. "Hell, Brigham, why don't you just come back to my place with me, spend the night there? This is insane."

She met his eyes and shook her head just once, left then right. "I'm not letting this thing chase me out of my house." Then she took her gaze off him and looked around the room. "You hear that, spook? This is my goddamn house now. I've sunk every penny I have into it, and I couldn't leave if I wanted to. So you and I are just gonna have to come to terms! Got it?"

Jack half expected the house to reply, even found himself looking around at the empty space, as she had been doing. But the house said nothing.

Sighing, she strode past him to the dresser, yanking open a drawer and plucking a nightie from a stack of silky fabrics without even looking down. "You have got to get rid of it for me, Jack. You do this for me, and I swear, I'll lay off you forever."

He shook his head, his gaze stuck on the nightie she held. It was emerald-green, like her eyes. Satiny and smooth. Indecently short, with spaghetti straps and lace in the deep V of the neckline. He was actually curious to see how she was going to look in that thing.

If he were being honest with her, he supposed he might admit that he would actually miss it if she stopped bugging him all the time, trying to get the best of him. But he wasn't being honest with her. Far from it.

And he was about to begin living the lie of a lifetime.

She hurried out of the bedroom into the hall. He followed, pulling the bedroom door closed behind him, wishing he could lock it, wondering if locks could keep ghosts incarcerated and guessing probably not. He followed her down the hall to the stairs. On the way she opened a closet and tugged out a stack of sheets and blankets. Back downstairs, in the living room, she yanked the cushions off her sofa, and Jack assisted her in pulling it out. Then he stood there watching in some kind of surreal trance while she made up the bed. For two.

"Turn your back."

"What?"

"I want to get undressed and I'm afraid to leave the room by myself. Pathetic and stupid, I know, but there it is. So turn around."

He turned around. "And what am I supposed to sleep in?"

"Your shorts?" she asked.

He could hear her peeling off her clothes, the fabric brushing over her skin. It was interesting, trying to guess what she was taking off, what remained. He chided himself for having impure thoughts about his worst enemy, but then decided he was sleeping with her, so it was only natural.

She finally said, "Okay," and he turned again.

Then he saw her in the green nightie, the way it hung from her shoulders, flowing like a satin river over her skin, except for where it tripped over her breasts. He could see them clearly through the fabric, nipples and all. He found himself licking his lips and told himself to knock it the hell off.

"What?" she asked.

He jerked his gaze upward, to her eyes again. "You do realize you've left nearly every light in the house on?"

"And you think I want to sleep in the dark after that little exhibition upstairs?"

He shrugged. "You don't even want to brush your teeth?"

"Planning to kiss me before morning, Jack?"

"Not if you begged me, sweetie."

"Then why are you worried about it?"

"Because you might roll over and breathe on me."

She rolled her eyes. "My breath is fine. And I showered this morning. But if you need to, you can use the shower in the downstairs bathroom."

"I think I will."

"Good." She came to him, taking his hand as if he were a child being led to the school bus for the first time. "This way." She led him through the living room, down a hallway and in through the third door on the left. "Here we go."

"Great. Thanks."

He stood there for a minute, waiting. She leaned back against the countertop, also waiting.

"Uh, were you planning to stay for this?" he asked at length.

She licked her lips. "Figured I could brush my teeth while you were washing up."

She didn't wait for an answer, just turned to face the sink, opened the medicine cabinet and located a toothbrush that was still in its wrapper. "I always keep extras around. There's one for you, too." She took out a second toothbrush and laid it on the counter. Then she glanced over her shoulder with a frown. "Well, go on, take your shower. I'm not going to look at you."

"You're looking at me now."

"That's because you weren't moving." She turned to face the sink again, cranked on the water.

Sighing in resignation, Jack turned on the taps, adjusted the temperature and began stripping off his clothes.

CHAPTER SIX

SHE KEPT HER EYES LOWERED, everything in her focused on brushing her teeth, as he peeled off his clothes. The mirror was dead ahead. She could catch a glimpse of him if she wanted to, but she didn't want to. Hell, she couldn't think of anything she wanted less. Besides, by the time the thought had time to pass through her mind, he was under the spray. She heard him yank the curtain shut, heard the way the flow of water changed when he stepped underneath it.

From the shower he called, "I can't believe you're too scared to even go into the bathroom by yourself."

She frowned, her eyes rising to the mirror, where she could see very little—just his shadow on the shower curtain. "I am not scared."

"No?"

"No. I just want to make sure you're close by in case anything weird happens again."

"So I can protect you from the bogeyman?"

"So you can witness it. You're my ghost buster, after all."

"Uh-huh."

"So I figure you need access to this thing—so you can figure out how best to deal with it. So you'll know which rattles to shake and which weeds to burn, that kind of shit."

"Helpful of you."

"I do what I can." She rinsed her mouth, spit, gargled, spit again. "Don't let it fool you, though. I'm no more convinced than I've ever been that you're for real."

"Then why ask for my help?"

She thought on that for a long moment, then sighed. "You're the best shot I have. There's not really anyone else."

"So it's one of those 'last man on earth' situations?"

"More like one of those 'any port in a storm' situations."

"I see."

She sighed. "So, have you?"

"Have I what?"

"Figured out which rattles to shake and which weeds to burn?"

He was quiet for a moment. "I have some ideas."

"Good. How much longer are you going to be?"

"Two minutes, why?"

She glanced at the toilet, decided not to risk it, reached for a clean washcloth and turned on the taps.

"Hey!"

She looked up fast at the exclamation, realized her blasting hot water into the basin must have given him a shot of cold. "Sorry." She shut the water off. Then she smeared some of her facial cleanser on, dipped the cloth into the basin and washed her face. She was applying moisturizing night cream when she glimpsed his long, tanned arm snaking out of the shower, groping for a towel. She handed him one.

"Thanks."

"You're wel—" Before she could finish, he yanked back the curtain and stepped out of the shower. And then she was stuck there. She couldn't force her errant gaze to move from his body. Good God, it was incredible. Who would have thought such a jerk would have a body like that? Muscular shoulders, smooth and hard. Sculpted chest, and abs—oh, hell, his abs belonged in *Playgirl.* She could wash laundry on those abs.

"I'm wel…?" he asked.

"Built," she said.

"Compliments, from you?"

"More like an expression of surprise."

"Shock and awe?"

"Shock, yeah. Not so much of the awe."

He shrugged. "And what would it take to up your awe factor? Just out of curiosity, mind you."

She shrugged right back. "Hell, I don't know. Maybe if you lost the towel?"

He gaped. She grinned, and then he relaxed. "Funny," he said. He reached for his clothes, which he'd draped over the towel bar. The briefs he tugged free were small, dark blue and clingy. She finally worked up the willpower to stop gawking at him and turned around again. But she was all too aware that he was dropping the towel and pulling those briefs on, and some little devil inside was trying to talk her into peeking.

She resisted. Barely.

"You want to stay while I drain the snake?"

"Drain the…? Oh. That's the tackiest thing I've ever heard."

He shrugged and moved toward the toilet.

She darted out of the bathroom at the speed of light.

But she didn't go far. After closing the door behind her, she remained right there, just outside it. Hell, it pissed her off to no end that she was afraid to be alone in her own house. But damn.

She heard the flush, the water running in the sink. Then he finally stepped out of the bathroom. He didn't close the door, just held it open. And stood there looking at her.

"What?"

"Oh, come on. You know you have to. Go on, I'll wait right out here."

She thinned her lips, thought about snapping at him. But hell, he was right. She did have to go, and as a matter of fact it was borderline decent of him to offer to stay close by while she did.

"I don't need you to wait out here for me," she said as she went into the bathroom.

"No, I know you don't. But I'll wait here, anyway."

If she didn't dislike him so much, she'd have been grateful. As it was, she could only wonder if he was storing up all these weaknesses he was discovering in her for future use in the unending battle between them.

When she came out again, she noticed him looking at her body, and decided she wasn't the only one with weaknesses. He looked often, every time he thought she might not notice. Could her nemesis be attracted to her? Damn, she would never let him hear the end of it if he admitted that one!

She led the way back to the living room, flung back the covers and crawled into bed. She really hadn't been worried about spending the night with Jack. Now, though…

"You aren't going to put on a shirt?" she asked.

"Wasn't wearing a T-shirt," he said. "Can't very well sleep in my button-down."

"I don't know why not. I could."

His eyes changed just a little, lowering slowly. And she got the distinct impression he was picturing her sleeping in his button-down shirt, and liking the image.

"This isn't going to be a problem, is it, Jack?" she asked, sliding to one side to make room for him.

He got into the bed beside her, pulled the covers over them both and lay back on the pillows with his hands folded behind his head. "What isn't?"

The attraction, she thought. The fact that his body turned her on like nobody's business and the feeling she got that he was having the same reaction to hers. But she wasn't going to be the one to admit it! "Nothing," she said. "Never mind."

He nodded. "'Night, Brigham."

"'Night, Jack."

She closed her eyes, knowing good and damned well she would never sleep.

He did not seem to have the same problem. In fact, he was snoring softly within ten minutes. And five minutes after that, he rolled over, and before she knew what to expect, he had wrapped her up tight against him, imprisoning her there with one arm and one leg. Her face was pressed to his utterly unclothed chest, one arm caught between his belly and hers, and her pelvis was mashed to his groin.

"Oh, great," she whispered.

"Mmm," he replied. And then one of his big hands burrowed into her hair, stroking just a little before settling down.

Something in her stomach turned a somersault. She tried to tug her arm from where it was trapped between them, but in the process her hand brushed over his abs, and she stopped what she was doing as her heart skipped a beat. Lifting her head away from his chest, just a little, she peered up at his face. His eyes were closed, his breaths deep and steady. Sound asleep. So…

She let her palm rest lightly on his abdomen, and when he didn't stir or react, she moved it just a little, up and down over the rippling muscles there. God, he must work out like a man driven to have a belly like this. She'd never touched anything so perfect. So arousing. Too bad it was attached to a man she didn't like.

"Hey, Kiley?"

She froze, her hand going still.

"You awake?"

That was it, that was it. Just pretend to be asleep. Perfect. She tried to breathe the way a sleeper breathed, but gradually, so he wouldn't notice the sudden change.

"Kiley?"

She didn't respond, just kept breathing, kept still.

He drew his arm from around her, eased her from her side onto her back so slowly she knew he was trying not to wake her. She guessed he didn't want her to realize he'd been holding her so…intimately.

But no, that wasn't it. A second later, she knew that wasn't it, because he was sitting up, just a little, and she felt his hand pushing her hair away from her face, slowly, softly. The warmth of his touch trailed over her jaw to her neck, to her shoulder, and slowly, slowly, lower, drifted over her satin-covered breast, making her want to slap him and arch closer all at the same time. But he kept going, sliding his hand to her belly, sideways to trace the curve of her waist, and back again to her abdomen.

Enough. Hell, it was enough. He was making her hot without even trying, and if he kept it up she was going to have an orgasm right in front of him.

She made a little noise in her throat and slowly rolled onto her side, facing away from him, just so he'd get thc idea that, even asleep, she was rejecting him.

He went still for a moment. And then he was touching her again. His hands, both of them now, on the small of her back and sliding lower, boldly, right to her buttocks, cupping her cheeks and squeezing.

Furious and more turned on than she could believe, she jerked onto her other side, facing him, and said, "Just what the hell do you think you're doing?"

He smiled slowly. "Same thing you were doing to me a few minutes ago, Kiley. Fair is fair."

"I don't have a clue what you're talking about. I wasn't doing anything but sleeping a few minutes ago."

"Liar." His hand closed on her wrist, and he put her hand on his abdomen again, held it there with his hand over it. "Go on, touch to your heart's content. It's not like I mind."

"You damn well should mind. You don't even like me."

He shrugged. "I'm a guy. Liking you doesn't have to enter into it. Go on, satisfy your curiosity. Feel me up."

She slid her hand upward over those rock-hard abs even as she pulled it away. "You are so full of yourself."

"I'd far prefer you to be full of me."

She blinked hard and fast. "What?"

He shrugged. “We’re both adults. Unmarried, uncommitted.”

“One of us ought to be committed, though.”

He smiled slowly, pushing her hair away from her face. “If we’re not gonna be enemies anymore—are, in fact, becoming allies in the war against your spooks—then there’s really no reason we shouldn’t.”

“There are a million reasons we shouldn’t.”

“You want to. I want to. It’s surprising, I admit that, but—”

“I do not want to.”

“No?” He ran the back of his hand over her breast again, and then again as her nipple grew hard and tight. “Gee, Kiley, your body says otherwise.”

She narrowed her eyes on him. “I hate you.”

“You want me, though. I want you, too.”

“You son of a—”

His hand slid down over her belly, and she felt herself wanting it to keep going, wanting him to touch her.

“Tell me to stop,” he whispered.

She didn’t. And he was right, liking didn’t even enter into it.

His fingers touched the top of her panties. He slid them inside. “You can tell me to stop anytime, you know,” he whispered again. He was leaning over her now, his face very, very close to hers. “But I hope you don’t.”

She told herself to tell him to stop, and then tell him to go away. But instead, she felt her thighs ease a little farther apart, her hips push against his hand, just a little.

He moved his hand farther, sliding his fingers between her moist lips, parting them, and rubbing against the softness they hid. "Damn, woman. I haven't been this hot for anyone in ten years. Why the hell did it have to be you?"

She tried to answer, but all that came out was a soft moan, and that just made him rub her harder, exploring new places, probing to new depths. Shameless, she opened up to him and moved against his hand, and her breaths came faster. She reached for him, desperate to know this was hitting him as hard as it was hitting her, and her hand closed around him, thick and hard and pulsing with need. So she rubbed, teased him the way he was teasing her.

He drew his hand away, got up onto his hands and knees, above her. She felt cold, empty, ached to be in his arms again. But he was kneeling over her, stripping away her panties, peeling off her nightgown, staring down at her naked body. "God, Brigham. You never told me you were a goddamn goddess." He closed his hands on her breasts, squeezing, kneading them.

She wanted him as naked and vulnerable as she was, so she tugged at his briefs until they came down and she had complete access to his erection.

He slid off the foot of the bed, grabbed her ankles and dragged her lower on the mattress until her butt was at the very edge. He slid his hands up her legs to her knees and bent them up, back, wide. She was aching for him by now. Squirming and pleading in soft whimpers for him to do it, already. Holding her like that, he pushed himself slowly, deeply inside her, farther, and still farther.

"Oh, yes," she moaned, her eyes falling closed.

He buried himself inside her, filled her to her very depths. And then, for some reason, he went still and swore softly under his breath.

CHAPTER SEVEN

THE LIGHTS WERE OUT. He was kneeling between her warm, firm thighs, buried inside her, every nerve ending in his body electrified. And every single light in the place had just gone out, making Jack wonder if someone had come in. Or maybe the storm going on inside him was actually happening outside, and the power had gone out.

He stopped moving, and she whimpered in protest. Then he wondered what the hell demon lived in this house, that it would possess him to do something as stupid as to sleep with his worst enemy. And yet, when he looked at her, lying beneath him, squirming against him, head moving side to side, eyes closed, he wanted to ignore the sudden blackout and keep up what he was doing. It would be a mistake, but damn, what a pleasant mistake to make.

He hovered there, deep inside her, debating, mind against body. He drove himself just a little deeper, loving the sounds she made as she took him. And then the light in the stairway flashed on, flickered, went off again. "Hell," he muttered.

"What?"

Her eyes blinked open, just as the TV set flashed on,

its volume full throttle, blasting a hard rock video. The surprise of that blast of noise sent her eyes flying wider. He withdrew from her fast, as startled as she was.

She blinked at the TV screen, then at the flickering stairway light. “Jack?”

“I’ll shut it off.” He went to turn off the television. The volume was deafening.

“Wait.” She said it loud, then reached out and grabbed the remote from the end table beside the sofa bed. She hit the power button on the TV, and it went dark, silent. The stair light flicked again, then stayed on. One by one the other lights came back on as well.

She pursed her lips, drawing the sheet up to her chest as if suddenly embarrassed to be naked in front of him. “Maybe my ghost is the jealous type.”

He smiled, not because she was funny, but because she was making jokes when she must be frightened half out of her mind. Kiley was a tough one, but then again, he’d always known that. “Maybe it’s just as well,” he said, and couldn’t believe he was saying it.

“I was thinking the same thing. Sex probably isn’t the best idea we ever had. We don’t even like each other.”

“Oh, I don’t know. You’re growing on me, Brigham.”

“Yeah, and us being naked in the same bed has nothing to do with that whatsoever?”

“I didn’t say that.”

She shook her head. “Whatever just happened here—”

“Almost happened,” he corrected her.

“Almost?” She pursed her lips. “We didn’t finish, Jack, but we definitely got started.”

“It was a goddamn good start, too.”

She averted her eyes. "It wasn't based on affection. Or caring. Or any tender feelings whatsoever."

"Oh, come on. Don't pretend you can speak for me on that."

"Jack, we didn't even kiss first."

He mulled that over, realized she was right. So no kissing, to a female, equaled no caring, no tenderness. Good to know. "Okay, so there was no kissing. So if this thing that almost happened—that started to happen—wasn't based on affection, then what was it based on?"

She shrugged. "Libido? Fear? Chemistry?"

"And those are the wrong reasons to have sex?" he asked.

"All the wrong reasons. But it's okay. The ghost caught us in time."

"Gives me even more motivation to help you get rid of it," he said, sending her an evil grin.

She smiled back, and a lump formed in his throat as he watched the movement of her lips, and he realized he wanted to kiss her. He regretted not taking his time, before. Just as well, though. Hell, what would she have read into it then? Still, the thought persisted.

"Think you can sleep?" she asked. She was getting out of the bed, tugging the covers with her. He glimpsed as much of her as possible, figuring it would be his last chance for a while.

He surprised himself by answering honestly. "Not next to you, no."

She picked up her nightie, pulled it on over her head, letting the covers go only when she was concealed. Didn't matter. He'd seen her and the image was burned into his mind. He almost groaned aloud when she stepped into the panties and pulled them up.

Then she tossed him his briefs, because he was sitting there on the bed with a pillow over his privates. "Good," she said.

"Good what? That I'm not going to be able to sleep?"

"Exactly. I won't sleep, either. Between almost jumping your bones and the damn ghost, I'll be lucky if I can sleep again for a week."

"You sound like you have a plan—something we can do instead."

She nodded, padding across the room and taking the book she'd had in her car earlier from the fireplace mantel. He used the opportunity to pull on his underwear and prop the pillow behind his head. She said, "We can read. I already got started, but nothing that really explains any of this has shown up so far."

She handed him the book. He looked at it and nodded.

"There's an entire chapter on this house, in fact." She climbed back into the bed beside him. "I think I might have a case against the real estate agency. Do you?"

"Failure to disclose ghosts. Yeah, it's probably in the law books, right in the same section where they have to disclose termites and leaky roofs."

She smiled again. "Go on, open to the chapter. We may as well read it together, though I'm not altogether sure I want to know any more than I already do."

He nodded, flipped to the chapter that opened with a photo of her house and started reading.

BY THE TIME THEY FINISHED the chapter it was nearly dawn. The "ghost" or whatever was raising hell in

Kiley's new home had been quiet for the rest of the night, and she was starved.

She closed the cover. "Well, that was helpful."

"Not."

She stretched and got to her feet. "Hungry?"

"Don't tell me you're offering to cook me breakfast?"

"What are you, insane? You're taking me to IHOP."

He glanced at his watch. "They won't be open for an hour and a half."

She pouted. "Oh, hell. Well, I can scramble an egg, but the whites might be runny. I never seem to get them quite—"

"How about if I make breakfast?"

She raised her eyebrows.

"Yeah, I can cook. Just don't let it get around." He got up, pulled on his jeans.

She led the way to the kitchen, showed him where things were, put on a pot of coffee, then sat at the table and watched him work. He knew his way around a kitchen, whisking eggs in a large bowl, adding milk, cinnamon, nutmeg, soaking slices of bread in the concoction, and dropping them onto a sizzling griddle.

"Wow," she said.

"I'm a man of many talents." He glanced at her. "As you would have found out last night, had we not been so rudely interrupted."

She let herself grin back. This was something new, this flirting going on between them. She wasn't sure how to react to it. Was this going to be the new nature of their relationship, now that she'd vowed to stop trying to discredit him and put him out of business? How odd it would be not to be his worst nightmare. She wasn't sure how to deal with it, or whether she even liked it. She'd enjoyed tormenting him, hounding him.

So she decided to change the subject. "Let's nutshell this, shall we?"

"Sure." He expertly flipped the French toast.

"What do we know about this house that we didn't know before?" she asked.

"Well, the last couple who lived here moved out within six months, but refused to cite a reason or be interviewed by the book's author," Jack said.

"The couple before that claimed that the place was haunted. Talked about lights and things going on and off, items being moved around, footsteps in the middle of the night."

"Nothing as drastic as what's been happening to you, though."

She nodded. "Same as the family who lived here before them. They actually liked the ghost, said it watched out for them. I wonder why. I mean, the ghost has never seemed hostile to anyone else—"

"That we know of," he said.

She nodded. "But prior to that, there was nothing—not until the suicide."

"Yeah. You know, I had no idea Phil Miller had ever lived in this house, much less that his first wife had committed suicide."

"You mean you know him?"

He nodded. "He's a music teacher in a neighboring school district. Must be close to retirement age by now. But I've seen him around."

"He comes into your shop? Seems interested in the spiritual?"

"Nah. We eat in the same diner a lot."

"Oh." She was disappointed. For a moment there, she thought she might be onto something. Then she brightened again. "Still, it was right after her death that the haunting began. Do you think it's Sharon Miller, Jack? Do you think she's the ghost?"

He shrugged. "Need a plate, here."

She hopped up, got two plates from the cupboard and handed him one. He stacked three slices of the toast onto it, handed it back to her and threw in three more. "Go ahead and start without me."

She set her plate on the table, went to the fridge for margarine, maple syrup and got out a bottle of orange juice while she was at it. Then she got silverware and glasses for them, and when that was done, poured two mugs full of coffee and set the creamer and sugar on the table.

"There."

By then he was flipping his three slices onto his plate and joining her. He sat down. She said, "So where should we begin?"

"Well, you can tell me what your life was like before you came to Burnt Hills," he said.

She looked up quickly. "I meant with the ghost. Can you just exorcise this thing, or do you need to know more about it, first?"

He seemed to be taking his time, thinking it over while adding syrup to his toast, cream to his coffee. "Well," he said at length. "The more information we have, the more effective the exorcism will be."

"That's what I figured. So what's the plan?"

"Right now, eating breakfast. And talking. Where are you from, Kiley?"

She sighed. "You really wanna know?"

"Yeah. I know, it seems odd to me, too."

She shrugged, took a bite and moaned in ecstasy. When she'd swallowed, she said, "This is incredible."

"I know."

She licked her lips. "I was a spoiled little rich girl from Richmond, Virginia. Inherited my parents' entire fortune. Fell for a con man who married me, took me for every red cent, and then left me high and dry."

She felt his eyes on her, realized he'd stopped eating. Slowly she looked up at him.

"That's why you're so down on people you perceive to be hucksters?"

She nodded. "It's why I stopped believing anything I couldn't find proof of." She shrugged. "Maybe I've been wrong. Maybe my own bitterness has warped my vision."

"Maybe." He wasn't quite meeting her eyes anymore, and he dug back into his breakfast as if it were the most important thing he would do all day.

When she finished and was sipping her coffee, she leaned back in her chair. "God, I feel like patting my belly. That was delicious."

"Glad I managed to satisfy at least one of your physical cravings."

She smirked at him. "Oh, I don't think you'd have had any trouble with the other."

"No?"

She didn't answer. Since when did she stroke this man's ego? Not that that's what she was doing. He'd been good. God, it would have been mind-blowing. But it didn't pay to think about that now. It hadn't happened. It wasn't going to.

"Okay, so here's what I'm thinking," she said.

"About what?"

"About the ghost. I think we should contact the last couple who lived here."

"The ones who wouldn't talk to the author?"

She nodded. "They might be more willing to talk to me. I mean, I'm living here, after all."

"You're also a journalist who enjoys exposing people as frauds. They might be suspicious of you."

"Hmm, you have a point. Okay, so you'll have to help me talk to them. Meanwhile, we'll do a little investigative digging into Mr. Miller. See if we can find out anything more about his wife's death."

"Like what?"

"Like how she killed herself, and why. And what she might want from me." She licked her lips. "Maybe you could consult the Ouija board or whatever the hell you use, see if you can get any answers from her directly."

"Naturally. That was going to be my first move."

She nodded, swallowed more coffee. Outside the sun was coming up, its orange-yellow rays beaming in through the kitchen windows. "I suppose I should take a shower."

He nodded. "Yeah. I should wash up and shave, myself. You want me to stand in the bathroom while you shower?"

She licked her lips. That would be a bad idea. Very bad. She would be all too tempted to reach out and yank him into the water with her. "I think I'll be okay, now that it's light outside. So long as I use the downstairs bathroom."

He lifted his chin, cleared his throat. "Tell you what, I'll go use the upstairs one. Just to see what happens."

"You're a better man than I am," she told him. He was either very brave or very foolish, she wasn't sure which. "Let's both leave the doors open, okay?"

"Deal."

Gathering her nerve, she cleared the table and tossed the dishes into the dishwasher, just as a delaying tactic. Then she went to her bathroom, listening to Jack's footsteps on the stairs as he went to his.

It wasn't freezing cold. That was a good sign. The sun was beaming in through the window, higher now than before. The lights were working. She opened the cabinet, taking out her body wash, bath oil, shampoo, conditioner, loofah. Then, with all those items loaded in her arms, she turned to face the tub.

And then she dropped everything on the floor and screamed at the top of her lungs.

The tub was full to the brim, water sloshing over the top onto the floor. And lying there, beneath the clear, warm water, was a woman. Her blond hair floated like a nest of yellow snakes around her head. Her mouth was slightly agape. And her eyes were wide open, focused on Kiley's, and pleading.

CHAPTER EIGHT

THE SOUND OF HER SCREAM split his mind wide open and let a slew of nightmarish images flow in, each more horrific than the one before. Even though he was running before the sound died, he couldn't seem to get to her fast enough.

And then he did.

She was backed into the farthest corner of the downstairs bathroom, with one hand fisted near her mouth and the other one pointing, trembling, at the tub.

He looked at the bathtub, half afraid to. But there was nothing there.

"Kiley?" He moved closer to her. "What, what is it?"

When he stood right in front of her, blocking her view of the tub, her glazed eyes focused on him. "It was there. Jack, it was there, in the tub, she was—"

"Wait, wait, hold up a sec." The tempo, pitch and decibel levels of her voice had been rising steadily, and he sensed she was close to panic, so he closed his hands on her shoulders, intending to lead her out of the bathroom, into something more nearly resembling safe ground. As soon as he touched her, she fell into his arms, sliding her arms around his back, burying her face in his chest and holding on so tight he thought she might crack his ribs.

He buried a hand in her hair, snapped the other around her waist and tried to keep holding her that way while maneuvering them both out of the bathroom. He took her all the way through the house, and outside, to her car—she in her nightgown, and he in his jeans. He paused only long enough to snag her key ring from the hook by the door.

"Jack, what are we…?"

"Screw this. You need to get the hell out of that house. For now, just for now."

"I haven't even showered."

"You can shower at my place."

"But my clothes—"

"I'll come back and get you some."

"Alone?"

"Not on your life." He put her in her car, shut the door, went around to the driver's side and got behind the wheel. Only when they were heading down the road did he turn to face her, to ask her, "What did you see in the bathtub, Kiley?"

She licked her lips, sat a little straighter in the seat. "I think I know how Mrs. Miller killed herself," she said softly.

He lifted his brows. "How?"

"Drowning. In the bathtub, I think."

"And you think this because?" He was almost afraid to ask.

"Because I saw her. That tub was full of water. Overflowing, even, and she was there, lying there on the bottom. Her eyes were open and she was looking right at me."

The last few words came out in a whisper. He ached for her, literally felt pangs in his belly for her pain.

She sent him a searching look. "She was there. She was really there."

"I believe you."

"She was young, beautiful, when she died. Long honey-blond hair. Green eyes. She could've been a model."

He nodded. "We're here," he said, pulling her car into his driveway. He lived in a modest-size log home, one story with a loft. Just big enough for him. He liked it, maybe more now than ever. No history, no ghosts. Not that he believed in the damn things, anyway. He stopped the car. The look of relief on Kiley's face was something to see. He got out, went to open her door for her, but she beat him to it.

He led her inside, unlocking the place, holding the door. "I'd show you around, but it would be a short trip. Kitchen's in there. Bedroom's up in the loft. Bathroom's through there, and there's a den in back.

"And this is the living room."

He nodded. "Go on, go take your shower. And then sack out in my bed for a while. You're dead on your feet."

"I should go in to work."

"Call 'em. Phone's in the kitchen."

"Okay. Yeah. Okay, I can rest here." She looked around, sighed. "This is a nice place, Jack. It feels good here."

"And not a ghost in sight," he said.

She smiled. "Thanks for this."

He nodded. "I need to go to the shop, see Chris, and then I'll head back to your place and pick you up a few things. Okay?"

"Don't go there alone, Jack."

"I won't. But I will bring you back some clothes and stuff. I'll be a couple of hours. No more. And if you need me, my cell phone number is programmed into the phone. Number nine."

She nodded. "I really do owe you for all of this."

He sent her an evil smile. "And I fully intend to collect, Brigham. So don't fret about it too much."

CHRIS WAS ALREADY TURNING the Closed sign around to the Open side when Jack walked up to the door of the shop. The kid stepped aside to let him in, but before Jack could so much as say "good morning" the questions were pouring out.

"So? What happened last night? You didn't go home. I know, 'cause I called six times. Did you spend the night with her? Did anything happen? I thought you hated each other. What's going on, Jack?"

Jack held up two hands and hurried through the shop toward the section in the back that was devoted entirely to books. Then he stood there, perusing the rack.

"Jack?" Chris asked. "C'mon, aren't you going to tell me anything?"

Sighing, Jack looked down at the kid. "It's not good, I'll tell you that."

"No? Not even…?"

"No, not even. And don't ask again, kid. That's none of your business. Besides, it has nothing to do with whatever the hell is haunting Kiley Brigham's house."

Chris licked his lips. "I, uh—thought you didn't believe in ghosts, Jack."

"Didn't. Not until last night."

Chris widened his eyes. "You saw it?"

He shook his head. "Lights flashing, drawers flying around the bedroom, doors slamming."

Chris licked his lips. "So you were in her bedroom."

He sent the kid a glare. "Part of the job, kid."

"Job?" Then Chris went pale. "You don't mean—"

"The lady has hired me to get rid of her ghost."

"B-but…you—"

"Believe me, I know. So now I'm in one hell of a predicament. I either admit to her that I'm a fake, or I fake my way through this, fail, and then she'll know I'm a fake, anyway." He lowered his head. "And she's been burned by a fraud like me before, Chris. Hell, when she finds out the truth—" He made himself stop there, before he gave away more than he wanted to. Not that he had a clue what he'd be giving away. He was confused as hell right now.

Chris shrugged. "One way to solve the whole mess," he said. "You just have to get rid of the ghost for her."

"Oh, come on, kid."

"It's not like you haven't done it before. You've cleared a dozen houses right in Burnt Hills alone."

"That wasn't real and you know it. I read a few books, went through the motions and eased the minds of some extremely nervous people with vivid imaginations."

"You helped them. None of them had any visitations after you finished."

"None of them had any visitations before I started."

"How can you be so sure of that?"

Jack didn't reply.

"And what about all the readings, Jack? The advice you give these people, the way it helps them?"

"It's not hard to give people good advice."

"As good as yours, and all the time? Jack, did you ever stop to think that maybe the reason Kiley Brigham can't prove you're a fraud is because you aren't?"

He rolled his eyes.

"You knew that client was a fake the other day. You knew Ms. Brigham was in the shop. Hell, I'll bet you knew there was something in her house the second you walked through the door, if not sooner."

Jack thinned his lips. "Listen, none of this matters, anyway. We've got work to do here. I need to find the last people who lived in that house, and see if they're willing to talk to us, and I need to figure out how the hell to get rid of a ghost. A real ghost."

The kid shrugged. "The first part's easy. Brad and Cindy Stark moved to Saratoga Springs."

"You know how to reach them?"

The kid shrugged, walked to the checkout counter and pulled a telephone directory from underneath. Flipping it open, he ran his fingers along a list of names, and said, "Here you go."

Jack turned the book around, saw the listing, couldn't believe it was this easy. Then he picked up the phone.

KILEY HAD SHOWERED, DRESSED in one of Jack's clean T-shirts, and then crawled into his bed and slept like a log. She only woke when something touched her cheek, gentle as a breeze, making her eyes flutter open. Jack was crouching beside the bed, looking at her oddly.

"Oh. Hi again," she said.

"I hated to wake you, but we have a date."

She blinked sleepily. "A date?"

"Yeah. Here, I brought you some clothes." He nodded toward the stack of neatly folded garments he'd placed on the nightstand.

She sat up in the bed, raking her hair with one hand. "You went back to the house?"

"Yep."

"Alone?"

He smiled sheepishly. "Hell, no. Took Chris along."

She laughed, shaking her head.

"What? That's funny?"

"Just that a guy built like you are would drag scrawny little Chris along for protection."

"I didn't take him for protection—I took him as a witness, in case something too odd to believe happened to go down, and—" He stopped there. "A body like mine, huh?"

She pursed her lips, threw back the covers and got out of the bed, though she had to slide by him to do it. He was still sitting on the edge. "So did anything happen?"

"What? Uh, no. Nothing. Just grabbed you some clothes—although, I kind of wish I hadn't."

Frowning, she swung her gaze his way. But his eyes weren't on hers; they were sliding up and down her body instead.

He said, "You look so damn good in my T-shirt it's a shame you have to change."

"Oh, yeah. And what is it you're hoping to accomplish with that line of bull?"

He shook his head slowly. "It's not a line, Kiley. I'd have said something sooner—I just…never thought of you that way. Till last night, at least." He gave a little shrug, met her eyes with a teasing light appearing in his own. "Guess it took sleeping with you to open my eyes."

"Yeah, that'll do it every time." She held her clothes to her chest and headed into the bathroom, muttering, "Men." Then she closed the door behind her. She tried to put his words out of her mind as she dressed. It was only his libido talking. He didn't like her, much less give a damn about her. This was all based on the heat that had flared up between them last night, and that had been based on nothing more than pure idiocy, combined with bowstring-taut tension and bone-chilling fear. All that adrenaline pumping. All that unbelievable shit happening in her house. Sure, they'd reacted. Why the hell wouldn't they?

It was a mistake, and it meant nothing. And God, she wanted to do it again—and not be interrupted this time.

The look in his eyes had been so intense just now. She'd felt an answering heat rise up under her skin everywhere his gaze lingered. His voice had gone all soft and throaty and it felt like a touch when he said her name.

"Knock it off, Brigham." She said it to her reflection, and she said it firmly.

Her reflection looked back at her, wearing the tight, low-slung jeans he'd picked out, with a tiny T-shirt that hugged every curve. She wondered if he'd done it on purpose.

"Did you say something?" he asked from beyond the door.

"Uh—what's this date you mentioned?" It was the only thing she could think of on short notice. Besides wondering how he would react when he saw her in these jeans, and then chiding herself for wondering. Still, her tummy tightened in anticipation.

"I found the people who lived in the house before you. Turns out Chris knew who they were. Moved out to Saratoga Springs."

She went to the bathroom door, a hairbrush in her hand, and yanked the door open. "You called them?"

He nodded.

"And they agreed to meet us?"

"For lunch today at— Holy shit. I take it back."

"You take what back?" But she already knew. She knew by the way his eyes were wandering down her body, even before he reached out to clasp her arm and draw her farther into the room, so he could walk around behind her.

"I take back wishing I hadn't brought you any clothes. How come I've never seen you in those jeans before?"

She shrugged. "You wouldn't have noticed if you had."

"A dead man would have noticed you in those, lady."

She sighed, turned to face him and looked him square in the eye. "Jack, what the hell are you doing?"

He looked surprised, but not confused. He knew exactly what she meant, and he didn't pretend otherwise. Sighing, he lowered his eyes. "Damned if I know."

"Well, do you think you could knock it off?"

"You really want me to?"

She licked her lips. "I don't know. But I do know it keeps me so off balance I can't think straight. It's goddamn surreal to have my worst enemy flirting with me like this. Almost as fucked up as the ghost in my house."

"Yeah. Okay, I get that. Although I think we're way

past that "worst enemy" stage. It's bull and we both know it."

She lowered her head. "Okay, it's bull."

"I never hated you as much as I pretended to."

"Me, neither," she admitted.

"It feels odd to me, Kiley, to be so into you all of a sudden. But I am."

She looked at him, questioning him with her eyes.

"I'm still not sure if you really want me to rein it in."

Kiley sighed, looking away. "Hell, Jack, neither am I."

He lifted his brows, tipped his head to one side. "Maybe if we just did it, got it out of our systems…"

She looked at the clock on the nightstand. "That's such a freakin' brilliant idea, it's a crying shame we don't have time."

He eyed her. "You're being sarcastic."

"No, I mean it. I'd bang you right here if it wasn't already twenty to twelve. 'Cause God knows that would fix everything."

"I never said it would fix everything."

"Jerk."

"Bitch."

She held his gaze, then smiled slowly. "Now, *that* feels normal." Then she preceded him out of the bedroom and down to the car.

CHAPTER NINE

JACK SAT ACROSS FROM the couple he couldn't stop thinking of as Ken and Barbie, and watched their eyes as they spoke.

"I really don't know why we agreed to this. It's kind of silly," Cindy Stark said.

"You agreed because I told you there was a perfectly nice, innocent woman living in that house now, and that she was going through hell," Jack said. "You agreed because I laid a big guilt trip on you."

The woman pursed her lips and met her husband's eyes. "Still, that's got nothing to do with us." She slanted her gaze toward Kiley. "Whatever you're going through, it's got nothing to do with us."

"I know that," Kiley said. "But if you could just tell me what happened to drive you out of that house…?"

"Nothing drove us out," her husband, Brad, said with a nervous laugh. "We found a great place in the Springs."

"Oh, it's gorgeous," Cindy beamed. "Totally restored Victorian. We did it in shamrock, with three shades of maroon in the trim."

Jack nodded, translating their words. "You have a nice, clean, spook-free life now, and you don't want to pollute it with thoughts about the trouble you left behind. It's almost as if you might accidentally conjure the same trouble in the new place if you admit to what happened in the old."

Cindy widened her eyes. "How can you—how does he…?"

"Don't be silly, dear," Brad said, silencing her by covering her hand with his own. "He's taking shots in the dark."

"No," she whispered. "He's reading my mind."

Kiley shot Jack a look, surprise or something like it in her eyes. Then she drew her gaze back to Cindy's. "He's going to help me clear the house."

"It's not going to work. We had three different people come in and try to clear it, but nothing worked."

"Maybe not, but if anyone can clear this place, Jack can," Kiley went on. "The thing is, our chances of success are much better if we can figure out what's really going on, what's causing this. To do that, I need to know what happened. What did you see, what did you hear, what did you feel in that house?"

Brad looked at Cindy, willing her not to say a word.

Jack said, "Knock it off, pal. If you don't want to help us, that's your choice. Don't try to make her responsible for your bad karma."

Brad rolled his eyes and looked away. "I don't believe in karma."

"I do," Cindy said. "I believe in a lot of things I never did before." She licked her lips. "There's more than one ghost in that house, Ms. Brigham. There's the woman in the tub, she's the main one."

"You mean you saw her, too?" Kiley asked.

Cindy nodded. “Once in the upstairs bath, once in the downstairs one. But there are others. So many others. And some of them are angry. Some of them—lash out.”

“Where have you seen these others?”

“We never saw them.” Brad was speaking now. “But there were—incidents. Mostly in the cellar, but once in a while they’d come into the main parts of the house. Threaten us. Shit like that.”

“Not us,” Cindy said. “Just you, Brad. They never tried to harm or frighten me the way they did you.”

“What did they do to you?” Jack asked the other man.

Brad pursed his lips, lowered his head, shook it.

“There was the time he was going down the cellar stairs to check a circuit breaker, and the light bulb exploded. He was in total darkness, and when he turned to come back up for a flashlight, there was a wound-up piece of wire on the stairs.”

“I’d have sworn it wasn’t there when I went down,” he said.

“You fell?” Kiley asked.

He nodded. “Broke a leg and two ribs.”

“And there was the incident with the water heater. The way the pilot kept going out, the matches kept blowing out, the gas was running into the cellar. And when Brad tried to come up the stairs, the door was jammed. Wouldn’t open.”

“My God, how did you get out?” Kiley asked.

“I don’t know. Eventually they just…let me.”

“They didn’t want you dead,” Jack said. “They just wanted you to pay attention. What do you do for a living?”

The man looked up slowly. “I’m a cop.”

KILEY SPENT THE AFTERNOON at her office, trying to at least look as if she were working on a story. But the pages she keyed into her computer were not work. Not the kind she was paid to do, at least. Instead, she filled screen after screen with a detailed account of everything that had been happening in her house, everything she had learned and everything she feared.

It accomplished little, she decided later on. In fact, it accomplished nothing, except to keep her mind focused on her fear. She supposed that was better than leaving it focused on the change in her relationship with Jack McCain, which was something that scared her more than any ghost ever could. What the hell was up with that, anyway?

Sighing, she glanced at the clock, realized the day was spent and thought it was time to go home. Then she shivered. Damn, but she didn't want to go back there. And yet, her spine straightened and she got to her feet. She was not going to let anything scare her out of her home. She was not going to become so needy that she couldn't go into her own house without a chaperone. No way in hell.

She shut down her computer, shouldered her purse and picked up her keys. Fifteen minutes later, she was standing beside her car, staring at the house. The lights were still on. She'd never turned them off. She was glad of that now, even though it wasn't completely dark yet. Taking a breath, she marched up to the door, punched in her access code and went inside. And then she stood there, with the door wide open and the entire house spread out before her. Empty, she told herself. But it didn't feel empty. It felt as if there were eyes on her, watching her, waiting.

Kiley looked around the empty house. "Listen up, okay?" She said the words loudly, and felt like an idiot for standing in her open doorway talking to herself. "I don't even know if you can hear me, but if you can I have something to say, so pay attention."

She felt something. Or maybe it was her imagination. Whatever, her courage rose a notch, and she found herself stepping farther inside. "I know you're here. I know there's something wrong, something you want me to understand. I know that now. And I'm going to find out what it is. I'm going to do everything I can to figure it out and make it right. I'm going to dig until I uncover the truth, and—"

She stopped there, because a vase tipped right off a stand and shattered on the floor.

Kiley jerked backward, almost turned and fled right back through the door, but then she stopped herself. "What?" she asked. "Something I said?"

Nothing. No sound.

"Okay, then. Okay. I just...wanted to let you know I'm on your side, here. All right?"

She listened, half expecting the ghost or whatever the hell it was to reply. But it didn't.

"Of course, if you hurt me, or scare me out of the house, the deal's off. So how about you give it a rest for a while, give me a few days to get to the bottom of this?"

Again, there was no reply. Then again, she hadn't really expected one. She sighed and moved through to the living room, sinking into a chair and sighing again. "I'll be fine here by myself," she muttered. "Until I have to use the bathroom. What the hell am I going to do then?"

"Kiley?"

She lifted her head, startled by the voice calling her name, but only for a brief instant. It was only Jack. He stood in the doorway, a large pizza box balanced on one hand, a brown paper bag in the other.

Hell, she thought. She shouldn't be so damned glad to see him. And yet she had to fight to keep herself from smiling ear to ear and running to him.

"I stopped by the office, but you'd already left."

"Figured I had to face it sooner or later. You didn't have to come, Jack."

"I couldn't have slept a wink with you out here alone. Besides, I've been doing some research, and I think I've come up with an idea."

"Yeah?"

He nodded, striding through the formal dining room and into the cozier kitchen. She followed him.

"Sit," he said. "I brought dinner." He put the pizza box on the table, set down the bag, and then went to the cupboards for plates and tall glasses.

"Health food, I see."

"Hell, yeah."

She peeked inside the bag, found a six-pack of cola and a large bag of potato chips, and smiled. "What, no tofu? No herbal tea?"

He put the plates on the table, went to the fridge and filled both glasses with ice. He glanced her way, seemed a little nervous.

"What is it, Jack? What's wrong?"

He sighed. "I...don't really eat tofu and bean sprouts or drink herbal tea. You were right about that stuff. And I'm telling you this now, because it's suddenly very important to me that you not think of me as some garden variety con man. So I figure honesty is the best policy."

She tipped her head to one side. "So…the flaky fake diet is just to go with the image?"

"Exactly."

She sighed, flipped open the pizza box, pulled out a gooey slice and put it onto her plate.

"You're…disappointed," he said.

"No. Actually, I'm relieved. Just…worried."

"Relieved?"

She almost told him she couldn't imagine herself being with a man who subsisted on nuts and twigs, but she bit her tongue in time. "Never mind why I'm relieved. It's why I'm worried that's important here."

"Okay, then why are you worried?"

She looked across the table at him. "I'm worried about whether the rest of your claims are just as false. Tell me the truth, Jack. Can you help me, or are you just playing along to keep me from finally getting the goods on you?"

He licked his lips, lowered his head. "If I can't help you, Kiley, then I don't know who can." Then he met her eyes again. "To be honest, I've never dealt with anything like what's going on here in this house before. I really don't know if I can do it. After tonight, though, maybe you and I will both know."

She sighed, nodding. "What happens tonight, Jack?"

He studied her, looking a little relieved. "You aren't throwing me out?"

She smiled a little, shook her head. "I appreciate you being straight with me. Now, will you tell me what you have planned for tonight?"

He seemed to relax, took a bite of his slice of pizza,

then chewed while pouring cola into both their glasses. He said, "Tonight, Ms. Brigham, we are going to hold a séance."

Kiley blinked and held his gaze. "A séance," she repeated. "Like, where you conjure up spirits from the other side?"

"Exactly."

She blinked twice. "Jack, we already have spirits from the other side. What we need to do is boot them out, not call them in."

He nodded, smiling a little, an act that made his lips far more attractive than they should have been. "When we figure out what the ghosts are trying to tell us, we'll know how to get rid of them, right?"

"I…guess."

"So, we hold the séance, give them the perfect way to try to tell us."

"And we're going to do this ourselves? Just the two of us?"

He averted his eyes. "Well, I tried to get some of the local mediums to help us out, but seeing as how they've all been the subjects of your columns at one point or another, they all said thanks, but no thanks."

She thinned her lips, lowered her head. "They didn't put it quite that nicely, did they?"

"No. I think one of the more memorable phrases was, I hope the ghost eats her skinny white ass."

She pursed her lips. "Well, I can't blame them, I suppose. But then again, why would I want any of them? I caught each and every one of them faking, otherwise they wouldn't have made my column in the first place."

Jack caught her chin, lifted it and held her gaze. "Just

because they weren't one hundred percent genuine, Brigham, that doesn't mean they were one hundred percent phony."

"No?"

"No. This isn't black and white. There are shades of gray. All kinds of them, apparently."

"You sound surprised by that."

He pursed his lips. "I never used to believe it. Then again, until recently, I'd never—"

He stopped himself. She could almost see him stomping on a mental brake pedal. "You'd never what?" she asked.

Jack shook his head. "Nothing. Never mind, it doesn't matter. What matters is that we make this work."

"You think it will?"

"I think neither of us has any better ideas. Do we?"

She gnawed her lower lip. "I tried to contact Mr. Miller today, but he wouldn't take my call, much less return it. He wants nothing to do with this place."

"Then we're left with the ghosts. We can't solve this unless they tell us what it's about. No one else will."

She pursed her lips, lowered her head. Then raised it again when she felt his hand sliding over hers where it rested on the table.

"I know you're scared," he said.

"I'm not—"

"The hell you're not. I'm scared too, Kiley. And not just about the damn ghosts."

A frown tugged at her brow and she stared down at their hands. Then, jittery for reasons beyond her understanding, she got up from the table, slipping her hand from beneath his, turned and began pacing across the room.

Jack got up, came to stand behind her, very close behind her. "I want this thing solved as badly as you do," he whispered. "I want it out of the way, so I can see what's left when it's gone."

"I don't know what you mean," she said, turning to face him as she spoke.

"Yeah, you do." He lifted a hand and gently pushed her hair away from her face, tucking it behind her ear. Then, slowly, he lowered his head, brushed her lips with his. Once, then again.

Kiley's heart fluttered and her stomach tied itself in knots. The soft, tender kisses went on, until, trembling, she slid her hands up his chest, over his shoulders, and then linked her arms around his neck. His arms closed around her waist, and he pulled her tight to him and kissed her long and deeply. She let her lips part, tasting him, loving it.

Finally, he lifted his head away, and when she opened her eyes she found his probing them. Kiley licked her lips, tasting him on them. She sought for words, and heard herself muttering, "B-but I don't even like you."

He smiled, and it made her want to kiss him all over again. "Yeah, you keep telling yourself that, Kiley. But trust me, it isn't gonna change a thing. It didn't for me, anyway." He leaned in, nibbling at her mouth again. "And you can get rid of that notion that there's no affection involved here, lady. We kissed this time."

"Is that why you kissed me? To prove it's not just physical so you can get me into bed?"

"No. I kissed you because I wanted to. I'd like to keep on kissing you all night. But we've got other things to worry about, unfortunately."

Kiley wanted him. She wanted to make love to him, now, tonight. She pushed her hands through her hair. "This is so much to deal with. And with everything else going on—ghosts and hauntings and dead women in my bathtub—"

He nodded, sliding his arms from around her waist. "I know. I'm sorry, Kiley, I shouldn't have—no. Hell, I'm not sorry."

She smiled up at him. "I'm not, either."

"Good. So now maybe you understand why I'm in such a hurry to get all that other stuff out of the way."

She nodded. "Yeah. Okay. So…we'll have the séance."

"Great. I've got everything we need out in the car."

He turned as if to go out and fetch his props. "No, Jack," she said, stopping him in his tracks.

He turned to face her. "Don't tell me you've changed your mind?"

She shook her head. "We're not doing anything," she told him, "until I've finished my pizza."

CHAPTER TEN

JACK WAS SETTING UP the table in the formal dining room, feeling more nervous than he'd ever been in his life, when the doorbell chimed. Kiley was in the kitchen, putting away the leftover pizza, stacking the dishes in the dishwasher. So he went to the door and pulled it open.

Chris stood there, smiling. Behind him were two of the psychics Kiley had nailed in her column over the past year. Maya, a thirtysomething witch, blond, blue-eyed and petite, nodded hello to him as he stepped aside to let them in. She wore jeans, a cozy-looking sweater, and a pentacle around her neck. Right behind her was John Redhawk, a shaman. Aside from the turquoise beads and ponytail, he, too, was dressed casually, jeans and a green polo shirt under a denim jacket.

Jack heard Kiley come in from the kitchen. She started to say something, then stopped in her tracks.

To break the awkward silence, Jack said, "I, uh—thought you two couldn't make it."

John sent a tight look at Kiley. "If there are spirits trapped here, they need help to get across."

Maya nodded. "We can't punish them for her actions."

"Great," Kiley said. "They're on the goddamn ghosts' side."

"Fortunately your interests and theirs are the same," John said, moving farther into the room. "As are your goals and ours—to free them, so they can move on."

Jack turned to Kiley, knowing she was about to roll her eyes or make some sarcastic comment. But he caught her in time.

"No doubt, Ms. Brigham, you think we can't be of any help anyway," Maya said.

Kiley pursed her lips. "I did catch you faking."

"You caught us being inaccurate," John explained. "There's a very big difference."

"You totally ignored all the times we were dead on target with our work," Maya added, "and focused only on the times when we missed the mark."

Chris nodded hard, then put his own two cents in. "You failed to take into account all the people they helped. And the fact that no one was ever harmed by what they did."

Kiley pursed her lips, lowered her head. "I get it, Chris." Then she lifted her eyes again, took a breath. "You two just admitted you're not always right. I suppose I need to do the same."

John nodded slowly. "Some of the people you condemned in your column were frauds, Ms. Brigham. Some of them were doing harm, and were sorely in need of exposure. I was glad to see them go. They just make the rest of us look bad. But it's a mistake to paint all psychics with the same brush. And it's just as bad to hold us up to standards that are impossible for anyone short of a god to meet."

She nodded. "I'm starting to realize that." Then she frowned. "But if you're not batting a thousand, then how the hell can an outsider ever tell the difference?"

"They can't," Maya said. "But we can. We know who's for real and who's just running a scam to make a buck. Maybe in the future, you could work with us, instead of against us."

Kiley blinked, clearly stunned. "You…would do that? Work with me? My God, I never thought—"

"Because you never asked," John said. "But believe me, we'd love to help you put the frauds out of business."

Kiley shook her head in something that looked like wonder.

"Chris filled us in on the details," Maya said, changing the subject. "So where are we doing this?"

"I'm setting up in the dining room." Jack led the way, looking with hypercritical eyes at the stuff he'd set up. Candles around the room in holders, lots of them, all white. Charcoal tablets, already lit and turning slowly white with heat, filled censers in various spots, each with a small dish of herbs beside it.

"Anything else you want to have in here?" he asked.

John lifted a dish of the herbs. "What are you using?"

"Dandelion, sweetgrass and thistle," Jack said.

"Mmm." John tugged a pouch from his jacket pocket. "I'll add a little tobacco. I've had good results with it."

"And vervain," Maya said, adding a pinch of something from her own knapsack. "To make it go." She looked around the room. "I'd feel better if we did this within a circle and if we marked the boundary with salt, and placed representations of the elements in the quarters."

John nodded his agreement.

Chris looked at Kiley. "C'mon, I'll tell you what we need and you can help me find it." The two of them went into the kitchen.

Jack sighed, turning to the others. "Thanks for coming. I mean it, I'm in way over my head here."

"Why?" Maya asked. "It's not as if you haven't done this before."

Jack glanced toward the kitchen. "I always assumed the problem was in the minds of the clients. That's where I solved it. Hell, I went through the motions, but I wasn't really doing anything. You know that, you just finished saying you could tell the real psychics from the frauds."

They looked at each other, then slowly back at him. John said, "We can, Jack. And you're one of the real ones."

Jack stood there gaping, even as Kiley and Chris returned. She carried a bowl of water, and he had a box of salt.

"Good," Maya said. "Set the bowl in the west—that would be over here." She pointed. "Move one of those censers so it sits opposite it, in the east, and put one of the taper candles in the south." She took the salt from Chris, and poured a small pile of it in the north position.

"Ready, everyone?" she asked.

Kiley looked at Jack. He found himself moving closer, taking her hand. "We're ready."

John was moving around the room, lighting each candle, and adding pinches of the herbal mixture to each censer. Chris shut off the lights. Then they took their seats around the table, as Maya walked in a large circle around them, pouring a boundary line of salt as she moved. When it was all poured, she set the salt box down and walked the perimeter again, moving her hands like a mime as she created a circle of protection and power.

When she took her seat at the table, all was silent.

John looked at Jack. "Take the lead, my friend. This is your project, we're just here for backup."

Jack almost refused, but then he realized how that would look to Kiley. Even though he thought things had changed between them, he wasn't ready to admit to her that he was a fraud. He was terrified—not that she would expose him. Hell, he didn't even care about that anymore. No, his greatest fear was that she would turn away from him. And he didn't think he could stand that.

So much more than his business was at stake now. He cared what she thought of him now.

He took a breath, tried to remember all the usual mumbo jumbo, and said, "Join hands." Beside him, Kiley slid her hand into his. Impulsively, he drew it to his lips, and pressed a kiss there. She squeezed a reply. He closed his eyes and instructed everyone through several deep breaths in an effort to relax them. Finally, he addressed the spirits.

"Those of us here at this table call out to those of you elsewhere in this house. We know you're here. We know you have something you want to tell us. We've created this sacred space and we invite you in. You are welcome here, provided you mean us no harm. You are welcome here, so long as your intentions are for the highest good. Come now, join us."

A door slammed.

Jack's head came up, eyes flying open and he saw the others on high alert as well. They met each other's eyes around the room, in the flickering candle glow. And then, suddenly, a gust of icy wind blew through, and every candle in the room went out.

Jack felt himself sinking, as if his chair had dissolved

beneath him. He fought it, tried to cling more tightly to the hands on either side of him, but it was no use. They fell away and he plummeted downward, right through the floorboards, hitting the basement floor so hard it knocked the wind out of him.

He swore and got up, brushing himself off, rubbing his tailbone gingerly. Looking up, he expected to see the hole above him, but the ceiling was perfect. Flawless.

And then he heard someone speaking softly, and he turned to look.

There in the corner was a man of perhaps thirty. His slicked-back hair and dated glasses made him look like something out of a '70s sitcom. Knife-sharp crease on his plaid pants, thick belt with an oversized buckle and a tie so wide it was almost funny.

Jack said, "Hey. Who the hell are you and what are you doing down here?"

But the man didn't hear him. He went right on with what he was doing. And what he was doing, Jack realized, was smoothing new concrete over a portion of the floor. He knelt there, moving a trowel over the smooth, slick gray mush.

Jack strode across to him. "What the hell are you doing?" he demanded. And when the man didn't answer, he reached for him, to spin him around and make him talk. But his hand moved right through the guy.

"Jack?"

The voice was Kiley's. It was coming from above.

"Jack, are you all right? Come on, Jack, wake up!"

He felt her hands on his face, her breath on his skin. And then he was rising again, rising as if on an elevator at top speed, leaving his stomach somewhere below.

He jerked his head up, opened his eyes. Kiley was standing over him. The lights were on. Maya, John and Chris surrounded him. "Jesus, what happened?"

"You passed out," Kiley said.

"He went into a trance," Maya corrected.

"He left his body, journeyed into the realm of the spirits," John put in.

"Well? Which is it, Jack? What happened to you?"

He sat up straighter in the chair, rubbed his forehead. "How long was I out?"

"Fifteen minutes or so," Kiley said.

"It felt like about fifteen seconds."

She stroked his face. "Are you okay? I knew this was a bad idea. I just knew it."

Jack licked his lips. "No. No, it was a good idea. I…I saw something."

She frowned, staring at him. "What?"

"I think it was Mr. Miller. He was spreading concrete in the cellar."

CHAPTER ELEVEN

KILEY STOOD OVER THE SOFA, where she'd made Jack lie down. John, Maya and Chris had left, at Jack's insistence. He swore he knew what he needed to know now, thanked them for their help and told them to go.

"I'm not sure what happened back there, Jack."

He closed his eyes and pressed a hand to his forehead. "Neither am I." He held her gaze. "Only thing I am sure of, is that I need to see that basement."

An icy shiver rippled through her entire being. "I don't know if that's such a good idea."

"I think it's the only way to end this thing, Kiley."

She pursed her lips. "It's not safe down there."

"You stay up here. I just need to take a look."

Firming her jaw, she shook her head. "No. Not alone. If you're going down there, I'm going with you."

He studied her face for a moment. "You sure?"

She nodded.

Sighing, Jack reached out to cup her cheek. It was a touch that seemed tender, protective in some strange way. "You're braver than you look, you know that?"

"Is that supposed to pass for a compliment?"

"Just a fact." He got to his feet.

"Oh," she said. "You meant, right now?"

"No. No, not right yet. There's something else, first."

"Is there?"

He smiled softly, reached for her and pulled her to him. "This." He cupped her face and tipped it, so that he could kiss her the way it suited him. He took his time, probed and licked, tasted and explored. Kiley felt herself melting for him.

"Jack," she whispered.

"I know. This is no time for—but God, Kiley, I can't stop thinking about how it felt when we—"

"I know. I know."

He slid his hands down to her waist, then up again, raising her little T-shirt with them. She lifted her arms overhead, so he could take it off her. No bra. He hadn't brought her one when he brought her clothes, and she had no doubt that was deliberate. His hands covered her breasts, then he bent her backward and used his mouth instead, tasting, suckling. She let her head fall backward and stopped fighting the moans of pleasure. He was wrestling her jeans free now, shoving them off her hips and driving a hand down the front of her panties, cupping her there. He held her, arched backward over one arm, mouth attacking a breast, hand attacking her center. It was almost too good.

"Jack, please..."

He laid her on the sofa, tugged the jeans off the rest of the way, stripped away her panties. Then he yanked off his own jeans, frenzied now in his rush. She was on fire, gripping him, pulling him to her even before he had his jeans off. And then he was there, sliding inside her, filling her just as he had before. But this time he didn't stop. He drove into her, and when she clutched his buttocks and dug her nails into his firm flesh he did it again, harder and deeper with every thrust. She twisted her legs around him, tilted her hips to take him, cried out his name with every breath he forced from her lungs. His hands held her butt, pulling her hard to him so he could plunge even deeper. His mouth took her nipple, and he used his teeth now, in gentle bites and nibbles that made her cry out in sweet anguish. He moved faster, harder, driving her to the edge of what she could bear, and finally, beyond that edge, into sweet oblivion. The orgasm broke like a tidal wave, and she shrieked his name as her entire body shuddered in spasms of release. And then he was there, too, groaning deep in his throat as he drove more deeply than ever, and held her to him as he poured into her. She felt the rhythmic pulse in him, the milking contractions in herself, and she clung to it, rode it out, until slowly the waves receded and her muscles relaxed.

He slid onto his side, pulling her close, wrapping her in his arms. "That was incredible."

"It was supernatural," she agreed. "Why did we waste so much time hating each other?"

He leaned up, kissed her earlobe and held her for another ten minutes while their heart rates returned to normal. And then, finally, she sighed and got to her feet. "Shall we get this over with?" she asked.

"It's as good a time as any." He got up, found their clothes, helped her to dress, sliding her panties over her feet and pulling them slowly up for her. Every touch was a caress. He repeated the process with the T-shirt. She took the jeans from him, because if he kept this up he was going to make her decide to do something else besides explore the basement.

Hell, what was this now? Were they casual sex partners, or something more?

She looked past him at the darkened windows, heard the wind picking up outside. Branches moved, scraping gnarled limbs over the sides of the house, like demons trying to claw their way in. She shivered, all the fears he'd made her forget returning in force.

Jack slid an arm around her shoulders. "Don't worry, Kiley. I'm not going to let anything happen to you. Especially not now."

The way his voice thickened on those words made her look up at him quickly. "Don't wax mushy on me, Jack. That would be scarier than the basement."

"Come on."

She walked with him, wished he couldn't feel her shaking, but not so much that she would give up the reassuring arm around her. In fact, she walked as close beside him as she could. At the basement door, she drew a breath.

Jack reached out, closed his hand on the knob and opened the door. She stared into a rectangle of utter blackness. Then she reached past him, into the inky dark, which felt like a physical thing, cold and dense. She found the light switch, flicked it.

Light flooded the stairway. She swallowed her fear. "We're coming down here to keep our promise, ghost. We're checking out the things you've been trying to tell us, but I'll tell you right now, at the first sign you're fucking with us, we're out of here. Understood?"

There was no sound, no sign of any reply.

She looked at Jack. He nodded. "Let's go, then." Still holding her near his side, he started down the stairway.

It was a solid stairway, modern, obviously not the original set. They walked down, thirteen stairs, to the bottom, a smooth concrete floor.

"So?" she asked. "Where was it you saw in this…vision?"

He looked at the ceiling, evenly spaced studs, with cross-pieces in between them. Steel pipe ran along the edges of some boards, laying a hot-and-cold running trail from the basement to the bathrooms and the kitchen. Then he lowered his gaze, scanning the basement. "Over here, I think."

She walked with him across the basement. He moved slowly, and Kiley wondered if he was feeling the same things she was. It seemed to grow colder with every step they took. And there was something else in the air. Something electric and alive.

He stopped, and seemed to be staring at the floor.

"Is this it?"

He nodded. "Yeah. I think so."

"What do you think we should do about it, Jack?"

He sighed, looking around the room. She followed his gaze. There were some old tools hanging from hooks in the wall. Hoe, rake, shovel. They were old, battered, dusty. They'd been here when she bought the place, and she hadn't bothered to get rid of them. She hadn't even touched them. Hell, she'd only been in the basement once, with the real estate agent. For some reason she hadn't been able to come back down here since she'd moved in.

He seemed about to answer her, when a loud clattering sound made Kiley jump six inches and clutch her chest. Her heart racing, she scanned the basement to find the source of the sound. The old shovel lay on the concrete floor. It had fallen off its hook. She swallowed her fear, took a calming breath and looked up at Jack.

He said, "I think we need to dig up the floor."

"Yeah. I kind of picked up on that."

He nodded. "We'll need something stronger than a shovel to break through concrete." Taking her hand, he turned and started back toward the stairway.

From the corner of her eye, Kiley saw something flying toward them. She swung a hand to the back of Jack's head, pushing him forward and down, ducking along with him, and the thing whizzed over their heads so fast and so close that she felt the breeze it caused, heard the sound of it passing. It slammed into the wall on the other side of them and stayed there.

"Holy Christ," Jack muttered, straightening and staring.

She stared, too. The rounded end of the shovel was embedded in the wall, its handle sticking straight out, still quivering from the impact.

"That could have taken off your head," Kiley whispered.

"Yeah." He was staring behind him, eyes wide and watchful.

"Goddamn it!" Kiley turned and shouted. "What are you, stupid or something? We can't dig the effing floor up with a shovel. It's concrete, you blithering idiot. We're going to need a jackhammer or something. So unless you've got one of those to hurl at us, knock it the hell off!"

Jack stared at her, then looked around the basement. "You think it got the message?"

"Hell, you scared me. Should've worked on the ghost."

She searched his eyes, suddenly, acutely aware of how ridiculously much he had come to mean to her. “It better have,” she said. She ran a hand through his hair, kissed his chin.

Then, turning, they took another step toward the stairs. Nothing happened, so they started up them. They made it almost all the way to the top, before the creaking, splitting, cracking sounds alerted them to trouble. Jack grabbed her waist and shoved her ahead of him and through the open doorway. Then he vanished behind her. Kiley shrieked, and spun around in time to see the entire staircase collapsing and taking Jack with it. “Jack!” She shouted his name, reaching for him. But the door slammed in her face.

JACK HIT THE FLOOR HARD, then curled into a protective ball as debris rained down on him. He was pummeled, his head, back, shoulders, his hands and arms where he clutched them around his face like a makeshift helmet, pounded by falling debris. He thought he heard Kiley screaming his name, but he couldn't be sure with the roar around him. And then, suddenly, there was just silence.

Swallowing hard, Jack tried to move. It hurt when he straightened. Boards fell off his body, clattering to the floor around him. He got upright, brushed some of the dust from his shoulders and tried to take stock. His shoulder throbbed. Lower back wasn't feeling too pleasant, either. Above him, he could hear Kiley, pounding on the door, shouting and swearing.

He cupped his hands and hollered in her direction. It took two or three tries before she heard him and stopped her own shouting to listen. “Jack?” she called.

“Yeah. I'm okay.”

"Thank God." He lowered his head, smiling a little at the level of relief that came through in that one simple declaration. "Jack, I can't get the door open." But he was looking at the floor now, frowning at the way the debris had come to rest on the other side of the basement. Broken boards formed a rectangle, framing the area where he'd seen the man laying concrete. He walked over there, bending low, moving the boards away. Frowning, he looked more closely.

"Jack?"

"Just a sec!" he called.

He bent closer, noticing now the way the dust had gathered into a tiny crevice, which, like the broken boards, formed a rectangle in the floor. He brushed at the dust, running his fingers along the fissure, realizing this piece of concrete was separate from the rest, not a part of the floor, but something else.

He looked across the room then, at the forgotten tools in the corner. Spotted a crowbar. "Okay, I get it," he said softly. "We don't need a jackhammer."

He heard a soft creaking sound and turned to see the cellar door swinging slowly open. On the other side, Kiley stood with a baseball bat in her hands, and it was raised up as if she'd been about to pound the door with it. She blinked down at him.

He said, "Is there another way in and out of here?"

She nodded. "A hatchway door that leads outside."

He nodded.

"You going to come out that way, Jack?"

He thinned his lips. "I'm afraid if I try, that exit will get annihilated, too. No, I think we need to dig this thing up now."

"But—"

"The cement's sectioned here. I think I can pry it up."

She stared at him, then at the area around him. "What, you couldn't just say so? You had to risk killing him?"

The lights flickered off, then on again. Jack said, "Maybe you should stop yelling at them, Kiley?"

"Fuck them. I'm coming back down. See you in a minute."

She vanished from the doorway. Jack went to the corner to grab the crowbar, then tugged the shovel from where it was embedded in the wall and carried both back to the spot with him.

A few minutes later, Kiley arrived at his side. She had found another crowbar and knelt on the basement floor beside him. "Are you really okay?"

"Yeah. I'll be a little sore, but nothing serious." He was jamming the flat end of the bar into the crack, moving it back and forth. The crack grew wider with every movement.

She did what he was doing, working in the other direction, and thcy made their way around the entire rectangle. She said, "You have a little blood on your face."

"A few of the boards landed on me when the stairs collapsed."

She pursed her lips, frowning hard. He smiled at her. "It does my ego a world of good to know you care, Kiley."

"It's not by choice, Jack."

The edge he was prying rose up a little. "Here, quick, get your bar over here," he said. Kiley hurried to his side and jammed her bar underneath, helping him pry the slab of concrete upward. Jack dropped his own bar, gripping the edge with his hands, pushing and lifting. Kiley used her bar to help him, until finally they managed to overturn the slab. It hit the floor and split into several pieces.

Jack looked at Kiley and she licked her lips as if she was nervous before handing him the shovel. He eyed the dirt, began scraping it aside with the shovel blade, felt something underneath. "It's shallow," he said.

She nodded. "It's cold again. Hell, Jack, I can see your breath." She rubbed her arms. "We must be close."

He nodded and continued scraping away the soil, revealing a square of metal, two feet by two feet.

"What is it? A box, is it some kind of box, Jack?"

He ran his hands over the thing, tracing its edges. "I feel…hinges." He lifted his gaze to meet hers. "Jesus, Kiley, I think it's some kind of a…a door."

"A door?"

He nodded.

"A door to what?"

Goddamn good question. The word hell popped into his mind, but he decided not to share that with her.

CHAPTER TWELVE

"JACK, I'M AFRAID." For once Kiley didn't mind admitting it, as she stood there staring down into pitch-black darkness.

"Me, too."

"I think it's time we call the police. Don't you?"

He shrugged. "No proof a crime's been committed." He glanced down into the darkness. "Though I'd bet the farm on it."

She gripped his arm, as if she could convince him by squeezing her words into him. "Let's at least try. If the police won't come out here, then we'll do it ourselves."

He tipped his head to one side, started to speak, but then seemed to decide against it.

"Come on, Jack. We'll call the police, we'll do it right now."

He nodded, so she tugged him away from that inky maw and toward the shallow concrete steps that led up out of the cellar to an angled hatchway door. She pressed her palms to it, to push it open. But it wouldn't budge. "Hell, I know it's not locked. I thought I left it wide open, but—" She pushed again.

Jack said, "I was afraid of something like this."

She frowned at him, then she understood. "They

won't let us out, will they? Not even if it's to tell their story?"

"They don't trust us, Kiley. What's to stop us from getting out of here and running like hell? Never looking back? God knows that's what everyone else who's lived here has done."

She licked her lips, and turned slowly to face the now-open metal trapdoor in the floor. "I don't want to go down there, Jack."

"I know, honey. I know. Neither do I."

"Do we even have a light?"

"Yeah." He pulled a flashlight from somewhere. "I remembered about the lights going out before. Brought backup."

"Good thinking."

He drew a breath. "Stay up here, kid. As close to the hatchway door as you can."

She shook her head. "I'm more afraid to be here alone than I am to go down there with you. We do this together."

"If you're sure…"

She gave a firm nod.

"Okay, then." He put her behind him, drawing her hands to his waist just above his hips, and she knew it was because there wasn't enough room for them to go side by side down the concrete steps that led deep into the earth. "Stay close."

"No problem there," she said.

He flicked on the flashlight, holding it in front of them as they moved slowly down the steep, narrow stairs. He kept his free hand over one of hers on his waist. The darkness closed in around them. She knew there was light behind her from the cellar, but without turning she couldn't see it. And knowing it was there wasn't nearly reassuring enough. Feeling Jack's warmth suffusing her hand helped more. But it didn't dispel the chill of foreboding that gripped her more thoroughly with every step. It was more than blinding darkness that surrounded her. It was physical, real. It hugged her with cold dampness. She smelled it—dank and sour. She tasted its bitter, stale, putrid air. She even heard it, containing and muffling every sound.

"God, there's a smell."

"I know."

At the bottom of the stairs, the floor leveled off. Concrete, perfectly rectangular, just tall enough for an adult to walk upright, and only wide enough for one to pass through. Jack's shoulders brushed the walls if he leaned even slightly to one side or the other. It was a concrete tunnel, with only the occasional cobweb blocking the way.

And at its end, the darkness widened.

Jack paused, shining the flashlight's beam around. "It's a room, I think." He traced three walls, then examined the fourth, the one with the doorway in which they stood. "I don't see any other exits. This is the only way in."

"Or out," she whispered. "Jack, do you feel that? We're not alone."

He pulled her up beside him, now that there was room to stand two abreast, sliding an arm around her and holding her close, even as he moved the flashlight beam around the room again, lower this time, tracing the floor from end to end. The light beam stopped when it hit the body.

Kiley yelped and turned her head into Jack's chest. But then she forced herself to look again. Trembling, straining against her own will to turn her head once more, she looked.

The darkly stained bones and leatherlike flesh slumped against the wall. Tangled blond hair clung in patches to the skull.

"There are chains," Jack said. "Look."

She followed the beam of light to the manacles on the wrists and the chains mounted to the walls behind. "This is a nightmare."

"It was for her," Jack said.

And suddenly, the gut-wrenching, bone-numbing fear she had been feeling vanished—replaced by a wave of grief as it hit her that this scary, smelly, partially decomposed body had been a person. A woman, or even a girl. Brought down here, chained up and…

"Oh, God, there are more," Jack said.

She opened her eyes and saw the light moving around the floor, illuminating another corpse, and then another, and another. "Sweet Jesus," she whispered. Tears were welling in her eyes. "It's over, I promise you. God, no wonder you can't rest. No wonder. I promise you, all of this is coming to light. Now."

No.

The word was spoken, she heard it, and yet it felt as if it were not a word at all, but a feeling. A powerful emotion. She heard the trapdoor slam down, behind and above them.

"The spirits of this place aren't ready to let us leave," Jack whispered.

"Maybe they never will be," Kiley said.

Jack touched her shoulders. "Don't think that way."

"How can I not? God, Jack, we could be trapped

down here. We could die the same horrible way they did." Pulling away from him, she started back along the tunnel, hurrying through the darkness to the stairway, and seeing just what she had expected to see. The closed door at the top. She went up, pushed at it, but nothing.

Jack was behind her, his arms around her, and she turned into them, let him hold her. Eventually she calmed enough to sink onto a step, and he handed her the flashlight and tried to open the door himself, but it was no use.

Sighing, he sank down beside her. "It's going to be all right. Chris knows we're here, he knows we were planning to dig."

"You think anyone will find us if these ghosts don't want them to?"

He sighed. "I think they do want us to be found. Just as they wanted to be found themselves. We just have to wait until they're ready."

"Why the delay? What could they hope to gain?"

He pulled her closer, held her beside him. They sat there on the second step from the bottom, the terrible stench of death permeating the air. And slowly, Kiley realized that Jack was shivering. At first it was just a mild ripple, but then it seemed to grow until his entire body vibrated with it. Kiley pulled free of his embrace to look at him. She lifted the flashlight and he shielded his eyes, averted his face.

"What is it, Jack? What's wrong?"

"I don't...know."

Kiley swallowed hard. He'd been shaking earlier, during the seance, too. Just like this. No, not this bad. "What should I do?"

The shaking stopped suddenly, and Jack went very still. His head fell forward, and the rest of his body tried to follow. Kiley gripped his shoulders and kept him from toppling to the floor. She eased him backward instead, lowering his head carefully until it rested on a stair, wishing for a pillow. "Jack? Jack, can you hear me?"

His eyes flashed open then. So suddenly, with such an unnatural look in them that she jerked away from him.

Blinking, calming herself, she leaned closer again. "Jack?"

She was dizzy as she studied his face. He wasn't responding, but at least he'd stopped shaking. God, she had to sit down. She sank onto the step again, let her head fall forward. If she could just rest her eyes for a moment.

But when she lifted her head again she wasn't in the basement anymore. She was upstairs, running herself a hot bath, alone again, and sad at being always so alone.

Her husband was always going on business trips, and he must think she was pretty stupid if he thought she didn't realize something more than business was going on. She felt tears hot on her cheeks and glanced into the mirror.

The face of a beautiful woman looked back at her. Buttery blond hair, piercing, sad eyes. "He doesn't love me anymore," Sharon Miller whispered through Kiley's lips. "He never touches me. Something's terribly wrong. There's a coldness in his eyes that wasn't there before."

She turned at the sound of an engine in the driveway. Phil was home early. He would expect her to be asleep, not up weeping. But she had to confront him, now, tonight, before she lost her courage.

She padded downstairs in her nightgown. Only—he didn't come inside. Why wasn't he coming inside?

She moved to the window to peer out at his car in the driveway, and then she noticed that the hatchway door was open. "What is he doing in the cellar?" she asked herself.

Turning from the window, Sharon went down into the basement. There was a trapdoor in the floor. One she never knew was there. Oh, God, she could hear a woman crying. Distant, echoing.

Sharon's heart was beating fast. Somewhere deep inside, Kiley was begging her not to go down there. But she went. She knew she was Kiley, not Sharon, and she knew this was something like being trapped in someone else's nightmare. But she couldn't wake up and she couldn't make it stop.

Turning, she walked the length of the tunnel, ending in the room of horror, where the young wife of long ago had no doubt ended up. And then Kiley saw them, through Sharon's eyes, or was it Sharon reliving it through Kiley's? Women, beautiful young women, chained to the walls. They were dirty, their hair in tangles. They were naked. One hung limply, dead or close to it, but the others were alive and terrified. And her husband, the man she had loved, was forcing the new one to her knees, fastening the chains around her wrists, hitting her when she whimpered and pleaded. "God, what is this?"

Jack—no, not Jack—Phil spun around and saw her there.

"Help me," the girl he'd been chaining up begged. "Please, get out and help me!"

Sharon turned to run, but Phil was too fast for her. He caught her before she made it out, flung her to the floor.

She was frightened. God, she had never been frightened like this. She couldn't believe this was her husband.

He bent over her, clutched her head between his palms. "You have to understand, Sharon. I have needs. Dirty, secret needs. You're too fine a woman for me. I could never use you the way I can these filthy sluts."

"Phillip, they're girls! They're only girls!"

"Whores. I pick them up in the city, bring them here to satisfy my needs. No one misses them, Sharon. It's just as well I take them out of the world."

"You...kill them?"

"They don't last well, those whores. Get sickly, weak. Eventually they die on their own, or I take mercy on them, put them out of their misery."

She clutched her stomach, doubling over and fighting the urge to vomit. When she got it under control, she tried to straighten again. "How—m-many?" Tears were flowing from her eyes now, she could barely see, despite the lights he had strung through the place, trouble lights like they used on construction sites.

He smiled slowly. "Oh, many. Lots and lots of them." He drew a breath, sighed. "Come on, my love. I promise, nothing so unpleasant is going to happen to you."

He slid his arm around her shoulders. She shivered, wondering what he would do to her now.

"I...won't tell your secret, darling. I would wish things were different. I would ask that you stop this and let them go, but I would never betray you."

"No, of course you wouldn't. Not to your mother, nor your priest. Good Christian that you are. You'll stay with me, continue loving me, though you think me a rapist and murderer."

The trapdoor was open as he led her up the stairs. Somewhere down deep inside her, Kiley thought that was odd. It had been closed before. Somehow, she was aware that she and Jack were being used as puppets, as the play unfurled again. And she wondered how far it would go.

But then the other overtook her again. Behind her she could hear the moans and weeping, pleading voices. "Get away from him. Run. Tell someone!"

Ahead of her, she saw light. Her husband yanked the plug from the wall, and the trouble lights went black. The women sobbed, growing hysterical as they were plunged into darkness, but he didn't care. He slammed the steel door down again, never releasing the death grip he had on her arm.

"You're hurting me."

"Not for much longer, love. I promise. Come along now." He took her up the stairs. She felt his grip on her arm relax and she pulled free, racing as fast as she could through the house, toward the door. But he beat her there, blocking her escape. Turning, her heart pounding in her chest, she ran upstairs, seeking the safety of a room with a door she could bolt against him, and a telephone. She went into the bedroom, pushing the door shut.

He slammed into it, but she braced with all her strength, then slid the bolt home. Slowly, she backed away. But he was pounding the door, howling with rage. Bang! Bang! Bang!

"Stay away!" she cried, grabbing the telephone, dialing O.

The door crashed open, and he surged toward her. She heard the line ringing, but he was too close. She dropped the phone, racing into the bathroom and slamming the door.

He kicked it in so fast and hard it hit her full in the chest, knocking her off balance, and she hit the floor. Her head cracked against the porcelain tub. And then it swam. She was dizzy, darkness creeping in around the edges of her vision.

"There, now. You won't die dirty, buried alive, as they do. No, nothing so horrible for my lady." He smiled down at her as he bent over her. "And you've already run the water. That was thoughtful of you." He picked her up, lowered her into the bathtub. His palm to her face, he pushed it beneath the water.

She couldn't breathe! Her arms flailed, legs kicked, but he held firm. And then the water rushed into her lungs. It was gentle, cleansing, soothing. Her body calmed, relaxed. And darkness crept over her.

And then she was standing there, in the bathroom, watching him. He was still leaning over the tub, she realized, puzzled. Then she looked past him and saw her own face in the water.

"He's killed you," a woman said. "He killed us, too."

Sharon turned and saw them. Women, beautiful women, all around her. So many faces and soulful eyes. "I'm so sorry," she said.

"We have to tell someone. He'll keep on doing it until we make someone stop him."

She nodded and turned to look at her husband again.

He was sitting on the floor beside the tub, his head lowered, sobbing.

And then he wasn't her husband, and they weren't in the bathroom. He was Jack McCain, sitting on the bottom steps in the hidden basement bunker, his head in his hands.

Kiley went to him, knelt in front of him. "Jack, it's okay. It's okay, it wasn't real."

He lifted his head slowly, blinked the confusion from his eyes. "Kiley?"

She nodded, and he pressed her face between his palms, pulled her to his face, kissed her lips over and over. "Jesus, you're okay. I thought I—I thought I'd—"

"I'm okay. So are you, and you're not Phillip Miller. You're Jack. All that was—I don't know, it was…it was someone else. It was the past coming in. Sharon Miller reliving it through us, so we'd finally understand."

He nodded, holding her closer.

"It wasn't real, Jack," she told him.

"You're right about everything but that." He brought his head up, looking past her, into the darkness. "It was very real."

She turned to follow his gaze, and she saw them. Faint wisps in the shapes of women. Some were more defined than others, mists shaping into faces and limbs and hands. Others were just vague shapes, silhouettes of light in the darkness. "God, there are so many of them," she whispered. "But there were only four in the room."

Jack rose, clasping her shoulder. "They're buried in the back lawn."

She closed her eyes. "Oh, God."

"It gets worse," he said softly. "He's still doing it."

Her head came up fast. *"What?"*

"Phillip Miller isn't dead, Kiley. He's alive and well and living not far from here. And he's still murdering women."

And then she remembered. "The missing prostitutes from Albany. Oh, my God, Jack! We have to get out of here, we have to stop him and—"

There was a groaning sound, and a powerful crash, followed by light spilling in from behind. The trapdoor lay open, the way to the cellar clear.

Kiley met Jack's eyes. "I am so sorry I ever called you a fraud, Jack. You're—you're so amazing it's scary."

He shook his head slowly. "Remind me to tell you later why you're dead wrong about that."

She frowned at him. But then she turned to look back at those shapes, the spirits of women, all of them. "It's over. We'll stop him. We promise. And then you can rest in peace."

EPILOGUE

KILEY'S ENTIRE HOUSE WAS surrounded in yellow police tape. Police cars, SUVs and vans lined the street, and heavy equipment growled and belched in the back yard. News crews were everywhere, but Kiley wasn't giving any interviews. She'd written what she could about all of this in her latest column, and the rest was going into a book.

She stood on the sidewalk, watching the bodies being exhumed and carried in plastic bags out to waiting vehicles, one by one. Jack sat on the curb close beside her, fallen leaves in brilliant colors carpeting the sidewalk around him, reading the paper.

Officer Hanlon came over to where she stood. "They've arrested Phillip Miller. There were three women in his basement when they arrived."

Jack looked up from the newspaper. Kiley's throat tightened up. "Alive?"

"Yes. Thanks to you."

She swallowed hard. "Thanks for telling me."

Hanlon nodded and headed back to the house. Kiley looked down at Jack. "Well?"

He met her eyes, then refocused on the page and began reading aloud from her latest column. "'So to sum it up, I've learned that not everything I don't understand or believe in is necessarily make-believe. There are good psychics, and there are bad ones. And the only way to judge which is which is by how they make you feel. If their advice helps you, heals you, answers a need you have, then they are as genuine as any minister, priest, pastor or shrink. I'm retiring from my former career of debunking everything I don't happen to believe in. After what I've seen in my house, I know now that there is far more in this world than I will ever understand. And it humbles me to admit that the extraordinary and genuine skills and gifts of three psychics I called fakes—two of them in this very column—were what enabled me to find the truth about the women who were murdered and buried on my property, and to stop a killer at the end of a thirty-year spree. Those psychics were for real, even though I claimed to have proven otherwise. I will never question what I don't understand again.'"

Jack folded the newspaper and got to his feet. "It's wonderful. Your best column ever."

She shrugged. "If a psychic as gifted as you are doesn't know whether he's a fraud or not, how the hell can I pretend to?" She shook her head. "I can't believe you were as convinced you were a fake as I was, all this time. How can you have a gift like that and not know?"

Jack shrugged. "Chris knew. He knew all along. I guess it just took a case I cared this much about to make me aware of it."

"Yeah? And what was it about this case that made you care so much?"

He gave her a slow, sexy smile, reached out to clasp

her nape and pulled her to him for a long, lingering kiss. His lips moved against hers when he said, "I think you know."

"No way," she whispered back. "You're the one who's psychic, remember?"

"Right. So I suppose I have to spell it out for you."

She sent him a smile and nodded. "Please."

"I'm nuts about you, Kiley. I don't know when I went from hating you to loving you—maybe it was from the very start. But I know I do."

She nodded. "I was hoping you'd say that."

"Why?"

"Well, I'm going to need a place to crash for a while, for one thing."

He made a face at her. She smiled fully. "And you know, there is that pesky fact that I love you, too."

"Do you?"

"Mmm-hmm."

He kissed her once more, tucked her under his arm and led her back down the sidewalk toward the car. "When the police have finished here, we should have the other psychics in town come back here, do a cleansing ritual, make sure those spirits have made it across to the other side. They deserve to be at peace. God knows they've suffered long enough," Jack said.

"I agree. But I have a feeling they made it just fine. I think they're at peace now, Jack."

"Yeah, I feel as if they are, too."

They reached the car, and he opened her door for her.

"Where are we going?"

"My place, or I guess I should say our place now."

She shot him a loving look. "You mean I can move in?"

"Yeah. Just one rule, Kiley."
"What?"
"You can't bring any ghosts with you."

SOMEONE ELSE'S SHADOW

BARBARA HAMBLY

For George…and Baby

CHAPTER ONE

"TESSA?"

Dim light shone at the top of the first long flight of stairs. Maddie Laveau hitched her duffle coat closer around her shoulders, glancing warily back at the plate-glass door onto East Twenty-ninth Street. Yellow street-lights glared through the glass doors into the narrow lobby, barely more than a widened corridor with a care-taker's booth. Quincy the caretaker had gone home an hour ago at ten, which was just as well, since Maddie wasn't in the mood for a forty-five-minute monologue on the subject of taxes and the Republican party. The place smelled of moldy carpets and cigarettes smoked decades ago. The street door had been locked, and Mad-die had locked it again behind her the minute she'd let herself in with Tessa's key.

But if her roommate had a key, she told herself—du-plicated from that of another dancer, who'd duplicated it from one of the instructors who was no longer teach-ing at the Dance Loft—God knew who else in New York had them.

Heart pounding, Maddie mounted the dark stairs.

"Tessa, are you there?"

Silence. Though the Glendower Building had always

given Maddie the creeps, it housed one of the most respected dance schools in the city. Maddie wasn't sure why this was so—God knew there were other buildings in New York City, including the one she lived in, just as old, just as shabby, just as dingily lighted.

But from the first time she'd walked through its doors, twenty-two months ago now, it had made her nervous, as if there was always something there looking over her shoulder.

She climbed the long stairway quickly, two stories past the dancewear shop on the first floor and the storerooms and offices on the second, glancing repeatedly over her shoulder: *Like someone could have been hiding in the lobby?* A Barbie doll couldn't have taken cover there. Someone had repainted the stairwell during the last remodeling in the eighties with the neutral pinks and grays fashionable then, but hadn't stripped the old wallpaper underneath or put in modern lighting. The result was simply dingy, and Maddie guessed that underneath the gray industrial carpeting lurked layers of carpet tiles and the brown linoleum still visible on the upper floors. Uncovering the original wood, laid back in the 1890s, would be like revealing the stratification in some archaeological dig.

During the several months she'd taught belly dancing in one of the Dance Loft's smaller studios, Maddie had always hated being in the building at night. Charmian Dayforth, the owner, seemed to have no qualms about handing out keys to students, instructors and the part-time office help that came and went with the speed of Hollywood wives. After seven and a half years of living in New York, Maddie moved through the building with great wariness, with one hand in her coat pocket curled around a can of pepper spray.

Her roommate, Tessa, had been in town exactly six months. And while the girl had a self-reliant barrio toughness to her, she *was* only eighteen.

Which was why Maddie was climbing the long flight of stairs from the lobby in the semidark at eleven-fifteen on a January night, after dancing all evening at the Al-Medina Restaurant on Lexington Avenue. The advanced ballet class officially ended at ten, but the instructor frequently ran late, especially now, with the auditions for the American Ballet Academy coming up.

With the auditions approaching, Tessa would stay on later still.

This was not a good idea, in a neighborhood that wasn't anything to write home about… Not that Tessa had anyone back in El Paso to write home *to*.

From the small and gloomy lobby at the top of the first flight of stairs, Maddie followed the light to the door marked *The Dance Loft* and pulled out the second of Tessa's much-duplicated keys. The front office of the dance school was identical to the dozens Maddie had seen in Baton Rouge, in New Orleans and in New York over the twenty-three years since her first ballet class when she was five: threadbare carpet, plywood paneling, posters displaying the names of teachers. Rows of black-framed eight-by-tens of ballerinas floating weightless and serene onstage, or head shots scribbled with autographs. Looking at the little room through its glass door, Maddie had to smile as she put the key in the lock….

But the door wasn't locked.

Damn it! Maddie was shocked. *Tessa, for God's sake, when you're in here by yourself, lock the door behind you! Didn't being raised by two drunks in a domestic demilitarized zone teach you any distrust? This is the big city!*

Tessa's dance bag lay in a corner of the big studio, where the fluorescents still blazed twenty feet above the sprung wooden floor. From the door, Maddie scanned the room. The mirrors threw back her own reflection, medium height and still slim, though she'd put on ten pounds since her own stick-thin ballerina days. Belly dancers might not get the respect ballerinas did, she reflected, but at least they didn't have to starve themselves to get into productions. Her light-brown hair hung nearly to her waist, still curled into a maze of braids and twists, the jeweled clasps in it incongruous against the drab green duffle coat and jeans.

There was no sign of Tessa.

Bathroom, thought Maddie. She walked over to the black canvas bag: pink silk pointe shoes repaired with duct tape, worn and holed knit warm-ups wadded into a ball, jeans hanging over the barre. They brought back to her so clearly the first time Tessa had slipped apologetically through the door of the Dance Loft's front office last July, as if she expected to be thrown out for daring to breathe the air in there. "I'm Theresa Lopez," she'd said in her soft voice. "Is there, like, a bulletin board where I can put up a notice asking if anyone needs a roommate?"

Maddie had shown her—the board was crammed with similar ads—and because it was midmorning and Maddie had just finished teaching her own class, she'd got her a cup of coffee and they'd sat on the spavined old sofa in the front office and talked.

Though there was ten years difference in their ages—Tessa was just eighteen—Maddie had liked her immediately. Maybe because her response to Maddie's teaching belly dancing had been a heartfelt "How cool!" instead of a condescending "Oh… like those girls in the clubs?" Maybe because of the careful expression in the back of those huge brown eyes that had identified Theresa Lopez as a survivor of the same sort of war that Maddie herself had, at that time, only recently gotten out of alive, though in Theresa's case the enemy had been parents, and in Maddie's case…

Sandy.

Maddie's mind still flinched from the recollection of her ex-husband.

And the flinch woke her to the fact that a good five minutes had passed.

"Tessa?" The hall outside the Dance Loft's front office was dim and it seemed like miles to the bathroom. When Maddie reached it and pushed the door open a crack, she saw that the room was dark.

Tessa wasn't there. Hadn't been there, at least not when Maddie had come upstairs.

Maddie stood for several minutes in the gloom of the hall, listening to the silence of the building around her.

Not empty silence. Silence that breathed, and listened.

Well, duh, she told herself quickly, *Of course it's not empty, Tessa's here someplace….*

But a part of her knew it wasn't Tessa whose presence she sensed.

Maddie walked back to the office, checked the big studio again, hoping against hope she'd find Tessa there, folded into some impossible stretch and simply oblivious of the fact that it was now eleven-thirty.

Nada. She called out Tessa's name, hesitantly, but there was no reply from the other, smaller rehearsal rooms that the Dayforths rented to freelance instructors in tango, Hawaiian, hip-hop and, yes, belly dancing…so long as they didn't need them for ballet classes of their own.

Now truly uneasy, she let her bag slip down off her arm and knelt quickly to fish through the gaudy jumble of gold sequins and green silk for her cell phone. *Damn it,* she thought, *I knew this would happen…*without being precisely certain what "this" was. There was a miniflashlight in the bag, too—the electricity in the Glendower Building was notoriously erratic—and Maddie's wallet, which she transferred to her coat pocket along with the pepper spray.

Getting into the ABA was one thing—Maddie knew well how few new students they took each year, and how, with a direct feed from the most prestigious ballet company in the country, they chose none but the absolute best.

Putting your life in danger was another.

Not, she thought wryly, that you didn't do just that, cheerfully, when you were driven to succeed as Tessa was driven. She recalled her own teenage days of diet pills and bloodstained toe shoes. A few nights ago she'd come here at midnight, to see Tessa still in this studio, practicing *grand jetés* and *sautes de basque* back and forth across the huge floor with the gem-hard concentration of a gladiator training for a death fight. The younger girl's brilliance was matched only by her hunger for perfection of technique, a hunger sharpened by a short lifetime of denial.

In that first conversation six months ago, Tessa had spoken only of parents who "think I'm crazy." It wasn't until later—a week after their first meeting, to be exact, when Charmian Dayforth had dropped Maddie's two belly dancing classes in favor of another children's ballet class and Maddie had had to take a roommate to make ends meet—that Maddie had learned how hard that slim, dark-eyed girl had fought to dance at all.

Tessa knew the competition she was up against. Without a dime coming in from El Paso, she worked two jobs, getting up at four-thirty in the morning and putting in hours doing Mrs. Dayforth's clerking, filing and phone answering in trade for her classes, wanting only to learn. There were nights when Maddie had come up to the school after her own gigs at Al-Medina or the Algerian Marketplace and had found her asleep from sheer exhaustion on the front office couch.

Maddie flicked on the flashlight, left her bag beside Tessa's in the studio, stepped back into the dark hall.

"Tessa!" Her voice echoed in the halls, grating horribly on that watchful silence. "Tessa, can you hear me?" The flashlight was less than the length of her hand and had a beam that broke up a yard from the lens. It took her several minutes to find the light switches in the hall, and the dreary grayish glare was barely less depressing than absolute darkness.

Big studio, small studio, tap studio…dark. There was another big studio, though without the two-story ceiling, on the floor above, and a medium-size one where Maddie had taught her belly dance ladies the preliminary mysteries of isolation, shimmies and hip drops. Tessa was in neither of those, nor in the big changing room, though something that Maddie suspected was a rat darted out of sight under a locker. At that size she hoped it was a rat and not a cockroach, anyway.

That was another reason she disliked the Glendower Building.

Her heart pounded as she turned on the lights to the stairway up and mounted the narrow carpeted steps. The two floors above the Dance Loft—she thought there were two floors, anyway—had been divided and subdivided and redivided over the course of nearly a century into a maze of small offices and tiny studios where a couple of fly-by-night music companies did business, along with three literary agencies and a handful of freelance computer technicians. There were little workshops and padded sound booths, reached by odd little passageways that turned back on themselves or dead-ended into blank walls; windowless cubicles surrounding dreary waiting rooms with names on the doors like Wild Adventure Tours—*as opposed to tame adventures?* Maddie wondered.

Maddie thought she'd covered the fifth floor—the one immediately above the two floors of the Dance Loft—thoroughly, trying every locked and silent door. But it was also completely possible that she'd missed a hallway or a whole section of doors. There was no way of telling.

There were definitely rats up here.

And a silence that seemed to look over her shoulder, waiting to grin at her if she turned around.

Grimly, Maddie turned on the lights of the next stairway up, pushing from her mind the question of what on earth Tessa would have come up here for. She wouldn't have left her bag, wherever she was: Bloch pointe shoes cost upward of eighty dollars a pair.

Maddie was halfway up the stairs when the lights went out.

She cursed, froze as blind darkness shut around her, as if someone had dropped a blanket over her head. Damn the management and its cheap wiring—or were the lights on some kind of timer to save money? Anger carried her through the first half minute while she dug in her pocket for the flashlight....

"Stand still, you little bitch."

The whispered words came so soft that they might almost have been inside her head. Only they weren't. She knew they weren't.

Her heart constricted, then raced like a NASCAR engine as her hand scraped, pawed for the damn flashlight. *Oh, God, where the hell is it...?*

"...little sluts are all alike...good for one thing..."

She couldn't tell whether that thick, slurring voice was in front of her or behind her. But it was close, close and very clear, for she could hear the hiss of breath, smell a faint whiff of some cloying cologne laid over the stink of sweaty wool and alcohol. *Oh, God, where is that flashlight...?*

Her fingers touched it, buried deep in the folds of the left-hand pocket, slipped away from it, then grabbed it and flicked it on. Nothing above her on the stairs—she whipped around fast, shaking with shock, saw him....

Saw his shadow.

He was farther away than she'd thought, at the bottom of the stairs behind her, beyond the range of the flashlight's weak beam. A man's shape, tall and looming, a darkness against the deeper dark of the hall. Still his voice seemed to be right up against her ear as he whispered, "Bitch…"

And was gone.

Maddie climbed the stairs fast. The light switch was farther from the top than any sane remodeler would find useful, and as she hunted for it, sweeping the feeble beam along the walls, she listened desperately behind her, wondering if she'd just heard the stair creak, the floor creak.

Tessa, she thought, *Jesus Christ, Tessa, be okay….*

She flipped the switch. One light went on, far down at the end of the hall. Nothing worked near the stairwell.

In her mind she still heard the whispering. She couldn't tell where it was coming from, for it seemed to fill the air around her, some of it intelligible, some half heard and foul beyond the borders of sanity.

He's down there. Behind me.

Maddie retreated down the main hall toward the light. A corridor gaped to her right and she whipped the watery flashlight beam down it, the knobs of locked doors gleaming furtively in darkness. Something lay on the floor, something small—Maddie didn't know why she recognized it as one of the bandannas Tessa wore in her hair, but she did. She looked for a light switch but there was none, turned a corner into a dead end, retraced her steps, turned another…

Damn it, thought Maddie with a sinking heart, *I miscounted. Looks like there's another floor above this one….*

Stairs, narrower yet and as unlit as the fire escapes in hell, ascended at the end of the short hall....

The next second she realized that Tessa was standing at the foot of them, her back to Maddie, looking up.

"Tessa!"

The girl swung around, startled, catching at the corner of the wall for support. In her tights and leotard she looked about thirteen, her thin form half concealed by a baggy T-shirt, whose old rock-concert logo had been nearly chipped away by time and laundering. Her marvelous black hair was wound up into a neat ballerina's bun on top of her head.

"Maddie?" She sounded puzzled rather than afraid.

"Are you all right?" Maddie strode down the hall, put a hand behind Tessa's back, drew her toward the faint light still visible from the main hall. Through leotard and T-shirt she could feel every vertebra, as if she'd put her hand on a pile of jacks. "I was coming back from Al-Medina, and I thought I'd walk you home...."

They turned the corner by a locked door marked, *Vulgarian Records*, Tessa looking around her uncertainly, as if not entirely sure of where she was.

Maddie herself was just praying that the main hall would be empty when they reached it. "I saw your stuff still in the studio...."

There were still, of course, the stairs to get down....

"Thank you." Tessa sounded hesitant, but then made herself smile. "How was your gig? You get a lot of tips?"

"Decent." *And I left them downstairs in my bag, like an idiot, for our pal Whispering Smith to help himself....* "Tessa, listen, there's somebody else in the..."

They stepped around the corner and there he was.

Maddie's breath jerked in her lungs, and Tessa stepped toward the tall shadow and said, "So what happened to the lights?"

"When I fired up the Doomsday Machine to destroy the planet, I had the microwave on and I blew a circuit." He stepped into the weak glimmer of the flashlight: brown eyes, pleasantly craggy features, dark, stiff hair hanging in disarray over his forehead. Under a greenish-brown wool sweater the tails of a much-faded denim shirt protruded, finished off by patched and battered jeans. "You need something? Other than a better flashlight?"

"Maddie," said Tessa, "this is Phil Cooper. He plays piano for the ballet classes—he's got a studio here in the building."

"Hi." Maddie's heart was still pounding so hard it almost nauseated her. Her fingers closed around the pepper-spray can in her pocket, though her common sense told her that unless he were armed, the man probably couldn't take on the two of them. She wanted to pull Tessa back out of arm's reach but didn't know how to manage it unobtrusively.

"Maddie's my roommate," continued the girl blithely. "She dances over at Al-Medina—*and* reads tarot cards." Her pride and delight in both of these accomplishments rang in her voice. "She's really good."

"Remind me to consult you the next time I get offered a recording contract." His voice was pleasant, husky and a little hesitant, but Maddie could see that he didn't miss the way she drew back from him.

"I suggest you save your money for a lawyer," she said. "Tessa, we've got to get out of here. It's almost midnight."

Tessa's eyes widened with shocked guilt. "No way! Oh, sweetie, I'm sorry…." She let Maddie pull her down the stairs, Phil trailing behind. Maddie almost told him to get lost but decided that it was better if she knew where he was. The lights worked fine once they got down to the Dance Loft.

"Makes sense," said Phil cheerily as the bright glare flooded the halls. "If the Dayforths left, the owners would be stuck with two whole floors to rent out. They don't give a rat's ass what we think about them up on the sixth floor."

Maddie said nothing. As they collected their bags Tessa chatted with Phil about the long explanation Quincy the caretaker had given her concerning the building's electricity—"I swear the man took twenty minutes to tell me about buying a lightbulb! Well, first he told me about how electricity worked, *then* he told me about the lightbulb…."

"They've got a twelve-step program for that," said Phil as he followed the two women down that last long spooky flight of stairs to the lobby. "On-and-On-Anon. You ladies be okay walking over to the subway?"

"We're fine," Maddie snapped, and stepped out onto the stoop. Phil remained in the building and gave them a polite wave as Tessa followed Maddie out the door.

The night's icy mist had almost thickened to rain. Maddie's boots knocked sharply on the wet pavement as they headed for the subway stop on Park, making her glance back more than once, as if she expected to see someone drifting behind them in the dark. "Is he the night watchman for the school as well as the piano player?" she asked after they had walked a little way in silence. "Or does he just like sneaking around old buildings in the dark?"

"I think he lives there these days." Tessa huddled her pea coat more closely around her and glanced worriedly at the sharp note in her roommate's voice. "But don't tell Mrs. Dayforth, okay? He rents this studio on the top floor and writes music, and about two weeks ago his roommate at his apartment told him his girlfriend was moving in, so Phil had to vacate—way harsh, I thought. I mean," Tessa added contritely, "if you wanted me to boogie so you could bring in a boy, I know you'd give me more than a day to find someplace else. Horny is one thing, but you don't got to be rude."

"Sweetheart," smiled Maddie, "after my previous experience in the male-roommate department, I promise you, you have nothing to worry about." They walked on for another half block, detouring around the ubiquitous clusters of trash cans at the curb, glancing down narrow areaways where lights burned in tailor shops, button stores, basement clubs full of smoke. At the corner of Lexington Avenue an all-night Korean grocery glowed like a jewel with produce, bottles, steam trays filled with Oriental chicken salad and lasagna. At length—so as not to let her mind return to the male-roommate department—Maddie asked, "What were you doing up on the sixth floor? Why did you go there?"

"I don't..." Tessa hesitated. "I guess I thought I heard a noise or something. Or...or voices talking." In the yellow glare of the grocery's lamps her dark pixie brows drew down over the straight little nose; her glance darted sidelong to Maddie again. "I think maybe it had to have been my imagination."

"Did someone call you? Or…or whisper to you?"

Theresa shook her head. "Whisper what?"

Maddie shivered, remembering the note of vile gloating in the voice, as much as the obscenity of the words. Had it really been Phil Cooper? It was hard to put that hoarse voice together with the piano player's easygoing friendliness. But then, she thought, she'd trusted Sandy, too.

LYING AWAKE IN HER BED later, staring at the street lamps' distant glare reflected on the hanging sheets that separated her "bedroom" niche from the rest of the big studio apartment, Maddie thought about Sandy.

Had it really been ten and a half months since that deep voice had spoken to her over the phone: "Mrs. Weinraub?"

"I *was* Mrs. Weinraub," Maddie had replied carefully. "But I'm no longer married to Sandy Weinraub." And she'd thought, *Oh, God, not another collection agency….* Though she could no longer be responsible for his debts after the date separation was filed, she still lived with the nightmare of some unsuspected creditor crawling out of the woodwork, some hitherto unrevealed legal technicality that would haul her back into the craziness of poor Sandy's existence.

But the deep voice had said, "I'm Officer O'Neill of the NYPD. Mr. Weinraub's body was found by his landlord this morning. His death appears to have been from natural causes. We'd like you to come down and identify it."

It still seemed like last week.

Had he always lied to her? Maddie was still trying

to figure that one out. Nothing in her peaceful—if rather obsessive—childhood had prepared her for marriage to a man whose life was a surreptitious quest for chemical oblivion. Certainly nothing had prepared her to look behind Sandy's intelligence and charm into the nightmare of addiction and lies. Asking him to leave had been one of the hardest things she'd ever done, and for nearly a year she'd lived with the pleading phone messages, the desperate requests for money, the fear that she'd encounter him one day panhandling, homeless, in the street.

And then he was gone.

Natural causes, if you could call the results of a lifetime of drug and alcohol abuse "natural."

And looking back at nine years of memories, from the moment she'd walked into that first writing class at Tulane and been struck speechless by the youthful teacher's slow, wry smile, Maddie still couldn't hate him, or be angry at him. He certainly had not torn her life to pieces in malice.

According to everyone she'd talked to, that was just something addicts did.

Or something men did. Maddie wasn't sure which. All the promises, and all the lies, and all the things she'd given up, trying to make a relationship work with someone who wasn't present in his body upward of fifty percent of the time. Had it been different, she wondered, when first they'd met? When first she'd dropped out of college to go to New York with him, to be his adored one and his admiring wife? Or had she just been too naive to notice?

She stretched out her hand to scratch Baby's black-

and-white ears. The cat put a paw over Maddie's wrist and began to lick her hand; at times Maddie thought Baby considered herself Maddie's kitten, at times, Maddie's mother. Baby had been Sandy's cat, a useful lesson, Maddie thought, in human relations. Animals only understood what you did, not what you said. When Maddie had begun looking at what Sandy did, and not listening to what he said, the mist of infatuation started to clear from her eyes.

But she'd never ceased loving him.

On the other side of the sheet-wall, she heard the springs of the old sofa creak softly under Tessa's too-slight weight. The girl cried out something, a muffled sob in her sleep. Maddie half sat up, for her young roommate suffered occasionally from nightmares. Maddie couldn't imagine how, after three hours of class, ten hours of work and individual practice on top of that, Tessa had the energy even to dream. She listened, ready to go out and wake her if her nightmare continued, but the sound was not repeated.

Did she dream of her parents? Maddie wondered. Of the chaos she'd only hinted at in their conversations: her father's drunken rages, her mother's screaming efforts to control him, the ugly separation battle that had resulted in Tessa traveling back and forth from El Paso to San Francisco several times a year? Was she imagining herself at the age of eight, alone on a Greyhound bus?

Or the fears about what she'd do if she couldn't get into a ballet company, couldn't get a job doing what she loved?

Or did she dream of the darkness of the Glendower Building? Closing her eyes, Maddie saw Tessa again, standing in the darkness at the bottom of the stairway to the seventh floor, listening to a man's voice whispering obscenities while he reached out to her with his shadow hands.

CHAPTER TWO

"CAN I JOIN YOU?"

Maddie turned, startled, from watching the dirty granite doorway of the Glendower Building across the street, and looked up to see Phil Cooper standing beside her table.

So he exists in daytime, and outside the building.

And the next instant, *What's* that *about?*

...little sluts are all alike...good for one thing...

He seemed very tall, standing over her in the heatless morning brightness from the window of the Owl Café. She took a deep breath.

"Okay."

He drew back a bit from the chill in her tone. For a moment she thought he was going to say, *Well, don't do me any big favors,* and walk off. She couldn't tell whether she'd feel angry at him or immensely relieved if he did.

He set his coffee cup on the table and said—without sitting— "Look, I'm sorry if I pissed you off with that stupid crack about consulting you next time I signed a contract. Tessa tells me you take your card-reading pretty seriously...." He winced and added, "So now that I've shoved my *other* foot into my mouth, I'll just roll myself out the door. But I really didn't mean it to sound like it did." He picked up the cup and was turning to go when Maddie laughed.

"You'll never make it out the door with both feet crammed in your mouth."

"Hide and watch me." His shoulders relaxed and he came back. "If the lady in the yoga studio on the fifth floor can walk around on her hands with her ankles crossed behind her neck, I can sure get out with both feet in my mouth." He must have read the look in Maddie's eye, because he set his cup on the table again and sat down. For a man who was presumably sleeping on the floor of a practice studio he was clean and shaved, if scruffy. His hair was clean and still slightly damp—Maddie guessed he was sneaking showers in the Dance Loft's dressing rooms.

Mrs. Dayforth would be beyond pissed if anyone ratted on him.

At this hour, shortly after two, the Owl was emptying out, the clerical staff and warehouse handlers from all the small companies in the neighborhood heading back to work and leaving the battered tables and the hard-worn bentwood chairs to the dance students, the lawyers from the offices overhead and their clients, and stray shoppers from Lexington Avenue.

He added with a rueful grin, "I've had lots of practice at it."

"And I've had lots of practice hearing people make cracks about the cards. People believe in them or they don't. There's no reason why you should." Maddie spread her hands. "You didn't..." She hesitated again, looking into those brown eyes and wondering, *Was it the same man?*

Was it the same voice?

The smell of him certainly wasn't the same, that horrible rancid stink of grimy wool and cologne.

If she asked him, would he tell her the truth?

"You didn't hear anyone else in the building the other night, did you?" And as she spoke the words something in her flinched and she wished she could snatch them back, shove them in her pocket and walk away and be safe.

"Did you?"

It was him.

Was it him?

He'd drawn back from her at the question, suddenly wary. Maddie shook her head. "Tessa tells me you're sleeping there these days."

"Shh!" He hunched his shoulders and put a finger dramatically to his lips. "If the building management heard that they'd terminate my lease, and then I'd *really* be in trouble. I'm hoping it's just temporary, till I build up enough of a nest egg to get a place…but in this town you need a nest egg the size of a forklift. Between playing for the ballet classes I teach private piano students in my studio. If I lost that place I'd be back bustin' rods in Tulsa."

Maddie's eyebrows went up. "So you're really in construction?"

"I *was* really in construction," said Phil, then he looked down at his coffee cup, turning it so the handle lined up with the edge of the table. "Or rather, I was always really a musician but I had to do the construction thing when I lived at home. My dad would pay for me to go to college in engineering or business—he's a contractor—but music?"

He shrugged and glanced up to meet her eyes again. "That's one reason I wasn't in the best mood last night. It was my birthday—the big three-oh. Sleeping on the floor in an empty building wasn't the way I thought I'd be spending it."

Maddie looked down at his hands. Big hands, knotty from carrying steel rebars—"bustin' rods," the lowest level of the construction trade—but long-boned and supple. A musician's hands. His face, in daylight, seemed younger than it had last night in spite of the lines around the corners of the eyes, the few flecks of silver in the thick dark hair.

She found herself wondering under what circumstances he'd acquired the old break in the bridge of his nose, the short scar under his left eye. Wondering what he'd gone through to come here, and what kind of music he wrote in that desperately held studio on the sixth floor.

"I sent him the two CDs I cut," said Phil, more quietly. "Last time I was home I found them in a drawer, still wrapped in plastic. My stepmom keeps asking me how come I don't write the kind of music real people like?" He caught himself and glanced up at her, apologetic. "Sorry. You're not into classical music, are you?"

"You know," said Maddie solemnly, folding her hands beneath her chin, "I tried for years to work out a belly dance routine to Mozart's *Eine Kleine Nachtmusik,* and I just couldn't fit in a drum solo."

"Ow!" He flinched ruefully. "I'm sorry. 'Man develops third foot, shoves it in mouth—film at eleven.' I don't seem to be doing too well. It's just after years of having people's eyes glaze over when I talk about music…"

"I run into the same thing," said Maddie gently, "from all those people who think a belly dancer is the same as a stripper."

Phil looked away. In a Victorian novel, Maddie reflected, he would have blushed.

"Have you ever seen a good belly dancer perform?"

"Um…uh…"

In a topless bar with the other construction workers, she thought—she knew.

And then, like the recollection of a nightmare, in her mind she heard again…*little sluts are all alike….*

And saw the wary look that had come into his eyes when he'd dodged her question and asked instead, *Did you?*

What are you doing sitting here talking to this man? Much less imagining what he'd look like on a construction site at the age of twenty-four in an undershirt?

Maddie got quickly to her feet. Instead of saying, *You should come on over to Al-Medina and check it out some evening,* she opened her mouth to retort, *You figure anyone who dances for tips couldn't tell the difference between Rossini and Tchaikovsky without a crib sheet and a copy of* 101 Classical Favorites *in her Discman?*

Sandy had had the same attitude—it was due to his good-natured contempt for the art that Maddie had abandoned dancing, nine years ago.

But the genuine distress in Phil's eyes as he looked up at her—the helpless apology for having, as he thought, inadvertently angered her yet again—stopped her. For a moment there was silence between them, Maddie looking down into his face as he sat with his big hands around the coffee cup, an exile like herself who couldn't go home.

She let her breath out. "There's Tessa," she said, nodding across the street at the thin pea-coated figure on the steps of the Glendower Building. "I guess I'll see you around the school."

And she added, though she didn't know why, "Good luck."

"Thank you," he said. "These days I sure need it."

SHE INTERCEPTED TESSA halfway across the street and suggested a quick lunch at the Twenty-ninth Street Café—a little to her roommate's surprise, since they usually had a sandwich at the Owl on the days when Maddie taught at the SoHo YWCA. Tessa, Maddie noticed, barely ate anything; she hoped her young roommate would go back to the apartment and take some rest between her afternoon class and the start of her late shift at Starbucks, but she knew it wasn't likely.

Afterward, Maddie managed to put Phil Cooper from her mind for the rest of the day. She had five scheduled card readings in the candlelit back room of the Darkness Visible bookstore in the West Village, and two more walk-ins while she was there—forty dollars per half hour, a substantial contribution to the rent.

Only that night, as she took the subway home from her usual Al-Medina gig, did Phil return to her mind.

This was partly due to Josi, the other dancer at the restaurant that night, a kittenish California blonde who had, Maddie suspected, gotten most of her experience in topless clubs. She was younger than Maddie and stunningly pretty, and had a habit of taking drinks from customers' glasses, or wiping her face with a napkin filched off a businessman's lap, or casually adjusting her overflowing bra mid-shimmy. If she thought a man would stump up a bigger tip she'd invite him to tuck the money into her bra, which was adorned with large, pink, rhinestoned lips, rather than her belt. Everyone was thoroughly entertained: the Americans in the audience didn't know the difference, and the Arabs and Iranians were simply enchanted. But, as Abdullah, the owner, confided to Maddie later, it wasn't really dancing.

But when Maddie's own set came, and she trailed out in a swirl of purple veils and Farid Al-Atrash's timeless dance music, all her annoyance washed away—with Josi, with Phil, with the scheduling directors of the SoHo Y, with her mother....

For a time there was just dancing. The Moroccan and Egyptian waiters—and Abdullah himself—drifted in from the other dining rooms to watch, clapping along with the music and gathering up dropped dollar bills and her discarded veil for her after the set was done.

Josi, thought Maddie as she rode home on the subway later—though the girl was perfectly sweet and good-natured—was probably what Phil thought of when he heard the word *belly dancer.*

Yet he would not leave her mind. As she sat wedged between a couple of home-going green-haired club rats and an elderly gentleman reading a Yiddish newspaper, their conversation at the Owl returned to her. She remembered again the shape of those long hands, strong and work-hardened and deft-looking as they cradled the coffee cup. Remembered the fleeting downward quirk of the corner of his mouth. Spending your birthday sleeping on the floor of an empty building was probably enough to make anyone flippant.

Had that disappointed father, that clueless stepmom, even remembered to send him a card?

I was always really a musician but I had to do the construction thing when I lived at home....

Maddie's stomach curled in sympathy as she recalled the look on her mother's face, patronizingly amused when Maddie had come in breathless over that first belly dance class. *Honestly, what will they be teaching at that studio next?* And later, in those glass-sharp accents of disapproval, *Dearest, I understand you wanting to branch out a little bit, to improve your ballet, but what's wrong with tap? Your cousin Lacy takes tap.*

Cousin Lacy was also a cheerleader, a modeling-school graduate, a steady participant in teen and subteen beauty pageants since kindergarten and a practicing bulimic who was routinely two hours late to everything because it took her that long to get her makeup and hair perfect before emerging from her room.

Maddie couldn't explain what it was about the visceral joyfulness of Middle Eastern dance that drew her. Only that when she entered that first class at sixteen, for the first time she had felt that she could dance uncriticized and imperfect, for herself and not for her mother, her teachers, some future competition judges.

Only for herself.

She wondered if Tessa would know where she could get hold of one of Phil's CDs. Or both of them.

She dreamed about Phil that night.

Dreamed of the warm, lapping waters of the Gulf of Mexico, on whose shores her parents used to rent a summer house. Dreamed of lying on the beach, below the yellow-flowered tangles of wild jasmine, in the perfect restful stillness of the gathering dusk. Phil was lying beside her, on one of those faded old blankets that came with the rental house—only there was no house in sight, no other houses at all, just two crumbling Roman pillars marking the path down to the beach, and the luminous colors of the sky.

She said, "I wanted you to see this place. It's quiet. The world is too noisy."

And Phil's hand stroked her shoulder, drawing her down to him, so that her long hair veiled his face. "Were you happy here?" he asked, and she said, "Yes."

His hand slid up to the back of her neck and she lowered her face to his, their lips meeting, the soft whisper of his breath warm on her cheek. "It's safe," she said for no reason she could recall.

They were making love, Phil's hands exploring her face, her throat, her shoulders and the soft flesh over her ribs, as if it had been a long time since he'd lain with a woman, or as if he had never felt free to touch bare skin before. Maddie's hands trailed over the heavy muscle of his forearms, the too-pale skin—so surprisingly soft—and corded muscle of chest and belly; touched the sharp cheekbones and the tucked-away half grin that always decorated one corner of his mouth.

The dream was slow and wordless, the strength of him pressing her down into the blanket, powerful without roughness, deft and light. When he cupped and cradled her breasts, the warmth that ran through her flesh was like the sand beneath her reflecting the heat of that afternoon's sunlight. When he entered her, she pressed her lips to his shoulder, to his throat, tasting and smelling his flesh and his sweat.

It was so good to feel simple passion, simple trust, after years of deception and lies.

She said, "I didn't think I'd be able to come here again," and tightened her arms around his shoulders, her legs around his thighs. The scent of him, the feel of him, were absolutely different from Sandy, and even in her dream she felt glad of that, glad that this was really Phil. Even when she'd dreamed about other men during her marriage—the delightfully silly fantasy parade of improbably costumed Johnny Depps and Brad Pitts and Nicolas Cages—their flesh had tasted like Sandy's. The way they'd held her had been with Sandy's light nervous touch, and they had all kissed her with Sandy's lips.

When she had asked Sandy to leave, she had ceased dreaming about men at all.

She woke with a gasp of delight, and for that first instant she felt that if she turned her head Phil would be there in bed beside her, beach sand still in his hair.

What the hell am I thinking?

...little sluts are all alike, whispered a voice in her thoughts, *...good for one thing...*

The intense joy she'd taken from his touch washed away in cold shock.

But lying in the dark, staring at the ghostly trapezoids of streetlights reflected on the ceiling, she felt no surprise. It was as if she knew she was drawn to Phil from the first moment she saw him in the feeble glow of her flashlight....

Only of course that hadn't been the first time.

The first time was the dark shape bulking at the bottom of the stairs, blackness against blackness deeper still, whispering…reaching out to her.

Maddie sat up in bed, trembling, her arms clasped around her knees. Fearing that if she lay down she'd sleep again, and dream about him.

Dream about making love to him—or dream about the shadow at the bottom of the stairs.

Sandy returned to her mind, and her own crazy blaze of passion and tenderness for him. Even all those nights of drunken ramblings, all those nights of being wakened with demands that she go out to the pharmacy *right then* and get him more of whatever he needed that week—all those moments of murderous rage and humiliation—had not erased her love. Knowing about him what she knew, though every single specific memory of Sandy was the memory of awfulness, the pain in her heart was the pain of loss.

Of course I'd have frenzied dreams of making love to a maniac who lurks around deserted buildings at night!

Dim illumination revealed the shapes of her little alcove, separated from the long axis of the apartment with its neat wall of sheet. Dresser, nightstand, bronze lamp in the shape of a dancing elf, closet crammed with costumes and veils, a print of an Alma-Tadema painting on the wall. From Eleventh Avenue far below a horn honked—New York never really slept—and very faint music trickled in from the apartment next door. Baby slumbered on the pillow at her side.

No sound from the other side of the curtain. Tessa

had been asleep when Maddie had come in from Al-Medina, a tangle of Indian-black hair on the pillows of Sandy's pink-and-turquoise Populuxe couch. Knowing how poorly the girl slept, Maddie had not even turned on the light as she'd put up the burglar bar and the chains, and slipped through to her own cubicle.

The memory of Phil's lips, even through the surrogacy of a dream, wouldn't leave her.

The memory of his hands, a laborer's hands with a pianist's touch.

The weight of his body pressing down onto hers.

The slow grin in his eyes as he said, *I can get out with both feet in my mouth,* and his distress with himself that he'd angered her.

If she slept again, she wondered, would she be back with him?

It's safe, she had said in her dream. But she no longer trusted her dreams.

Moving carefully so as not to disturb Baby, Maddie switched on the bronze lamp to its lowest glow and reached into the bottom drawer of the nightstand for the cards.

Being a card reader, Maddie had discovered, was similar in many ways to being a belly dancer: one was constantly getting tarred with the same brush that categorized the Josis of the world. Most of the people who made appointments to come to her little cubbyhole in the back of the Darkness Visible bookstore—or who just walked in off the street saying, *Hey, can you tell my fortune?*—had firm preconceptions of what the tarot cards were and did, and most of those preconceptions varied so widely from person to person that Maddie sometimes wondered if they were all thinking about the same objects.

Seventy-eight symbols.

Pictures that embodied truths or situations, or clusters of possible events.

If there is a pattern, an intentionality, to Is-ness, her teacher had told her, *the cards line up with that pattern, like iron filings in a magnetic field. Those who touch the cards affect the local swirls of the pattern of All That Is. Those who study them see different meanings in those alignments.*

If the dances of the Maghreb and the Middle East were Maddie's road to self and joy, the cards were her parallel road of connection to the world, in its widest sense. She couldn't imagine thinking in terms other than the shadowy armature of their infinite combinations.

This should at least be able to give me some insights about who this man is, reflected Maddie, fishing from the same drawer a small scented candle on a green glass saucer, *and whether I'm crazy to feel toward him what I do.*

It may even mention whether or not he was the whisperer in the shadows…or why he chose to screen the whisperer when I asked, Did you hear anyone else?

Her hands shook a little as she lit the candle, switched out the bedside lamp.

What kind of an answer is Did you?

Maddie took three deep breaths and shuffled the cards.

After a little hesitation, she chose the King of Pentacles to represent Phil. Pentacles was the suit of

Earth, of craftsmen and artists, of money and property—which Phil didn't have any of, apparently. The king was used as a significator for a dark-haired man, a brown-eyed man and—if his birthday was yesterday—a Capricorn, one of the signs of Earth. She could as easily have used the Knight of Pentacles—Phil was, like the knights, a seeker and a traveler—but it was one of the several cards she'd used for Sandy, who had been a Capricorn, too. Poor Sandy had never had the core of adult strength in him to be King of anything.

Usually, the card she had used for Sandy was the card he had chosen to represent himself: the Fool. The blithe traveler so rapt in contemplation of his thoughts that he doesn't see the cliff that gapes before his feet.

Maddie closed her eyes, whispered her prayer to be shown what she needed to see, and laid out the cards.

And sat back, disgusted and appalled.

It was not anything she had expected to see in connection with Phil.

As if she had opened what she had thought to be a scented lingerie drawer, and found it filled with roaches and worms.

Even the most tolerant reading could not make the scattered gold circles of the Pentacles into anything other than warnings of blind greed. The five of that suit spoke of fear of poverty, the six—reversed—of chicanery, bribes and legalized theft, financial oppression. And with the greed, the swords: strife, violence, coercion, rampant self-will.

Maddie saw Tessa—or a card that she assumed to be Tessa—in the dreamy Page of Cups, but everything else in the spread was harsh, frightening and dark as the halls of the Glendower Building itself.

There was the Devil, holding the captive lovers chained.

There was the ten of Swords—a worse card than the skeletal Death card, in Maddie's opinion—a dead man lying pierced with ten swords, in the last light of a fading yellow sky.

And the "outcome" card, the final card of the reading, was the Tower, struck by lightning and collapsing in flames, destroying all within.

Do not have anything to do with this man or you will be very, very sorry.

Her hands trembling, her heart pounding, Maddie gathered up the cards, slipped them at random back into the pack and shuffled again. Generally she accepted what the readings told her—acceptance was part of the mental discipline of the tarot—but she couldn't believe that Phil…

Her mind stalled on the sentence: *You mean, you can't believe that the man who whispered those half-heard obscenities to you in the darkness would have the cards give him a bad reading?*

Grow up, princess!

The second reading was also virtually all swords and pentacles, and contained both the Devil and the Falling Tower.

As did the third, with the Tower once again in the "outcome" position.

Maddie put the cards away, shivering. She had occasionally had this happen—the same cards coming up over and over again despite continual shufflings. It usually occurred when there was something she was trying not to look at, didn't want to see. The presence of Tessa's card—the Page of Cups—in all three readings didn't reassure her, either. She, Maddie, wasn't the one who could have been expected to be in the Glendower Building last night. And now that she came to think of it, what was Phil doing in the Owl, watching the entrance of the Glendower Building across the street?

If I go to sleep, will I dream about him again?

And do I want to?

She hadn't made up her mind about this when she drifted off to sleep, and spent the rest of the night dreaming about going to a vast and colorful amusement park with Abraham Lincoln—an entertaining enough way to pass the rest of the night.

CHAPTER THREE

IN THE LIGHT OF THE following morning, the possibility that Phil Cooper would be stalking Tessa seemed far less likely. Three appearances of the Falling Tower notwithstanding, the man simply seemed too sane—and appeared to have too much of a sense of humor—to be creeping around dark hallways whispering. *Something* of that insanity would show.

Wouldn't it?

Nevertheless, over the course of the next week Maddie watched and listened to her roommate with uneasy attention, mentally flagging those occasions when the piano player's name surfaced in conversation, noting where he showed up in Tessa's life, and when.

The result was totally inconclusive. The afternoon after her dream—and the card reading that followed—Phil wandered into the Owl while Tessa and Maddie were having a sandwich, caught Maddie's eye and raised his brows. *Mind if I join you?* She looked away, and when she looked back, he was gone.

Which was just as well, Maddie reflected, considering the rush of almost physical memory that flooded her, as if she had in fact felt his hands stroking her, his lips light and gentle on hers, instead of just dreaming the whole incident.

If he'd followed Tessa there, he didn't do it again.

And with ABA auditions coming up, Maddie doubted if Tessa would have been aware of it if Phil had been slouching around behind telephone poles in a trench coat and a ski mask with a chainsaw sticking out of his pocket. She worked early and late, to leave herself time to attend as many classes as she could, training in beginner classes early in the morning to "warm up," as she put it, and practicing alone late into the night. Unlike many of her classmates—some of whom had parents who paid for personal nutritionists and trainers—Tessa wasn't a deliberate self-starver, but she tended to forget to eat, especially when she had a class coming up.

And these days she *always* had a class coming up.

It was just as well, Maddie reflected, that she herself was kept extremely busy between teaching, dancing and card readings. It kept things in perspective and kept her from acting like a mother hen—whatever she might be thinking. She'd seen how perilously easy it had been for her to take over responsibility for Sandy's disordered life: it was not something she wanted to do again.

Indeed, on the days when Tessa started work at Starbucks at five in the morning, if Maddie had a full lineup of readings to do after teaching her own classes at the SoHo Y—a Middle Eastern and a Senior Flexibility—the two girls often didn't see each other until ten or eleven at night, when Tessa would finish Darth Irving's advanced class. If Maddie had a belly dance gig, their paths wouldn't cross for days.

"Help, help, some stranger is breaking into the apartment!" squeaked Maddie on Wednesday night, when

Tessa came in at eleven to find her curled up with Baby on the couch watching *Casablanca.* "Do I know you, madame?" Tessa had replied.

And yet, behind this appearance of normalcy, Maddie's instincts told her that something was very wrong. Her uneasiness would come in flashes, leaving a dark stain of worry on her consciousness that couldn't be dismissed. Someone *had* been up in those tangled hallways on the fifth floor, someone mentally unbalanced if nothing worse. Tessa had promised to be careful, to lock the studio doors and not stay as late, but to her reassurance, "It's okay, Phil's there," Maddie could find nothing to say.

In her dreams she sometimes found herself back in those dark mazes, stumbling against walls that seemed to narrow on her like a trap, frantically searching for a light switch with a flashlight that didn't work. Listening to a thick, hoarse voice mumbling vile suggestions. Smelling the reek of sweaty wool, tobacco and cologne.

One evening Maddie went to the Dance Loft after doing readings until ten, and found Tessa, as usual, working alone after class, doing *grand jetés* back and forth across the big studio with Phil playing a crashing Tchaikovsky accompaniment: Maddie watched for a time from the darkness of the empty hall, then left silently, without making her presence known, and kicked herself all the way back to Thirty-second Street. But she was still awake an hour later when Tessa's key rattled in the door.

"Does he usually do that?" asked Maddie as the younger girl sorted out her threadbare, sweat-soaked tights from the gym bag, laid out clothes for the following morning, unfurled sheets and blankets from the chest that doubled as a coffee table. "Stay to play for you?"

"Phil?" Tessa looked surprised, then smiled. "He's such a champ about it. He's like, 'As long as I'm sleeping here, anyway, I might as well be of some use.' Like he hasn't been working on his own stuff all day, and teaching those awful brats up in his studio every time he gets a spare half hour. Why didn't you come in?"

"Because you were in the middle of your dance," said Maddie. Which, she told herself, was actually perfectly true. "And I know you don't get enough studio time to practice."

Tessa paused in the midst of pulling pins out of her tight-wrapped sable bun, perched on the back of the sofa like a disheveled fairy in her pink tights. "You are so sweet," she said softly. "I think you're the only friend I've got who doesn't just come barging in and figure I'm dying to drop what I'm doing and talk *right now.* Thank you." She unfolded her long legs and hopped down, prowled to the refrigerator, came back with orange juice in a thick green glass mug. "Did I look okay? Hobbs and I are going to do a *pas de deux* as part of the audition—" Hobbs was the most talented of the male students, a thoroughly gay and thoroughly good-natured young man from Detroit. "Most of the time I feel like I come down okay on my jumps, but then I'll wobble. The ABA only takes…"

She stopped herself, shook her head. "Sorry. I'll sit here and nitpick myself for hours, and that's got to be about as interesting as watching me brush my hair. How was your night?"

"Other than the woman who wanted me to do a reading on why her cat wasn't accepting the new Chihuahua she just got yesterday? Pretty calm. What do you think of Phil? Is he all right?"

"Oh, he's the bomb." Tessa nodded, suiting the action to the word by starting to brush out her hair. She looked like ten miles of bad road, drawn and fragile despite the thin striations of whipcord muscle in her chest, arms, back. "You aren't mad at him, are you? He asked me."

Phil's hands cupping her face as he pressed her back into the warm sand. The scent of his flesh and the feel of his skin under her fingertips.

The black-and-yellow Devil card, grinning at her amid the tangle of Swords.

The Falling Tower.

"No."

Tessa's smile returned, relieved. "I told him all that you told me, about how belly dancing is descended from some of the oldest tribal dancing in the world, and it traveled along the Silk Road, and all that about it turning up in flamenco and gypsy music and all kinds of other neat places. He's all like, *So* that's *why those ladies hang diamonds and fringe all over their secondary sexual characteristics.*"

She captured Phil's sardonic inflection perfectly, and Maddie thought of the infamous Josi in terms of traditional dances of the Silk Road and burst out laughing. "And you said?"

"*Don't you wish* you *could?* And he laughed."

Maddie tried to picture the Devil's face on the card laughing at himself, and couldn't.

"He really loves music," Tessa continued more quietly. "You should hear him play. Even if he's just playing for the classes, it's like… Sometimes your heart just hurts. He's one of those people who sees mathematical patterns in Bach, and all that."

Passion and lightness and beautiful technique, an integral part of Tessa's flying jumps rather than something simply to time them. A playful joy that echoed Maddie's own sense of what dance—whether ballet or hip-hop or Indian temple rites—was for.

Tessa stretched and went to pull her Sailor Moon nightgown out of the small drawer of her possessions. "I'm working on him, but he's still kind of like, *Oh, belly dancing…*" She raised one eyebrow in an exaggerated, patronizing sneer. "I think he just needs to have his consciousness raised."

"Come up to my place, little boy," purred Maddie in her best imitation of Mae West's throaty double entendre, "and I'll raise your consciousness."

Both girls went into gales of giggles.

But later that night Maddie woke to hear movement on the other side of the dividing curtain and, stepping out into the living room, found Tessa standing at the door in her nightgown, fumbling to get the burglar bar unfastened. Maddie said, "Tessa, what is it?" and Tessa's whole body jerked, her knees buckling. She caught herself on the doorknob as Maddie rushed to her. In the unearthly blue of the reflected street lamps Tessa's dark eyes were filled with panic; when Maddie caught her to steady her she could feel her friend shaking.

"Sweetie, what is it?"

Tessa shook her head, looked around her, baffled. "I…I must have sleepwalked," she stammered, breathless. Her hands, gripping Maddie's arm, were icy cold. "I used to do that when I was a little *niña,* when Mama and Dad broke up."

"Were you dreaming about something?" Maddie walked her back to the couch, switched on the small reading lamp at its head. Last night—or maybe the night before?—Maddie had been wakened by Tessa crying out in her sleep in Spanish: *No! No me toque!*

Tessa shook her head uncertainly, groping for some half-recalled image. But the next moment the fine arches of her brows pulled together, and she flinched away from the memory of whatever it was.

"What did you dream?" asked Maddie softly.

"I don't remember."

The father who'd leave her sitting in his truck outside the bars in El Paso until one in the morning on the way home from picking her up after school? The mother who'd come screaming drunk into her bedroom at midnight pulling dresser drawers out and throwing everything into the middle of the floor?

Maddie had heard about both of these individuals. Tessa answered too quickly, but Maddie didn't press her. Maybe she didn't remember.

FOUR NIGHTS A WEEK, Maddie danced at Al-Medina—sometimes with the incomparable Josi, sometimes with Zafira Mafous, a beautiful Lebanese girl who danced under the stage name of Lucy—and finished her last set at eleven. Upon occasion she'd get a private gig, a birthday party or bar mitzvah, and then it was anybody's guess when she'd get home, which was the case the following Saturday night.

She unlocked the door at one—tired, smelling a little of champagne thanks to a tipsy rabbi, and three hundred dollars richer—and saw in the ghostly glow of the reflected street lamps the tumble of Tessa's bedding on the couch and the bathroom door open and dark.

Tessa was gone.

Maddie crossed at once to the curtain of sheets and looked through to her own bed. But the only one there was Baby, curled up on the pillows with that *And where have* you *been all night, young lady?* look in her green eyes.

In a New York studio apartment there are very, *very* few places where even an anorexic ballerina can hide.

In her mind Maddie saw Tessa standing in her nightgown, her long black hair hanging down her shoulders, fumbling at the door. When one or the other of them was home they left the key in the lock. The only thing that had defeated her the other night was the burglar bar.

Maddie whispered, "Damn it!" The January night was freezing cold with an icy wind blowing off the harbor. A glance around the apartment showed Tessa's street shoes and coat still there, her jeans folded neatly on the arm of the sofa and the tights she'd had on earlier that evening when she'd left for class crumpled in the bathroom hamper. The clothes for tomorrow—white shirt and black trousers for work, tights and leotard for class—lay on top of her gym bag. The red sweatshirt she sometimes wore over her nightgown was gone, and that was all.

How far could someone walk in their sleep? Maddie couldn't imagine Tessa operating the elevator, for instance, but even the residents of the tenth floor sometimes used the stairs out of sheer exasperation with the single rickety car. The thought of her roommate heading blithely for the stairs—did she walk with her eyes shut?—turned Maddie cold inside. The thought of her wandering around the hallway of the tenth floor was worse, given some of the creeps the tenant of 10-C sublet to. Maddie dumped her dance bag onto the couch and was heading back to the door when the key rattled in the lock.

It was Tessa, shivering and wrapped in a navy pea coat far larger and shabbier than her own, underneath which were visible a pair of familiar, patched and superannuated jeans, rolled up at the ankle, and two pairs of wool socks.

Phil, beside her, wore frayed black dress pants, a muffler wrapped around his neck over two flannel shirts and his green wool sweater, and looked frozen to death.

"I found her outside the Glendower Building, trying to get in," he said, leading Tessa to the couch and settling her down, tugging the blanket over her. "God knows how long she'd been there. Probably not long, dressed like she was, in this town—she was just in her nightgown and a sweatshirt…."

"I must have sleepwalked." Tessa pulled the thick cotton quilt tighter around herself, shivering as if she would shake her bones loose. "Jesus, I've *never* sleepwalked that far! My dad told me I once got out of the house and halfway down the block, when I was about six. I don't remember that. But this time I woke up like in those crazy dreams, where you go to school in your pajamas, only it was for real. I was up in Phil's studio…."

Maddie's eyes widened and snapped to the man kneeling at Tessa's feet. She must have made some sound or move, because he looked up, met her furious gaze.

Saw the thought that screamed, *Oh, yeah?*

And she saw his startled, almost disbelieving shock that she'd suspect him of…what?

Kidnapping Tessa out of her apartment?

The absurdity of the suspicion doused her anger—and her suspicious demand, *And what were* you *doing happening along just at that moment…?*—and she said, "Thank you," and meant it. She drew a couple of deep breaths, trying to force herself calm. "You look frozen. There's another blanket in that chest over there. You both look like you need some cocoa."

Phil got to his feet, his cheekbones red. "I'm okay." He sounded like he, too, was keeping his voice neutral with an effort. "I better let you get her to bed…."

"No." Maddie stepped quickly to intercept him on the way to the door. "Please. I'll make you some cocoa," she repeated softly. "Is that your only coat you lent her?"

Phil nodded, looking down into her face. His own anger faded as he saw her look of mortified remorse. He followed her around the end of the counter, into the so-called kitchen, which was in fact a nook about the size of Maddie's mother's dining room table back in Baton Rouge. "I was just coming back from the Met," he said. "*La Bohème*—if you're up in the nosebleed seats they don't care what you wear. When I saw her from down the street I thought she was some poor crazy woman, the kind you see wandering around the subways in housecoats with crocheted afghans wrapped around them. Then I got close and saw who it was. She was just about unconscious with the cold…."

"I know she sleepwalks." While the milk was slowly warming Maddie dug the cocoa out of one sealed container and the sugar out of another, and a package of marshmallows out of a third, even the cleanest of New York apartments being what they are. "She tried to get out of here the other night. And I just…" She hesitated, looking up at him, wondering how the hell she could explain the shadow in the hallway. The deep-seated sense of danger that haunted her dreams.

Phil leaned a shoulder against the corner of the cupboard and folded his arms. "You don't think much of men, do you?" There was no mockery in his voice, no scorn. Just a question.

Maddie said, "No, I know I don't. I'm sorry." *I'm sorry I immediately assumed you were a stalker, a kidnapper, and a rapist. My bad.*

"Are you a dyke?" He used the word as he would have used any other, without venom or judgment, just a question. A one-syllable word instead of a three.

She shook her head, the gaudy jewels in her long hair glittering. "Just a survivor."

He nodded. The comprehension in his eyes was like the glimpse of a scar.

They stood for a minute looking at each other in the cold, white glare of the single fluorescent light over the stove.

Quietly, Maddie said, "That night I first met you, when Tessa was wandering around on the sixth floor, *did* you see or hear anyone else in the building? I asked you that before, and I think you ducked the question."

Phil was silent for a long time, the only sound in the kitchen the whisper of the wooden spoon as Maddie stirred the slow-heating milk in its pan. Then he said, "When you read tarot cards, does that mean you're psychic?"

Maddie shook her head. "Sometime—if you're interested—I'll explain why I think the tarot works, when it works. But you don't have to have second sight or be able to see auras or anything. They just…work." She said nothing for a time, swishing the spoon back and forth in the milk, then asked, "Have you seen something in the building?"

"No." Phil answered very quickly and looked away from her as he did so. Maddie said nothing.

After a long time he said, "You mean like a ghost?" and this time there was a biting note in his voice that spoke of all his feelings about the inherent bull of the supernatural.

And that spoke more deeply still of fear.

"I don't know what I mean," replied Maddie quietly. "What do *you* mean?"

Phil drew in his breath, let it out. His face in profile was expressionless, except for a small line in one corner of his mouth. He said, "I haven't seen a ghost. I haven't seen anything." He shifted his arms, one hand cupping his chin so that the fingers half hid his mouth, concealed the telltale line. "It's just I have these dreams."

"Since you've been sleeping in the building?"

He nodded, and his breath drew in, then rushed out

as if he were trying to flush out some darkness inside. Then his eye went past her and he half grinned. "You're going to lose that milk." Maddie turned quickly, shifted the pan from the stove and began stirring in cocoa and sugar. Phil stepped closer, looking down over her shoulder admiringly. "You're the first person I've met since I left Tulsa who makes it the real way."

"Down on the bayou *everybody* makes cocoa the real way. I heard tell from some Yankee once something about powder and microwaves, but I didn't believe it. There're things even Yankees couldn't possibly do."

"Don't trust us, Miss Scarlett." Phil shook his head as she handed him a mug. "We're capable of anything."

Maddie picked up her own mug and Tessa's, but when they carried them back into the living room they found Tessa curled up under the blankets, still wearing Phil's dilapidated pea coat, sound asleep. Phil switched off the main light and carried the cocoa back to the kitchen, where Maddie flicked on one of the fake candle-flame lamps she'd bought for a Halloween party a few years ago—the lowest light she could manage—and turned off the fluorescent light over the stove.

"Can I have her marshmallow?" asked Phil, and Maddie obligingly scooped it into his mug. They settled on the floor of the kitchen, lamp and cups between them, and Phil shrugged out of his sweater and one of the flannel shirts. She saw under the second one the rumpled white dress shirt he must have worn to the opera, and around his neck a loosened black satin tie. At the same time she noted that none of his clothes smelled of tobacco, the stench she remembered in the mix of smells that had hung around the whisperer.

Sweat and cologne could be cleaned away from clothing, cigar smoke almost never.

She drew in her breath, feeling as if she were slowly prying her fingers away from their grip on mistrust.

She had spent enough years reading the cards—dealing with people who had exhausted rational explanations for their feelings—to know that all this time while they'd been joking and kidding, he was working himself up to go back and look into the dark box of his dreams.

"The first week I was sleeping there I walked through the halls of that building six, seven times a night," he said in time. "Turning on lights, listening… And there was nobody there. Then I'd go back to my studio and double and triple lock the door—I'll take you up sometime and show you the burglar bar and chains I got for it. That was before I realized what I was hearing was just dreams, those awful dreams where you think you're awake."

He spoke with his face turned slightly away, talking to the air, as if he were answering questions in a military debriefing.

"What did you dream about?"

"Girls. Not like you think," he added, with a faint gleam of humor, and Maddie shook her head. "Sometimes I just hear their voices, or hear them crying. Once I heard—I thought I heard—one of them say 'Stop it,' or 'Don't touch me,' something like that…. And I heard him laugh."

"Who laugh?"

"I don't know. A man. Then I wake up and there's nothing." He looked again at her sidelong, not as if he expected she wouldn't believe him—she was pretty sure he knew she would—but as if he expected some reaction that would turn his dream into mockery in his own eyes.

Maddie asked, "Where are you in the dreams?"

Whatever reaction he'd expected—possibly a long account of *her* supernatural dreams and how she knew they were part of some past life experience, something Maddie had frequently encountered when speaking of the world of dreams—the matter-of-fact question seemed to reassure him.

"In my studio," he said. "That's the creepy thing. I'm in my sleeping bag on the floor and I can see the piano and the tape machine and the laptop and the boxes, everything exactly the way it really is. But I hear these girls crying—and I swear to you it sometimes sounds like they're right outside the door. And I hear this…this *bastard* chuckle, or sometimes words I can't make out. A couple of nights ago I heard him say, yell, 'You little sluts are all alike,' and it sounded like he was about three feet away, in the room with me."

He raked his fingers through his hair, rubbed the back of his neck, a gesture she'd seen him make before.

"Other times it's far off. Or it's just footsteps. Footsteps overhead, only I know there's nothing overhead… My studio's on the top floor." He shrugged.

"The first time I heard anything—I think it was the third night I slept there—it was…" He frowned, piecing together exactly what he had heard, or dreamed he'd heard. "That was weird. I did that dream-you're-awake number—which I've had maybe twice or three times in my entire life—and I heard this sound, this metallic rattling and pounding, like something being shaken or hammered on. Then I woke up sweating, and it was quiet. But I got up and got my flashlight and went out to look, and I went all around the halls switching on lights. And I not only didn't see anything that made the noise, but I didn't see anything that *could* have made a noise like that."

He finished his cocoa, set the cup on the floor between them, his long arms wrapped around his knees. The flickering orange of the artificial candlelight hid his eyes in shadow, but Maddie saw by the drawn look of their corners that there were memories uglier still.

"So about a week ago I dream about a fire. I dream I'm caught in this dark place, and there's smoke everywhere and I can't breathe. Lines of fire run along the wood floor and up the walls. And I'm scared. I don't know when I've been that scared in a dream." He looked down at the floor, turned his mug so that the handle lined up with the lines in the linoleum of the floor.

"These girls are all around me, tripping over these big tables down the center of the room, trying to get out of there. And there's no way out. The stuff on the tables is all catching fire, and sparks and bits of burning stuff are swirling around in the air. One girl I remember—her skirt caught fire, long skirts down to the floor…."

His voice cracked and he shook his head, trying to rid it of images that would not go away.

"Jesus, it was awful, and so goddamn clear. I look around for some way to help them, to get them out of there, but I can't. The girls all run to this door, this metal door, and try to open it. But it's locked. They're all shaking it and hammering on it and screaming, and I realize that's the noise I heard, the rattling of the metal door as they pounded on it with their fists.

"Some of them jump out the windows," he finished softly. "Through the smoke I can see the roofs across the street, and it's high up, seven or eight floors. But there's no other way out."

He stared straight ahead of him, his hands folded in front of his mouth again, fear and horror at what he had seen like a darkness in his eyes. After a while, he said, "I don't know where I got all that from. Too many video clips of 9/11, maybe."

Maddie shook her head, trying not to see the nightmare that his words summoned to her mind. "That's not what it sounds like," she said quietly. "It sounds to me like the building is haunted. There may have been a fire there years ago…."

"Yeah. Right." The twist of Phil's mouth was sardonic again. "So who we gonna call?"

Maddie didn't smile back at the *Ghostbusters* joke. She leaned a little to glance around the edge of the counter that separated the kitchen from the rest of the apartment, saw the bony little lump that was Tessa, a shadow on the couch in the shadowy dark. "What worries me," she said softly, "is that this seems to be having an effect on Tessa. What was she doing on the sixth floor that night, trying to go up those stairs? Even she couldn't tell me. She'd been up since four-thirty that morning. If she rested between exercises, dozed off and sleepwalked..."

"Whoa," said Phil. "What stairs? There's no stairway up from the sixth floor."

CHAPTER FOUR

MADDIE BLINKED AT HIM in surprise. "Yes, there is. When I caught up with Tessa she was standing at the bottom of a flight of stairs, leading up to the floor above. I asked her what she was doing and she said she'd heard a noise, or voices talking. But I got the feeling that she really didn't know."

"And you didn't hear anything? Or go looking for anything? Because if you came up another flight…"

"We didn't," insisted Maddie. "This was just before we met you. The lights went off when I was on the stairway from the fifth floor up to the sixth. I didn't go up any farther than that."

"Well, if the lights were off, how did you see a stairway?" asked Phil. "With that dinky little flashlight you had I'm surprised you didn't walk into a wall. You could have gone around a couple more turns of the stairs without knowing it…."

"Even in the dark I know up from down," pointed out Maddie. "Once I found Tessa there was no reason for me to climb any more stairs. And I saw the stairway. It was down one of those convoluted little hallways, away from the main stair…."

"You mean like a ladder up to the roof? Because there's one of those…"

"I mean like a staircase." She closed her eyes, picturing it again. Picturing Tessa standing at the bottom of that slot of blackness in her pink tights and Broken Glass U.S. Tour T-shirt, swaying a little on her feet as she'd swayed a few nights ago, when she'd stood fumbling with the burglar bar in her sleep. Slowly, calling the images back to her mind, she said, "The steps are wood. The walls are dirty, pale, there's paint peeling and water stains...."

There's evil up there, she thought. Something terrible, waiting in the darkness.

Maddie opened her eyes and saw Phil regarding her doubtfully, as if she'd begun a monologue about who she'd been in a past life, or how spirits channeled their thoughts through her while she meditated. She knew the look because she'd so frequently worn it herself.

It was quite common, when people got their cards read, for them to feel called upon to discuss every other aspect of their contacts with the supernatural, either because they felt themselves to be in the presence of a sympathetic ear or because they wanted to impress her. In her nearly two years of consulting in the back room of the Darkness Visible bookstore, Maddie had encountered large numbers of people who felt themselves to be reincarnated priestesses of Isis, or channelers of various spirits from realms beyond Earth, or returned alien abductees. And while she had met people whom she felt did, in truth, remember past lives, or have contact with spirits—she wasn't so sure about abductees, at least not the ones she'd met—she was fairly sure there weren't *that* many of them walking around.

Phil said—speaking as if he were choosing his words with care— "Look, Maddie... What I had were creepy dreams. But dreams are all they were. I don't know what you saw, but I've been over every inch of the sixth floor, and there isn't a stairway like that. I've been through the other floors, too, and yes, that place is like a Skinner-box rat maze, but I'm pretty sure I've never seen a stairway like that in the whole building."

"You must have been pretty shook up," said Maddie quietly, "to search the whole building."

He looked away from her, then back. "Yeah. I was pretty shook up."

Unless you're lying. The thought came so close behind the impulse to reach across the slight space that separated them, to put her hand on his wrist—to lean into his touch and see if his lips would taste the way they tasted in her dream—that she suspected that her wariness sprang more from the recollection of Sandy's manipulative vulnerability than from any true judgment of danger.

Their eyes met and she felt—she knew—that he was inches from drawing her to him, breaths from pressing her down to the floor beneath his gentle weight, uncaring that she was a raving kook or that he was a whispering stalker who rambled empty buildings in darkness. *It's safe,* she had said…

In my dream! she reminded herself.

Not in real life. There was no safe in real life.

If I step over the cliff, will I fall or be borne up on the wind and realize I can fly again?

He said, "I'd better go."

Stay. "All right."

You little sluts are all alike. Had the words come from something that whispered in the halls of the Glendower Building—in the dreams of whoever drifted off to sleep there? Or from the dark at the bottom of this man's mind?

Rather than wake Tessa, Maddie dug Sandy's old leather jacket out of the back of the closet. Sandy had been thinner than Phil and narrower through the shoulders—putting the sweater back on underneath didn't help the fit any—but the jacket would at least still zip, and it was better than freezing. Phil turned the leather shoulder over and grinned at the Cleveland Indians patch. "That looks like it dates from the days before the Tribe was any good."

Maddie smiled at the memory. "He never gave up on them."

"Your husband?"

Tessa must have told him. Had he asked?

Maddie nodded. "She'll bring your stuff back tomorrow—or the day after, if I can talk her into taking a break for a day and resting. Thank you for getting her here safe." She turned the key in the lock as she stepped out into the hall with him and walked him down to the elevator. It took its usual endless rattling time to arrive, though God knew where else it was or who else was using it at two in the morning.

"Like I was gonna leave her on the sidewalk?"

Maddie poked him with her elbow. "What do you want, me to act like it was something you owed us? Did you bring her in a cab?" She fished in her pocket for part of the dancing money, and Phil raised his hand, refusing.

"We walked." It was a blatant lie—the dry socks on Tessa's feet would have proved that even if Maddie *had* thought even for one moment that Phil would force a half-frozen girl to cross most of Manhattan Island on foot at one in the morning.

She gestured her surrender. "Then let me buy you lunch."

"You've got a deal. I'm glad she has someone to look after her," Phil added in a quieter voice. "So many of them don't. The girls at the Dance Loft," he explained at Maddie's inquiring look. "And the other schools where I play. When the ABA's auditioning, or when any of the big companies come through town, they—the girls—get crazy, starving themselves or fainting in class or driving themselves in class after class as if it was the end of the world. It's not good for them, I know it's not. And some of the little ones are the worst, with these wild-eyed mothers hanging on the sidelines like vultures."

Maddie thought of her own mother, taking her to the doctor for diet pills and paying one of the neighboring college students to write her school papers for her when she had an audition coming up, so she could fit in just one more class. "It's a fine line between supporting someone else's dream and seducing them into your own," she said. "I gather Tessa never had anyone to support hers."

"Which is why she's pushing herself like this." Phil folded his arms, leaned against the jamb of the dilatory elevator's door. "Trying to sleepwalk back to the studio to get in just one more *saute de basque* if it kills her…"

"Is that what you think she was doing tonight?"

Phil raised his eyebrows.

As opposed to falling under the evil influence of a haunted building?

Maddie drew a deep breath. In either case, the answer was the same. "I'll do what I can to look after her," she said. "I understand that craziness. I went through it myself for years. Sort of like sleeping on the floor in a haunted piano studio in New York in order to write music instead of making a good living bustin' rods in Tulsa."

Phil swallowed a grin and shook a finger at her nose. "There is absolutely no comparison," he said severely. "And don't you think it."

And then, because his pointing finger was so close to her face, he slipped his hand under the bejeweled waterfall of her hair and drew her mouth gently to his.

Maddie's lips parted, she felt the wall behind her shoulders, the hard grip of his arm around her rib cage and the cracked old leather under her palms. Felt the scratch of beard stubble against her chin, against her jaw and her throat as she turned her head aside to let him kiss her neck, the thin skin where her shirt opened above her sternum. Her own lips brushed his temple, the delicate rim of bone around the socket of his eye as her fingers tangled with the rough horsetail stiffness of his hair…and the whole world turned into a single dark, sweet torrent of need.

Where his body pressed hers she could feel him shake.

The elevator bell dinged.

Phil stepped back from her. They were both trembling, staring into each other's eyes, breathing deep and hard.

No possibility of pretense.

His rough-knotted fingers traced the shape of her

cheekbone, her lips, as they'd traced her breasts in her dream.

He said, "I'll see you?"

Maddie nodded. She felt as if her body had been rock, in a single instant shattering and turning to light.

He stepped into the elevator and was gone.

THE DARKNESS VISIBLE bookstore was down a flight of steps in one of those old brownstones of the West Village, the railed areaway below sidewalk level hosting, in summertime, a coffee machine and a couple of bins full of old Grateful Dead posters and battered prints of unlikely sixties rock-stars in historical garb. Now, in December, the bins and coffee machine occupied the front part of the tiny shop, along with shelves of dried sage bundles and packets of pennyroyal and hyssop, assorted versions of the tarot deck, from Aleister Crowley's to the Barbie tarot, boxes of crystals, sets of runes, a small harp, yarrow stalks and small bronzes of Ganesh, Athene and Quetzalcoatl. From there back it was books, on every conceivable and inconceivable subject and, at the rear of the store, a stairway leading up to two small chambers draped in sari fabrics and chiffon, where Maddie and various other part-time diviners consulted with their clients. Beside the stair—its contents spilling over onto the surrounding wall—was the bulletin board, half an inch thick with flyers for drum circles and healing seminars, with lost-and-found announcements and the cards of every psychic counselor, personal trainer, computer consultant, dancer, musician, baby-sitter and housekeeper who had passed through the West Village since 1964.

Under an enormous painting of Shiva dancing with Rita Hayworth, Diana Vale sat at her tall Victorian desk, a square-faced, gray-haired, kindly woman who looked like she could have been the Good Witch of Someplace or Other or somebody's mother. She was in fact both, and a good deal besides. She said, "Hello, sweetheart," and hopped down from her stool to hug Maddie as she came in. "Did you have readings this afternoon? I don't have anything written down."

Maddie shook her head. "I have a gig tonight out on Long Island. A Turkish gentleman's ninetieth birthday party, given to him by five of his daughters. I have to catch the train in about an hour and a half, but I need some advice. Have you ever heard of the Glendower Building?"

Diana's eyes narrowed. "It rings a bell...." Between running the bookstore and serving on the board of the local low-cost day care center, Diana wrote articles for a dozen magazines and journals concerning the occult. There was very little about haunted buildings that she didn't know or at least know how to find out about. "Where is it?"

"Here in town, over on Twenty-ninth Street. It's the building the Dance Loft is in. There's a dancewear store downstairs and storerooms on the second floor, then the Dance Loft has two floors and the upper two floors are rented out as studios and offices."

"I remember." Diana nodded. "You said you never liked it."

Maddie nodded. "It's a creepy building. I never could put my finger on what's wrong with it, and at the time it was the only place I could rent space to start dance classes. But I was actually glad when Mrs. Dayforth rescheduled the room out from under me."

"And you think you saw or heard something?"

"I saw a man—a shadow after the lights went out—whispering things to me, terrible things. At first I thought it was…well, someone Tessa knows who's staying in the building because he lost his apartment. But now I've gotten to know this person and he doesn't seem like someone who'd do that—aside from the fact that I smelled tobacco on this person and Phil doesn't smoke. And Phil says that while sleeping in the building he's had weird dreams, about a fire, and young girls being hurt. He says they're just dreams…."

Maddie fell silent, trying to sort out facts from feelings and fears. "And Tessa's been acting strangely. Phil—he's the piano player at the Dance Loft—says it's because of her audition for the ABA coming up, but I don't know. She's been sleepwalking, trying to get back into the building. Last night she managed to get out in just her nightgown and a sweatshirt. I think if Phil hadn't been coming back from the opera when he did she might really have froze to death."

She turned her head and glanced out into the little shop's areaway. The slushy snow that had fallen late last night had congealed into dirt-fringed grayish globs on the steps. Boots and the hems of coats flickered by at sidewalk level, barely seen through the bookshop's doors.

"Then sometimes I think it's my imagination, like one of those pictures that sometimes looks like one thing and sometimes another. Phil may be right and it may be just Tessa's own stress, and some combination of anxieties out of his past, that are doing this same thing to them at the same time. I don't know. The building feels leprous to me—diseased. Especially at night. But a lot of buildings in New York feel that way."

"A lot of buildings in New York have some ugliness in their past that doesn't bear looking at." Diana took a mug from a hook on the wall behind her desk and went to pour herself some coffee. Her long gray braids hung down her back nearly to her waist, over a shawl she'd loomed herself. "New York is an old city, and it has always been a place where men would seek to make money regardless of the cost to those they exploited. Such things leave their mark."

She perched on her high stool again, turning to face her computer screen, and clicked into stored files, tapping in the name *Glendower Building*. Maddie leaned an elbow on the corner of the desk and watched her older friend's keen, kindly face by the screen's reflected glow.

"Nothing here. I'll go online and look it up in the Spirit Guide Web site, but you can't find *anything* in the new edition since they rearranged the classifications. And I'll see what I can find in the block records of the insurance companies." She clicked on the DSL line, tunneling through the bright-colored ether of the Internet and dodging pop-ups like an X-wing fighter pilot evading attacking Imperial disintegrator beams.

"Do *you* think what your friend—Philip, is it?—says about Tessa's mental state is true? I haven't seen her in weeks, but the last time she came here to meet you she did not look well. Not all evils in the world have supernatural explanations, you know."

"No," agreed Maddie with a sigh. "And God knows back in my ballet days I went crazy enough when I had an audition coming up. She isn't eating, and though I can't imagine not being able to sleep after eight hours of work a day plus four ballet classes, she's having nightmares, crying out in her sleep. I know I was always so dead tired all I'd dream about was sleep…and food. And sometimes Brad Pitt."

"But you didn't have to work to pay your rent, on top of worrying about the audition," Diana reminded her quietly, sitting back from the glowing screen. "And you had parents who, for all their faults, were at least present, and supported you in your dancing. From what you've told me, Theresa has none of these things. Who knows what ghosts are arising from the dark of her mind?"

No, Tessa had cried in her sleep. *No me toque*….

Maddie had no idea what that meant, and wondered if Tessa had screamed in Spanish because it was the language of her childhood, the language of her dreams…or because it was the language her father and mother spoke.

The phone rang. Diana said, "Bother," and picked it up, setting aside the mouse and turning her eyes from the screen as she listened to the caller. "I don't think so, sir…. No, as far as I know, Barbie dolls were first marketed in 1956 and there's no evidence of a connection with ancient Egypt…. Of course not…"

Maddie glanced at the clock, estimating how long it would take her to paint up, assemble her dance gear, and get to Grand Central from West Thirty-second Street if she had to check in at Mrs. Buz's house at six. Outside snow had begun to drift down again. It would be a bitter night.

Tessa had taken Phil's jeans, socks and pea coat with her when she'd left that morning for work at Starbucks before the beginner class at nine. Since Phil had no phone, Maddie had folded a note in with them, saying that she'd be out until late, and was he off Saturdays?

She had dreamed last night, disturbingly, of Sandy. Dreamed of those long, maddening arguments in which he'd insisted that he was just tired, he'd taken a long walk and gotten dehydrated, and he had a liver ailment that acted up now and again and made him "wibbly," as he put it. Dreamed of searching the apartment, over and over, looking for hidden caches of pills. *What kind of love do we have if you don't trust me?* he kept asking her, in that slurred singsong she'd come to identify and hate. *Why can't you learn to trust?*

Just as Diana hung up the phone a stout young man with greasy hair and a complexion like a mushroom came in, asking for a book on occult minerology. "The very fact that the outer circle of Stonehenge is composed of igneous diorite *proves* that the stones were raised by levitation, since it's far easier to levitate igneous rock than it is to levitate sedimentary or composite...."

No wonder Phil had looked at her that way last night.

"I'm sure there's something in that section that will interest you," Diana finished, pointing the young truth-seeker to the archway lettered Lost Knowledge—Travel. She turned back to Maddie. "I'm sorry."

"It's all right. It was worth it to learn something I never knew about—uh—monolithic construction techniques of the Ancient World." Maddie wrapped her scarf back around her neck, covering the blue-and-silver Pakistani necklaces she wore when she taught dance, the strange-shaped Berber crosses that were said to protect one "in the four corners of the world." Though not a believer in magic amulets, Maddie wore them, anyway. In New York you needed all the help you could get.

"And you're right about Tessa. There's enough demons in peoples' own heads without imagining them coming out of the walls of old buildings as well. But if you get a chance, I'd still be very curious to learn anything you can find about the Glendower Building."

"I'll e-mail you tonight if I find anything," promised Diana. She took Maddie's hands in farewell, then stood for a moment, looking inquiringly into her face. "Is there anything else you want advice about?" she asked.

Maddie hesitated, seeing the Falling Tower in her mind, the stern-browed King of Pentacles crossed by the grinning Devil, with his down-thrust torch and his tiny slaves chained at the foot of his throne. "Do you have time to do a reading for me?"

"HE'S A CAPRICORN, a musician," said Maddie as she took one of the carved chairs beside the table in the front of the store. Some readers she knew could only work in the quiet surroundings of Diana's candlelit back rooms. Diana had lived with the tarot as an armature of her thought processes so long that she could drop in and out of the half-tranced state of contemplation at will.

The Seeker After Igneous Truth was still sitting on the floor in the Lost Knowledge section, deep in communion with *Hidden Secrets of the Lost Library.* Llyr and Mr. Gaunt, the two store cats, dozed heavily before the heater. Outside the usual ruckus of taxi horns and police sirens yowled from Washington Square, but the store itself was quiet.

Diana's large, competent hands flipped a card from the deck, then passed the remainder to Maddie. "The Nine of Pentacles?" asked Maddie, startled. "But Phil…"

"I don't know anything about Phil," replied Diana evenly. "Nor do you, if you've asked me to do a reading about him and, I assume, your feelings for him…?"

Maddie nodded.

"You can't learn about him through the cards. But you *can* learn about *you.* It's about where *he* fits into *your* life, not where you fit yourself into *his.*"

Maddie shuffled the deck, breathing deeply, as Diana had taught her, sinking herself into the state of light trance where she could be better able to act as a channel for the energies aligning the universe. When she'd first come to New York seven years ago and taken Diana's tarot class, she had done little the first year but learn techniques of trance and meditation. Diana did not believe in hurrying too quickly to knowledge: *It's like picking up a hot pan off the stove, before you've made yourself a glove to protect your hand,* she would say. *The knowledge isn't going anywhere. The energies that rule the cosmos will still work the same way a year from now.*

For the past year and a half, Maddie had used the Nine of Pentacles as her own card in readings. The picture on it was of a wealthy woman alone in her garden, a pet hawk on her fist. She watched it now as Diana built up the reading around it, Past and Future, Hopes and Fears. As well as the dark-browed King of Pentacles, the Knight of Cups rode his horse along the edge of the sea, "the coming of a matter of the heart." Maddie smiled as she recognized the Fool—Sandy stepping blithely off the edge of a cliff, the way he always did, his eyes on the illusion that it was possible to live without discomfort. It was in the position of a thing that influenced her outlook. Sandy had certainly done that.

Or was it herself, she wondered, who had stepped off the cliff edge of loving, without knowing whether it was safe or not?

In the position that marked the future, the Lovers clasped hands and smiled. Maddie saw also the Three of Cups, the Graces partying hearty. Above them was one of the best of the Greater Trumps, the sign of the Dancer at the Heart of the World.

"There's danger in the future." Diana touched the Nine of Wands, the beat-up hero defending the gap in the palisade. "And a warning here, about danger that arises out of the past...."

"The Devil has shown up in so many of my readings I'd be disappointed if he didn't put in an appearance here, too," sighed Maddie resignedly, looking down at the grinning shape with its torch and its chained slaves. When Diana read the cards, she often described how she saw pathways linking them. Maddie wondered if she saw them now.

"Is this Phil?" She tapped the King of Pentacles, lurking at the nadir of the reading, the basis from which the problem sprang. Yet looking at the card, she felt an echo of the darkness of the Glendower Building around her, heard the whisper in her ear. Like the pathways Diana saw, Maddie sensed that this wasn't Phil at all, but something else. Something wicked, and old.

Bitch...little sluts are all alike.

"It may be some aspect of him that you will need to deal with," said Diana slowly. "I'm more inclined to think that it may be someone else entirely, someone you haven't yet met. But there's another warning here, of danger, the Five of Wands." She glanced up at Maddie, her brown eyes troubled. "For something that has the promise of a joyful outcome, this is a bad reading, Maddie. A warning. But not, I think—" her fingers brushed the Lovers and she smiled "—about your friend Phil."

Her smile faded, and she gathered up the cards. "You be careful, dear."

"I try to be," said Maddie, and put on her coat and scarf again. "But the trick is always to know what to be careful *of.*"

CHAPTER FIVE

THROUGHOUT THE LONG RIDE to Westhampton, it was as if Sandy Weinraub occupied the seat at Maddie's side.

Her physical passion for Phil confused her. She wanted him, but knew in her heart that it was much more than that. The reawakening of desire was followed closely—as it had been last night—by misgivings about herself and her judgment.

She had loved Sandy, passionately and completely. It had seemed to her right and logical to surrender things she loved in order to be with him and to keep him happy. The first night they'd been together, she remembered very clearly, he had spent sipping vodka, never seeming really drunk. Not that it would have mattered, as long as they were together.

She had willed herself not to notice. Not to have it matter.

She let her breath out in a sigh, her body moving with the jostle of the train. In retrospect she couldn't imagine how she could have been that stupid.

Stupid to love him, she thought. Stupid to marry him. Stupid to pound her head against the wall of thinking she could change him, by threats to leave, by pleas, by reasoning, by all her offers of help. She still didn't know whether he'd actually loved her or not. Could addicts really love?

Had it *all* been lies?

She loved Phil. She knew that as surely as she knew her name, and the knowledge filled her with terror and despair.

If he was lying to her—about loving, about sanity—she didn't think she could go through all that pain again. Every instinct she possessed told her that Phil Cooper was a man she could love, a man she could trust. He was strong and funny and listened to what other people said, to say nothing of the fact that just being in the same room with him made her want to rip his clothes off and drag him into bed….

But every instinct she possessed had once told her that Sandy loved her. And that their love was good and right.

Which left her where?

Bay Shore. Patchogue. Exhausted shoppers bundled in overcoats and rubber boots trying to juggle purses, magazines, brown Bloomie's bags from the after-Christmas sales, umbrellas, crying children who should have been settled down for naps and cookies hours ago. Early darkness flashed by the windows of the train, hiding the long gray shape of cold beaches, colder sea.

In the river parishes along the Mississippi they'd be lighting bonfires, huge frames of logs whose orange glare was visible for miles through the dense winter fog. Everyone would be getting ready for Mardi Gras and holding King Cake parties—if you got the plastic baby in your slice of King Cake you'd have to throw the next party—and the whole world smelled of burning sugar from the refineries. Though it would be damply cold, it was seldom the wet, brutal, uncaring cold of New York.

"I came down here the minute I discovered there were places in the world where it didn't snow," Sandy had said to her, with his sly sidelong grin, as they'd walked up St. Peter Street to the Café du Monde from his apartment in the French Quarter, through that damp sugar-smelling fog and the glaring lights of Mardi Gras. Maddie had leaned into the shelter of his arm and laughed.

That first year of living in New Orleans—of her going to classes and pretending to all her friends that she wasn't having an affair with the writing teacher—there had been a lot of laughter.

After he came to New York to work as an editor for *Galactic* magazine, it seemed to Maddie that he had never actually worked again. She'd worked, mostly waiting tables. During his year at *Galactic* she had, in fact, done a lot of unpaid editing while he was "not feeling well." She'd gotten money once from her mother, but the emotional interest payments were simply too high: if she had to hear her mother one more time on the subject of the career as a professional dancer she'd just *thrown away,* she would have said something—as her aunts liked to put in—that did not do credit to her raising.

It had been easier to pretend that everything was all right.

Didn't he see what it was doing to me? she wondered. *Didn't he care?*

When Maddie had returned from Darkness Visible that afternoon to the apartment on Thirty-second Street to get ready for her gig, she'd found Sandy's leather jacket laid neatly over the back of the couch. Just the sight of it hit her hard. *Oh, my God, he's turned up again....*

Forgetting, for that first instant, that he was never going to turn up again.

The memory of her struggle against him was still burningly clear. When she'd asked him to leave she'd had the locks changed, but she knew Sandy was cunning. Her greatest fear, during the eleven months between his departure and his death, had been that he'd get evicted from whatever friend he was sponging off, or single flophouse room he was living in, and that she'd come home some afternoon and find his jacket on the back of the couch and his stuff piled in the living room: *This is just for a couple of days or weeks....*

And she'd have to go through the whole agony again of finding him a place, paying first-'n'-last, and getting him out of her apartment and out of her life. She'd have to steel herself against the panic attacks, the frantic declarations of love, the sobbed promises of reform.

She'd gone over and picked up the jacket, and found under it two CDs. *Wind on the Water* and *Dust Storm,* instrumental music by Phil Cooper. Produced by one of the myriad of tiny private music companies that had sprung up in the wake of inexpensive CD technology, complete with Photoshop covers and a not-quite-professional black-and-white picture of Phil on the back.

What her mother would say if Maddie informed her that she was in love with yet another penniless artist—and another Yankee at that—she didn't like to think.

I love him. Does he love me?

She didn't know whether she hoped he did, or not.

It would be easier to simply have a bone-shaking, teeth-rattling, back-clawing affair and call it quits. *See, I am* too *worth something.*

Easier all around to go on living with Tessa and Baby, to dance and teach and read the cards for those throngs of black-clothed Midwestern Goths and Gothettes who wandered through the West Village in search of sex, drugs and body-piercings. To seek her own strength, as Diana had advised, rather than spend her life guessing about someone else's weakness.

Like the Nine of Pentacles, the lady in her own garden, with the hawk on her fist. Alone.

The lights of Mastic Beach whipped by in the dark.

But the Nine of Pentacles, Maddie knew, like all the nines in the tarot deck, had the meaning of being one less than the ten. Nine was the place where you could stop the train and get off, if you didn't have the courage or the faith or the blind willfulness to continue to the ultimate outcome of the meaning of the suit. In the suit of the Swords, nine could mean—one of its several meanings—a wake-up call, the horror of realizing where violence and strife will lead. In the Wands it was a warning: *Is this what you really want?* before you reached the ambiguous burden of what your will has brought you. In the suits of the Cups and the Pentacles, it carried implications of settling for what seems best—worldly riches or solitary content—rather than pressing on to the joys of greater love that lay beyond.

Diana had seen danger around her. *Not from Phil,* she had said, and had smiled.

Why am I so ready to believe the spread that tells me

he is the whisperer in the dark of the Glendower Building, while my mind balks at the spread that tells me he isn't?

Maddie touched the insulated lunch box in which she carried her CDs—the party's hostess, Mrs. Buz, had promised her a live band but Maddie knew far better than to trust a client's assurances about anything. She fished out *Wind on the Water,* though it was too noisy in the train to play it, or anything, on her Discman. Gazed for a time at that grainy shot of the craggy, thoughtful face, the kitten he'd chosen to have photographed with him.

If the building isn't haunted, Phil may be a lunatic. If it is, Tessa is probably in danger. Or am I just ready to believe the worst of him because I'm looking for a reason to run back into my garden and slam the gate? Keep your distance, pal, or I'll sic my hawk on you.

FOUR SONS AND A GRANDSON of Mrs. Buz were waiting at the Westhampton station in an enormous SUV to drive Maddie to their mother's house. Maddie put the CD—and the subject of its composer—aside, and the rest of the evening passed in a kaleidoscope of music, chatter and enough lamb and couscous to feed the Turkish army. Resplendent in green and gold, she danced for a wildly appreciative audience, the men springing up to dance with her—or flipping showers of dollar bills onto her head in the far-more-polite Middle Eastern fashion of tipping the dancer—and the women howling and ululating behind their hands.

As every dancer of Maddie's acquaintance could attest, private parties were always very much of a toss-up. She'd performed at birthday and retirement gigs where she'd come away with liquor and worse things in her hair, swearing she'd quit dancing for good. There were always people who treated dancers as if they'd just jumped out of a cake or stepped off the walkway at some Jersey strip joint. Like all her dancer friends, she'd had her share of occasions where she'd showed up and found twenty-five drunks and only a boom box for the promised "sound system," and had ended up having to change into her costume in the pantry.

But this, for once, was the other kind of party. Completely apart from a five-hundred-dollar check and nearly half that much again in tips, Maddie enjoyed herself thoroughly. There was always something infinitely delightful about dancing with a live band—*oud, mizmar, doumbek* and accordion—and about dancing for an audience that knew the kind of dancing they were looking at, rather than Omaha tourists out to see belly rolls. As always, the dancing freed her mind, washing away any concerns about Phil, or Sandy, or whether or not she'd ever be able to love and trust again or if she wanted to try.

The energies that rule the cosmos aren't going anywhere, Diana had said. *There is no way that you can miss what you're intended to have.*

At times like this, it made great sense to Maddie that there were sects of Hinduism that saw the guiding god of the universe as a dancer.

Afterward, Mrs. Buz and her sisters packed up several pounds of leftover couscous, kebabs, *lokum* and *sarigi burma* and begged her to take it away with her "for your little roommate and your friends"—during the course of the evening the hostesses had gotten out of her all about Tessa and Phil. "You are too skinny—you need flesh to dance!"

Then they all hugged her, jammed more tips into her hands and put her in the family SUV to take her to the station for the last train to the city.

It was now midnight, freezing cold and snowing. It was the twelfth of January, the small hours of the year, when light and spring seem furthest away. A cold moon winked through bitter scuds of cloud. Almost no one was on the late train back to the city, leaving Maddie time and quiet to slip *Wind on the Water* into her Discman, and put the earphones over her ears.

Maddie had heard it said many times that you can't hide on the dance floor. She didn't know enough about music to know if it revealed the inner soul to the same degree—Richard Wagner at least seemed to be proof that one could compose exquisite melodies and still be a class-A prick—but if evil lurked in Phil Cooper's inner soul, it certainly didn't come out in his art.

Mostly piano, though he also played both mandolin and guitar, sometimes—according to the liner notes—multiple-tracking all three. He also played harpsichord, the light, jangly notes flowing into a style like jeweled ragtime. The music itself was beautiful, melodic, sometimes simple and sometimes complex, and absolutely nothing like anything either commercial or modern that Maddie had ever heard.

It delighted her, and she knew instinctively that it was too odd to be marketed as pop, too melodic to be what currently passed for classical style, and too unpretentiously old-fashioned for any of the New Wave stations she'd heard.

It was a beautiful anomaly, and it no longer surprised her that Phil was scratching to make ends meet.

Nor was it strange that he was getting a ration of grief over it from an elderly contractor in Tulsa.

She turned the jewel case over, regarded the harsh features and the gently smiling dark eyes. *You can't learn about him through the cards,* Diana had said. *It's about where he fits into your life, not where you fit yourself into his.*

The last song on the disk was called "Step Off the Edge and Fly." Something in the soaring cascades of notes told her that he understood.

You can't learn about him through the cards. The only way was the real way, the hard way everybody did it: putting in the time, putting out your heart, and seeing how you felt about it at the end of every day.

PENN STATION WAS NEARLY deserted—hard, flat surfaces echoing coldly the voices of those few unfortunate travelers still en route to someplace or other at one-thirty on a Sunday morning in January. Though it was only a few blocks, Maddie got a cab to the apartment on Thirty-second Street. "And another thing," the driver ranted at her the moment she shut the door, "there were videotapes of Kennedy's assassination, and Bobby Kennedy's and Martin Luther King's. *How come there wasn't a videotape of John Lennon's assassination?* You tell me *that!*"

It was fortunately a short ride. Maddie paid him and he zoomed away without pausing for breath.

When she slipped through the door of the apartment as silently as she could, the first thing she did was look at the couch. Her stomach sank with dread.

No Tessa. The bedding hadn't even been made up.

Maddie dumped her bag on the floor, looked at the clock.

Ten to two.

Shit.

She scooped up the telephone, tapped through to the message service. The first was from Diana. "Maddie, I've sent you an e-mail about what I could learn of the Glendower Building. Even if it's late when you get in, I think you'd better read it right away."

The second was from Phil. "I hope you pick up your messages the minute you get in. There's something weird going on here and I think you'd better come down. I'll be in the lobby waiting to let you in. If I'm not there, please wait for me, I won't be more than a few minutes. Love you."

The next three were hang-ups. Phil, probably—there was one per hour, nearly on the hour, as if he was walking across to the Owl—which closed at midnight—or down to the all-night liquor store on the corner to make them. Part of her mind tagged the information, and the fact that whatever "weird" was, it obviously was something that couldn't be explained to a 911 operator.

Part of her mind jarred breathlessly on his first message's closing.

What did you say to me?

Love you.

Quick and casual, like a kiss in passing or a pat on the shoulder.

Love you.

She was already on her way through the curtain to her alcove, where the laptop was set up on the tiny dresser under the soft glow of the bronze lamp. She clicked onto the Net and an obnoxiously perky droid voice informed her, *You have mail.*

To: BeautifulDancer909
From: ValedGoddess@DarknessVisible.com
Maddie,

Here's what I've been able to find out about the Glendower Building and the man who built it, and what happened there in January 1908.

The Glendower Building was constructed in 1884 by Lucius Glendower, who owned a number of construction companies, tenement buildings, clothing factories and match factories on the Lower East Side. It was eight stories tall, the upper three floors of which were occupied by the Pinnacle Ready-Made Shirt Company, which Glendower owned.

As you probably know, in the days before trade unions there was not only no regulation of how little an employer could pay—or how many hours' work he could demand of employees, firing at will those who refused to do as they were told—but there were no safety regulations, either. Glendower had a bad reputation even among the garment workers of the Lower East Side.

Maddie thought, Yikes! Her grandfather had been a reporter covering labor strikes early in the century, so she knew a little about the people who were running the garment business then. It was saying something for one man to have a "bad reputation" among that gang of robber barons.

Glendower paid four dollars a week and hired mostly Russian, Jewish, Italian, Irish and Cuban girls whose families desperately needed any income they could get. The girls worked a twelve-hour day in the winter, sixteen hours in the summer, and Glendower's floor managers routinely locked the doors of the factory loft except for a brief break at lunchtime. They said this was to check pilfering (the only toilets were in the yard behind the building and fabric could be sneaked over the fence) and also to make sure the girls didn't go down to the yard simply to loaf. This was common practice then.

The windows were locked for the same reason, also usual business practice in the garment industry. If nothing else it led to several faintings a day in the summertime and at least one girl's death from heat stroke and dehydration. Glendower paid off the city inspectors rather than go to the expense of putting fire escapes on the building, though they were added later.

What gave Glendower a smelly reputation was his sexual abuse of the girls who worked for him. His office was on the sixth floor and he would routinely take girls there and molest them, with the threat of being fired—and blacklisted from work in any of the other garment factories on the East Side—if they refused. This wasn't that uncommon, either, by the way. Back then it was thought that a girl who worked—

especially an immigrant girl—was fair game. Judging by complaints to the fledgling ILGWU, it sounds like Glendower—a massive dark-haired man whose father made a fortune selling guns to both sides in the Civil War—was a sex addict and, if not clinically a sadist, at least got a kick out of roughing up girls.

Phil had said, *I hear them crying.... And I heard him laugh.* Maddie heard again in her mind the whispering voice from the darkness: *little sluts are all alike...good for one thing...*

She thought of the endless stream of bright-faced children trotting up and down those stairs in their pink beginner's leotards, their wispy little practice skirts. The floors that had been trodden by girls not much older, on their way to earn enough money to keep their parents and siblings from being thrown out of their tenement rooms, were buried these days under God knew how many layers of subsequent linoleum and paint.

But it was as if the walls remembered, and wept with shame in the dark.

Like most loft garment factories at that time, Pinnacle Ready-Made was a disaster waiting to happen. Rags soaked with sewing-machine oil weren't taken out nearly often enough—it would be a nuisance to maneuver anything down the stairways, which were about two feet wide to get maximum advantage of space in the building for office and warehouse rental—and were allowed to pile up under the worktables. This was long before any kind of flame retardant was used on cloth, and the factory floors were piled with rags, scrap, lint from the machines and cotton dust, and cotton dust, which is highly flammable, permeated the air.

On the morning of January 13, 1908, the inevitable happened and fire broke out in the seventh-floor factory.

Maddie closed her eyes, hearing in her mind the sound Phil had described, the frantic clattering of fists pounding on a locked metal door.

Ninety girls were killed. The seventh and eighth floors were destroyed completely and the sixth floor gutted. Lucius Glendower's body was found in one of the stairwells, where he'd apparently become disoriented in the smoke and confusion and burned to death. The consensus of local opinion was that this was only a preliminary to a similar but more lasting destiny.

His estate was divided between his second wife and his nephew, Grayson, who married one another in order to consolidate the stock holdings. They repaired the building, which they sold in 1925.

Maddie tried to imagine someone that coldheartedly calculating and greedy, and felt a little glow of gladness that Lucius Glendower had spent a portion of his life with not one, but two of them. Served them all right.

She scrolled down, expecting only an account of subsequent remodeling and sales.

The first time a girl disappeared in the building after the fire was in 1919. I couldn't find much about her except that she was one of Grayson Glendower's factory girls, but there doesn't seem to be any doubt that she never left the building, and that her body was never found.

Maddie thought, her heart curling in on itself with shock, The first time…?

She scrolled down fast through the succeeding paragraphs of Diana's e-mail. Counting names and dates. Too appalled, at first, to believe what she read.

In all, since 1919, at least ten girls had gone into the Glendower Building and had not come out.

New York's finest had come up with a number of logical explanations to account for as many of them as possible. Some of them may even have been correct. One of the girls, a sewing machine operator who vanished in 1943, was called a "troublemaker" by her family and was apparently dating a Protestant boy they didn't like, a boy who'd gone into the army. There was speculation she'd run off to join him before he was shipped off to fight in Italy, where he was killed a few months later; there was little surprise that no one had ever heard from her again. And the one who'd disappeared while working late one night in December 1967 had been a sixteen-year-old runaway from Portland, whose true name her fellow hippies in her East Village crash-pad didn't even know.

But even discounting those—and the few witnesses involved swore that neither girl had left the building—that still left eight girls whose families, boyfriends and roommates were positive they had no reason to drop out of sight. Eight girls who had simply disappeared in the mazes of the Glendower Building's dark upper floors.

Eight girls between the ages of sixteen and twenty. All of them except Eileen Kirkpatrick dark-haired, like most of the girls who'd been fodder for the East Side garment shops at the nineteenth century's turn. All of them between mid-December and the thirteenth of January, the dark midnight of the year.

Little sluts are all alike...good for one thing...

CHAPTER SIX

DIANA VALE HAD ENOUGH friends in difficult living situations that Maddie knew she never left her phone turned off at night or refused to pick up calls, even at two in the morning. After eleven rings it was obvious that the owner of Darkness Visible wasn't at home that night. Maddie tried, without much hope of success, calling the shop, but not much to her surprise got only the answer-droid. She hung up, her heart pounding and her breath coming fast.

There's something weird going on here and I think you'd better come down....

Maddie dumped out her costume bag, shoved her big flashlight into it and a pack of spare batteries. Two balls of string and a sharp folding knife, from the apartment's utility drawer, at the thought of those dark mazes of little halls on the upper floors. The household hammer and a pry bar that could double as a club. What else?

Garlic? Silver bullets? Cold iron? A crucifix? She slung the bag over her shoulder, headed for the subway.

Love you...

She saw Phil across Twenty-ninth Street, coming out of—as she had suspected—the all-night liquor store where there was a phone. Even at that distance she recognized the tall, angular shape, the way he walked. She called "Phil!" without even considering what she'd do or say if it wasn't him; he stopped and turned.

"Maddie!"

She crunched through a clotted drift of snow and dirt piled up at the curb, dashed across the icy street. At this hour there was almost no one abroad even on the avenues, let alone in this slightly run-down block. A few dim streetlights glittered on the ice-slick pavement, and turned Phil's breath into a cloud of diamonds. When he caught her in his arms—when he kissed her, quick and hard and relieved, on the lips, and when she returned both the embrace and the kiss—it felt like something they'd been doing for years.

"Jesus, am I glad to see you...."

"Where is she?"

"I don't know." He fumbled in his pocket for the lobby key as they walked the last few yards to the door. The reconverted lofts and boutiques and the emporia hawking Korean electronics, which had taken over the old brick factory buildings, were shut down and dark. Dingy utility lights made a yellowish square of the Owl's window behind an iron grille. The serviceways and alleys between the buildings were slabs of primordial night, and the cold defeated even the faint pong of old garbage and backed-up drains that seemed to be ground into the very fabric of Manhattan. Between the angular outlines of towering walls, black cloud made a matte nothingness of the sky.

"She stayed after Darth Irving's advanced class tonight and asked if I'd play for her. I said yes and went up to my studio to get a cup of coffee—Tessa had unplugged and washed out the office pot when she went off work before class. When I came back to the big studio she was gone. Her bag was there, so I waited…."

He let them into the gray little coffin of the front hall, locked the door and bolted it behind them, led her past Quincy the caretaker's empty booth and up the stairs. As she ascended that first long flight—two floors past the ground-floor shops' storerooms—Maddie found herself wondering if the door onto Twenty-ninth Street was the same as it had always been. If that had been the entrance by which all those Russian, Jewish and Cuban girls had gone into the building every day, to work at Pinnacle Ready-Made.

She thought of them, girls who these days would be the little green-haired Gothettes going in groups to the Village to get butterflies tattooed on their hips, or hooking up their laptops to do their NYU homework at Starbucks. Saw them in her mind, hugging faded shawls around themselves and gathering up their long, flammable skirts to hurry past the sixth floor, praying Mr. Glendower wouldn't step out of his office just then and say, *Come in here. I want to see you.*

"I went through this whole building," Phil said. "Quincy'd left by then, and I've been trying to reach him all night. No answer. I called for her—yelled up and down those creepy hallways. Turned on every light and tried every doorknob in the place, looked in the men's rooms and the ladies'…everywhere. Her key to the front door was in her bag, she couldn't have got out."

"No," said Maddie. "No, I don't think she did."

They crossed through the Dance Loft's seedy front office, stepped into the fluorescent blaze of the big studio, the glare of the lights off its walls of mirrors all the more shocking after the gloom elsewhere. According to Diana's e-mail the third floor had been a silk warehouse in January 1908. In the winter of 1962 it had contained three or four "to-the-trade" showrooms for wholesalers in artificial flowers and feathers, where a girl named Hannah Sears had worked…and where her purse, coat and galoshes had been found one morning, with the key to the locked downstairs lobby door lying on top of them.

Looking up, Maddie could see where one of the partition walls had been removed, a rough band like a welt in the wall above the line of the mirrors, painted over a dozen times.

"Phil," said Maddie, "I would rather say anything in the world to you other than this." She looked up at him, with his dark rough hair falling forward into his eyes and his shirt half-unbuttoned under his pea coat; the face that was already so familiar to her, so much a part of her thoughts. She was very aware that she had the choice to say *Call the cops—they'll be able to put a trace on her if she left the city….*

It would be the rational and sensible thing to do.

And it would mean Phil wouldn't look at her as he'd looked at her last night, sitting on the floor of the kitchen, when she'd spoken of the narrow stairway leading up from the sixth floor, the stairway that he claimed didn't exist.

Who is *this nutball? And why am I wasting my time talking to her?*

And nobody could say she hadn't done her best.

Only she knew that the police had been called in

when Maria Diaz had disappeared in 1956, and Vera Rosenfeldt in 1972, and little Moongirl in 1967...and for others as well.

See where he fits into your life, Diana had said. *Not where you can fit yourself into his.*

Which included, she supposed, his idea of how the universe was supposed to work.

She took a deep breath. "Tessa isn't the only woman to disappear in this building," she said, and told him, as quickly and in as few words as she could, the content of Diana's e-mail. "Now, people disappear in New York all the time," she said. "I have no idea what the statistics are for any single building, chosen at random, for people who're last seen in it and never heard from again. Sometime when we're free, I'll be perfectly happy to go down to City Hall and look up other buildings as a control group."

Phil said nothing. Only looked down at her, his eyebrows drawn together, listening and thinking... What?

"But every one of those girls disappeared between mid-December and the thirteenth of January—the anniversary of the 1908 fire. That's today. And every one of those girls was of the same age and general appearance of the girls that Lucius Glendower victimized here in his life—first- or second-generation Americans, mostly Latin or Jewish."

"Except for the last one, Padmini Raschad." His voice was quiet in the brightly lit box of the studio, and there was a flicker of anger in his dark eyes. "Quincy told me about her. Quincy has sat in that lobby every day since 1980, and since I can't piss him off by walking away too fast or too often, believe me, there isn't a thing that's gone on in this building that I haven't heard about, several times."

He slid out of his pea coat, draped it over the bench of the piano in the corner of the studio as he spoke, like a man preparing himself for a fight. "Padmini Raschad disappeared in 1994. She worked at a travel agency up on the fifth floor. There was a little bit of a stink when she disappeared—Quincy said they had the police in, but nobody ever found anything. But that means the Dayforths knew about her. They had to, the Dance Loft's been here since the eighties. And they never bothered to tell anybody that there was, or might be, something strange about the building. Probably didn't want to scare away customers."

Maddie had never had much use for Charmian Dayforth since the time her own classes had been dumped without notice. From what she knew of her, Phil was undoubtedly right. She couldn't see Mrs. Dayforth notifying anyone even if she'd seen Lucius Glendower's ghost prowling around the halls.

Phil continued, "I suppose a Pakistani would look pretty much like an Italian to someone who didn't really care."

Maddie shut her eyes briefly and whispered a prayer of thanks for the garrulous old vet who watched over the lobby.

"So what do we do?"

"Let's go up to the sixth floor."

The silence of the building pressed around them as they climbed the flights of stairs. Even with all the lights on, the sense of cold evil persisted, of something waiting for them, of something walking behind them, something that disappeared every time Maddie turned her head. A dark-haired man, Diana had said Glendower had been: a wealthy man and a ruler of industry.

The King of Pentacles, whose shadow Maddie had mistaken for Phil.

The king who fed on the spirits of the girls whose bodies he broke to his will.

The king who still stirred alive in the winter months, when the nights were long at the midnight of the year. Who, when he grew hungry enough, whispered to girls in the dark.

In her mind she saw Tessa again, standing at the foot of that narrow stairway, looking up. Listening. She was exhausted emotionally and pushed to her physical limits; Maddie had seen her too many nights stumble home and doze off before she could finish dinner. If Lucius Glendower's voice murmured to her in her dreams, it would find an easy entry to the dark part of the mind where the consciousness goes in sleep.

No me toque, she had cried in her sleep. Maddie had looked it up in a Spanish dictionary, before leaving for Mrs. Buz's wingding earlier that afternoon. *Don't touch me.*

She wondered where Lucius Glendower's office had been, in what was now the maze of subdivided offices and cubicles, studios and windowless rehearsal halls of the sixth floor. Near the main stair, where his shadow had hissed obscenities at her in the dark?

"Do you want to make another search?" asked Phil when they got to the top of the stairs and Maddie halted and began to dig through her bag.

"Do you feel satisfied that she's not up here?"

He nodded. "I searched every nook and cranny." From his pocket he produced the blue chalk that Mrs. Dayforth used to mark the scheduling board at the Dance Loft. "I marked every place I checked—which means I'd better make sure there's not a molecule of blue chalk dust anywhere on me when Quincy has to come up here and clean it up, or I'll be sucking sidewalk by nightfall. What you got?"

"Insurance." Maddie tied one end of the string to the banister of the main stair that led down to the fifth floor.

Phil raised his eyebrows. "What do you think's going to be chasing us, that we have to find the way through the halls that fast?"

"Things you don't believe in," said Maddie. "And neither do I. Not really."

Phil said softly, "Like Hamlet said, I guess there are more things in Heaven and Earth than are dreamt of in my philosophy. You really think there's something up here?"

"I do," said Maddie. "Something that's been up here for a long time." She handed him the flashlight and closed her eyes.

It was one thing to read the cards, to accept that the random arrangement of symbols would line up along the intricate networks of energy and destiny comprising Time and Space. It was one thing to go with Diana to certain places in Central Park, or to old buildings upstate in the Hudson Valley, and watch her friend pass her hands along the stone of the walls, scrying deep-buried energies there. When Diana had talked her down into a deep trance, and had shown her how to seek the minute changes in temperature that indicated active psychic residue, Maddie had thought she felt them.

But looking back now, she wasn't sure.

And it was quite another thing, to breathe deep and slow, to empty and order her mind into the state of trance, knowing that the life of someone she cared about might be—was—at stake. *I shouldn't be doing this,* she thought desperately. *I should be watching Diana do it, Diana who's had years of trance-work and spirit-watching, who has crossed back and forth over the curtain that separates the world as we know it from those unseen places where energies have form. Diana knows what she's doing. I don't.*

But her instincts told her that the longer she waited, the less chance there would be of following Tessa to wherever she'd been lured. The less chance there was of bringing her back safe.

The deeper she breathed, the more she relaxed her mind, the greater Maddie's sense of peril grew. She remembered clearly her feelings the first time she'd stepped through the door of the Glendower Building, seeking a studio to rent to teach dance less than a month after she'd found Sandy a furnished room and helped him move his stuff there.... That sense of uncleanness. Of ugliness. Of energies that screamed at her, *Don't come in here....*

Only she'd needed a place to teach a class, if she were going to make her rent. Like the little Jewish and Russian and Cuban girls who'd gone up and down the stairs each day to a factory floor they knew was a firetrap, to work for a man who summoned them into his office under threat of blacklist, she did what she needed to do to survive.

And as she relaxed her mind, she felt those early feelings of dread sharpen and crystallize, as if the veils that shrouded and blurred them were being drawn, one by one, aside.

She heard no voices, and saw no shadows, but she was very conscious of those girls now, slipping along the hall in twos and threes with their shawls wrapped around them in the cold, their long hair braided up to keep it out of the machines. Names flickered through her mind and were gone.

She put out her hand, fingers spread as Diana had taught her, and brought it slowly close to the wall. She felt the energy at once, like the prickly horror of ants crawling on her skin. It took all her will not to jerk her hand away.

He was here. He was here everywhere in the building, as if his mind had spread like fungal fibers through the old brick that underlay all those layers of wallpaper and paint. Not living, but holding on to the living world, to the material pleasures and power that all his life he had refused to give up. A psychic monster that fed on what it could get.

Maddie walked forward slowly, following the fast-streaming energy along the wall. "There was a lobby here," she whispered through lips that felt numb, "outside the office door." She could see it, as if she'd visited the place in a dream. The stairway had continued up, where that wall now was. Farther down the main hall the energy ceased, turned cold. Unwinding the string behind her she entered one of the smaller halls, she was dimly aware of the blue chalk X at the corner and of Phil walking behind her, the flashlight in one hand and the pry bar in the other. He seemed barely more than a shadow to her, half unreal.

More real, a thousand times, was the sense of vile consciousness, the anger that seemed to vibrate the air. He was muttering, snarling like a caged dog, that hoarse, thick voice that had spoken to her ten nights ago at the foot of the stairway. He was somewhere just out of clear hearing, savage, furious, but she could smell his sweaty woolen suit, his expensive cologne, the brandy on his breath and the cigar smoke that permeated his flesh and his hair. His need—for women, for power, for domination over those too weak to fight back—was a second stench, deeper than the first.

She turned a corner and then another, the string trailing from her fingers. Office doors, then another little hallway branching off toward a suite, but she knew where the stairway lay. She turned right again and was conscious that the hallway and all the floor behind her was dark, though she didn't know just when the lights had gone out.

The glow of the flashlight touched the stairway. Narrow, barely wider than her shoulders, wooden steps splintery and dirty, walls stained.

She could hear Glendower talking now. Hear him cursing. *Uppity women…come here organizing…man can do what he wants to with his property. Mind your own business. I'll get you…. You little tramps don't like it, you go someplace else and work. Lazy foreigners, steal me blind, spend all your time sneaking cigarettes in the toilets while I'm paying you to work….*

Vile whisperings, chewed over and fermented for nearly a century. Resentment and rage, and under them the red strength of a soul that absorbs power from the pain of others. The death of others.

"He's up there," Maddie whispered, and put her hand on the fouled paint of the wall. "Tessa?"

And out of the darkness above—the darkness at the top of a stairway that had been destroyed ninety-five years before—came the stifled wail of a terrified girl.

Maddie put her foot on the lowest step, and the blast of rage that pounded down on her from the darkness was like the physical force of an explosion. *Get out of here! Get out of here, goddamn do-gooder hag! Rob a man of what's his! Tell a man what he can do on his own property, with his own girls!*

Nearly a hundred years ago to the day, the thing in the darkness above her had died, and in dying had swallowed up the strength of those who had perished with it in the inferno. As she climbed the steps, Maddie could feel those from whom that life force had been taken, the walls around her twittering, like trapped birds. Russian, Spanish, Yiddish, Italian—fragments of horror and pain. A warm hand closed on her wrist, reassuring and strong. "What *is* it?" breathed Phil. "This wasn't here…."

Maddie's mouth felt like she'd had an injection of lidocaine at the dentist. "It's the world he created," she mumbled. "The world that still exists in his mind…"

Pain stabbed at her, so sudden that she staggered. With the pain was a horrible and frightening sensation she'd never felt before, but she knew at once what it was: a cold grip twisting at her mind, seeking to tear her soul free of her brain. She gasped, turned her hand in Phil's and clutched at his fingers— "Hold me…"

His arms were around her, supporting her as the steps seemed to tip under her feet, or else there was something thrusting at her, shoving her, trying to knock her back down the inky slot of the stairway. A voice was shouting in her ears, black thunder that shook the walls around them, and under it Phil's voice, "I've got you, baby, I'm here…."

And like a wind-whirled bird, somewhere came Tessa's cry, "Maddie…!"

The pain ceased with a suddenness that made her gasp. The shouting ended in silence like the fall of an ax. But as Maddie led the way, stumbling, up the last few stairs, she felt the darkness taking shape above them, waiting for them, drawing in on itself. Preparing another blow.

The world at the top of the stairs was the world that had been the Glendower Building before the fire, mutated into a lightless nightmare by the mind that had remembered and maintained it for nearly a hundred years. The high-ceilinged loft room stretched away into darkness, the air a fog of cotton dust that clogged the lungs and throat. The dark shapes of bales, boxes, machines loomed everywhere. The walls and floor shuddered with the dull throbbing of engines, growing louder as the beam of the flashlight weakened and failed. Phil called out "Tessa!" but the roaring of the machines boomed louder still around them. "Tessa!"

We'll never hear her! thought Maddie in despair. *She's growing weaker, she can't fight him!*

For a moment she wanted to weep, to flee back to the stairway—if she could find it—to get herself out of this place….

She concentrated on her breathing, on steadying her mind. "Help me find her," she said, her voice quiet in the shaking darkness. "Help me get her out."

She felt the energy running over her hands again, tugging gently at her arms and her long hair. Touching her cheeks with feathery warmth, like stiff fingers callused by needles and pins. *Allá, hermana,* a voice seemed to breathe in her ear, patting, guiding. *Oi, the* momzer, *is he gonna be mad....*

She followed the energy through vibrating darkness, through what felt like a maze of corridors, loft rooms, then up another stairway whose walls brushed her shoulders on either side. Rats sat up and hissed at her on the steps ahead, red eyes glaring. Phil gave Maddie the flashlight, strode forward with the pry bar, never letting go of her wrist. His face was expressionless: he, too, was a man, thought Maddie, who would do what he had to do.

The rats retreated, but their stink was everywhere around them as they ascended the dark stairway. Partway up, Maddie felt the walls seeming to close in on them, felt the greedy, angry power of Lucius Glendower's mind grip and tear at hers. Pain pounded in her head again, cramped in her body, and she heard him howling: *I'll get you, you troublemaker! I'll get you....*

Like the Devil on the tarot card, raving and ugly, with the lovers held in chains at his feet. *But the chains*—she recalled the image clearly—*are loose. We can take them off, anytime we please.*

Then he was gone. The cold, tearing pain in her mind vanished, into a silent stillness more terrible than before.

There may have been some warning, some movement or sound, or the sudden reek of Glendower's tobacco and cologne. Maddie didn't know. But she looked quickly up into Phil's face and saw his eyes change, saw the blaze of greed and lust and triumph kindle there, in the instant before he snapped off the flashlight, slammed her against the wall of the narrow staircase, fell upon her in the dark.

She may have screamed his name—she didn't afterward recall. He bit her neck, her shoulders as he ground his body against hers, ripped open her shirt, tried to drag her to the floor. She'd had a split second to brace herself, to pull away, but he was terrifyingly strong. The next instant he thrust her away, turned as if he would flee, and Maddie grabbed his arm, the violence of his effort to wrench from her nearly breaking her wrist.

"Goddamn you, you bastard!" he screamed into the darkness. "You son of a bitch, you catch fire and die!" And he fell against the wall, his breath coming in harsh sobs.

Maddie clung to his arm, felt the shudder of his flesh gradually lessen. She knew exactly what had happened, what Glendower had tried to do. For one instant, she had seen Lucius Glendower looking out of Phil's eyes.

After a time she said, "He's trying to split us up. Trying to get me to run from you, or you from me, so he can get us lost, deal with us separately. Don't let go of me."

Phil caught her wordlessly against him, his strength just as frightening as it had been a moment before when the evil old man's spirit had possessed his mind. But he only held her to him, desperate, for a long minute, his breath burning against the side of her face.

Maddie whispered, "Come on. He's going to try again."

She felt him nod. The flashlight came on again, the

light of its beam fading and uncertain, as if the psychic forces loose in this madhouse dimension were even drinking the chemical energies of the batteries. Maddie pulled her shirt closed around her bleeding shoulders, clung to Phil's hand as they ascended the last of the stairs.

Tessa lay in what Maddie guessed to be the original eighth floor of the Glendower Building, the loft that had been one of the factory floors. They saw her through the loft's open doors, crumpled unconscious on the rag-strewn planks. The room was hellishly cold, snow falling onto the plates of glass of the big windows overhead. Beyond that snow—beyond the glass of the windows lower in the walls—only darkness. Maddie wondered what she would have seen, could she have looked out in the daytime, if it was ever daylight here.

Dust hazed the air, furred the long tables down the center of the room, the oily black shapes of the sewing machines. Rats scampered along the walls. As Phil and Maddie hurried through the open iron doors into the loft, Phil whispered, "Here. I saw this room in my dream…."

"Tessa!" Maddie knelt beside her friend. "Tessa, are you all right?" For a moment she feared, as the younger girl opened her eyes, that she would see in them, too, the demon-glare of Lucius Glendower's consciousness, as she had seen it in Phil's.

But Tessa only blinked up at her, dazed. "Get me out of here," she whispered in a broken voice. "He said he'd kill me—he'd keep me here…. Keep me here forever."

"You'll be okay, honey." Phil knelt beside her, picked her up in his arms. "Can you walk?"

Tessa nodded, reaching down with her long legs, her arms still around Phil's neck. The flashlight beam showed his eyebrows standing out very dark against a face blanched with shock and strain. Maddie wondered if Glendower's cold, ripping mind were twisting even now at Phil's thoughts, struggling to take over again. She swung the flashlight around the loft, but the beam was too weak to penetrate the darkness. In contrast to the roaring of the machines downstairs, this place was silent, with a silence that watched their every move.

In her mind she heard that evil voice again, a muttering babble of half-heard words. *Mine...mine...come in and tell me what I can and can't do...show them... Get them. Get them. Show them. Little tramps...only good for one thing...*

Only good to feed his lust, Maddie thought. *To fuel the undead greediness of his mind.* She said, "We'd better get out of here." The voice was growing louder. Coming closer.

Beneath the smells of machine oil and rats and cotton dust, beneath the sudden reek of tobacco and cologne, she could smell smoke.

Supporting Tessa between them, Phil and Maddie headed for the door. Stumbling, running, as Maddie realized what would happen...

The iron door swung shut with a booming clang.

Far off in the blackness, she heard a girl scream, *Fire!*

CHAPTER SEVEN

PHIL CURSED, FLUNG HIS weight against the door. The hollow metallic clatter turned to obscene laughter in the dark. "Pry bar," Maddie said, feeling strangely calm. "Hinges." She dug the hammer out of her bag and stood back, holding Tessa by the hand.

"The laws of physics goddamn better apply around here." Phil swung the hammer at the bar, the crash like cannon fire in the dark. "If this doorjamb is made of something other than wood…"

"Maddie!" Tessa screamed, and red light poured over them as fire burst out under the tables in the center of the room.

It was horrifying how fast the fire spread. Oil, rags, dust went up; lines of fire raced across the wooden floorboards, climbed the walls where the film of cotton dust exploded into sheets of flame. Heat smote them, driving Tessa and Maddie back toward the door where Phil hammered at the end of the pry bar, like a dark-haired, desperate Thor. Though Maddie could see no one else in the long spaces of the loft, she could hear them, hear their voices screaming: *Fuego!* And *Dear Jesus in Heaven, save us….*

The wooden jamb splintered and both girls flung

themselves at the door, felt it give. Maddie cried again, "Help us!" and whether the wild, terrified energies in the burning room responded—whether they *could* respond—she didn't know. But when she and Tessa hurled their weight against the metal again it tore free of the broken jamb, opening a narrow space where the hinges were half torn free.

Phil slid through first, swore again—smoke poured through and it seemed to Maddie for a moment that the broken door, the shattered jamb, tried to close up again around him, crushing his body like a huge mouth. He braced his back, fought the iron and the wood apart and gasped, "Can you get through past me?" As the two women slithered through the narrow gap, Maddie heard Glendower's voice shouting, not in her mind this time but seeming to come from the fire-saturated darkness all around them.

The string that stretched down the stairway was burning already, a thin line of fire through opaque black billows of smoke. The air burned in Maddie's lungs, grit blinded her eyes. Somewhere she heard the sound Phil had described, the wild, despairing hammering of fists against a locked metal door. Screaming, a dim and far-off echo, like the wailing of storm winds above the guttural roar of the flames.

They plunged down the stairs, through the holocaust of burning walls, flame-wreathed corridors below, desperately running for the next set of stairs. Swirling energies tore at Maddie's mind, wild spirits of panic and terror, eternally trapped in the darkness and the flame. Maddie clung grimly to Tessa's wrist, dragged her forward, following the burning streak of the string. She saw the flame race along the string ahead of them, as it plunged down the next flight of stairs; saw flame burst out of the walls, roar up in grabbing hands from the floor. The stairwell vomited smoke, hot wind pouring up it like a chimney, and in the smoke she saw him....

The shadow she'd seen, whispering to her at the foot of the stairs.

He blocked the stair below them, massive arms spread across it from wall to wall. His eyes were red, like the glaring eyes of the phantom rats. Nothing else of him could she see, but it seemed to Maddie, as she plunged down the stairwell toward him, that his whole body was formed of smoke, and of the writhing energies that he held twisted around his core. Beyond him lay the doorway to the real world, to the real Glendower Building as it existed in the twenty-first century, and the dingy glare of cheap electric bulbs, far off around the corners, framed him, illuminating the billow of the smoke.

She flung herself at that ghastly shape of smoke and hatred, swinging the flashlight like a club. Instead of the solid impact of flesh she felt a burning jolt of energy, like an electrical shock that numbed her arm. Yet his hands were solid as they seized her, shoved her against the wall as Phil had shoved her, with a force that knocked the breath out of her. She felt his weight buffet her, twist her, felt his teeth tear at her flesh.

Then Tessa dragged her free, and she heard the crackle and roar of energies as Phil slashed through the shadow of the ghost with the iron of the pry bar and hammer. Phil cried out, doubling over with shock and pain, but Glendower's shadow had broken up. The next instant it re-formed in the burning air, even as Maddie and Tessa turned back, caught Phil as he staggered, dragged him down toward the lights of the sixth floor.

I'll get you! Glendower screamed. *I'll show you.... No one takes from me what's mine!*

Phil stumbled, collapsed on the battered brown linoleum of the sixth-floor hall, and as Maddie bent down to drag him to his feet Tessa cried, "Look out!" Maddie raised her head and saw the glass windows of a nearby office door shatter, as if kicked by some monstrous energy within. Smoke poured out, red-stained by the flame that licked up close behind.

Maddie turned back, horrified. Smoke and fire belched from the stairway to the haunted realm above, the flames spraying, burning on the many-times-painted wallpaper, the wood of wainscots and doors. Against the flame the dark shape of Lucius Glendower rose, fists upraised, shouting incomprehensible curses, and fire poured forth around him and into the remainder of the building that had been his.

Maddie dragged Phil to his feet, thrust her shoulder under his arm on one side, Tessa supporting him on the other. His hand flailed, but Maddie felt the whole of his weight on them—smoke inhalation? The shock of breaking through the black energies of Glendower's spirit? She gasped, trying to breathe and choking on the smoke. Somehow she dragged them on through the tangle of hallways toward where she knew the stairway down had to lie. In the smoke and darkness she could barely see the white line of the string, except where the blaze raced along the walls, seared in frames of fire around burning doors.

I'll show you! Glendower's voice screamed behind them. *I'll get you!*

Tessa gasped, staggered, coughed, and when she fell the whole of her weight and Phil's nearly pulled Maddie to the floor. Her eyes burning, her vision blurred, Maddie fell to her knees beside them. "Get up! Please, get up!"

A dark shape emerged from the smoke beside her, reached down to drag Phil to his feet. Gasping, beyond speech, Maddie pulled Tessa up, hauled the younger girl's arm around her shoulders, as a voice shouted something to her. She thought it was *This way...*but couldn't be sure. Through the flaring horror of glare and smoke she could see the dark shapes of Phil and his rescuer following the line of the string, and she staggered after them.

The lights were gone, the fire spreading below them from floor to floor as they stumbled down the smoke-filled stairwell. Maddie heard, far off, the wail of sirens, New York's heroes to the rescue again. She could see nothing, only clung to the banister, wondering how she would or could make it down five floors. Now and then a gleam of reflected red light showed her the two shapes descending ahead, and once she heard Phil cough.

He's still breathing, she thought. *He's still alive.*

Dear God, don't let him die.

She glanced beside her at Tessa but could tell nothing in the superheated smoky black of the stairwell. Only, she could occasionally feel when the girl tried to help her, tried to walk, only to sag against her, gasping for breath. "Hang on," she panted. "Please, hang on...."

Light reflected from below, the glare of searchlights

from the street pouring into the lobby mingling with the firelight from above. The groan and screech of pry bars in the door frame, the confusion of shouts, sounding far away still at the bottom of that long double flight of final stairs.

The dark form that led Maddie stopped at the head of those stairs, lowered Phil down with his back to the wall. Maddie let Tessa slip down as well, stood with her hand against the wall, panting, getting her breath for the final descent. She turned her head to gasp something to the man who had helped her….

It was Sandy.

Sandy before drink and drugs had eroded him away to a man he himself would have despised. Sandy not as she'd last seen him on that cold metal table in the morgue, but as she'd first seen him, with a wry smile under his mustache and the old elfin gleam sparkling in the darkest eyes Maddie had ever seen. Sandy as he had always wished and hoped and wanted to be.

He smiled at her, and held out his hand.

With the amount of power and energy swirling around in the air—with the half-materialized forces Glendower had so long summoned into being—Maddie realized she shouldn't be surprised. Of course Sandy would figure out a way to mooch some of those energies, to come to her aid—to pay her back for nearly a decade of bailing him out of trouble. To save the life of the man she now loved. In his life, she recalled, Sandy had never been anything but generous.

She took his hand. Like Lucius Glendower's, it had solidness and strength to it, and Sandy's old lightness of touch. She said, "Thank you," feeling no fear or shock. Only happy to see him…happy that he looked so well.

He glanced down at Phil, then back at her, and grinned, the old shy Sandy grin. He stepped forward and kissed her, very gently, on the lips, his mustache tickling as it always had.

Then he turned and stepped off the edge of the final flight down—like the Fool stepping off his cliff—and faded into darkness and smoke.

DIANA WAS AT THE APARTMENT when Maddie woke up the following afternoon. Maddie's memories of the emergency room at Roosevelt Hospital were confused, due to shock and, she suspected, whatever the paramedics had given her while they were wrapping Phil and Tessa in wet sheets and dousing them with distilled water. She had a handful of sharp, clear images in her mind, like stills from a movie she barely recalled seeing: Phil propping himself up on his elbows on the gurney and saying groggily, "Wouldn't it be cheaper to take a cab?" and, later, Tessa sitting next to her in the dreary ER waiting room while the triage nurses tried to sort them out from the cases of trauma, OD and gunshot wounds all around them—a typical night in New York.

While the paramedics had been loading Phil and Tessa into an ambulance—Maddie huddled in the doorway of the Owl to stay warm—the Glendower Building had collapsed, like the Falling Tower, in a shower of flaming debris.

"They kept Phil overnight." Diana carried a plateful of kebabs and *sarigi burma* from the refrigerator to

Maddie's bedside. "Tessa's gone down to help Charmian Dayforth try to talk the fire department into letting her salvage what records she can from the Dance Loft's offices. I think she's one of the few students who did. All the rest are evidently scrambling to find practice space to get ready for the ABA auditions tomorrow." The white witch's voice was wryly amused at this evidence of artistic dedication. "The building was nearly gutted."

Maddie said, "Good. It should have been gutted—and razed—ninety-five years ago. Let's hope they'll finish the job this time."

When the Tower fell, she remembered from some interpretations of the tarot deck, the prisoners within it were freed. Lucius Glendower, and the spirits of all those girls whose souls had fed his greed. Freed to their final crossing, and to whatever, for them, would come next.

She sat up in bed, rubbed her neck, her arms. There were bandages where Glendower had bitten her, bruises where Phil had seized her by the arms. Her body felt as if she'd fallen down a flight of stairs, and her throat was sore as nobody's business. "Is Phil all right?"

"He seems to be." Diana glanced at the clock in the living room, through the white sheet curtains that had been opened wide. With her gray hair wound into a topknot and the sleeves of her homespun dress rolled over powerful forearms, she looked like a samurai denmother. "I went down to Roosevelt Hospital this morning and talked to him. He asked several times if you were all right, and Tessa. He said Glendower had 'gotten into his mind'; he was afraid you would not forgive him."

"I hope you told him it was all right."

"I told him you had enough experience with the supernatural to understand what had happened. He said, 'I'm not sure that's the kind of experience you want to have a lot of, but I'm glad.' He seemed very shaken up."

"Well, he just had it proved to him that the world isn't put together the way he thought it was," said Maddie. She picked a fragment of chicken off a skewer, held it out to Baby, who sniffed for a moment, then condescended to taste. "And so did Tessa…and really, so did I. It isn't that I didn't believe it was real, but… You can read about this, and hear about it, and even talk to people who've had experiences with the Other Side, but…" She shook her head at the memory of flame and darkness and smoke, of the cold brutal clutch of Lucius Glendower's mind, and of Sandy's farewell smile.

She glanced shyly up at her teacher and asked, "Did he say anything else?"

"To tell you that he loves you." Diana smiled and wiped the sticky syrup from the Turkish dessert from her fingers with a paper towel. "He said, 'Tell her I love her to hell and back, which I think is what we just did.' I don't know him well, but he seems to be a very remarkable man."

"I don't know him well, either," said Maddie. Baby climbed into her lap, settled down to washing her paws; there was great comfort in the soft black-and-white fur, the familiar presence. Maddie wondered if Sandy had ever appeared to his cat.

She wouldn't have put it past him.

"I love him—I want him—but…how can you love someone you don't really know?"

"Of course you can. You loved Sandy, and there were parts of him that you never knew. And he loved you, enough to return from beyond the grave to help you—you weren't his dupe, and his words of loving to you were not a lie. We love people differently at different stages of our knowledge of them. As love changes its shape and its nature, we have to decide what we're going to do about that love on any given day. And on *this* given day," added Diana, "your Philip may be out of the hospital already—the doctors said they were going to release him this morning, and it's past noon now."

"They'll release him," said Maddie quietly. "But with the Glendower Building burned to the ground, I don't think he has anywhere to go."

PHIL CAME THAT EVENING with Tessa, Tessa filthy with soot and exhausted, but determined to catch an audition prep class being given at one of the other studios. "I mean, like, everybody else in the school has spent the whole day prepping for the audition while I've been shoveling out files," she said, emerging from the bathroom already resplendent in tights and leotard, winding her wet hair into a bun. "I'd like to know who Mrs. Dayforth bribed. Thank God I wasn't trying to break in my new shoes last night, so the ones I lost were the old ones.... That sounds so cold, when poor Mrs. Dayforth just lost her studio. I mean, it was insured up the wazoo, but there were all her posters of herself, and mementos of when she was dancing.... Will you stay here tonight?"

She turned to Phil, who was sitting on the end of

Maddie's bed devouring kebabs and couscous as if he were a starving man. He ducked his head a little and said, "I'm lining up a couch at Hobbsie's place in Queens." Maddie had thought she recognized the shirt Phil was wearing as belonging to the Dance Loft's star male pupil.

Tessa looked a little surprised, and Maddie said shyly, "It would be all right if you stayed here."

Phil scooted a last fragment of onion around the plate with an empty kebab skewer, not looking up. "Thank you. I figured you ladies would have enough to worry about, without me sleeping on your carpet." He glanced sidelong at Maddie as he said it and added, "Right now you don't need to spend your energy wondering if I'm going to turn into the Thing That Wouldn't Leave."

Maddie smiled. "I trust you."

Their eyes met. Phil said, for her ears only, "That's a scary thing to say. Thank you."

"Well, if you ever get tired of Beefcake on Parade over in Hobbsie's apartment," said Tessa, stuffing her shoes and a towel into a plastic grocery sack from a Chinese market in lieu of a gym bag, "the door is open here. We'll even give you your own dish."

She and Phil left together—Phil had gotten a job playing for one of the audition classes at a studio in Brooklyn—and Maddie dropped at once into deep sleep untroubled by dreams of either Sandy, Philip or the nightmare that had burned to ashes on Twenty-ninth Street. She dreamed of flying, of dancing wreathed in clouds at the heart of the world.

She didn't see Phil until two nights later, at Tessa's I-Got-Into-the-ABA! party at Al-Medina.

Abdullah had offered the girls the Big Room, a long chamber two stories tall with a gallery around it that was never used these days. The curtained booths that overlooked the main floor were given over mostly to storage, or served as changing rooms for the dancers. Maddie and Tessa invited everyone they knew—the Dayforths didn't come, having little use for belly dancers, but Quincy and Diana both did—and Tessa borrowed one of Josi's pink veils and did the Spirits of Coffee Dance from the *Nutcracker,* to the music of flute and *doumbek* and wild applause.

It was while Maddie was dancing that she saw Phil. He sat on one of the wall divans near the small band, a bottle of Moroccan beer in hand, watching with fascinated delight. Since this was a party and not a gig, Maddie was doing a sword dance, the curved blade balanced across the top of her head, a form of the art that she enjoyed but that was not much in demand. She caught his eye and gave him half a smile, sank to the floor in front of him—long, rippling movements of each arm, of the chest, the hips, the rest of her body still, the weapon on her head never wavering. The band gave her flourishes, to let her show off each isolated motion: her eyes touched Phil's again.

Do you understand?

It's all dancing. Skill infused with joy. Weaving jewelry out of dreams.

He returned her smile.

"YOU'RE GOOD," SAID HIS VOICE behind her when she'd whirled herself off and climbed the narrow stairs to the curtained gallery booth she was using as a dressing room. She turned, still panting a little from the last frenzied drum solo. Saw him standing framed in the dim light of the corridor, rumpled and a little tired-looking in jeans and a gray linen shirt.

It seemed impossible to her that she could ever have mistaken Lucius Glendower's shadow—or Sandy's memory—for him.

"So're you. I played those CDs on my way back from a gig the other night—I never got a chance to tell you."

"I'm glad you like them. Thank God most of my stock, and the master tapes, were in storage. That music down there tonight—the rhythms they use, and the way they use them. I'll have to try that."

"You'll look great," promised Maddie with a grin. "I'll get Josi to lend you that little pink outfit of hers with the valentines on it...."

The curtain fell over the door behind him and he crossed the booth to where she stood, with her back to a curlicued pillar. Put one hand on the wall on either side of her shoulders. Looked down into her eyes. "You know what I mean."

"I know what you mean."

"Do you?" His hand touched her face, slipped beneath the heavy swags of her hair.

"I think so."

His thumb traced her cheekbone, her lips and her chin. Then lower, brushing the bruises on her neck and shoulder that she'd covered with an elaborate necklace of ersatz topaz and diamonds. "I never got a chance to say I'm sorry," he said. "You know I'd never hurt you."

"I know."

"I love you."

She reached behind her hair and unfastened the necklace, the jewels sliding, glittering, over his hand and down her breasts, where he gathered them like a fistful of stars. She whispered, "It's hard to say. It's not something I ever wanted to feel again."

"You don't have to say anything. Or feel anything." He drew back from her. "It's what *I* say. And what *I* feel. I'm not expecting you to do anything about it."

She put her arms behind his neck, drew his mouth down to hers. "It would be a lie," she murmured, "for me to say anything else. I love you."

His hands smoothed the bare skin of her belly and sides, stroked her back when she unfastened the heavy, jeweled bra. Her own hands parted his shirt, slipped over the heavy muscle, the washboard bones of his ribs, slow music from below spiraling through the red velvet curtains, mingling with the sound of their breath.

He lifted her, carried her to one of the divans, her hair spread out over the pillows as he stood above her, looking down. "You're so beautiful." He knelt and stretched out at her side. His hands cupped her breasts, gently exploring, then slid up under the silken clouds of skirts. Maddie arched her back, moving like a cat with his caresses, her world and her consciousness narrowed to the rough friction of his hands, the scent of his body, and widened, it seemed, to take in all of night, and all of life.

She took her time, endless time in the crimson gloom, as if she were dancing to the music down below. Her fingernails scraped lightly across his back and arms, and later his butt and thighs, teasing and sampling, in no hurry. Later they locked together, tighter and tighter, as if their bones would meld. He was patient, exploring the secrets that differ from woman to woman, and sometimes in the same woman from night to night. Maddie groaned and clung to him, guiding sometimes, sometimes taken by surprise at sensations she'd never guessed she could feel—later she was not the only one with bite marks on her neck and arms.

She thought as he entered her, *Why did I wait?* But she knew she hadn't been waiting for *a* man, but for *this* man. And for the healed woman that she was only now becoming. The Dancer at the Heart of the World.

Afterward they lay together panting on the dusty velvet, listening to the voices of Josi and Tessa in the corridor outside, to the quiet in the dining room downstairs. The music had ceased. The chatter had turned desultory.

Hobbsie's voice drifted up from below, "Anybody seen him? I said I'd give him a ride back to my place."

Phil started to sit up; Maddie laid a hand on his back. "Tell him you're coming home with me."

He lay down again at her side. Maddie felt she could have spent the whole night that way, the whole winter, close to his warmth. Relearning what it was to spend nights alternately talking and dozing, and sinking into loving like young animals mating in spring.

"I meant what I said, about not wanting to become something you get sick of seeing. I don't want…" His fingertips stroked her palm. "I don't want it to turn into that. I don't want *us* to turn into that. In a couple of months I'll have the money to get my own place—I never planned to spend longer than that sleeping on the studio floor. Rather than risk losing what I think we can have, I'll couch-surf until then."

Drowsily, Maddie reached across to touch his face. "Now who doesn't trust who?" she asked. "Do you think we'll lose what I think we're going to have?"

"No." There wasn't a trace of doubt in his voice. "I don't think anything in the world can touch us. Or in any other world."

Maddie smiled. "Nor do I." She felt very calm as she said it, lifted out of herself, beyond the shadows of a haunted past. As if more than a building full of ghosts and memories had burned down the other night, releasing those imprisoned within. "Do you want to move in?"

He sighed. "I should be a sensitive New Age guy and say no, no, you need your space.... But ever since I met you, I've been wondering what it's like to wake up next to you in the morning." He brought her palm to his lips. "And I want to be next to you when I fall asleep at night."

"We can't know the future," said Maddie softly. "We can only know ourselves. And maybe, if we're lucky, each other."

He leaned over her, pressed his lips to hers. "Then I think you've got yourself another roommate."

They rose from the divan and dressed, then went down to join their friends, afterward walking to the subway together through the icy January night.

DANCERS IN THE DARK

CHARLAINE HARRIS

ACKNOWLEDGEMENT:

My thanks to dancers past and present:
Coco Ihle, Larry Roquemore, Jo Dierdorff,
Shelley Freydont and the very helpful Molly McBride.
Special thanks go to Doris Ann Norris,
reference librarian to the stars, who can look up
the inner dimensions of a sarcophagus
faster than I can whistle "Dixie."

CHAPTER ONE

RUE PAUSED TO GATHER herself before she pushed open the door marked both Blue Moon Entertainment and Black Moon Productions. She'd made sure she'd be right on time for her appointment. Desperation clamped down on her like a vise: she had to get this job, even if the conditions were distasteful. Not only would the money make continuing her university courses possible, the job hours dovetailed with her classes. *Okay, head up, chest out, shoulders square, big smile, pretty hands,* Rue told herself, as her mother had told her a thousand times.

There were two men—two vampires, she corrected herself—one dark, one red-haired, and a woman, a regular human woman, waiting for her. In the corner, at a barre, a girl with short blond hair was stretching. The girl might be eighteen, three years younger than Rue.

The older woman was hard-faced, expensively dressed, perhaps forty. Her pantsuit had cost more than three of Rue's outfits, at least the ones that she wore to classes every day. She thought of those outfits as costumes: old jeans and loose shirts bought at the thrift store, sneakers or hiking boots and big glasses with a very weak prescription. She was concealed in such an ensemble at this moment, and Rue realized from the woman's face that her appearance was an unpleasant surprise.

"You must be Rue?" the older woman asked.

Rue nodded, extended her hand. "Rue May. Pleased to meet you." Two lies in a row. It was getting to be second nature—or even (and this was what scared her most) first nature.

"I'm Sylvia Dayton. I own Blue Moon Entertainment and Black Moon Productions." She shook Rue's hand in a firm, brisk way.

"Thank you for agreeing to see me dance." Rue crammed her apprehension into a corner of her mind and smiled confidently. She'd endured the judgments of strangers countless times. "Where do I change?" She let her gaze skip right over the vampires—her potential partners, she guessed. At least they were both taller than her own five foot eight. In the hasty bit of research she'd done, she'd read that vampires didn't like to shake hands, so she didn't offer. Surely she was being rude in not even acknowledging their presence? But Sylvia hadn't introduced them.

"In there." There were some louver-doored enclosures on one side of the room, much like changing rooms in a department store. Rue entered a cubicle. It was easy to slide out of the oversize clothes and the battered lace-up boots, a real pleasure to pull on black tights, a deep plum leotard and fluttering wrap skirt to give the illusion of a dress while she danced. She sat on a stool to put on T-strap heels, called character shoes, then stood to smile experimentally at her reflection in the mirror. *Head up, chest out, shoulders square, big smile, pretty hands,* she repeated silently. Rue took the clip out of her hair and brushed it until it fell in a heavy curtain past her shoulder blades. Her hair was one of her best features. It was a deep, rich brown with an undertone of auburn. The color almost matched that of her deep-set, dramatic eyes.

Rue only needed her glasses to clarify writing on the blackboard, so she popped them into their case and slipped it into her backpack. She leaned close to the mirror to inspect her makeup. After years of staring into her mirror with the confidence of a beautiful girl, she now examined her face with the uncertainty of a battered woman. There were pictures in a file at her lawyer's office, pictures of her face bruised and puffy. Her nose—well, it looked fine now.

The plastic surgeon had done a great job.

So had the dentist.

Her smile faltered, dimmed. She straightened her back again. She couldn't afford to think about that now. It was show time. She folded back the door and stepped out.

There was a moment of silence as the four in the room took in Rue's transformation. The darker vampire looked gratified; the red-haired one's expression didn't change. That pleased Rue.

"You were fooling us," Sylvia said. She had a deep, raspy voice. "You were in disguise." *I'd better remember that Sylvia Dayton is perceptive,* Rue told herself. "Well, let's try you on the dance floor, since you definitely pass in the looks department. By the way, it's Blue Moon you want to try out for, right? Not Black Moon? You could do very well in a short time with Black Moon, with your face and body."

It was Blue Moon's ad she'd answered. "Dancer

wanted, must work with vamps, have experience, social skills," the ad had read. "Salary plus tips."

"What's the difference?" Rue asked.

"Black Moon, well, you have to be willing to have sex in public."

Rue couldn't remember the last time she'd been shocked, but she was shocked now. "No!" she said, trying not to sound as horrified as she felt. "And if this tryout has anything to do with removing my clothes..."

"No, Blue Moon Entertainment is strictly for dancing," Sylvia said. She was calm about it. "As the ad said, you team with a vampire. That's what the people want these days. Whatever kind of dancing the party calls for—waltzing, hip-hop. The tango is very popular. People just want a dance team to form the centerpiece for their evening, get the party started. They like the vamp to bite the girl at the end of the exhibition dance."

She'd known that; it had been in the ad, too. All the material she'd read had told her it didn't hurt badly, and the loss of a sip of blood wouldn't affect her. She'd been hurt worse.

"After you dance as a team, often you're required to stay for an hour, dancing with the guests," Sylvia was saying. "Then you go home. They pay me a fee. I pay you. Sometimes you get tips. If you agree to anything on the side and I hear about it, you're fired." It took Rue a minute to understand what Sylvia meant, and her mouth compressed. Sylvia continued. "Pretty much the same arrangement applies for Black Moon, but the entertainment is different, and the pay is higher. We're thinking of adding vampire jugglers and a vampire magician—he'll need a 'Beautiful Assistant.'"

It steadied Rue somehow when she realized that Sylvia was simply being matter-of-fact. Sex performer, magician's assistant or dancer, Sylvia didn't care.

"Blue Moon," Rue said firmly.

"Blue Moon it is," Sylvia said.

The blond girl drifted over to stand by Sylvia. She had small hazel eyes and a full mouth that was meant to smile. She wasn't smiling now.

While Sylvia searched through a stack of CD cases, the blonde stepped up to Rue's side. She whispered, "Don't look directly in their eyes. They can snag you that way, if they want to, turn your will to their wishes. Don't worry unless their fangs run all the way out. They're excited then."

Startled, Rue used her lowest voice to say, "Thanks!" But now she was even more nervous, and she had to wonder if perhaps that hadn't been the girl's intention.

Having picked a CD, Sylvia tapped the arm of one of the vampires. "Thompson, you first."

The dark-haired taller vampire, who was wearing biking shorts and a ragged, sleeveless T-shirt, came to stand in front of Rue. He was very handsome, very exotic, with golden skin and smooth short hair. Rue guessed he was of Eurasian heritage; there was a hint of a slant to his dark eyes. He smiled down at her. But there was something in his look she didn't trust, and she always paid attention to that feeling…at least, now she did. After a quick scan of his face, she kept her eyes focused on his collarbone.

Rue had never touched a vampire. Where she came from, a smallish town in Tennessee, you never saw anything so exotic. If you wanted to see a vampire (just like if you wanted to go to the zoo), you had to visit the city. The idea of touching a dead person made Rue queasy. She would have been happy to turn on her heel and walk right out of the room, but that option wasn't open. Her savings had run out. Her rent was due. Her phone bill was imminent. She had no insurance.

She heard her mother's voice in her head, reminding her, "Put some steel in that spine, honey." Good advice. Too bad her mother hadn't followed it herself.

Sylvia popped the disk in the CD player, and Rue put one hand on Thompson's shoulder, extended the other in his grasp. His hands were cool and dry. This partner would never have sweaty palms. She tried to suppress her shiver. *You don't have to like a guy to dance with him,* she advised herself. The music was an almost generic dance tune. They began with a simple two-step, then a box step. The music accelerated into swing, progressed to jitterbug.

Rue found she could almost forget her partner was a vampire. Thompson could really dance. And he was so strong! He could lift her with ease, swing her, toss her over his head, roll her across his back. She felt light as a feather. But she hadn't mistaken the gleam in his eyes. Even while they were dancing, his hands traveled over more of her body than they should. She'd had enough experience with men—more than enough experience—to predict the way their partnership would go, if it began like this.

The music came to an end. He watched her chest move up and down from the exercise. He wasn't even winded. Of course, she reminded herself, Thompson didn't need to breathe. The vampire bowed to Rue, his eyes dancing over her body. "A pleasure," he said. To her surprise, his voice purely American.

She nodded back.

"Excellent," Sylvia said. "You two look good together. Thompson, Julie, you can go now, if you want." The blonde and Thompson didn't seem to want. They both sat down on the floor, backs to one of the huge mirrors that lined the room. "Now dance with Sean O'Rourke, our Irish aristocrat," Sylvia told her. "He needs a new partner, too." Rue must have looked anxious, because the older woman laughed and said, "Sean's partner got engaged and left the city. Thompson's finished med school and started her residency. Sean?"

The second vampire stepped forward, and Rue realized he hadn't moved the whole time she'd been dancing with Thompson. Now he gave Sylvia a frigid nod and examined Rue as closely as she was examining him.

Dust could have settled on Sean, he stood so still. He was shorter than Thompson, but still perhaps two inches taller than Rue, and his long straight hair, tied back at the nape of his neck, was bright red. Of course, Sean was white, white as paper; Thompson's racial heritage, his naturally golden skin, had made him look a little more alive.

The Irish vampire's mouth was like a capital *M*. The graven downturns made him look a little spoiled, a little petulant, but it was just the way his mouth was made. She wondered what he would look like if he ever smiled. Sean's eyes were blue and clear, and he had a dusting of freckles across his sharp nose. A vampire with freckles—that made Rue want to laugh. She ducked her head to hide her smile as he took his stance in front of her.

"I am amusing?" he asked, so softly she was sure the other three couldn't hear.

"Not at all," she said, but she couldn't suppress her smile.

"Have you ever talked to a vampire?"

"No. Oh, wait, yes, I have. A beauty contest I was in, I think maybe Miss Rockland Valley? He was one of the judges."

Of all the ways Sean the vampire could have responded, he said, "Did you win?"

She raised her eyes and looked directly into his. He could not have looked more bored and indifferent. It was strangely reassuring. "I did," she said.

She remembered the vampire judge's sardonic smile when she'd told him her "platform" was governmental tolerance toward supernatural creatures. And yet she'd never met a supernatural creature until that moment! What a naive twit she'd been. But her mother had thought such a topic very current and sure to attract the judges' attention. National and state governments had been struggling to regulate human-vampire relationships since vampires had announced their existence among humans five years before.

The Japanese development of a synthetic blood that could satisfy the nutritional needs of the undead had made such a revelation possible, and in the past five years, vampires had worked their way into the mainstream of society in a few countries. But Rue, despite her platform, had steered clear of contact with the undead. Her life was troublesome enough without adding an element as volatile as the undead to the mix.

"I just don't know much about vampires," she said apologetically.

Sean's crystalline blue eyes looked at her quite impersonally. "Then you will learn," he said calmly. He had a slight Irish accent; "learn" came out suspiciously like "lairrn."

She focused safely on his pointed chin. She felt more at ease—even if he was some kind of royalty, according to Sylvia. He seemed totally indifferent to her looks. That, in itself, was enough to relax her muscles.

"Will you dance?" he asked formally.

"Yes, thank you," she said automatically. Sylvia started the CD player again. She'd picked a different disk this time.

They waltzed first, moving so smoothly that Rue felt she was gliding across the floor without her feet touching the wood. "Swing next," he murmured, and her feet did truly leave the floor, her black skirt fluttering out in an arc, and then she was down again and dancing.

Rue enjoyed herself more than she had in years.

When it was over, when she saw that his eyes were still cool and impersonal, it was easy to turn to Sylvia and say, "If you decide you want me to work for you, I'd like to dance with Sean."

The flash of petulance on Thompson's face startled Rue.

Sylvia looked a bit surprised, but not displeased. "Great," she said. "It's not always easy…" Then she stopped, realizing any way she finished the sentence might be tactless.

Julie was beaming. "Then I'll dance with Thompson," she said. "I need a partner, too."

At least I made Julie happy, Rue thought. Rue's own partner-to-be didn't comment. Sean looked neither happy nor sad. He took her hand, bowed over it and let it go. She thought she had felt cold lips touch her fingers, and she shivered.

"Here's the drill," Sylvia said briskly. "Here's a contract for you to sign. Take it home with you and read it. It's really simple." She handed Rue a one-page document. "You can have your lawyer check it over, if you want."

Rue couldn't afford that, but she nodded, hoping her face didn't reflect her thoughts.

"We have personnel meetings once a month, Blue Moon and Black Moon together," Sylvia said briskly. "You have to come to those. If you don't show up for an engagement, and you're not in the hospital with a broken leg, you're fired. If you fight with Sean, it better not show in public."

"What are the meetings for?" Rue asked.

"We need to know one another by sight," Sylvia said. "And we need to share problems we have with clients. You can avoid a lot of situations if you know who's going to be trouble."

It was news to Rue that there could be "trouble." She crossed her arms over her chest, suddenly feeling cold in the plum leotard. Then she looked down at the contract and saw what she would be paid per appearance. She knew that she'd sign; she'd have the contract in Sylvia's hands the next day, so she could start work as soon as possible.

But after she'd gotten back to her cheap apartment, which lay in a decidedly unsafe part of Rhodes, Rue did study the contract. Nothing in the simple language was a surprise; everything was as Sylvia had told her. There were a few more rules, covering items like giving notice and maintaining any costumes she borrowed from the company stock, but the contract was basic. It was renewable, if both parties wanted, after a year.

The next morning, Rue bundled up in the brisk mid-west spring morning and set out early to the campus so she would have time to detour. There was a mail slot in the door of the old building that housed Blue Moon/Black Moon. Rue poked the folded paper through the slit, feeling profound relief. That night Sylvia called Rue to schedule her first practice session with Sean O'Rourke.

CHAPTER TWO

WEARING CUTOFF SWEATPANTS and a sleeveless T-shirt, Sean waited in the studio. The new woman wasn't late yet. She would be on time. She needed the job. He'd followed her home the night she'd auditioned. He'd been cautious all the years he'd been a vampire, and that had kept him alive for more than 275 years. One of his safety measures was making sure to know the people he dealt with, so Sean was determined to learn more about this Rue.

He didn't know what to think of her. She was poor, obviously. But she'd had years of dance lessons; she'd had good makeup, a good haircut, the good English of privilege. Could she be an undercover operative of some kind? If she were, wouldn't she have taken the opportunity to work for Black Moon, the only remotely interesting thing about Sylvia's enterprises? Perhaps she was a rich girl on a perverse adventure.

His first fifty years as a vampire, Sean O'Rourke had done his best to conceal himself in the world of humans. He'd stayed away from others of his kind; when he was with them, the temptation to explore his true nature had grown too strong. Sean had been abandoned by the man who'd made him what he was. He'd had no chance to learn the basic rules of his condition; in his ignorance, he'd killed unfortunates in the slums of Dublin. Gradually, Sean had learned that killing his victims wasn't necessary. A mouthful of blood could sustain him, if he had it every night. He'd learned to use his vampiric influence to blot out his victims' memories, and he'd learned to blot out his own emotions almost as successfully.

After fifty years, stronger and colder, he'd begun to risk the company of other vampires. He'd fallen in love a time or two, and it had always ended badly, whether the woman he loved was another vampire or a human.

His new partner, this Rue, was beautiful, one of the most beautiful women he'd seen in centuries. Sean could admire that beauty without being swayed by it. He knew something was wrong with the girl, something hidden inside her. He hadn't watched people, observed people, all these years without learning to tell when a human was concealing something. Maybe she was an agent for one of the fanatical organizations that had formed to force vampires back into the darkness of the shadows. Maybe she suffered from a drug addiction, or some physical condition she was hoping to hide for as long as possible.

Sean shrugged to himself. He'd speculated far too much about Rue's possibilities. Whatever her secret was, in time he would learn it. He wasn't looking forward to the revelation. He wanted to dance with her for a long time; she was light and supple in his arms, and she smelled good, and the swing of her thick mahogany hair made something in his chest ache.

Though he tried to deny it to himself, Sean looked forward to tasting her more than he'd looked forward to anything in decades.

THE PRACTICE ROOM WAS a larger studio behind the room in which she'd met Sylvia and the others. "Sean/Rue" was scrawled on the sign-up sheet for the six-thirty to eight o'clock time slot. Julie and Thompson would be practicing after them, Rue noticed.

She was nervous about being alone with the vampire. He was waiting for her, just as still and silent as he'd been two nights before. As a precaution, she'd worn a cross around her neck, tucked under the old gray leotard. The black shorts she'd pulled on over the leotard were made out of a shiny synthetic, and she'd brought ballet shoes, tap shoes and the T-strap character shoes she wore for ballroom dancing. She nodded to Sean by way of greeting, and she dumped the shoes out on the floor. "I didn't know what you'd want," she explained, all too aware that her voice was uneven.

"Why are the initials different?" he asked. Even his voice sounded dusty, as though it hadn't been used in years. To her dismay, Rue discovered that she found the slight Irish accent charming.

"What do you mean? Oh, on the shoe bag?" She sounded like an idiot, she thought, and bit her lip. She'd had the shoe bag for so many years, she simply didn't notice anymore that it was monogrammed.

"What is your real name?"

She risked a glance upward. The brilliant blue eyes were just blue eyes; they were fixed on her at the moment, but he wasn't trying to rope her in, or whatever it was they did. "It's a secret," she said, like a child. She smacked herself on the forehead.

"What is your true name?" He still sounded calm, but it was clear he was going to insist. Actually, Rue didn't blame him. She met his eyes. She was his partner. He should know.

"I go by Rue L. May. My name is Layla LaRue LeMay. My parents liked the song? You know it?" she asked doubtfully.

"Which version? The original one by Cream, or the slower Eric Clapton solo?"

She smiled, though it was an uncertain smile. "Original," she said. "In their wilder years, they thought it was cool to name their daughter after a song." It was hard to believe, now, that her parents had ever had years of not being afraid what people would think, that once they'd been whimsical. She looked down. "Please don't tell anyone my name."

"I won't." She believed him. "Where do your parents live now?" he asked.

"They're dead," she said, and he knew she was lying.

And though he would need to sample her blood to be sure, Sean also suspected that his new partner was living in fear.

AFTER THEY WARMED UP, that first practice session went fairly well. As long as they both concentrated on the dancing, the conversation was easy. When they touched on anything more personal, it wasn't.

Sean explained that they were almost never called on to tap dance. "People who hire us want something flashy, or something romantic," he said. "They want a couple who can tango, or a couple who can do big lifts, for the charity balls. If it's something like an engagement party or anniversary, they want a sexy, slow dance, always ending with the bite."

Rue admired how impersonally he said it, as if they were both professionals in this together, like actors rehearsing a scene. In fact, that was exactly appropriate, she decided.

"I've never done this," she said. "The biting thing. Ah, do you always bite the neck?" As if she didn't care, as if she was quite matter-of-fact about the finale. She was proud of how calm she sounded.

"That's what the audience likes. They can see it best, and it's traditional. In real life, of course—if I can use the phrase 'real life'—we can bite anywhere. The neck and the groin have the big arteries, so they're preferred. It isn't fatal. I'll only take a drop or two. We don't need much as we get older."

Rue could feel her face flood with color. This matched what she'd learned from the university's computers, though she'd felt obliged to have Sean confirm what she'd read. She needed to know all this, but she was embarrassed, just the same. It was like discussing sexual positions, rather than the more comparable eating customs: missionary vs. doggy-style, rather than forks vs. chopsticks.

"Let's try a tango," Sean said. Rue put on her character shoes. "Can you wear a higher heel?" her partner asked impersonally.

"Yes, I can dance in something higher, but that would put me too close to your height, don't you think?"

"I'm not proud," he said simply. "It's all in how it looks."

Aristocrat or not, he was a practical man. To Rue's

pleasure, Sean continued to be a great partner. He was very professional. He was patient, and since she was rusty, she appreciated his forbearance. As the session continued, Rue grew more confident. Her body began to recover its skills, and she began to enjoy herself immensely.

She hadn't had fun in forever.

They ended up with a "cool-down" dance, a dreamy forties romantic song performed by a big band. As the music came to a close, Sean said, "Now I'll dip you." Then he lowered her, until her back was almost parallel with the floor. And he held the position. A human couldn't have sustained it for long, but his arm under her shoulders was like iron. All she had to do was keep her graceful alignment with his body. "Then, I bite," he said, and mimed a nip at her neck. He felt her shiver and willed her to relax. But she didn't, and after a moment, he assisted her in standing up again.

"We could have a booking this weekend, if you feel you're up to it," he said. "We'd have to practice every night, and you'd have to have your costumes ready."

She was relieved to have a safe topic to latch on to. Julie and Thompson were standing by the door, waiting for their turn in the practice room. They were listening with interest.

"Sylvia said there was a wardrobe of costumes?"

"I'll show you," Sean said. He sounded as calm and indifferent as he had at the beginning of the session.

After she'd glanced in the room off Sylvia's office, where costumes were hanging in rows on rolling racks, she went to the ladies' room. As she was washing her hands, Julie came in. The young blonde looked especially happy, with flushed cheeks and a big smile.

"I gotta tell you," Julie said. "I'm really glad you picked Sean. I always thought Thompson was pretty hot, and Sean is as cold as they come."

"How long have you been dancing for Sylvia?" Rue asked. She wanted to steer clear of discussing her partner.

"Oh, a year. I have a day job, too, clerking at an insurance agency, but you know how hard it is to get along. I settled in Rhodes because I thought a city in the middle of the country would be cheaper than either coast, but it's hard for a girl to make it on her own."

Rue was able to agree with that wholeheartedly.

"Hard to understand why the vampires do this," she said.

"They gotta live, too. I mean, most of them, they want a nice place to live, clean clothes and so on."

"I guess I always thought all vampires were rich."

"Not to hear them tell it. Besides, Thompson's only been a vamp for twenty years."

"Wow," Rue said. She had no idea what difference that would make, but Julie clearly thought she was revealing a significant fact.

"He's pretty low down on the totem pole," Julie explained. "What's unusual is finding a vamp as old as Sean performing. Most of the vamps that old think it's beneath their dignity to work for a human." She looked a wee bit contemptuous of Sean.

Rue said, "You all have a good practice, Julie. I'll see you soon."

"Sure," Julie said. "Have a good week."

Rue hadn't meant to be abrupt. But she had some sympathy for Sean. Just like her, he was making a living doing what he did best, and he didn't have false pride about it. She could draw a lesson from that herself.

That sympathy vanished the next night, when Rue discovered that Sean was following her home. After getting off the bus, she caught the barest glimpse of him as she walked the last block to her apartment. She ran up the steps as quickly as she could, and tried to act normally as she unlocked the common door and climbed up to her tiny apartment. Slamming the door behind her, her heart hammering, she wondered what she'd let herself in for. With the greatest caution, she left the lights off and crept over to the window. She would see him outside, looking up. She knew it. She knew all about it.

He wasn't there. She fed her cat in the dark, able to see the cans and the dish by the light of the city coming in the windows. She looked again.

Sean wasn't there.

Rue sat down in the one chair she had, to think that over. Her heart quit hammering; her breathing slowed down. Could she have been mistaken? If she'd been a less-experienced woman she might have persuaded herself that was the case, but Rue had long since made up her mind not to second-guess her instincts. She'd seen Sean. Maybe he wanted to know more about his partner. But he hadn't watched her once she was inside.

Maybe he'd followed her to make sure she was safe, not to spy on her.

It was hard for Rue to pay attention in her History of the British Isles class the next morning. She was still fretting. Should she confront him? Should she stay silent? She'd let her hair go all straggly for class, as she usually did, and she tucked it behind her ear while she bent over her notebook. She was so jangled by her indecision that she let her mind ramble. Her professor caught her by surprise when he asked her what she thought of the policy of the British during the Irish potato famine, and she had a hard time gathering up an answer to give him. To make the day even more unpleasant, while Rue was working on a term paper in the college library, she realized that the brunette across the table was staring at her. Rue recognized that look.

"You're that girl, aren't you?" the girl whispered, after gathering her nerve together.

"What girl?" Rue asked, with a stony face.

"The girl who was a beauty queen? The one who—"

"Do I look like a beauty queen?" Rue asked, her voice sharp and cutting. "Do I look like any kind of queen?"

"Ah, sorry," stammered the girl, her round face flushing red with embarrassment.

"Then shut up," Rue snarled. Rudeness was the most effective defense, she'd found. She'd had to force herself, at first, but as time went on, rudeness had become all too easy. She outstayed the flustered student, too; the girl gathered up her books and pencils and fled the library. Rue had discovered that if she herself left first, it constituted an admission.

After dark, Rue set out to dance rehearsal with anger riding her shoulders.

She debated all the way to Blue Moon. Should she confront her new partner? She needed the job so badly; she liked dancing so much. And though it embarrassed her to admit it to herself, it was a real treat to sometimes look as good as she could, instead of obscuring herself.

Rue reached an internal compromise. If Sean behaved himself during this practice as well as he had during the first, if he didn't start asking personal questions, she would let it go. She could dance this Friday and make some money, if she could just get through the week.

She couldn't prevent the anger rolling around her like a cloud when he came in, but he greeted her quite calmly, and she crammed her rage down to a bearable level.

The dancing went even better that night. She was on edge, and somehow that sharpened her performance. Sean corrected a couple of arm positions, and she carefully complied with his suggestions. She made a few of her own.

If he followed her home, she didn't catch a glimpse of him. She began to relax about the situation.

The next night, he bit her.

"You don't want the first time to be in front of a crowd," he said. "You might scream. You might faint." He seemed quite matter-of-fact about it. "Let's do that thing we were working on, that duet to 'Bolero.'"

"Which is maybe the most hackneyed 'sexy dance' music in the world," she said, willing to pick a fight to cover her anxiety.

"But for a reason," Sean insisted. "Reason" came out "rayson." His Irish accent became more pronounced when he was upset, and Rue enjoyed hearing it. Maybe she would irritate him more often.

The duet they'd been working on was definitely a modern ballet. They started out with Sean approaching Rue, gradually winning her, their hands and the alignment of their bodies showing how much they longed to touch. Finally they entwined in a wonderful complicated meshing of arms and legs, and then Sean lowered her to finish up in the position they'd practiced the night before, leaning Rue back over his arm.

"We'll go very low this time," he said. "My right knee will touch the ground, and your legs should be extended parallel to my left leg. Put your left arm around my neck. Extend your right."

"Can you sustain that? I don't want to end up in a heap on the floor."

"If I brace my right hand on the floor, I can hold us both up." He sounded completely confident.

"You're the vampire," she said, shrugging.

"What's my offense?" He sounded stung.

"I didn't realize you were going to be the boss of us," she said, pleased to have jolted him out of his calm remove. "Aristocrat," Sylvia had called him. Rue knew all about people who thought their money provided them with immunity. She also knew she wasn't being reasonable, but she just couldn't seem to stop being angry.

"You'd like to be the one in charge?" he asked coldly.

"No," she said hastily, "It's just that I—"

"Then what?"

"Nothing! Nothing! Let's do the damn finale!" Every nerve in her body twanged with anxiety.

She got into position with a precision that almost snapped. Her right leg extended slightly in front of her, touching his left leg, which he swept slightly behind him. He took both her hands and clasped them to his chest. His eyes burned into hers. For the first time, his face showed something besides indifference.

It wasn't smart of me to have a fight with him right before he bites me, Rue told herself. But the music began. With a feeling of inevitability, Rue moved through the dance with the vampire. Once she moved too far to the right, and once she lost track of her place in the routine, but she recovered quickly both times. And then she was leaning back gracefully, her left arm around Sean's neck, her right arm reaching back, back, her hand in an appealing line. Sean was leaning over her, and she saw his fangs, and she jumped. She couldn't help it.

Then he bit her.

All her problems were over, her every muscle relaxed, and she was whole again. Her body was smooth and even, and everything inside her was perfect and intact.

The next thing Rue knew, she was weeping, sitting on the floor with her legs crossed. Sean was sitting by her side, leaning over with his arm around her shoulders.

"It won't be like this again," he said quietly, when he was sure she would understand him.

"Why did that happen? Is it that way for everyone?" She rubbed her face with the handkerchief Sean had handed her. Where he'd kept it, she couldn't imagine.

"No. The first time, you can see what makes you happiest."

Can, she noted. She was sure it could also hurt like hell. Sean had been generous.

"It will feel pleasant next time," Sean said. He didn't add, "As long as I want it to," but she could read between the lines. "But it won't be so overwhelming."

She was glad he'd had enough kindness to introduce her to this in private. Of course, she told herself, he hadn't wanted her to collapse on the dance floor, either. She would look stupid then, and so would he. "Can you tell what I'm feeling?" she asked, and she deliberately turned to look him in the eyes.

He met her dark eyes squarely. "Yes, in a muffled way," he said. "I can tell if you are happy, if you are sad—when I bite."

He didn't tell her that now he would always be able to tell how she felt. He didn't tell her that she had tasted sweeter than his memory of honey, sweeter than any human he'd ever bitten.

CHAPTER THREE

THEY DANCED TOGETHER FOR two months before Sean discovered something else about Rue. He wanted to call her "Layla," her real name, but she told him he would forget and call her that in front of someone who…and then she'd shut down her train of thought and asked him to call her Rue like everyone else.

He followed her home every night. Sean wasn't sure if she'd seen him that second night, but he made sure she never saw him again. He was careful. His intention, he told himself, was simply to make sure she arrived at her apartment safely, but he inevitably analyzed what he saw and drew conclusions.

In all those nights, Sean saw her speak to someone only once. Late one Wednesday night, a young man was sitting on the steps of her building. Sean could tell when Rue spotted him. She slowed down perceptibly. By then Sean had bitten her five times, and he could read her so closely that he registered a tiny flinch that would have gone unnoticed by anyone else.

Sean slid through the shadows silently. He maneuvered close enough to be able to help Rue if she needed it.

"Hello, Brandon." Rue didn't sound pleased.

"Hey, Rue. I just thought I might…if you weren't

busy… Would you like to go out for a cup of coffee?" He stood up, and now the streetlight showed Sean that the young man was a little older than the common run of students, maybe in his late twenties. He was very thin, but attractive in a solemn way.

Rue stood for a second, her head bowed, as if she were thinking what to do next. The parts of her that Sean had begun to know were brittle and fragile, forged by fear. But now he felt her kindness. She didn't want to hurt this man. But she didn't want to be in his company, either, and Sean was dismayed by how happy this made him.

"Brandon, you're so nice to think of taking me out for coffee," she said gently. "But I thought I made myself real clear last week. I'm not dating right now. I'm just not in that mode."

"A cup of coffee isn't a date."

Her back straightened. Sean considered stepping out of the shadows to stand by her side.

"Brandon, I'm not interested in spending time with you." Her voice was clear and merciless.

The man stared at her in shock. "That's so harsh," he said. He sounded as though he was on the verge of crying. Sean's lip curled.

"I've turned down your invitations three times, Brandon. I've run out of courtesy."

The man pushed past her and walked down the street in such a hurry that he almost knocked over a trash can. Rue swung around to watch him go, her stance belligerent. She might look ruthless to the human eye, but Sean could tell she was full of shame at being so stern with a man as guileless as a persistent puppy. When she went up the steps, Sean drifted down the street, wondering all the while about a beautiful woman who didn't date, a woman who camouflaged what she was under layers of unattractive clothing, a woman who was deliberately rude when her first inclination was to be kind.

Rue May—Layla LaRue LeMay—was hiding. But from what? Or who? He'd been dancing with her for two months now, and he didn't know anything about her.

"WE GOT A CALL FROM Connie Jaslow," Sylvia said two weeks later. "She wants to hire three couples to dance at a party she's putting on. Since it's warm, she's determined to have a tropical theme."

Rue and Sean, Julie and Thompson, and the third pair of dancers, Megan and Karl, were sitting in the padded folding chairs that Sylvia usually pushed against the walls. For this meeting, they'd pulled the chairs in front of Sylvia's desk.

"She'd like the gals to wear sort of Dorothy Lamour-style outfits, and the guys to wear loincloths and ankle bracelets. She wants some kind of 'native-looking' dance."

"Oh, for God's sake!" said Karl, disgust emphasizing his German accent.

"Connie Jaslow is one of our big repeat customers," Sylvia said. Her eyes went from one to the other of them. "I agree the idea is silly, but Connie pays good money."

"Let's see the costumes," Julie said. Rue had decided Julie was a good-hearted girl, and almost as practical as Sylvia.

"This was what she suggested," Sylvia said. She held

up a drawing. The women's costume showed belly button; it was a short flowered skirt, wrapped to look vaguely saronglike, with a matching bra. The long black wig was decorated with artificial flowers.

Rue tried to imagine what she would look like in it, and she thought she'd look pretty good. But then she re-evaluated the low-rider skirt. "It would be that low?" she asked.

"Yes," Sylvia said. "Showing your navel is in right now, and Connie wanted a sort of update to the island look."

"Can't do it," Rue said.

"Something wrong with your button?" teased Thompson.

"My stomach," Rue said, and hoped she could leave it at that.

"I can't believe that. You're as lean as you can be," Sylvia said sharply. She wasn't used to being thwarted.

Rue had a healthy respect for her employer. She knew Sylvia would demand proof. Better to get it over with. Dancers learned to be practical about their bodies. Rue stood abruptly enough to startle Sean, who was leaning against the wall by her chair. Rue pulled up her T-shirt, unzipped her jeans and found she'd worn bikini panties, so she hardly had to push them down. "This would show," Rue said, keeping her voice as level as she could.

The room was silent as the dancers gazed at the thick, jagged scar that ran just to the left of Rue's navel. It descended below the line of the white bikinis.

"Good God, woman!" Karl said. "Was someone trying to gut you?"

"Give me a hysterectomy." Rue pulled her clothes back together.

"We couldn't cover that with makeup," Sylvia said. "Or could we?"

The other two couples and Sylvia discussed Rue's scarred stomach quite matter-of-factly, as a problem to solve.

The debate continued while Rue sat silently, her arms crossed over her chest to hold her agitation in. She became aware that she wasn't hearing a word from Sean. Slowly, she turned to look up at her partner's face. His blue eyes were full of light. He was very angry, livid with rage.

The dispassionate attitudes of the others had made her feel a bit more relaxed, but seeing his rage, Rue began to feel the familiar shame. She wanted to hide from him. And she couldn't understand that, either. Why Sean, whom she knew better than any of the other dancers?

"Rue," Sylvia said, "are you listening?"

"No, sorry, what?"

"Megan and Julie think they can cover it up," Sylvia said. "You're willing to take the job if we can get your belly camouflaged?"

"Sure," she told Sylvia, hardly knowing what she was saying.

"All right, then, two Fridays from now. You all start working on a long dance number right away, faux Polynesian. You'll go on after the jugglers. Julie and Thompson are booked for a party this Saturday night, and Karl and Megan, you're doing a dinner dance at the Cottons' estate on Sunday. Sean, you and Rue are scheduled to open a 'big band' evening at the burn unit benefit."

Rue tried to feel pleased, because she loved dancing to big band music, and she had a wonderful forties dress to wear, but she was still too upset about revealing her scar. What had gotten into her? She'd tried her best to conceal it for years, and all of a sudden, in front of a roomful of relative strangers, she'd pulled down her jeans and shown it to them.

And they'd reacted quite calmly. They hadn't screamed, or thrown up, or asked her what she'd done to deserve that. They hadn't even asked who'd done it to her. To Rue's astonishment, she realized that she was more comfortable with this group of dancers than she was with the other college students. Yet most of those students came from backgrounds that were much more similar to hers than, say, Julie's. Julie had graduated from high school pregnant, had the baby and given it up to the parents of the father. Now she was working nonstop, hoping to gather enough money to buy a small house. If she could do that, she'd told Rue, the older couple would let her have the baby over for the weekends. Megan, a small, intense brunette, was dancing to earn money to get through vet school. She'd seen Rue's stomach and immediately begun thinking how to fix it. No horror, no questions.

The only one who'd reacted with deep emotion had been Sean. Why was he so angry? Her partner felt contempt for her, she decided. Scarred and marred, damaged. If Rue hadn't felt some measure of blame, she could have blown off Sean's reaction, but part of her had always felt guilty that she hadn't recognized trouble, hadn't recognized danger, when it had knocked on her door and asked her out for a date.

That night, when they both left the studio, Sean simply began walking by her side.

"What are you doing?" Rue asked, after giving him

a couple of blocks to explain himself. She stopped in her tracks.

"I am going in the same direction you are," he said, his voice calm.

"And how long are you gonna be walking in that direction?"

"Probably as far as your steps will take you."

"Why?"

There it was again, in his eyes, the rage. She shrank back.

"Because I choose to," he said, like a true aristocrat.

"Let me tell you something, buddy," she began, poking him in the chest with her forefinger. "You'll walk me home if I ask you to, or if I let you, not just because you 'choose' to. What will you do if I *choose* not to let you?"

"What will you do," he asked, "if I choose to walk with you, anyway?"

"I could call the police," she said. Being rude wasn't going to work on Sean, apparently.

"Ah, and could the police stop me?"

"Not human cops, maybe, but there are vamps on the force."

"And then you wouldn't have a partner, would you?"

That was a stumper. No, she wouldn't. And since vampires who wanted to dance for a living were scarce, she wouldn't be able to find another partner for a good long while. And that meant she wouldn't be working. And if she wasn't working…

"So you're blackmailing me," she said.

"Call it what you choose," he said. "I am walking you home." His sharp nose rose in the air as he nodded in the right direction.

Frustrated and defeated, Rue shouldered her bag again. He caught the bus with her, and got off with her, and arrived at her building with her, without them exchanging a word the whole way. When Rue went up the steps to the door, he waited until she'd unlocked it and gone inside. He could see her start up the inner stairs, and he retreated to the shadows until he saw a light come on in the second-floor front apartment.

After that, he openly walked her home every night, in silence. On the fourth night, he asked her how her classes were going. She told him about the test she'd had that day in geology. The next night, when he told her to have sweet dreams, he smiled. The *M* of his mouth turned up at the corners, and his smile made him look like a boy.

On the sixth night, a woman hailed Sean just as he and Rue got off the bus. As the woman crossed the street, Rue recognized Hallie, a Black Moon employee. Rue had met all the Black Moon people, but she did her best to steer clear of them all, both vampire and human. Rue could accept the other Blue Moon dancers as comrades. But the Black Moon performers made her shrink inside herself.

"Hey, what are you two up to?" Hallie said. She was in her late twenties, with curly brown hair and a sweet oval face. It was impossible not to respond to her good cheer; even Sean gave her one of his rare smiles.

"We just left practice," Sean said when Rue stayed silent.

"I just visited my mother," Hallie said. "She seems to be a little better."

Rue knew she had to speak, or she would seem like the most insufferable snob. *Maybe I am a snob,* she thought unhappily. "Is your mom in the hospital?"

"No, she's in Van Diver Home, two blocks down."

Rue had walked past there a couple of times, and thought what a grim place it was, especially for an old folks' home. "I'm sorry," she said.

"She's in the Alzheimer's wing." Hallie's hand was already waving off Rue's expression of sympathy. "If I didn't work for Sylvia, I don't know how I could pay the bills."

"You have another day job, too?"

"Oh, yes. Every day, and nights I don't work for Sylvia, I'm a cocktail waitress. In fact, I'm due back at work. I ran down to see Mom on my break. Good to see both of you."

And off Hallie hurried, her high heels clicking on the pavement. She turned into a bar on the next block, Bissonet's.

Rue and Sean resumed the short walk to Rue's building.

"She's no saint, but it's not as simple as you thought," Sean said when they'd reached her building.

"No, I see that." On an impulse, she gave him a quick hug, then quickly mounted the steps without looking back.

Two weeks later, Blue Moon's three male vampires and three human women were dressing in a remote and barren room in the Jaslow mansion. Connie Jaslow had no consideration for dancers' modesty, since she'd provided one room for both sexes. To an extent, Mrs. Jaslow was correct. Dancers know bodies; bodies were their business, their tools. At least there was an adjacent bathroom, and the women took turns going in to put on their costumes and straighten the black wigs, but the men managed without leaving.

Rick and Phil, the two vampires who ordinarily worked together at "specialty" parties for Black Moon, had polished a juggling act. They would go on first. They were laughing together (Phil only laughed when he was with Rick) as they stood clad only in floral loincloths. "At least we don't have to wear the wigs," the taller Rick said, grinning as he looked over the dancers.

"We look like a bunch of idiots," Julie said bluntly. She tossed her head, and the shoulder-length black wig fell back into place flawlessly.

"At least we're getting paid to look like idiots," Karl said. The driver of the van that had brought them all out to the Jaslow estate, Denny James, came in to tell Karl that the sound system was all set up and ready to go. Denny, a huge burly ex-boxer, worked for Sylvia part-time. Megan and Julie had told Rue that Denny had a closer relationship with Sylvia than employer/employee, much to Rue's astonishment. The ex-boxer hardly seemed the type to appeal to the sophisticated Sylvia, but maybe that was the attraction.

Anxious about the coming performance, Rue began to stretch. She was already wearing the jungle-print skirt, which draped around to look like a sarong, and matching bikini panties. The bra top matched, too, a wild jungle print over green. The shoulder-length wig swung here and there as she warmed up, and the pink artificial flower wobbled. Rue's stomach was a uniform color, thanks to Julie and Megan.

Karl had brought the CD with their music and given it to the event planner who'd designed the whole party, a weirdly serene little woman named Jeri. On the way into the estate, Rue had noticed that the driveway had been lined with flaming torches on tall poles. The waiters and waitresses were also in costume. Jeri knew how to carry through a theme.

Rue went over the whole routine mentally. Sean came to stand right beside her. On his way out the door with Phil, Rick gave her a kiss on the cheek for luck, and Rue managed to give him a happy smile.

"Nervous?" Sean asked. It came out, "Nairvous?"

"Yes." She didn't mind telling him. *Head up, shoulders square, chest forward, big smile, pretty hands.* "There. I'm okay now."

"Why do you do that? That little…rearrangement?"

"That's what my mother told me to do every time I went on stage, from the time I was five to the time I was twenty."

"You were on stage a lot?"

"Beauty pageants," Rue said slowly, feeling as though she were relating the details of someone else's life. "Talent contests. You name it, I was in it. It cost my parents thousands of dollars a year. I'd win something fairly often, enough to make the effort worth it, at least for my father." She began to sink down in a split. "Press down on my shoulders." His long, thin fingers gripped her and pressed. He always seemed to know how much pressure to apply, though she knew Sean was far stronger than any human.

"Did you have brothers or sisters?" he asked, his voice quiet.

"I have a brother," she said, her eyes closed as she felt her thighs stretch to their limit. She hadn't talked about her family in over a year.

"Is your brother a handsome man?"

"No," Rue said sadly. "No, he isn't. He's a sweet guy, but he's not strong."

"So you didn't win every pageant you entered?" Sean teased, changing the subject.

She opened her eyes and smiled, while rising to her feet very carefully. "I won a few," she said, remembering the glass-fronted case her mother had bought to hold all the trophies and crowns.

"But not all?" Sean widened his eyes to show amazement.

"I came in second sometimes," she conceded, mocking herself, and shot him a sideways look. "And sometimes I was Miss Congeniality."

"You mean the other contestants thought you were the sweetest woman among them?"

"Fooled them, huh?"

Sean smiled at her. "You have your moments." The sweetness of that downturned mouth, when it crooked up in a smile, was incredible.

"You knock my socks off, Sean," she said honestly. She was unable to stop herself from smiling back. He looked very strange in his costume: the flowered loincloth, ankle bracelets made of shells and the short black wig. Thompson was the only one who looked remotely natural in the get-up, and he was gloating about it.

"What does that mean?"

She shook her head, still smiling, and was a little relieved when Denny knocked on the door to indicate that Jeri, the party planner, had signaled that it was time for their appearance. Karl lined the dancers up and looked them over, making a last-minute adjustment here and there. "Stomach looks good," he said briefly, and Rue glanced down. "Julie and Megan did a good job," she admitted. She knew the scar was there, but if she hadn't been looking for it, she would have thought her own stomach was smooth and unmarred.

After Karl's last minute adjustment of the bright costumes and the black wigs, the six barefoot dancers padded down the carpeted hall to the patio door, and out across the marble terrace into the torch-lit backyard of the Jaslow estate. Rick and Phil loped past them on their way inside, burdened with the things they'd used in their act. "Went great," Rick said. "That backyard's huge."

"It's probably called the garden, not the backyard," Thompson muttered.

Karl said, "Sean, is this the sort of place you grew up in?"

Sean snorted, and Rue couldn't tell if he was deriding his former affluence, or indicating what he'd had had been much better.

Since Rue was shorter than Julie, she was in the middle when the three women stepped out across the marble terrace and onto the grass to begin their routine. Smiling, they posed for the opening bars of the drum music. Julie looked like a different person with the black wig on. Rue had a second to wonder if Julie's own mother would recognize her before the drums began. The routine began with a lot of hulalike hip twitching, the three women gradually rotating in circles. The intense pelvic motion actually felt good. The hand movements were simple, and they'd practiced and practiced doing them in unison. Rue caught a glimpse of Megan turning too fast and hoped the torchlight was obscuring

Megan's haste. In her sideways glance, Rue caught a glimpse of a face she'd hoped she'd never see again.

All the years of training she'd had in composure paid off. She kept her smile pasted on her face, she kept up with the dance, and she blanked her mind out. The only thought she permitted herself was a reminder—she'd thought even Julie's family wouldn't recognize her, in the costume and the wig. Neither would her own.

Maybe Carver Hutton IV wouldn't, either.

CHAPTER FOUR

THE MUSIC WAS MOSTLY DRUMS, and the beat was fast and demanding. While Megan, Julie and Rue held their positions, the men leaped out, and the crowd gave the expected "Oooooh" at how high the vampires could jump. Sean, Karl and Thompson began their wild dance around the women. It was a good opportunity for her to catch her breath. Without moving her head from its position, she looked over at the spot where she'd seen him standing. Now there was no one there who reminded her of Carver. Maybe it had just been an illusion. Relief swept through her like sweet, cool water through a thirsty throat.

When Sean came to lift her above his head, she gave him a brilliant smile. As he circled, stomping his feet to the beat, she held her pose perfectly, and when he let her fall into his waiting arms, she arched her neck back willingly for the bite. She was ready to feel better, to have that lingering fear erased.

He seemed to sense her eagerness. Before his fangs sank in, she felt his tongue trace a line on her skin, and her arm involuntarily tightened around his neck. As the overwhelming peace flooded her anxious heart, Rue wondered if she was becoming addicted to Sean. "Hi,

I'm Rue, and I'm a vampire junkie." She didn't want to become one of those pitiful fangbangers, people who would do almost anything to be bitten.

The audience gave them a round of applause as the women stood up, the men sweeping their arms outward to mark the end of the performance. The crowd goggled curiously at the two dots on the women's necks. Rue stepped forward with Julie and Megan to take her bow, and as she went down she thought she saw Carver Hutton again, out of the corner of her eye. When she straightened, he wasn't there. Was she delusional? She pasted her smile back onto her face.

The six of them ran into the house, waving to the guests as they trotted along, like a happy Polynesian dance troupe that just happened to (almost) all have Caucasian features. They were expected back out on the terrace in party clothes in fifteen minutes. Meanwhile, Denny James would be dismantling their sound system and loading it into the van, because an orchestra was set up to play live music.

When they were scrambling out of the costumes, Rue made her request. "Julie, Megan…do you think you could leave your wigs on?"

The other dancers stopped in the middle of changing and looked at her. Julie had pulled on some thigh-high hose and was buckling the straps of her heels, and Megan had pulled on a sheath dress and gotten her "native" skirt half off underneath it. The male dancers had simply turned their backs and pulled everything off, and now all three were in the process of donning the silk shirts and dress pants they'd agreed on ahead of time. Rick and Phil were helping Denny gather up the costumes and all the other paraphernalia, to store in the van.

But they were all startled by Rue's request. There was a moment of silence.

Julie and Megan consulted with each other in an exchanged glance. "Sure, why not?" Julie said. "Won't look strange. We're all wearing the same outfit. Same wig, why not?"

"But we won't be wearing ours," Karl said, not exactly as if he were objecting, but just pointing out a problem.

"Yeah," Megan said, "but we look cute in ours, and you guys look like dorks in yours."

Karl and Thompson laughed at the justice of that, but Sean was staring at Rue as if he could see her thoughts if he looked hard enough. Phil, who never seemed to talk, was looking at Rue, with worry creasing his face. For the first time, Rue understood that Phil knew who she was. Like the girl in the library, he'd matched her face to the newspaper photos.

The black wig actually looked better with the shining burgundy sheath than Rue's own mahogany hair would have. She would never have picked this color for herself. Megan was wearing a deep green, and Julie, bronze. The men were wearing shirts that matched their partner's dress. Burgundy was not Sean's color, either. They looked at each other and shrugged simultaneously.

Out on the terrace, minutes later, the three couples began dancing to music provided by the live band. After watching for a few minutes, other people began to join them on the smooth marble of the terrace, and the professional couples split up to dance with the guests. This was the part of the job that Rue found most stressful. It was also the most difficult for her partner, she'd noticed.

Sean didn't enjoy small talk with companions he hadn't chosen, and he seemed stiff. Thompson was a great favorite with the female guests, always, and Karl was much admired for his sturdy blond good looks and his courtesy, but Sean seemed to both repel and attract a certain class of women, women who were subtly or not so subtly dissatisfied with their lives. They wanted an exotic experience with a mysterious man, and no one did mysterious better than Sean.

John Jaslow, the host, smiled at Rue, and she took his hand and led him to the dance floor. He was a pleasant, balding man, who didn't seem to want anything but a dance.

Men were much easier to please, Rue thought cynically. Most men were happy if you smiled, appeared to enjoy dancing with them, flirted very mildly. Every now and then, she danced with one who was under the impression she was for sale. But she'd met hundreds of men like that while she was going through the pageant circuit, and she was experienced in handling them, though her distaste never ebbed. With a smile and a soothing phrase, she was usually able to divert them and send them away pacified.

Rue and John Jaslow were dancing next to Megan and her partner, who'd introduced himself as Charles Brody. Brody was a big man in his fifties. From the moment he'd taken Megan's hand, he'd been insinuating loudly that he would be delighted if she went to a hotel with him after the party.

"After all, you work for Sylvia Dayton, right?" Brody asked. His hand was stroking Megan's ribs, not resting on them. Rue looked up at her partner anxiously. John Jaslow looked concerned, but he wasn't ready to intervene.

"I work for Blue Moon, not Black Moon," Megan said, quietly but emphatically.

"And you're saying you just go home after one of these affairs, put on your jammies and go to bed by yourself?"

"Mr. Brody, that's exactly what I'm saying," Megan said.

He was quiet for a moment, and Rue and Mr. Jaslow gave each other relieved smiles.

"Then I'll find another woman to dance with, one who'll give a little," Brody said. Abruptly, he let go of Megan, but before he turned to stalk off the terrace, he gave the small dancer a hard shove.

The push was so unexpected, so vicious, that Megan didn't have time to catch herself. She was staggering backward and couldn't catch her balance. Moving faster than she'd thought she was able to move, Rue got behind Megan in time to keep her from hitting the ground.

In a second, Megan was back on her feet, and Mr. Jaslow and Sean were there.

The gasp that had arisen from the few people who'd watched the little episode with Brody gave way to a smattering of applause as Megan and bald Mr. Jaslow glided across the terrace in a graceful swoop.

"Smile," Rue said. Sean had gotten everything right but that. As he two-stepped away with her, his lips were stiff with fury.

"If this were a hundred years ago, I'd kill him," Sean said.

He smiled then, and it wasn't a nice smile. She saw his fangs.

She should have been horrified.

She should have been scandalized.

She should have been mortified.

"You're so sweet," she murmured, as she had to a thousand people during her life. This time, she meant it. Though Sean had defused the situation, she had no doubt he would rather have punched Brody, and she liked both reactions.

In five more minutes, their hour was up, and the six dancers eased themselves out of the throng of party guests. Wearily, they folded and bagged the costumes for cleaning and pulled on their street clothes. They were just too tired to be modest. Rue saw a pretty butterfly tattoo on Megan's bottom, and learned that Thompson had an appendectomy scar. But there was nothing salacious about knowing one another like this; they were comrades. Something about this evening had bonded them as no other event ever had.

It had been years since Rue had had friends.

Denny was waiting at the side entrance. The van doors were open, and when Rue scrambled into the back seat, Sean climbed in after her. There was a moment when all the others stared at Sean in surprise, since he always sat in front with Denny, then Megan climbed in after Sean. The middle row was filled with Karl, Julie and Thompson; Rick and Phil clambered in the front with Denny.

It was so pleasant to be sitting down in circumstances that didn't require polite chatter. Rue closed her eyes as the car sped down the long driveway. As they drove back to the city, it seemed a good idea to keep her eyes closed. Now, if she could just prop her head against something…

She woke up when the car came to a stop and the dome light came on. She straightened and yawned. She turned her head to examine her pillow, and found that she'd been sleeping with her head on Sean's shoulder. Megan was smiling at her. "You were out like a light," she said cheerfully.

"Hope I didn't snore," Rue said, trying hard to be nonchalant about the fact that she'd physically intruded on her partner.

"You didn't, but Karl did," Thompson said, easing his way out of the van and stretching once he was on the sidewalk.

"I only breathe loudly," Karl said, and Julie laughed.

"You gotta be the only vampire in the world who takes naps and snores," she said, but to take any sting out of her words, she gave him a hug.

Rue's eyes met Sean's. His were quite unreadable. Though she'd had such a good time with him before they had danced at the Jaslows', he was wearing his usual shuttered look.

"I'm sorry if you were uncomfortable the whole way back," she said. "I didn't realize I was so tired."

"It was fine," he said, and got out, holding out a hand to help her emerge. He unlocked the studio door; Karl and Thompson began unloading the sound system and the dancers set the costumes on a bench outside Sylvia's office. Denny drove off in the empty van.

The small group split up, Megan and Julie getting in the cab they'd called, Karl and Thompson deciding to go to Bissonet's, the bar where Hallie worked. "Why don't you come, Sean?" Karl asked. "You could use some type O."

"No, thanks," Sean said.

"Showing your usual wordy, flowery turn of phrase." Karl was smiling.

"I'll see Rue home," Sean said.

"Always the gentleman," Thompson said, not too fondly. "Sean, sometimes you act like you've got a poker up your ass."

Sean shrugged. He was clearly indifferent to Thompson's opinion.

Thompson's fangs ran halfway out.

Rue and Karl exchanged glances. In that moment, Rue could tell that Karl was worried about a quarrel between the other two vampires, and she took Sean's arm. "I'm ready," she said, and actually gave him a little tug as she started walking north. Sean's good manners required that he set off with her. They took the first two blocks at a good pace, and then turned to stand at the bus stop.

"What frightened you?" he said, so suddenly that she started.

She knew instantly what he was talking about: the seconds at the party when she'd thought she'd seen an all-too-familiar face. But she couldn't believe he'd noticed her fear. She hadn't missed a beat or a step. "How'd you know?" she whispered.

"I know you," he said, with a quiet intensity that centered her attention on him. "I can feel what you feel."

She looked up at him. They were under a streetlight, and she could see him with a stark clarity. Rue struggled inside herself with what she could safely tell him. He was waiting for her to speak, to share her burden with him. Still, she hesitated. She was out of the habit of confiding; but she had to be honest about how safe she felt when she was with Sean, and she could not ignore how much she'd begun to look forward to spending time with him. The relief from fear, from worry, from her sense of being damaged, was like warm sun shining on her face.

He could feel her growing trust; she could see it in his rare smile. The corners of his thin mouth turned up; his eyes warmed.

"Tell me," he said, in a voice less imperative and more coaxing.

What decided her against speaking out was fear for his safety. Sean was strong, and she was beginning to realize he was ruthless where she was concerned, but he was also vulnerable during the daylight hours. Rue followed another impulse; she put her arms around him. She spoke into his chest. "I can't," she said, and she could hear the sadness in her own voice.

His body stiffened under her hands. He was too proud to beg her, she knew, and the rest of the way to Rue's apartment, he was silent.

CHAPTER FIVE

SHE THOUGHT HE WOULD STALK off, offended, when they reached her place, but, to her surprise, he stuck with her. He held her bag while she unlocked the front door, and he mounted the stairs behind her. While she sure couldn't remember asking him up, Rue didn't tell him to leave, either. She found herself hoping he enjoyed the view all the way up both flights. She tried to remember if she'd made her bed and put away her nightgown that morning.

"Please, come in," Rue said. She knew the new etiquette as well as anyone. Vampires had to be invited into your personal dwelling the first time they visited.

Her cat came running to meet Rue, complaining that her dinner was overdue. The little black-and-white face turned up to Sean in surprise. Then the cat stropped his legs. Rue cast a surreptitious eye over the place. Yes, the bed was neat. She retrieved her green nightgown from the footboard and rolled it into a little bundle, depositing it in a drawer in an unobtrusive way.

"This is Martha," Rue said brightly. "You like cats, I hope?"

"My mother had seven cats, and she named them all, to my father's disgust. She told him they ate the rats in the barn, and so they did, but she'd slip them some milk or some scraps when we had them to spare." He bent to pick up Martha, and the cat sniffed him. The smell of vampire didn't seem to distress the animal. Sean scratched her head, and she began to purr.

The barn? Scraps to spare? That didn't sound too aristocratic. But Rue had no right, she thought unhappily, to question her partner.

"Would you like a drink?" she asked.

Sean was surprised. "Rue, you know I drink..."

"Here," she said, and handed him a bottle of synthetic blood.

She had prepared for his visit, counting on it happening sometime. She had spent some of the little money she had to make him feel welcome.

"Thank you," he said briefly.

"It's room temperature, is that all right? I can heat it in a jiffy."

"It's fine, thanks." He took the bottle from her and opened it, took a sip.

"Where are my manners? Please take off your jacket and sit down." She gestured at the only comfortable chair in the room, an orange velour armchair obviously rescued from a dump. When Sean had taken it (to refuse the chair would have offended her), she sat on a battered folding chair that had come from the same source.

Rue was trying to pick a conversational topic when Sean said, "You have some of the lipstick left on your lower lip."

They'd put on a lot of makeup for the dance, and she thought she'd removed it all before they'd left the Jaslow estate. Rue thought of how silly she must look with a big crimson smudge on her mouth. "Excuse me for a second," she said, and stepped into the tiny bathroom. While she was gone, Sean, moving like lightning, picked up her address book, which he'd spotted lying by the telephone.

He justified this bit of prying quite easily. She wouldn't tell him anything, and he had to know more about her. He wasn't behaving like any aristocrat, that was for sure, but he easily suppressed his guilt over his base behavior.

Flipping through the pages, Sean copied as many numbers as he could on a small piece of notebook paper from Rue's pile of school materials. Several were in one town, Pineville, which had a Tennessee area code. He'd had a vampire friend in Memphis a few years before, and he recognized the number. He'd just replaced the address book when he heard the bathroom door open.

"You're taking the history of my country," Sean said, reading the spines of the textbooks piled on the tiny table that served as Rue's desk.

"It's the history of all the British Isles," she said, trying not to grin. "But yes, I am. It's an interesting course."

"What year have you reached in your course of study?"

"We're talking about Michael Collins."

"I knew him."

"What?" Her mouth fell open, and she knew she must look like an idiot. For the first time, she realized the weight of the years on Sean's shoulders, the knowledge of history and people that filled his head. "You knew him?"

Sean nodded. "A fiery man, but not to my taste."

"Could—would—you talk to my class about your recollections?"

Sean looked dismayed. "Oh, Rue, it was so long ago. And I'm not much of a crowd pleaser."

"That's not true," she said, adding silently, *You please me.* "Think about it? My professor would be thrilled. She's a nut about everything Irish."

"Oh, and where's she from?"

"Oklahoma."

"A far way from Ireland."

"You want another drink?"

"No." He looked down at the bottle, seemed surprised he'd drained it. "I must be going, so you can get a little sleep. Do you have classes tomorrow?"

"No, it's Saturday. I get to sleep in."

"Me, too."

Sean had actually made a little joke, and Rue laughed.

"So do you sleep in a regular bed?" she asked. "Or a coffin, or what?"

"In my own apartment I have a regular bed, since the room's light-tight. I have a couple of places in the city where I can stay, if my apartment's too far away when it gets close to dawn. Like hostels for vampires. There are coffins to sleep in, at those places. More convenient."

Rue and Sean stood. She took the empty bottle from him and leaned backward to put it by her sink. Suddenly the silence became significant, and her pulse speeded up.

"Now I'll kiss you good-night," Sean said deliberately. In one step he was directly in front of her, his hand behind her head, his spread fingers holding her in exactly the right position. Then his mouth was on Rue's, and after a moment, during which Rue held very still, his tongue touched the seam of her lips. She parted them.

There was the oddity of Sean's mouth being cool; and the oddity of kissing Sean, period. She was finally sure that Sean's interest in her was that of a man for a woman. For a cool man, he gave a passionate kiss.

"Sean," she whispered, pulling back a little.

"What?" His voice was equally as quiet.

"We shouldn't…"

"Layla."

His use of her real name intoxicated her, and when he kissed her again, she felt only excitement. She felt more comfortable with the vampire than she'd felt with any man. But the jolt she felt, low down, when his tongue touched hers, was not what she'd call comfortable. She slid her arms around his neck and abandoned herself to the kiss. When Rue felt his body pressing against her, she knew he found their contact equally exciting.

His mouth traveled down her neck. He licked the spot where he usually bit her. Her body flexed against his, involuntarily.

"Layla," he said, against her ear, "who did you see that frightened you so much?"

It was like a bucket of cold water tossed in her face. Everything in her shut down. She shoved him away from her violently. "You did this to satisfy your curiosity? You thought if you softened me up, I'd answer all your questions?"

"Oh, of course," he said, and his voice was cold with anger. "This is my interrogation technique."

She lowered her face into her hands just to gain a second of privacy.

She was half inclined to take him literally. He was acting as if she was the unreasonable one, as if all the details of her short life should belong to him.

There was a knock on the door.

Their eyes met, hers wide with surprise, his questioning. She shook her head. She wasn't expecting anyone.

Rue went to the door slowly and looked through the peephole. Sean was right behind her, moving as silently as only vampires could move, when she unlocked the door and swung it open.

Thompson stood there, and Hallie. Between the two, awkwardly, they supported Hallie's partner, David. David was bleeding profusely from his left thigh. His khakis were soaked with blood. The vampire's large dark eyes were open, but fluttering.

Thompson's gaze was fixed on Rue; when he realized that Sean was standing behind her, he was visibly startled.

"Oh, come in, bring him in!" Rue exclaimed, shocked. "What happened?" She spared a second to be glad none of her neighbors seemed to be up. She shut the door before any of them roused.

Hallie was sobbing. Her tears had smeared her heavy eye makeup. "It was because of me," she sobbed. "Thompson and Karl came in the bar. David was already there, he'd been having words with this jerk…." While she was trying to tell Rue, she was helping David over to Rue's bed. Thompson was not being quite as much assistance as he should have been.

Sean whipped a towel from the rack in the bathroom and spread it on Rue's bed before the two eased the wounded David down. Hallie knelt and swung David's legs up, and David moaned.

"It was the Fellowship," Thompson said as Hallie unbuckled David's belt and began to pull his sodden slacks down.

The Fellowship of the Sun was to vampires as the Klan was to African Americans. The Fellowship purported to be a civic organization, but it functioned more like a church, a church that taught its adherents the religion of violence.

"The other night I turned down this guy in the bar," Hallie said. "He just gave me the creeps. Then he found out I worked for Black Moon, and that I performed with David, you know, for the show, and he was waiting for me tonight…."

"Take it easy," Rue said soothingly. "You're gonna hyperventilate, Hallie. Listen, you go wash your face, and you get a bottle of TrueBlood for David, because he needs some blood. He's gonna heal."

Snuffling, Hallie ducked into the bathroom.

"He decided to get Hallie tonight, and David intervened?" Sean asked Thompson quietly. Rue listened with one ear while she stanched the bleeding by applying pressure with a clean kitchen towel. It rapidly reddened. She was not as calm as she'd sounded. In fact, her hands were shaking.

"David likes her, and she's his partner," Thompson said, as if David's intervention required an excuse. "Karl had left earlier, and David and I came out just in time to catch the show. The bastard had his arm wrapped around Hallie's neck. But he dropped her and went for David real fast, with a knife."

"Out on the street, or in the bar?"

"Behind the bar, in the alley."

"Where's the body?"

Rue stiffened. Her hands slipped for a moment, and the bleeding began again. She pressed harder.

"I took him over the rooftops and deposited him in an alley three blocks away. David didn't bite him. He just hit him—once."

Rue knew no one was thinking of calling the police. And she was all too aware that justice wasn't likely to be attainable.

"He'll heal faster if he has real blood, right?" she said over her shoulder. She hesitated. "Shall I give him some?" She tried to keep her voice even. She had hardly exchanged ten words with David, who was very brawny and very tall. He had long, rippling black hair and a gold hoop in one ear. She knew, through Megan and Julie, that David was often booked to strip at bridal showers, as well as performing with Hallie in private clubs. In her other life, Rue would have walked a block to avoid David. Now she was pulling up the sleeve of her sweater to bare her wrist.

"No," said Sean very definitely. He pulled the sleeve right back down, and she stared at him, her mouth compressed with irritation. She might have felt a smidgen of relief, but Sean had no right to dictate to her.

Hallie had emerged from the bathroom, looking much fresher. "Let Sean give blood, Rue," she said, reading Rue's face correctly. "It won't make him weak, like it would you. If Sean won't, I will."

David, who'd been following the conversation at least a little, said, "No, Hallie. I have bitten you already three times this week." David had a heavy accent, perhaps Israeli.

Without further ado, Sean knelt by the bed and held his wrist in front of David. David took Sean's arm in both his hands and bit. A slight flexing of Sean's lips was the only sign that he'd felt the fangs. They all watched as David's mouth moved against Sean's wrist.

"Sean, what a dark horse you are, me boyo, visiting the lady here after hours." Thompson's attempt at an Irish accent was regrettable. His eyes lit on the empty TrueBlood bottle by the sink. "And her all ready for your arrival."

"Oh, shut up, Thompson." Rue was too tired to think of being polite. "As soon as Sean finishes his, ah, donation, all of you can leave, except David. He can rest here for a while until he feels well enough to go."

After a few minutes, David put Sean's arm away from him, and Sean rolled his own sleeve over his wrist. Moving rather carefully, Sean picked up his jacket, carefully draped it over his arm.

"Good night, darlin'," he said, giving her a quick kiss on the cheek. "Kick David out after a couple of hours. He'll be well enough by then."

"I'll stay," Hallie said. "He got hurt on account of me, after all."

Sean looked relieved. Thompson looked disgruntled. "I'll be shoving off, then," he said. Hallie thanked him very nicely for helping her with David, and he was unexpectedly gracious about waving her gratitude away.

"We'll practice Sunday night," Sean said to Rue, his hand on the doorknob. "Can you be there at eight?" He'd been making plans for Saturday night while David had been taking blood from his wrist.

"I forgot to tell you," Thompson said. "Sylvia left a message on my cell. We have a company meeting Sunday night, at seven." It would just be dark at seven, so the vampires could attend.

"I'll see you there, Rue," Sean said. "And we can practice, after."

"All right," Rue said, after a marked pause.

Thompson said, "Good night, Rue, Hallie. Feel better, David."

"Good night, all," she said, and shut the door on both of them. She had one more bottle of synthetic blood, which she gave to David. She sat down in the chair while Hallie perched on the bed with David as he drank it. She tried valiantly to stay awake, but when she opened her eyes, she found two hours had passed, and her bed was empty. The bloody towels had been put to soak in the bathtub in cold water, and the empty bottles were in the trash.

Rue was relieved. "You and me, Martha," she said to the cat, who'd come out of hiding now that the strangers were gone. Rue's bed looked better than anything in the world, narrow and lumpy as it was. In short order, she'd cleaned her face and teeth and pulled on her pajamas. Martha leaped onto the bed and claimed her territory, and Rue negotiated with her so she'd have room for her own legs.

Rue was really tired, but she was also shaken. After all, there was a human dead on the street. She waited to feel a wave of guilt that never hit shore. Rue knew that if Hallie had been by herself, it would be Hallie lying bleeding on the street.

Been there, done that, Rue told herself coldly. *And all I got were the lousy scars to prove it.*

As for the shock she'd gotten at the Jaslows', a glimpse of the face she feared above all others, she was now inclined to think she'd imagined it. He would have made sure she noticed him, if he'd known she was there. He would have come after her again.

He'd sworn he would.

But it was funny that tonight, of all nights, she'd thought she'd seen him. At first, she'd imagined him everywhere, no matter how many times she'd called the police station to make sure he was still in the hospital. Maybe, once again, it was time to give Will Kryder a call again.

She imagined Sean lying in a coffin and smiled, just a curve of the lips before she drifted off to sleep.

Actually, Sean was on the road.

SEAN HAD A FEELING HE WAS doing something wrong, going behind Rue's—Layla's—back like this, but he was determined to do it anyway. If he'd asked Thompson to help, he had no doubt the younger vampire could have tracked down any information Sean needed on the damned computer. But Sean had never gotten used to the machines; it might take him twenty more years to accept them.

Like cars. Cars had been tough, too. Sean hadn't learned to drive until the sixties. He had loved phonographs from their inception, though, because they'd provided music for dancing, and he had bought a CD player as soon as he could. Words were hard for Sean, so dancing had always been his means of expression, from the time he'd become free to dance.

So here he was, off to collect information the old-fashioned way. He would get to Pineville tonight, find a place to hole up until he woke the next night, and then get his investigation under way.

Sean knew Rue had a fear that ran so deep she couldn't speak of it. And once he'd decided Rue was his business, it had become his job to discover what she feared. He had done some changing through the centuries, but the way he'd grown up had ingrained in him the conviction that if a man claimed a woman as his family—or his mate—he had to protect her.

And how could he protect her if he didn't understand the threat?

While Rue rose late to have a leisurely breakfast, clean her apartment and wash her clothes, Sean, who had consulted his housing directory, was sleeping in the vampire room of the only motel large enough to boast one, right off the interstate at the exit before Pineville. He had a feeling it was the first time the clerk had rented the room to an actual vampire. He'd heard that human couples sometimes took the room for some kinky playacting. He found that distasteful. The room—windowless, with two aligned doors, both with heavy locks, and a black velour curtain in between—had two coffins sitting side by side on the floor. There was a small refrigerator in the corner, with several bottles of synthetic blood inside. There was a minimalist bathroom. At least the coffins were new, and the padding inside was soft. Sean had paid an exorbitant amount for this Spartan accommodation, and he sighed as he undressed and climbed into the larger of the two coffins. Before he lay down, he looked over at the inner door to make sure all its locks were employed. He pulled the lid down, seconds before he could feel the sun come up.

Then he died.

CHAPTER SIX

WHEN SEAN FELT LIFE FLOWING back into his body that night, he was very hungry. He woke with his fangs out, ready to sink into some soft neck. But it was rare that Sean indulged himself in fresh human blood; these days, the sips he took from Rue were all he wanted. He pulled the synthetic blood from the refrigerator, and since he didn't like it cold, he ran hot water in the bathroom and set the bottle in the sink while he showered. He hated to wash the scent of Rue from his skin, but he wanted to seem as normal as possible to the people he talked to tonight. The more humanlike a vampire could look and act, the more likely humans were to be open to conversation. Sean had noticed that interactions were easier for Thompson, who still had clear memories of what it was like to breathe and eat.

He'd written down the numbers and names from Rue's book, just in case his memory played tricks with him. One of the numbers was self-explanatory—"Mom and Dad," she'd written by it. "Les," she'd written by another, and that was surely one he would have to explore; a single man might be a rival. The most interesting numbers were by the notation "Sergeant Kryder." She'd labeled one number "police station" and the second number "home."

Pineville looked like almost any small town. It seemed to be dominated by one big business—Hutton Furniture Manufacturing, a huge plant that ran around the clock, Sean noted. The sign in front of the library read Camille Hutton Library, and the largest church complex boasted a whole building labeled Carver Hutton II Family Life Center.

The tire company was owned by a Hutton, and one of the car dealerships, too.

There was no sign crediting the Huttons with owning the police force, but Sean suspected that might be close to the truth. He found the station easily; it was right off the town square, a low redbrick building. The sidewalk from the parking area to the front door was lined with azaleas just about to bloom. Sean opened the swinging glass door to see a young policeman with his feet up on the counter that divided the public and private parts of the front room. A young woman in civilian clothes—short and tight civilian clothes—was using a copier placed against the wall to the left, and the two were chatting as Sean came in.

"Yes, sir?" said the officer, swinging his feet to the floor.

The young woman glanced at Sean, then did a double take. "Vampire," she said in a choked voice.

The man glanced from her to Sean in a puzzled way. Then he seemed to take in Sean's white face for the first time, and he visibly braced his shoulders.

"What can I do to help you, sir?" he asked.

"I want to speak with Sergeant Kryder," Sean said, smiling with closed lips.

"Oh, he retired," called the girl before the young man

could answer. The man's name tag read "Farrington." He wasn't pleased at the girl's horning in on his conversation with the vampire.

"Where might I find him?" Sean asked.

Officer Farrington shot a quelling glance at the girl and pulled a pencil out of his drawer to draw Sean a map. "You take a left at the next stop sign," he told Sean. "Then go right two blocks, and it's the white house on the corner with the dark green shutters."

"Might be gone," said the girl sulkily.

"Barbara, you know they ain't left yet."

"Packing up, I heard."

"Ain't left yet." Farrington turned to Sean. "The Kryders are moving to their place in Florida."

"I guess it was time for him to retire," Sean said gently, willing to learn what he could.

"He took it early," the girl said. "He got all upset about the Layla LeMay thing."

"Barbara, shut up," Officer Farrington said, his voice very sharp and very clear.

Sean tried hard to look indifferent. He said, "Thank you very much," and left with the instructions, wondering if they'd call ahead to the ex-sergeant, warn him of Sean's impending visit.

SERGEANT KRYDER HAD INDEED gotten a call from the police station. His front light was on when Sean parked in front of his modest house. Sean didn't have a plan for interrogating the retired policeman. He would play it by ear. If Rue had written the man's phone number in her book, then the man had befriended her.

Sean knocked at the door very gently, and a slim,

clean-shaven man of medium height with thinning fair hair and a guarded smile opened the door. "Can I help you?" the man asked.

"Sergeant Kryder?"

"Yes, I'm Will Kryder."

"I would like to speak with you about a mutual friend."

"I have a mutual friend with a vampire?" Kryder seemed to catch himself. "Excuse me, I didn't mean to offend. Please come in." The older man didn't seem sure about the wisdom of inviting Sean in, but he stood aside, and Sean stepped into the small living room. Cartons were stacked everywhere, and the house looked bare. The furniture was still there, but the walls were blank, and none of the normal odds and ends were on the tables.

A dark-haired woman was standing in the doorway to the kitchen, a dish towel in her hand. Two cats rubbed her ankles, and a little Pekingese leaped from the couch, barking ferociously. He stopped when he got close to Sean. He backed up, whining. The woman actually looked embarrassed.

"Don't worry," Sean said. "You can never tell with dogs. Cats generally like us." He knelt and held out a hand, and the cats both sniffed it without fear. The Pekingese retreated into the kitchen.

Sean stood, and the woman extended her hand. She had an air of health and intelligence about her that was very appealing. She looked Sean in the eyes, apparently not knowing that he could do all kinds of things with such a direct look. "I'm Judith," she said. "I apologize for the appearance of the house, but we're leaving in two days. When Will retired, we decided to move down to our Florida house. It's been in Will's family for years."

Will had been watching Sean intently. "Please have a seat," he said.

Sean sank into the armchair, and Will Kryder sat on the couch. Judith said, "I'll just go dry the dishes," and vanished into the kitchen, but Sean was aware that she could hear them if she chose.

"Our mutual friend?" Will prompted.

"Layla."

Will's face hardened. "Who are you? Who sent you here?"

"I came here because I want to find out what happened to her."

"Why?"

"Because she's scared of something. Because I can't make it go away unless I know what it is."

"Seems to me if she wanted you to know, she would tell you herself."

"She is too frightened."

"Are you here to ask me where she is?"

Sean was surprised. "No. I know where she is. I see her every night."

"I don't believe you. I think you're some kind of private detective. We knew someone would be coming sooner or later, someone like you. That's why we're leaving town. If you think you can get rid of us easy, let me tell you, you can't." Will's pleasant face was set in firm lines. He suddenly had a gun in his lap, and it was pointed at Sean.

"It's easy to see you haven't met a vampire before," Sean said.

"Why is that?"

Before Will could pull the trigger, Sean had the gun. He bent the barrel and tossed it behind him.

"Judith!" Will yelled. "Run!" He dove for Sean, apparently intending to grapple with Sean until Judith could get clear.

Sean held the man still by clamping Kryder's hands to his sides. He said, "Calm yourself, Mr. Kryder." Judith was in the room now, a butcher knife in her hands. She danced back and forth, reluctant to stab Sean but determined to help her husband.

Sean liked the Kryders.

"Please be calm, both of you," he said, and the quiet of his voice, the stillness of his posture, seemed to strike both of the Kryders at the same time. Will stopped struggling and looked at Sean's white face intently. Judith lowered the knife, and Sean could tell she was relieved to be able to.

"She calls herself Rue May now," he told them. "She's going to the university, and she has a cat named Martha."

Judith's eyes widened. "He does know her," she said.

"He could have found that out from surveillance." Will was not so sure.

"How did you meet her?" Judith asked.

"I dance with her. We dance for money."

The couple exchanged a glance.

"What does she do before she goes on stage?" Judith asked suddenly.

"Head up, chest out, shoulders square, big smile, pretty hands." Sean smiled his rare smile.

Will Kryder nodded at Judith. "I reckon you can let go of me now," he told Sean. "How is she?"

"She's lonely. And she saw something the other night that scared her."

"What do you know about her?"

"I know she was a beauty queen. I know she danced in a lot of contests. I know she never seems to hear from her family. I know she has a brother. I know she's hiding under another name."

"Have you seen her stomach?"

"The scars, yes."

"You know how she got that way?" Kryder didn't seem to be concerned with how Sean had come to see the scars.

Sean shook his head.

"Judith, you tell him."

Judith sat on the couch beside her husband. Her hands clasped tightly in her lap, she appeared to be organizing her thoughts.

"I taught her when she was in tenth grade," Judith said. "She'd won a lot of titles even then. Layla is just…beautiful. And her mother pushed and pushed. Her mother is an ex-beauty queen, and she married Tex LeMay after she'd had two years of college, I think. Tex was a handsome man, still is, but he's not tough, not at all. He let LeeAnne push him around at home, and at work he let his boss stomp on what was left of his…manhood."

Sean didn't have to feign his interest. "His boss?"

"Carver Hutton III." Will's face was rigid with dislike as he spoke the name.

"The family that owns this town."

"Yes," Judith said. "The family that owns this town. That's who Tex works for. The other LeMay kid, Les, was always a dim bulb compared to Layla. Les is a good boy, and I think he's kept in touch with Layla—did you say she calls herself Rue these days? Les is off at college now, and he doesn't come home much."

"Carver IV came back from his last year of college one Christmas, two years ago," Will said. "Layla'd been elected Christmas Parade Queen, and she was riding in the big sleigh—'course, it's really a horse-drawn wagon, we don't get snow every year—and she was wearing white, and a sparkly crown. She looked like she was born to do that."

"She's a sweet girl, too," Judith said unexpectedly. "I'm not saying she's an angel or a saint, but Layla's a kind young woman. And she's got a backbone like her mother. No, I take that back. Her mother's got a strong will, but her backbone doesn't even belong to her. It belongs to the Social God."

Will laughed, a small, choked laugh, as if the familiar reference sparked a familiar response. "That's the god that rules some small towns," he said to Sean. "The one that says you have to do everything exactly correct, follow all the rules, and you'll go to heaven. Social heaven."

"Where you get invited to all the right places and hang around with all the right people," Judith elaborated.

Sean was beginning to have a buzzing feeling in his head. He recognized it as intense anger.

"What happened?" he asked. He was pretty sure he knew.

"Carver asked Layla out. She was only seventeen. She was flattered, excited. He treated her real well the first two times, she told me. The third time, he raped her."

"She came over here," Judith said. "Her mom wouldn't listen, and her dad said she must be mistaken. He asked her didn't she wear a lot of perfume and makeup, or a sexy dress." Judith shook her head. "She'd—it was her first time. She was a mess. Will called the chief of police at the time. He wasn't a monster," Judith said softly. "But he wasn't willing to lose his job over arresting Carver."

"She shut herself in the house and wouldn't come out for two weeks," Will said. "Her mother called us, told us to quit telling lies about the Huttons. She said Layla had just misunderstood the situation. Her exact words."

"Then," said Judith heavily, "Layla found out she was pregnant."

The buzzing in Sean's head grew louder, more insistent. He had never felt like this before, in his hundreds of years.

"She called Carver and told him. I guess she thought something so serious would bring him to his senses. Maybe she imagined that his parents had brought on all his violence. Maybe she thought he would do right by her somehow. She was just seventeen. I don't know what she thought. Maybe she wanted him to take her to a doctor, I don't know. She didn't want to tell her parents."

"He decided to take care of it himself," Sean said.

"Yeah," Will said. "He lost his mind. Usually, he can act like a real person when other people are around." Will Kryder sounded as detached as if he were discussing the habits of an exotic animal, but his hands were clasped in front of him so tightly that they were white. "Carver couldn't maintain the facade that night. He pulled up in front of the LeMays' house, and Layla came out, without saying anything to Tex or LeeAnne about where she was going. But Les was watching out the window, and he saw…he saw…"

"After he socked her in the face a few times, he broke his soda bottle and used that," Judith said simply. There was a long moment of silence. "Les got him off in time to save Layla's life, by hitting Carver with his baseball bat…he was on the high school team, then."

"Go on," Sean managed to say. They'd been lost in these tragic memories, but when they heard his voice, they looked up, to be absolutely terrified by Sean's face. "I'm not angry with you," Sean said, very quietly. "Go on."

"The scene at the hospital was—you can imagine," Will said, his voice weary. "She lost the baby, of course, and there was considerable damage. Permanent damage. She was in the hospital for a while."

"No one could ignore *that,*" Judith said bitterly. "But the Huttons got a good lawyer, of course, and he made a case for insanity. Here in Pineville, of course, a Hutton won't get convicted of jaywalking. He was declared temporarily insane, and the judge sentenced him to time in a mental institution and ordered his family to pay all Layla's medical expenses. He did grant Layla a restraining order against Carver ever contacting her again, or even coming within a hundred feet of her. I guess that's worth the paper it's printed on. When the mental doctors decided Carver was 'stabilized,' he could be released, and he had to go through so many courses of outpatient anger management and other therapy. That took four years." She shook her head. "Of course, that doesn't mean jack."

"He mutilates Layla, he causes the death of his own

child in her womb, and after a token sentence, he walks free." Sean shook his head, his expression remote. "Since I've lived in America, I've admired its justice system. So much better than when I was a boy in Ireland, when children could be hung for stealing bread when they were hungry. But this isn't any better."

The Kryders both looked embarrassed, as if they were personally responsible for the injustice. "That's another reason we're moving," Will said. "Sooner or later, when we least expect it, Carver III will make us pay for backing Layla up. She stayed with us some, when she was convalescing. She didn't want to see her parents. Les used to come over, visit her. Not LeeAnne. Not Tex."

Sean didn't express incredulity, and he didn't comment on Layla's family's behavior. He'd seen worse in his long life, but he hadn't seen worse done to someone he cared about as much as he cared about Layla LaRue LeMay.

"Does she call you?" Sean asked.

"Yes, she does, from time to time. She'll call here, or she'll call the station to talk to Will, to find out if Carver's out yet."

"And is he?"

"Yes. After four years, he's off all supervision now. He's footloose and fancy-free."

"And is he living here?"

"No. He left town right away."

"She saw him," Sean said out loud.

"Oh, no. Where?"

"At a party, where we were dancing."

"Did he approach her?"

"No."

"Did he see her?" Judith had hit the nail on the head.

Sean said slowly, "I don't know." Then he said, "But I have to get back. Now."

Will said, "I hope you're planning on being good to her. If I hear different, I'll come back and track you down with a stake in my hand. She's had enough trouble."

Sean stood and bowed, in a very old-fashioned way. "We'll see you in Florida," he said.

He left Pineville, pushing the rental car to its limit, so he could make the last plane that would get him into the city in time to find a daytime resting place. There was a safe apartment very close to the airport, maintained by the vampire hierarchy. He called ahead to reserve a coffin, and got on the plane after making sure there was an emergency space in the tail where he could wait if sunlight caught them. But all went well, and he was in a room with three other occupied coffins by the time the sun came up.

CHAPTER SEVEN

THE PERSONNEL OF BLUE MOON Entertainment and Black Moon Productions were draped around the big practice room in various positions of weariness. It was a scant hour after darkness had fallen, and some of the vampires looked sluggish. Every one of them clutched a bottle of synthetic blood. Most of the humans had coffee mugs.

Rue had come in full disguise. The more she'd thought about the glimpse she'd had of the man who'd looked so much like Carver Hutton IV, the more spooked she'd gotten. Between that fear and her upsetting spat with Sean, and the remembered tingle she'd felt when they kissed, she hadn't been worth anything during the weekend so far. She'd performed her regular weekend chores, but in a slapdash fashion. She hadn't been able to study at all.

When Sean came in, wearing sweatpants and a Grateful Dead T-shirt, her pulse speeded up in a significant way. He folded to the floor by her, his back against the glass of the mirror as hers was, and scooted closer until their shoulders and hips touched.

Sean was silent, and she was too self-conscious to look up at his eyes. She'd half expected to hear from him the night before, and when the phone hadn't rung and there'd been no knock at her door, she'd felt quite disconcerted. Men had seldom walked away from her, no matter how rocky their relationship had grown. *I am not going to ask him where he's been,* she swore to herself.

Sylvia was talking on the phone and smoking, which all the human dancers detested. She was doing it to prove she was the boss. Rue made a face and tried to arrange herself so her back was comfortable. The wall wasn't friendly to her spine, which had been jolted when she caught Megan after Charles Brody had shoved her. Megan was moving a little stiffly. Hallie looked subdued and David seemed healed, as far as Rue could tell. She hoped this week would be a better one for the entertainment troupe as a whole.

Rue sighed and tried to shift her weight slightly to her right hip. To her astonishment, in the next moment she felt herself being lifted. Sean had spread his legs, and he put her down between them, so her back rested against his stomach and chest. He scooted his butt out from the wall to give her a little incline. She was instantly more comfortable.

Rue figured if she didn't make any big deal out of it, no one else would either, so she didn't say a word or betray the surprise she felt. But she relaxed against Sean, knowing he would interpret that signal correctly as a thank-you.

Sylvia hung up at last. A black-haired female vampire with beautiful clear skin and dead eyes said, "Sylvia, we all know you're top dog. Put out the damn cigarette." The vampire waved her elegant hand at Sylvia imperiously.

"Abilene, tell me how you and Mustafa are doing," Sylvia said, blowing out smoke, but then she stubbed out the cigarette.

A tall human with a full mustache, Mustafa had more muscles than any man needed, in Rue's opinion. He was very dark complexioned, and a slow thinker. Rue wondered about the dynamics of this team, since the vampire half was a woman. How did that work? Did she do the lifts? Belatedly, Rue realized that in Black Moon's form of entertainment, lifting was probably irrelevant.

"We're doing fine," Abilene said. "You got any comments, Moose?" That was her pet name for her giant partner, but no one else dared use it.

"The pale woman," he said, his voice heavily accented and deep as a foghorn. Moose seemed to be a man of few words.

"Oh, yeah, the last gig we did, the party for the senator," Abilene said. "The wife of one of the, ah, legislators… I don't know how she got there, why her husband brought her, but she turned out to be Fellowship."

"Were you hurt?" Sylvia asked.

"She had a knife," Abilene said. "Moose was on top of me, so it was an awkward moment. You sure I can't kill the customers?" Abilene smiled, and it wasn't a nice smile.

"No, indeed," Sylvia said briskly. "Haskell take care of it?"

For the first time, Rue noticed the sleek man leaning against the wall by the door. She seldom had dealings with Haskell, since the Black Moon people needed more protection than the Blue Moon dancers. Haskell was a vampire, with smooth, short blond hair and glacier-blue eyes. He had the musculature of a gymnast, and the wary, alert attitude of a bodyguard.

"I held her until her husband and his flunky could get her out of there," Haskell said quietly.

"Her name?"

"Iris Lowry."

Sylvia made a note of the name. "Okay, we'll watch for her. I may have my lawyer write Senator Lowry a letter. Hallie? David?"

"We're fine," David said briskly. Rue looked down at her hands. No reason to relate the incident, even though it had ended with a death…a death that hadn't even made the papers.

"Rick? Phil?" The two men glanced at each other before answering.

"The last group we entertained, at the Happy Horseman—it was an S&M group, and we gave them a good show."

They weren't talking about juggling. Rue tried to keep her face blank. She didn't want her distaste to show. These people had shown her nothing but courtesy and comradeship.

"They wanted me to leave Phil there when our time was up," Rick said. "It was touch-and-go for a few minutes." The two vampires were always together, but they were very different. Rick was tall and handsome in a bland, brown-on-brown kind of way. Phil was small and slim, delicate. In fact, Rue decided, she might have mistaken him for a fourteen-year-old. *Maybe when he died he* was *that young,* she thought, and felt a pang of pity. Then Phil happened to look at Ruc, and after meeting his pale, bottomless eyes, she shivered.

"Oh, no," said Sylvia, and Phil turned to his employer. "Phil?" Her voice became gentle. "You know we're not going to let anyone else touch you, unless you want that to happen. But remember, you can't attack someone just because they want you. You're so gorgeous, people are always going to want you."

Sylvia braced herself in the face of that continued, terrifying gaze. "You know the deal, Phil," Sylvia said more firmly. "You have to leave the customers alone." After a long, tense pause, Phil nodded, almost imperceptibly.

"So, you think we need another minder, like Haskell? For nights when we're double-booked on Black Moon shows?" Sylvia asked the group. "Denny's a great guy, but he's really just a lifting-and-setup kind of fellow. He's not aggressive enough to be a minder, and he's human."

"Wouldn't hurt to have someone else," Rick said. "It would've taken some of the strain off if there'd been a third party there. It looked like it was going to be me against all of them for a little while. I hate to injure the client base, but I thought I might have to. People who like that kind of show are ready for a little violence, anyway."

Sylvia nodded, made another note. "What about you Blue Moon people?" she asked, obviously not expecting any response. "Oh, Rue. Only a couple of the Black Mooners have seen you in your dancing clothes. Take off the other stuff, so they can see what you really look like. I'm not sure they could recognize you in a crowd."

Rue hadn't planned on becoming the center of attention, but there was no point of making a production of this request. She stood and unbuttoned the flannel shirt, pulled off the glasses and stepped out of the old corduroy pants she'd pulled on to cover her practice clothes. She held out her arms, inviting them to study her in her T-shirt and shorts, and then she sank down to the floor again. Sean's arms crossed over her and pulled her tightly against him. This was body language anyone could understand—"Mine!" The Black Moon people almost all smiled—Phil and Mustafa being the exceptions—and nodded, both to acknowledge Rue and to say they'd noted Sean's possessiveness.

Rue wanted to whack Sean across his narrow aristocratic face.

She also wanted to kiss him again.

But there was one thing she had to say. "We had some trouble," she said hesitantly. She could understand David and Hallie's silence. They hadn't been on a professional engagement—*and* a man had died. But she couldn't understand why Megan wasn't speaking out.

Sylvia said, "With whom?" Her eyebrows were raised in astonishment.

"Guy named Charles Brody. He got mad when Megan wouldn't take money to meet him afterward. He mentioned your name, Sylvia, but he wouldn't…he didn't accept it too well when we told him we didn't work for Black Moon. He acted like it was going to be okay, that he accepted Megan's refusal, but when he turned to leave, he shoved her down."

"I don't recognize the name, but he could've hired us before," Sylvia said. "Thanks, I'll put him in the watch-for file. Were you hurt?" She waited impatiently for Megan's reply.

"No," Megan said. "Rue caught me. I would've said something, but I'd pretty much forgotten it." She shrugged. She clearly wasn't too pleased with Rue for bringing up the incident.

"I want to speak," Sean said, and that caught everyone's attention.

"Sean, I don't think you've spoken at one of these meetings in three years," Sylvia said. "What's on your mind?"

"Rue, show them your stomach," Sean said.

She rose up on her knees and turned to look at him. "Why?" She was stunned and outraged.

"Just do it. Please. Show the Black Moon people."

"You'd better have a good reason for this," she said in a furious undertone.

He nodded at her, his blue eyes intent on her face.

With a visible effort, Rue faced the group and pulled down the front of her elastic-waist shorts. The Black Moon people looked, and Abilene gave a sharp nod of acknowledgment. Phil's dark eyes went from the ugly scar to Rue's face, and there was a sad kinship in them that she could hardly bear. Mustafa scowled, while Rick, David and Hallie looked absolutely matter-of-fact. Haskell, the enforcer, averted his eyes.

"The man who did this is out of the mental hospital, and he's probably here in the city," Sean said, his Irish accent heavier than usual. Rue covered her scars, sank to her knees on the floor and looked down at the linoleum with utter concentration. She didn't know if she wanted to swear and throw something at Sean or…she just didn't know. He had massively minded her business. He'd gone behind her back.

But it felt good to have someone on her side.

"I got a human to find a picture of this man in the

newspaper and copy it." Sean began to pass around the picture. "This is Carver Hutton IV. He's looking for Rue under her real name, Layla LeMay. He knows she dances. His family's got a lot of money. He can get into almost any party anywhere. Even with his past, most hostesses would be glad to have him."

"What are you doing?" Rue gasped, almost unable to get enough breath together to speak. "I've kept all this secret for years! And in the space of five minutes, you've told people everything about me. Everything!" For the first time in her life, Rue found herself on the verge of hitting someone. Her hands fisted.

"And keeping it secret worked out well for you?" Sean asked coolly.

"I've seen him," a husky voice said. Hallie.

And just like that, Rue's anger died, consumed by an overwhelming fear.

If any of the dancers had doubted Rue's story, they saw the truth of it when they saw her face. They all knew what fear looked like.

"Where?" Sean asked.

Hallie crooked her finger at her partner. "We saw him," she said to David. He put his white arm around her shoulders, and his dark, wavy hair swept over her neck as he bent forward.

"Where?" David asked Hallie.

"Two weeks ago. The bachelor party at that big house in Wolf Chase."

"Oh." David studied the picture a little longer. "Yes. He was the one who kept grabbing at you when you were on top. He said you were a bitch who needed to learn a lesson."

Hallie nodded.

Tiny shivers shook Rue's body. She made an awful noise.

"Jeez," Hallie said. "That's what he said to you, huh, when he cut you? We just thought he wanted us to do a little, you know, play spanking. We did, and he chilled. The host looked like he was upset with the guy's outburst, so we toned it down. Please the man who's paying the bill, right?"

David nodded. "I kept an eye on him the rest of the evening."

Sylvia said, "You watch out for this guy. That's all. Just let Rue know if you've seen him. Nothing else."

"You're the boss," Mustafa said. His voice was low and rumbly, like a truck passing in the distance. "But he will not hurt Abilene."

"Thanks, Moose," said the vampire. She stroked his dark cheek with her white hand. "I love ya, babe."

"Getting back on track," Sylvia said briskly. "Rick, you and Phil didn't turn in your costumes for a week after that Greek party. Hallie, you can't have your mail sent here. If you keep that up, I'll start opening it. Julie, you left the lights on in the practice room last night. I've talked to you about that before."

Sylvia read down a list of minor offenses, scolding and correcting, and Rue had a chance to calm herself while the other employees responded. She was all too aware of Sean standing behind her. She could not have put a label on what she was feeling. She went to sit on the high pile of mats that they sometimes spread on the linoleum floor when they were practicing a new lift.

When the others began leaving, Rue started to pull her outer layer of clothes back on.

"Not so fast," Sean said. "We have practice tonight."

"I'm mad at you," she said.

"Turn out the lights behind you, whichever one of you wins," Sylvia called.

Sean went out into the hall and locked the front door, or at least that was the direction his footfalls took. She heard him come back, heard him over at the big CD player in the corner, by the table of white towels Sylvia kept there for sweaty dancers.

Rue began to warm up, but she still wasn't about to look at Sean. She was aware he began stretching, too, on the other side of the room.

After fifteen minutes or so, she stood, to signal she was ready to practice. But she kept her eyes forward. Rue wasn't sure if she was being childish, or if she was just trying to avoid attacking Sean. He started the CD player, and Rue was startled to recognize Tina Turner's sultry voice. "Proud Mary" was not a thinking song, though, but a dancing song, and when Sean's hands reached out for hers, she had no idea what he was going to do. The next twenty minutes were a challenge that left her no time for brooding. Avril Lavigne, the Dixie Chicks, Macy Gray and the Supremes kept her busy.

And she never once looked up at him.

The next song was her favorite. It was a warhorse, and the secret reason she'd decided to become a dancer, she'd told him in a moment of confidence: the Righteous Brothers' "Time of My Life." She'd worn out a tape of the movie *Dirty Dancing,* and that song had been the climax of the movie. The heroine had finally gained enough confidence in herself and trust in her partner to attempt a leap, at the apex of which he caught her and lifted her above his head as if she were flying.

"Shame on you," she said in a shaky voice.

"We're going to do this," he said.

"How could you take over my life like this?"

"I'm yours," he said.

It was so simple, so direct. She met his eyes. He nodded, once. His declaration hit her like a fist to the heart. She was so stunned by his statement that she complied when he put his hand on her back, when he took her left hand and pressed it to his silent heart. Her right hand was spread on his back, as his was on hers. Their hips began to move. The syncopation broke apart in a minute as he began to sweep her along with him, and they danced. Nothing mattered to Rue but matching her steps to her partner's. She wanted to dance with him forever. At every turn of her body, every movement of her head, she saw something new in his pale face—a glint of blue eye, the arch of his brow, the haughty line of his nose, which contrasted so startlingly with the grace of his body. When the song began to reach its climax, Sean raced to one end of the long room and held out his hands to her. Rue took a deep breath and began to run toward him, thinking all the way, and when she was just the right distance from Sean, she launched herself. She felt his hands on her hipbones, and then she was high in the air above his head, her arms outstretched, her legs extended in a beautiful line, flying.

As Sean let her down the line of his body very slowly, Rue couldn't stop smiling. Then the music stopped, but Sean didn't let her feet touch the floor. She was looking right into his eyes, and the smile faded from her face.

His arms were around her, and his mouth was right by hers. Then it was on hers, and once again he asked admission.

Rue whispered, “We shouldn’t. You’re going to get hurt. He’ll find me. He’ll try to kill me again. You’ll try to stop him, and you’ll get hurt. You know that.”

“I know this,” Sean said, and he kissed her again, with more force. She parted her lips for him, and he was in her mouth, his arms surrounding her, and she was altogether overwhelmed. It appeared that she was his, as much as he was hers.

For the second time in her life, Rue gave herself up to someone else.

“This is different,” she whispered. “This is different.”

“It ought to be.” Sean said. “It will be.” He picked her up in one smooth move. Their eyes were locked.

“Why are you getting into my life?” She shook her head, dazed. “There’s so much bad in it.”

“You fought back,” he said. “You made a new life, on your own.”

“Not much of one.”

“A life with courage and purpose. Now, let me love you this way.” His body moved against hers.

“I’m not scared.” She was.

“I know it.” He smiled at her, and her heart wrenched in her chest.

“You won’t hurt me,” she said with absolute faith.

“I would rather die.” He was so serious.

“You know I can’t have children,” she said. She meant only to let him know he didn’t need to use birth control.

“I can’t, either,” he murmured. “We can’t reproduce.”

If she’d ever known that, she’d forgotten it. She felt

oddly jolted. She'd always supposed that her barrenness would be a terrible obstacle to forming another relationship, but instead it was a non-issue.

His tongue flicked in her ear. "Tell me what you like," he suggested, his breath tickling her cheek. He walked over to the pile of exercise mats, carrying her as if her weight was nothing.

"I don't know," she said, partly embarrassed at her own ignorance, partly excited because she was sure he would find out what she liked.

"Light out, light on?"

"Out, please."

In the space of a second, he was back beside her. He had a few towels with him. He spread them on the mats, and she was glad, because the vinyl surface was unpleasant to the touch.

"My clothes?" he asked. He waited for her answer.

"Oh…off." Ambient light came through the frosted glass in the door of the studio, and she could see the gleam of his skin in the darkness. He was built smooth and sleek, as dancers usually are, and he was purely white except for the trail of red hair starting below his navel and going down. She followed that trail with her eyes and found herself gasping.

"Oh…oh. Wow."

"I want you very much."

"Yeah, I get that." Her voice was tiny.

"Can I see you?" For the first time, his voice was tentative.

She sat up on the pile of mats and rose to her knees. She pulled off her white T-shirt very slowly, and her bra was gone in an instant.

"Oh," he said. He reached out to touch her, hesitated.

"Yes," Rue said.

His white hands with their long fingers cupped her breasts with infinite gentleness. Then his mouth followed.

She gasped, and it was an urgent sound. His hands began tugging her shorts, gathering up her panties with them, and she lay down so he could coax them over her feet. He stayed down there for a minute or two, sucking her toes, which made her shiver all over, and then he began working his way up her legs.

She was afraid her courage would run out. She wanted him so badly she shook all over, but her only previous experience with sex had been short and brutal, its consequences painful and disastrous.

Sean seemed to understand her misgivings, and he eased his body up her length until his arms wrapped around her and his mouth found hers again.

"I can stop now," he told her. "After this, I'm not sure. I don't want to hurt you or frighten you."

Rue said, "Now or never."

He gave a choked laugh.

"That didn't sound very romantic," she apologized. His hips flexed involuntarily, pressing his hard length against her stomach, and he began to lick her neck.

"Oh," she said, reaching down to touch him. "Oh, please." His fingers touched her intimately, making sure she was ready. The delicate movement of his fingers made Rue shudder.

Then he was at her entrance, the blunt head pushing, and then he was inside her. "Layla," he said raggedly.

"It's good," she said anxiously. After a few seconds, she said again, in an entirely different tone, "It's so good."

"I want it to be better than good." His hips began to move.

Then she couldn't speak.

CHAPTER EIGHT

SHE HAD NEVER IMAGINED she could be so relaxed, so content.

His hair had come loose from its ribbon and trailed across her breasts as he lay on his stomach looking down at her. He had never seen anything so beautiful as her face in the faint glow of the city night that lit the room through the frosted glass.

She wondered how he could have become so important to her in such a short time. She loved every line of his face, the power of his sleek white body, the passion of his love-making; but most of all she loved the fact that he was on her side. It had been years since anyone had been on her side, unconditionally, unilaterally. She thought, *I should still be angry that he went to Pineville.* But she searched for the anger she'd initially felt and found it was gone.

"I'm a wimp," she concluded, out loud.

"I know what that means," Sean said, his voice dreamy. "Why do you say that?"

"I'm glad you found out. I'm glad I don't have to tell you all about it. I'm glad you care enough to want to find...Carver."

The hesitation before she was able to say his name told Sean a lot.

"What did your parents do?" he asked. He hadn't had time to ask Will Kryder all the questions that had occurred to him.

"They didn't believe me," she murmured. "Oh, my brother Les stood by me. He saved me that night. But he's not a strong-willed, forceful kind of guy. See, my dad works for Carver's dad, and my dad probably couldn't get hired anywhere else now. He drinks a lot. I'm not sure he'd still have the job he's got if he wasn't my father. Dad knows Hutton's got to keep him on, or else he might talk. My mother…well, she decided to think it was a clever ploy on my part to get Carver to marry me. When she found out otherwise, she was…livid."

"She wanted you to marry him."

"Yes, she actually believed that I'd want to be tied to the man who raped me."

"In my time, we would have made him wed you," Sean said.

"Really?"

"If you were my sister, I would have made sure of it."

"Because no one else would have married me otherwise, right? Damaged goods."

Sean perceived he had made a massive error.

"And for the rest of my life I would have had to put up with Carver's little ways, like beating on me, because he'd raped me," Rue said coldly.

"All right, in my time, we would have been wrong," he conceded. "But we would have been on your side."

"I have you on my side," she said. "I have you on my side *now.* If this has meant anything to you."

"I don't get this close to anyone unless it means something to me."

"That come from being an aristocrat? In your time, were you like Carver?" There was an edge to her voice that hadn't been there before.

"The night we first make love, you can compare me to the man who raped you?"

She hadn't thought before she spoke. "After years of weighing every word I said to another person, all of a sudden I've gotten to be the worst—I'm so sorry, Sean. Please forgive me for the offense."

There was a long silence in the dark room. He didn't speak. Her heart sank. She'd ruined it. Her bitterness and mistrust had twisted her more than she knew. But she'd come by it naturally, and she didn't see how she could have existed otherwise.

After another unnerving two minutes of silence, Rue began to fumble around for her clothes. She was determined not to cry.

"Where are you going?" Sean asked.

"I'm going home. I've screwed up everything. You won't talk to me, and I'm going home."

"You offended me," he said, and his voice wasn't level or calm at all. He was saying, *You hurt me.* But Rue wasn't absorbing that. Before Sean could scramble into his own clothes, she was gone, wearing her flannel shirt tossed over her dance outfit. She'd thrust her feet into her boots without lacing them. She was out the door of the studio, then out the door to the building, before Sean could catch her. He cursed out loud. He had to check the studio and lock everything up; that was the duty of the last person out, and it was something he couldn't shirk. He could always catch up with Rue, he was sure; after all, he was a vampire, and she was human.

CARVER WAS WAITING FOR HER in the third alley to the north.

Rue was walking very swiftly. She was trying not to cry; and not having much luck. She wanted to reach the next corner in time for the bus, which would be the last one running on a Sunday night. As she passed the alley entrance, Carver burst out with such astonishing suddenness that he was holding her arm before she could react.

"Hello, Layla," he said, smiling.

The nightmares she'd had for four years had come to life.

Carver had always been handsome, but his present look was far from his preppy norm. He'd spiked his dark hair and he was wearing ragged jeans and a leather jacket. He'd disguised himself.

"I have a score to settle with you," he said, still smiling.

Rue hadn't been able to make a sound when he'd grabbed her arm, but now she began to scream.

"Shut up!" he yelled, and backhanded her across the mouth.

But Rue had no intention of shutting up. "Help!" she screamed. "Help!" She groped in her bag for her pepper spray with her free left hand, but this one night she hadn't been prepared, mentally or physically, and she couldn't find the cylinder she usually carried ready to use.

Pinning her with his grip on her right arm, Carver began pummeling Rue with his fist to make her shut up. She tried to dodge the blows, tried to find the spray, tried to pray that help would come. Where was the pepper spray? Abandoning her futile one-handed rummaging through her big bag, Rue yanked it off her shoulder, since it was only an impediment. Then she fought back. She wasn't nearly as big as Carver, so she went for his genitals. She wanted to grip and squeeze the whole package, but he pulled back. All she managed was a vicious pinch, but that was enough to double him over. When he heard a woman shouting from across the street, he staggered away from Rue.

"Leave that girl alone!" a female voice yelled. "I'm calling the police!"

Rue sank to her knees, too battered to stand any longer, but she stayed facing him, her hands ready to defend herself. She would not give up what she'd worked so hard to maintain. Carver began to hurry down the alley as swiftly as his injury would permit—she was proud to see he was walking funny—and though Rue remained upright, but still on her knees, he vanished from her sight as he passed out of the alley and onto the next street.

"I won't fall," she said.

"Are you okay?"

Rue wouldn't even take her eyes from the alley entrance to examine the woman beside her. This woman had saved her life, but Rue wasn't going to be taken by surprise again, if Carver decided to return.

"Rue! Rue!" To her immense relief, she heard Sean's voice. Now Carver couldn't hurt her anymore; no matter how angry Sean was at her, he wouldn't let Carver strike her. She knew that. With profound relief, she understood she didn't need to stay vigilant any longer, and she sat back on the pavement. Then she was lying on the sidewalk. And then she didn't know anything else.

WHEN SHE BEGAN TO RELATE to her surroundings again, Rue knew she was in a strange place. Hospital? Nope, didn't smell like a hospital, a smell with which she was all too familiar. It was a quiet place, a comfortable place. She was lying on clean white sheets, and there was someone next to her. She tried to move, to sit up, and she found out she was sore in several places. Before she could gain control of herself, she groaned.

"You okay? You need a drink of water?" The voice was familiar and came from a few feet away. Rue pried her swollen eyes open. She could see—a little. "Is that Megan?" she asked, her voice a dry thread.

"Yep, it's me. Julie and I been taking turns."

"Who else is here? Where *is* here?"

"Oh, we're at Sean's place, in his safe room. That's him in the bed with you, babe. It's daytime, so he had to sack out. He wasn't going to leave you without someone to help you, though. He made us swear on a stack of Bibles that we wouldn't leave. So you won't think we're these wonderful people, I gotta tell you that he promised to help us out with the money we're getting docked for missing work. I mean, I want to help you, and I would've come, anyway. But I just couldn't, ah, skip telling you. Okay?"

Rue nodded. It was an effort, but somehow Megan caught the motion. "Water would be good," Rue managed to say.

In just a moment, Megan was sliding her arm under Rue's back and helping her sit up a little. There was a glass of cool water at her lips, and Rue sipped gratefully.

"You need to get up and go to the bathroom?"

"Yes, please."

Megan helped Rue rise. To her relief, Rue discovered she was in the T-shirt and shorts she'd worn the night before. She shuffled to the bathroom. When she was through, she washed her face in the sink and brushed her teeth with a toothbrush she found still encased in a cellophane wrapper. That made her feel a great deal better, and she made her way back to the bed with a little more confidence.

"Megan, I'll be okay now, if you need to get to work."

"You sure, girlfriend? I can stay. I don't want Sean to be mad at me."

"I'm good. Really."

"Okay then. It's four o'clock. Sean ought to be up in about two hours. Maybe you can get some more sleep."

"I'll try. Thank you so much."

"Don't mention it. See you later."

Rue had left the light in the bathroom on, and when Megan had gone through the heavy curtain at one end of the room, Rue turned to her silent companion. Sean lay on his back with his hair spread out on the pillow. His lips were slightly parted, his eyes closed, his chest still. The absence of that rising and falling, the tiny motion of life, was very unnerving. Did he know she was there? Did he dream? Was he truly asleep, or was he just held motionless, like a paralysis victim? She'd almost forgotten what they'd fought about. She stroked his hair, kissed his cool lips. She remembered what they'd done together, and a flush suffused her face.

What Carver had done to her, when he'd attacked her years before, didn't qualify as sex. It had been an assault, using his sex organ as the weapon. What she'd done with Sean had been real sex, making-love sex. It had been intimate and primal and wonderful. Carver had made her into a shell of a human being overnight. Over the course of a few weeks, Sean had helped her become a full person once more.

She wasn't going to chicken out just because he was dead part of the time.

So, when darkness fell, Rue made sure her arm was across his chest, her leg lying over his. Suddenly she knew he was awake. The next second, his body reacted.

"Good evening to you, too," she said, startled and intrigued by his instant readiness.

"Where is Megan?" he asked, his voice still a little fuzzy from sleep.

"I told her to go. I'm better."

His eyes widened as he remembered. "Show me," he demanded.

"You seem to be ready for anything," she said, greatly daring, her hand wandering down his abdomen in a tentative way.

"I have to see your injuries first," he said. "I shouldn't even be…it's your smell."

"Oh?" she tried to sound insulted, failed.

"Just the smell of *you.* Your skin, your hair. You make me hard."

Not a compliment she'd ever gotten before, but she could see the evidence of the sincerity of it.

"Okay, check me out," she said mildly, and lay down. Sean raised himself on one elbow, and his left hand began to turn her face this way and that.

"It's my fault," he said, his voice steady but not exactly calm. "I shouldn't have stopped to lock up the studio."

"The only fault is Carver's," she said. "I've played

that blame game too many years. We don't need to start it all over again. For the first year after he attacked me, I thought, 'What if I hadn't worn that green dress? What if I hadn't let him hold my hand? Kiss me? Slow dance with me? Was it my fault for looking pretty? Was it my fault for treating him as I would any date I liked? No. It was his fault, for taking a typical teenage evening and turning it into the date from hell."

Sean's fingers gripped her chin gently and turned her face to the other side so he could examine her bruises. He kissed the one on her cheek, and then he pulled the cover down to look over her body. She had to stop herself from pulling it right back up. This level of intimacy was great and very exciting, but she sure wasn't used to it.

"This is the closest anyone's been to me in years," she said. "I haven't even seen a doctor who looked at this much of me." Then she told herself to shut up. She was babbling.

"No one should ever see this much of you," he said absently. "No one but me." His fingers, whiter even than her own magnolia skin, brushed a dark bruise on her ribs. "How much are you hurting?"

"I'm pretty stiff and sore," she admitted. "I guess my muscles were all tensed up, and then, when I got knocked around…"

He touched her side gently, his hand very close to her breast. "Will you be able to dance tonight? We need to call Sylvia and cancel if you will not be able. She can get Thompson and Julie to do it."

He was still hard, ready for her. She was having a difficult time remembering her sore muscles.

"I don't know," she said, trying not to sound as breathless as she felt.

"Turn over," he said, and she obediently rotated. "How's your back?"

She moved her shoulders experimentally. "Feels okay," she said. His fingers traced her spine, and she gasped. His hand rubbed her hip.

"Don't think I got bruised there," she said, smiling into the pillow.

"What about here?" His hand traveled.

"There, either."

"Here?"

"Oh, no! Definitely not there!"

He entered her from behind, holding himself up so his weight wouldn't press on her tender ribs. "There?" he asked, the mischief in his voice making something in her heart go all soft and mushy.

"You'd better…massage…that," she said, ending on a gasp.

"Like this?"

"Oh, yes."

After they'd basked in the afterglow for a happy thirty minutes, Rue said, "I hate to bring this up, but I'm hungry."

Sean, stung by his own negligence, leaped from the bed in one graceful movement. Before Rue knew what was happening, he'd lifted her from the bed, ensconced her in a chair, and clean sheets were on the bed and the old ones stuffed in a hamper. He'd started the shower for her and asked her what kind of food she liked to eat. "Whatever's in the neighborhood," she said. "That's what I love about the city. There's always food in walking distance."

"When you come out of the shower, I'll be back with food for you," he promised.

"You haven't bought food in years, have you?" she said, and the fact of his age struck her in a way it hadn't before.

He shook his head.

"Will it bother you?"

"You need it, I'll provide it," he said.

She stared at him, her lips pressed together thoughtfully. He didn't say this like a wimp who was desperate for a woman. He didn't say it like a control freak who wanted to dole out the very air his sweetheart breathed. And he didn't say it like an aristocrat who was used to having others do his bidding.

"Okay, then," she said slowly, still thinking him over. "I'll just shower."

The heat of the water and the minutes of privacy were wonderful. She hadn't been around people on a one-on-one basis so much for some time, and to be precipitated into such an intimate relationship was quite a shock. An enjoyable one, but still a shock.

Having clean hair and a clean body did wonders for her spirits, and in the light of Sean's determination to provide for her, she found a pair of his jeans she could wriggle into. She rolled up the cuffs and found a faded pumpkin-colored T-shirt to wear. It was pretty obvious she wasn't wearing a bra, but she didn't know where her bra was. Rue had a terrible conviction that it was still in the studio, which would be a dead giveaway to the other dancers. She left the bedroom and went out into the living room/kitchen/office to wait for Sean. It was small and neat, too, and had a couple of narrow windows through which she could see people's feet go by. For the first time, she realized Sean had a basement apartment.

Shortly after, he came in with two bags full of food. "How much of this can you eat?" he asked. "I find I have forgotten." He'd gotten Chinese, which she loved, and he'd bought enough for four. Luckily, there were forks and napkins in the bags, too, since Sean didn't have such things.

"Sean," she said, because she enjoyed saying his name. "Sit down while I eat, please, and tell me about your life." She knew how his face looked when he came, but she didn't know anything about his childhood. In her mind, this was way off balance.

"While I was in Pineville," he said, "I looked in the windows of your parents' home. I was curious, that's all. In the living room, your father was staring into a huge glass case that takes up a whole wall."

"All my stuff," she said softly.

"The crowns, the trophies, the ribbons."

"Oh, my gosh, they still have all that out? That's just…sad. Did he have a drink in his hand?"

Sean nodded.

"Why did you tell me this when I asked to know more about you?"

"You're American royalty," he said, supplying the link.

She laughed out loud, but not as if he were really amusing.

"You are," he said steadily. "And I know you've heard Sylvia say I was an aristocrat. Well, that's her joke. My origins are far more humble."

"I noticed you could make a bed like a whiz," she said.

"I can do anything in the way of taking care of a

human being," he said. He looked calm, but she could tell he wasn't—something about the way his hands were positioned on the edge of the table. "I was a valet for most of my human life."

CHAPTER NINE

"YOU WERE A GENTLEMAN'S gentleman?" Her face lit up with interest.

He seemed taken aback by her reaction. "Yes, my family was poor. My father died when I was eleven, so I couldn't take over his smithy. My mother was at her wits' end. There were five of us, and she had to sell the business, move to a smaller cottage, and my oldest sister—she was fifteen—had to marry. I had to find work."

"You poor thing," she said. "To have to leave school so early."

He smiled briefly. "There wasn't a school for the likes of us," he said. "I could read and write, because our priest taught me. My sisters couldn't, because no one imagined they'd need to." He frowned at her. "You should be eating now. I didn't get you food so you could let it grow cold."

She turned her face down to hide her smile and picked up her fork.

"I got a job with a gentleman who was passing through our village. His boy died of a fever while he was staying at the inn, and he hired me right away. I helped out his valet, Strothers. I went with them when they returned to England. The man's name was Sir Tobias

Lovell, and he was a strange gentleman. Very strange, I thought."

"He turned out to be a vampire, I guess."

"Yes. Yes, he was. His habits seemed very peculiar, but then, you didn't question people above you in social station, especially since anyone could see he was a generous man who treated people well. He traveled a great deal, too, so no one could wonder about him for too long. Every now and then, he'd go to his country house for a while. That was wonderful, because travel was so difficult then, so uncomfortable."

"But how did you come to be his valet? What happened to Strothers?"

"Strothers had already grown old in his service, and by the time I was eighteen, Strothers had arthritis so badly that walking was painful. Out of mercy, Sir Tobias gave him a cottage to live in, and a pension. He promoted me. I took care of his clothes, his wigs, his wants and needs. I shaved him. I changed his linen, ordered his bath when he wanted, cleaned his shoes. That's why I know how to take care of you." He reached over the table to stroke her hair. "Once I was in closer contact with Sir Tobias, it became obvious to me there was something more than eccentricity about the man. But I loved him for his goodness, and I knew I must keep his secrets, as much for my own sake as for his. We went on, master and man, for many years...maybe twelve or fifteen. I lost track, you see, of how old I was."

That seemed the saddest thing she'd ever heard. Rue lowered her gaze to hide her tears.

"I realized later that he'd take a little from the women he bedded," Sean said. "He pleased them very much, but most of them were weak the day after. In our small country neighborhood, he had the name of being a great womanizer. He had to go from one to another, of course, so no one woman would bear the brunt of his need. He seemed much healthier when we went to the cities, where he could visit houses of ill repute as much as he liked, or he could hunt in the alleys."

"What happened?"

"The village people grew more and more suspicious. He didn't age at all, you see, and people grew old very quickly then. But he lost money and couldn't afford to travel all the time, so he had to stay at the manor more often. He never went to Sunday church. He couldn't be up in the daytime, of course. And he didn't wear a cross. The priest began to be leery of him, though he donated heavily to the church.

"People began to avoid me, too, because I was Sir Tobias's man. It was a dark time." Sean sighed. "Then they came one night to get him, a few of the local gentry and the priest. I told him who was at the door, and he said, 'Sean, I'm sorry, I must eat before I run.' And then he was on me."

Rue had lost the taste for her food. She wiped her mouth and laid her hand over Sean's.

"He gave me a few swallows of his blood after he'd drained me," Sean said quietly. "He said, 'Live, if you have the guts for it, boy,' and then he was gone. The people at the front door broke in to begin searching the house for him, and they found me. They were sure I was dead. I was white; I'd been bitten, and they couldn't hear my heart. I couldn't speak, of course. So they buried me."

"Oh, Sean," she said, horror and pity in her voice.

"Lucky for me, they buried me right away," he said briskly. "In a rotten coffin, at that. Kept me out of the sunlight, and the lid was easy to break through when I woke." He shrugged. "They wanted to be through with the job, so they hadn't put me in too deep. And they didn't keep watch at the churchyard, to see if I'd rise. Another stroke of luck. People didn't know as much about vampires then as they did a hundred years later."

"What did you do after that?"

"I went to see my sweetheart, the girl I'd been seeing in the village. Daughter of the dry-goods dealer, she was." He smiled slightly. "She was wearing black for me. I saw her when she came out to get a bucket of water. And I realized I'd ruin the rest of her life if I showed myself to her. The shock might kill her, and if it didn't, I might. I was very hungry. Two or three days in the grave will do that. And I had no one to tell me what to do, how to do what I knew I must. Sir Tobias was long gone."

"How did you manage?"

"I tried to hold out too long the first time," he said. "The first man I took didn't survive. Nor did the second, or the third, or the fourth. It took me time to learn how much I could take, how long I could hold off the hunger before it would make me do something I'd regret."

Rue pushed her food away.

"Did you ever see him again?" she asked, because she couldn't think of anything else to say.

"Yes, I saw him in Paris ten years later."

"What was that like?"

"He was in a tavern, once again the best-dressed man in the place, the lord of all he saw," Sean said, his voice quite expressionless. "He always did enjoy that."

"Did you speak?"

"I sat down opposite him and looked him in the eye."

"What did he say?"

"Not a word. We looked at each other for a couple of minutes. There was really nothing to say, in the end. I got up and left. That night, I decided I would learn to dance. I'd done village dances as a boy, of course. I enjoyed it more than anything, and since I had centuries to fill and no pride to be challenged, I decided to learn all about dancing. Men danced then, almost all men. It was a necessary social grace if you were at all upper-class, and I could go from one group to another, acting like Sir Tobias when I wanted to learn the ballroom dances of the wealthy, and like my own class when I wanted to pick up some folk steps."

They both unwound as Sean talked about dancing. Rue even picked up her fork again and ate a few more bites. Gradually Sean relaxed in his chair and became silent. When she was sure he'd recovered from his story, she said, "I have to feed the cat. I need to go to my apartment."

"But you can't stay there," Sean said stiffly.

"Then where?"

"Here, of course. With me."

She did her best not to glance around the tiny apartment. She could probably fit her books and clothes in somewhere, but she would have to discard everything else she'd acquired with so much effort. How could they coordinate their very different lives? How much of his feeling for her was pity?

He could read her mood accurately. "Come on, let's get your things. If I'm right, you've missed one day of classes. You'll need to go tomorrow if you're able. How is walking?"

She was moving slowly and stiffly. Sean put socks on her feet and laced her boots in a matter-of-fact way. There was something so practical and yet so careful about the way he did such a lowly task that she felt moved in an unexpected way.

"At least I don't have a wig you have to powder," she said, and smiled.

"That was a great improvement of the twentieth century over the eighteenth," he said. "Hair care and shoes—they're much better now."

"Hair and shoes," she said, amusement in her voice. She thought that over while Sean got ready to go, and by the time they were outside in the night, she felt quite cheerful. She looked forward to lots of conversations with Sean, when he would tell her about clothes and speech patterns and social mores of the decades he'd lived through. She could write some interesting term papers, for sure.

She loved to listen to Sean talk. She loved it when he kissed her. She loved the way he made her feel like a—well, like a woman who was good in bed. And she loved the way he handled her when they were dancing, the respect in which he seemed to hold her. How had this happened over the past few months? When had he become so important to her?

Now, walking beside him, she was content. Though her life had just been shaken to pieces and her body was sore from a beating, she was calm and steady, because she had Sean. She loved every freckle on his face, his white strong body, his quirky mouth, and his dancing talent.

He'd done wonderful things for her. But he hadn't said he loved her. His blue eyes fixed on her face as if she were the most beautiful woman in the world, and that should be enough. The way he made love to her told her that he thought she was wonderful. That should be enough. She had a strong suspicion any man would laugh at her for wondering, but she wasn't a man, and she needed to hear the words—without having asked for them.

The next second she was yanked from her brooding by an unexpected sight. She'd glanced up at her apartment windows automatically, from half a block away, and she'd gotten a nasty shock.

"The light in my apartment is on," she said, stopping in her tracks. "The overhead light."

"You didn't leave it on last night?"

"No. The ceilings are high, and it's hard for me to change the bulbs in that fixture. I leave on the little lamp by my bed."

"I'll see," Sean said, pulling away from her grasp gently. She hadn't realized she'd been gripping his arm.

"Oh, please, don't go to the door," she said. "He might be waiting for you."

"I'm stronger than he is," Sean said, a little impatiently.

"Please, at least go up the fire escape, the one on the side of the building."

Sean shrugged. "If it'll make you happy."

She crept closer to the building and watched Sean approach the fire escape. He decided to show off at the last minute and scaled the brick wall, using the tiny spaces between bricks as hand- and toeholds. Rue was impressed, sure enough, but she was also disconcerted. It was unpleasantly like watching a giant insect climb. In a very short time, Sean had reached the level of the window and swung onto the fire escape. He peered inside. Rue could tell nothing from his stance, and she couldn't manage to see his face.

"Hey, Rue." Startled, she turned to see that her next-door neighbor, a part-time performance artist who called herself Kinshasa, had come up beside her. "What's that guy up to?"

"Looking into my apartment," she said simply.

"What were you doing last night? Sounded like you decided to rearrange the whole place."

"Kinshasa, I wasn't at home last night."

Kinshasa was tall and dreadlocked, and she wore big red-rimmed glasses. She wasn't someone you overlooked, and she wasn't someone who shrank from unpleasant truths. "Then someone else was in your place," she said. "And your friend's checking to see what happened?"

Rue nodded.

"I guess I should've called the cops last night when I heard all that noise," the tall woman said unhappily. "I thought I was doing you a favor by not calling the police or the super, but instead I was just being a typical big-city neighbor. I'm sorry."

"It's good for you that you didn't go knock on my door," Rue said.

"Oh. Like that, huh?"

The two stood watching as Sean came back down the fire escape in a very mundane way. He looked unhappy, so far as Rue could tell.

Sean, though not chatty or outgoing, was always polite, so Rue knew he had bad news when he ignored Kinshasa.

"You don't want to go back up there," he said. "Tell me what you need and I'll get it for you."

Suddenly Rue knew what had happened. "He got Martha," she said, the words coming out in a little spurt of horror. "He got her?"

"Yes."

"But I have to—" She started for the door of the building, thinking of all the things she needed, the fact that she had to find a box for the furry body, the grief washing over her in a wave.

"No," Sean said. "You will not go back in there."

"I have to bury her," Rue said, trying to pull away from his hand on her arm.

"No."

Rue stared up at him uncomprehendingly. "But, Sean, I have to."

Kinshasa said, "Baby, there's not enough left to bury, your friend is saying."

Rue could hardly accept that, but her mind skipped on to other worries. "My books? My notes?" she asked, trying to absorb the magnitude of the damage.

"Not usable."

"But it's four weeks into the semester! There's no way—I'll have to drop out!" The books alone had cost almost six hundred dollars. She'd gotten as many as she could secondhand, of course, but this late in the term, could she find more?

At least she had her dancing shoes. Some of them were in a corner at Blue Moon Entertainment, and the rest were in the bag she'd taken to Sean's. Rue's mind scurried from thought to thought like a mouse trapped in a cage.

"Clothes?" she mumbled, before her knees collapsed.

"Some of them may be salvageable," Sean murmured, but without great conviction. He crouched beside her.

"I know some people who can clean the apartment," Kinshasa said. "They just came over from Africa. They need the money."

This was an unexpected help. "But it's so awful in there, Sean says." Tears began to stream down Rue's face.

"Honey, compared to the mass graves and the slaughter they've had to clean up in their own country, this will be a piece of cake to them."

"You're right to give me some perspective," Rue said, her spine stiffening. Kinshasa looked as if she'd intended no such thing, but she bit her lip and kept silent. "I'm being ridiculous. I didn't get caught in that apartment, or I would've ended up like poor Martha." Rue managed to stand and look proud for all of ten seconds, before the thought of her beloved cat made her collapse.

"I'll kill him for you, honey," Sean said, holding her close.

"No, Sean," she said. "Let the law do it."

"You want to call the police?"

"Don't we have to? He'll have left fingerprints."

"What if he wore gloves the whole time?"

"I let him get away with hitting me last night, and what does he do? He comes here and kills my cat and ruins all my stuff. I should've called the police last night."

"You're right," Kinshasa said. "I'll call from my place right now."

Sean said nothing, but he looked skeptical.

THE POLICE WERE BETTER, kinder, than Rue expected. She knew what that meant. Her apartment must be utterly gory. Sean told the detective, Wallingford, that he'd be able to tell what was missing. "You don't need to go up there," Wallingford told Rue, "if this guy can do it for you." Sean and Wallingford went up to the apartment, and Rue drank a cup of hot chocolate that Kinshasa brought her. Rue found herself thinking, *I've had friends around me all the time, if I'd just looked.*

When Sean reappeared with a garbage bag full of salvaged clothes, he told Rue the only thing he knew for sure was missing was her address book. "Was my address in it?" he asked her quietly.

"No," she said. "Maybe your phone number. But I didn't even know where you lived until last night."

"The police say you can go now. Let's go back to my place." After an uneasy pause, he continued. "Do you think you can dance tonight? It's almost too late to call Sylvia to get a replacement team."

"Dance tonight?" She looked at him as they walked, her face blank. "Oh! We're supposed to be at the museum tonight!"

"Ballroom dancing. Can you do that?"

"If there's a dress I can wear at the studio." Though she had to wrench her thoughts away from her destroyed apartment, it would be a relief to think about something else. They would waltz a little, do a dance number to "Puttin' on the Ritz." They'd done the same thing several times before. It was a routine that pleased an older crowd, which the museum benefactors were likely to be.

"They asked for us specifically," Sean said. But then

he scowled, as if there were something about the idea he didn't like.

"Then we have to do it," Rue said. She was so numb, she couldn't have put into words what she was feeling. When Sean unlocked the studio, he insisted she stand outside while he checked it out first, and she did so without a word. He led her inside, looking at her eyes in a worried kind of way, trying to gauge her fitness. "Besides," Rue said, as if she was continuing a conversation, "I need the money. I have nothing." The enormity of the idea hit her. "I have *nothing.*"

"You have me."

"Why?" she asked. "Why are you doing this?"

"Because I care for you."

"But," she said, disgusted, "I'm so weak. Look at me, falling apart—like I couldn't have predicted this would happen. Why did I even get a cat? I should have known."

"Should have known you shouldn't love something because it might be taken away from you?"

"No, should have known he'd kill anything I loved."

"Come on," Sean said, his voice hard. "You're going to put on the pretty dress here, and I'm going to make some phone calls."

The dress was the palest of pinks. It was strapless, with a full skirt. In the trash bag she found some matching panties to wear under it, and a paler pink frothy half slip. There were panty hose in the costume room, and Rue pulled on a pair. Her shoe bag was there, thank God, since she'd walked out in such a huff the night before, and it contained the neutral T-strap character shoes that would suit the program.

Sean, who'd finished his phone calls, pulled on some

black dancer's pants and a white shirt with full sleeves. He buttoned a black vest over that and added his dancing shoes to Rue's bag. While he was buttoning the vest, he felt a brush running through his hair.

"Shall I braid it?" she asked, her voice so small it was barely audible.

"Please."

With the efficiency born of years of changing hairstyles quickly, Rue had his hair looking smooth and sleek in a minute.

"Will you leave yours loose?" Sean asked. "It looks beautiful as it is." Rue seldom left her long hair unbound for a performance, but he thought its color was brought out beautifully by the pale pink of the dress. "You look like a flower," he said, his voice low with admiration. "You would be wonderful no matter what you looked like, but your beauty is a bonus."

She tried to smile, but it faltered on her lips. She was too sad to appreciate his compliment, "It's nice to hear you say so," she said. "We need to go. We don't want to be late."

CHAPTER TEN

THEY TOOK A CAB, WHICH Sylvia would pay for; after all, they had to keep their clothes clean and fresh for the dancing. The Museum of Ancient Life had just opened a new wing, and the party was being held in the museum itself. All the attendees were patrons who'd donated very large sums toward the construction of the new wing. All of them were very well dressed, most of them were middle-aged or older, and they were all basking in the glow of being publicly acknowledged for having done a good thing.

The vampire and the dancer stood for a minute or two, watching limousines and town cars dropping off the well-heeled crowd. Then they made their way back to the entrance Sylvia had instructed them to use. The museum staffer at the door checked their names off a list. "Wait a minute," the heavy man said. "You're already here."

"Impossible," Sean said imperiously. "Here is my driver's license. Here is my partner's."

"Hmm," the man said nervously, his fingers drumming on the doorjamb. "I don't know how this happened. I shouldn't let you in."

"Then the Jaslows and the Richtenbergs will have to go without their dancing," Sean said. "Come, Rue."

Rue didn't have a clue what was happening, but she could tell Sean was quite indifferent that someone else had used his name, almost seemed to have been expecting it. If he was relaxed about it, so was she. "I'll call our employer on my cell," she said to the man. "You can explain to Sylvia Dayton that we're not being allowed entrance, so she won't blame us, okay?"

The man flushed even more, his eyes running up and down the printed list over and over, as if something different would pop up. When he glanced up at Sean and the vampire's eyes caught the guard's gaze, the man's face lost its belligerence instantly.

"I guess your names were checked off by mistake earlier. Come on in," he said.

Rue looked at Sean in awe. Vampire talents could come in handy.

It was lucky they'd dressed at the studio, because there wasn't a corner for them here. The back recesses of the museum weren't designed with parties in mind, as the Jaslows' home had been. The small rooms and narrow corridors were full of scurrying figures, and Rue realized that things were being handled by Extreme(ly Elegant) Events, Jeri's company, which had catered the Jaslows' party. The servers wore the traditional white jacket distinguished with the E(E)E logo on the shoulder. The halls were crowded with trays and trays of hors d'oeuvres, and cases and cases of champagne. Jeri was directing the staff, wearing the same serene smile.

And the man whose white jacket was straining across his shoulders was surely Mustafa, aka Moose, who worked for Black Moon. As soon as she'd identified him, Rue realized that the short-haired woman opening a champagne bottle was Hallie, and her partner, David, was busy filling a tray of empty glasses. David looked quite different with his thick, wavy black hair pulled back and clubbed.

"Sean," she said, tugging on his hand to make him stop, "did you see Moose?"

He nodded, without looking around at her. They continued to make their way through the narrow maze of corridors to the door indicated on the little map Sylvia had left for them.

"Okay, this is it," he said, and they paused.

There was no place special to leave their bags, so they dropped them right inside the door, then changed into their dancing shoes on the spot.

"They're all here," he told her, when she was ready. "I called them. All of them who aren't working tonight, that is. Thompson and Julie have an early gig in Basing, and Rick and Phil have a very private engagement right after this for a few select museum patrons. But all the rest are here, even Haskell."

"Sylvia knows about this?"

"No. But that's so she can deny it."

"It's wonderful that they'd do this for you."

"They're doing it for you. Moose and Abilene gave our names to get in. The others came with the triple E people. When I heard the board had asked for us, specifically, I figured Hutton was behind it. We'll stop him tonight," Sean said, and then looked sorry he'd sounded so grim. "Don't worry, Rue." He kissed her on the check lightly, mindful of her lipstick.

Rue was too numb to grasp what Sean meant. Automatically, they checked each other over, Sean looked at his watch, and they swung open the door.

Since they were "on" the minute they stepped out of the door, they walked hand in hand with a light, almost prancing walk, until they'd reached the center of a huge open area. The dome stretched upward for three stories, Rue estimated. She'd been to the museum before—when the new wing had been under construction, in fact—and she loved the wide expanse of marble floor. Wouldn't their music get lost in the huge space?

Sean and Rue reached the center of the floor, Rue trying not to stare at the glass cases of masks that lined the wall. The dancers stood there, smiling, arms extended, waiting for all the milling patrons to become aware of their presence and to clear the area for their performance.

"Aren't they lovely!" exclaimed a white-haired woman with sapphire earrings who wasn't standing quite far enough away. A scowling face seemed to disagree. Rue dimly recognized the obnoxious man from the Jaslows' party, Charles Brody.

Their music began over the public address system, and Rue had to fight to keep her face pleasant. Sean had another surprise for her. He'd switched routines. The music was "Bolero." This was their sexy number, the one they'd only performed once or twice at anniversary parties. Why had he picked that music for this night?

But as they began to twine together in the opening moves, Rue seemed to be able to feel the sensuousness in her bones. She felt the passion, the yearning, conveyed by the music.

Suddenly Sean lifted her straight up, his hands gripping her thighs, until they formed a column. She looked down at him with longing, and he looked up at her with desire. She extended her arms gracefully upward as he turned in a smooth circle. As he continued to hold her, changing his grip so she was soaring above him like a bird, her full skirt falling over his shoulders, the crowd began to applaud at their display of strength and grace. Sean let her down so gradually that her feet didn't jolt when they touched the floor. She was able to pick up her steps again smoothly. Then Sean leaned her back, back, over his arm, and put his lips to her neck. She felt her whole body come alive when she felt his touch, and she waited for the bite with the faintest of smiles on her face.

But in that second, she was aware of a difference. Her partner was far tenser than he'd ever been at the finale; in fact, he was like an animal expecting attack. His body covered hers more completely than it should, as if he were protecting her. The crowd was closer than it should be, and she distinctly saw Haskell's face turn sharply to the right, his mouth opening to shout, allowing a glimpse of his shining fangs. A woman screamed.

Carver, in a tux, stepped out of the polite circle that had formed around the temporary dance floor, then he reached in his pocket and pulled out a knife. He pressed a button in the hilt and a wicked blade leaped out. In the space of a second, he'd slashed Haskell, who faltered and fell. Megan grabbed for Carver's arm next, and she might have slowed him down if Charles Brody hadn't shoved her as hard as he could, just as he'd done that night at the party. Again Megan landed on the floor, and then Carver was in the center of the circle with them.

She knew what he would do. She was sure that Sean thought Carver would try to kill her, and he might—if there wasn't anything else he could do to her—but first, she knew, he would try to kill Sean. Their just-finished dance had shown clearly that she loved the vampire, and Carver would relish killing something else she loved. Because Sean wasn't expecting it, she was able to shove him off her just as the knife descended.

Black-haired Abilene tackled Carver from the rear. Carver couldn't make a killing blow that way, but he managed to sink the knife into Rue's abdomen and pull it directly back out to strike again. Then a wounded Haskell, bloody and enraged, piled on top of Carver. With a bellow of enthusiasm, as if he were on the football field, Moose threw himself on top of them all.

The pain wasn't immediate. Unfortunately, Rue remembered all too clearly when he'd done the same thing years before, and she knew in a very short time she would hurt like hell. She made a bewildered sound as she felt the sudden wetness. Amid the screams and shouts of the crowd, Sean was trying to get Rue to her feet so he could drag her out of the melee. "He may have hired someone to help him. You have to get out of here," Sean said urgently.

But Rue watched Karl take a second to deck Charles Brody before he joined the other vampires in pinning Carver to the marble floor. The trapped man was fighting like a—well, like a madman, Rue thought, in a little detached portion of her brain. Not all the museum patrons had seen the knife, and they were bewildered and shouting. There could have been twenty assassins in the confusion of staff, patrons and servers.

"Come on, darling," Sean urged her, holding her as he helped her clear the outskirts of the gathering crowd.

"Let's get out of here." He could feel her desperation and assumed he knew the cause. His eyes were busy checking the people moving around them, trying to be sure they were unarmed. "I thought if we did 'Bolero' we might provoke him to attack when we were ready for him, but this wasn't what I had planned." He laughed, a short bark with little humor.

Rue reached her free hand under her skirt and felt the wetness soaking her petticoats. It had begun trickling down her legs. She staggered after Sean for a few feet. She put her hand against a pillar to brace herself. When she lowered it to try to walk, she saw her perfect handprint, in blood, on the marble of the pillar. "Sean," she said, because he was still turned away from her, still looking for any other assault that might be coming their way.

He turned back impatiently, and his eye was caught at once by the handprint. He stared at it, his brow puckered as if he were trying to figure it out. He finally understood the tang of blood that he'd barely registered in his zeal to get Rue to safety.

"No," he said, and looked down at her skirt. If his face could become any whiter, it did.

His eyes looked like the lady's sapphire earrings, Rue thought, aware that she wasn't thinking like a rational person. But she figured that was probably a good thing. Because in just a minute the pain would start up.

"You're losing too much blood," he said.

"She's going to die," Karl said sadly. He'd materialized suddenly, pulling off his white jacket as he evaluated Rue's condition. "Even if you call an ambulance this minute, they will be too late."

"What..." For once, Sean seemed to be at a loss as to what to do.

"You have to hide her," Haskell said without hesitation, coming up to join them. The ordinarily tidy blond vampire, now disheveled and smeared with blood, was still cool-headed enough to be decisive. "If you want to save her, this is the last chance," he said.

"Find a place," Sean said. He sounded...afraid, Rue thought. She'd never heard Sean sound afraid.

Karl said, "The Egyptian room."

Sean picked Rue up like a child. Haskell and Karl followed, ready to ward off any attack from behind. But only a museum guard ran up to them, making some incoherent comment on Rue's wound. Haskell, clearly not in any mood for questions and maybe a little maddened by the scent of blood, pinched the man's neck until he slumped to the floor.

The Egyptian room had always been Rue's favorite. She loved the sarcophagi and the mummiform cases, even the mummies themselves. She'd often wondered about the ethics of exposing bodies—surely once people were buried, they deserved to stay that way—but she enjoyed looking on the long-dead features and imagining what the individual had been like in life—what she'd worn, eaten...who she'd loved.

Now Sean carried her to the huge sarcophagus in the middle of the floor. Made to contain the inner coffin of a pharaoh, the highly carved and decorated limestone sarcophagus was penned in by hard sheets of clear plastic, preventing people from touching the sides. Fortunately, this pen was open at the top. A vampire could clear the barrier easily.

Sean leaped over lightly, followed by Karl, while Haskell held Rue. Though the lid must have weighed hundreds of pounds, Karl and Sean easily shifted it to one side, leaving a narrow opening. Then Haskell carefully handed Rue to Karl, while Sean climbed in the deep stone box, which came to his lower chest. Karl handed Rue in, and Sean laid her on the bottom. She was able to lie flat on her back, with her legs fully extended. She felt as if she was looking up at Sean floating hundreds of feet above her. He lay down beside her, and she felt the numbness wearing away.

Oh, God, no. Please. She knew the onset of the pain. As she began to scream, Karl moved the lid back in place, and then there was almost perfect darkness.

"RUE," SAID SEAN URGENTLY.

She heard his voice, but the pain rendered it meaningless.

"Rue, do you want me to end the pain?"

She could only make a small sound, a kind of whine. Her fingers dug into him. There was hardly enough room side by side for them, and she had the feeling Sean couldn't straighten out, but that was the least of her concerns at the moment.

"You can be like me," he said, and she finally understood.

"Dying?" she said through clenched teeth.

"Yes. I wasn't quick enough. I didn't plan enough. And then you made sure he got you instead of me. Why, Rue? Why?"

Rue could not explain that she operated on instinct. She could not have borne to see the knife enter him, even though a moment's thought would have told her that he could survive what she could not. She hadn't had that moment. Her understanding was a tiny flicker in the bottom of a well that was full of agony.

"If I make you like me, you will live," he said.

This was hardly the best time to be making a huge decision, but she remembered the story Sean had told her about his master's sudden attack on him, the callous way the man had left Sean to cope with the sudden change. If Sean could survive such a metamorphosis, she could, because Sean was here to help her.

"Won't leave?" she asked. Her voice trembled and was almost inaudible, but he understood.

"Never." His voice was very firm. "If you love me as I love you, we'll weather the change."

"Okay." *Love,* she thought. *He loved her.*

"Now?"

"Now. Love you," she said, with great effort.

With no more hesitation, Sean bit her. She was already hurting so badly that it was just one more pain, and then she felt his mouth drawing on her, sucking her dry. She was frightened, but she didn't have the strength to struggle. Then, after a minute, the heavy grayness in her head rose up and took her with it.

"Here," said a voice, a commanding voice. "You have to drink, Rue. Layla. You have to drink, now." A hand was pressing her face to bare skin, and she felt something run over her lips. Water? She was very thirsty. She licked her lips, and found it wasn't water, wasn't cold. It was tepid, and salty. But she was very dry, so she put her mouth to the skin and began to swallow.

SHE WOKE AGAIN SOMETIME LATER.

She felt…funny. She felt weak, yes, but she wasn't sore. She remembered vividly waking up in the hospital after the last time she'd been attacked, feeling the IV lines, the smell of the sheets, the little sounds of the hospital wing. But it was much darker here.

She tried to move her hand and found that she could. She patted herself, and realized she was a terrible mess. And there was someone in this dark place with her. Someone else who wasn't breathing.

Someone *else*…who wasn't breathing.

She opened her mouth to scream.

"Don't, darling."

Sean.

"We're… I'm…"

"It was the only way to save your life."

"I remember now." She began shivering all over, and Sean's arms surrounded her. He kissed her on the forehead, then on the mouth. She could feel his touch as she'd never felt anyone's touch before. She could feel the texture of his skin, hear the minute sound of the cloth moving over his body. The smell of him was a sharp arousal. When his mouth fell on hers, she was ready.

"Turn on your side, angel," Sean said raggedly, and she maneuvered to face him. Together, they worked down her panty hose, and then he was in her, and she made a noise of sheer pleasure. Nothing had ever felt so good. He was rougher with her, and she knew it was because she was as he was, now, and his strength would not hurt her. Her climax was shattering in its intensity.

When it was over, she felt curiously exhausted. She was, she discovered, very hungry.

She said, "When can we get out?"

"They'll come lift the lid soon," he said. "I could do it myself, but I'm afraid I'd push it off too hard and break it. We don't want anyone to know we were here."

In a few minutes, she heard the scrape of the heavy lid being moved to one side, and a dim light showed her Rick and Phil standing above them, holding the heavy stone lid at each end.

Other hands reached down, and Julie and Thompson helped them out of the sarcophagus.

"How is it?" Julie asked shyly, when she and Rue were alone in the women's bathroom. The men were cleaning up all traces of their occupancy of the sarcophagus, and Rue had decided she just had to wash her face and rinse out her mouth. She might as well have spared the effort, she decided, evaluating her image in the mirror—delighted she could see herself, despite the old myth. Her clothes were torn, bloody and crumpled. At least Julie had kindly loaned her a brush.

"Being this way?"

Julie nodded. "Is it really that different?"

"Oh, yes," Rue said. In fact, it was a little hard to concentrate, with Julie's heart beating so near her. This was going to take some coping; she needed a bottle of True-Blood, and she needed it badly.

"The police want to talk to you," Julie said. "A detective named Wallingford."

"Lead me to him," Rue said. "But I'd better have a drink first."

It wasn't often a murder victim got to accuse her attacker in person. Rue's arrival at the police station in her bloodstained dress was a sensation. Despite his broken arm, Carver Hutton IV was paraded in the next room in a lineup, with stand-ins bandaged to match him, and she enjoyed picking him from the group.

Then Sean did the same.

Then Mustafa.

Then Abilene.

Three vampires and a human sex performer were not the kind of witnesses the police relished, but several museum patrons had seen the attack clearly, among them Rue's old dance partner, John Jaslow.

"There'll be a trial, of course," Detective Wallingford told her. He was a dour man in his forties, who looked as though he'd never laughed. "But with his past history with you, and his fingerprints on the knife, and all the eyewitness testimony, we shouldn't have too much trouble getting a conviction. We're not in his daddy's backyard this time."

"I had to die to get justice," she said. There was a moment of silence in the room.

Julie said. "We'll go over to my place so you two can shower, and then we can go dancing. It's a new life, Rue!"

She took Sean's hand. "Layla," she said gently. "My name is Layla."